STEALING EMBERS

Fallen Legacies Book 1

Stealing Embers

Julie Hall

AWARDS

Finalist, Speculative Fiction
Huntress
2018 ACFW Carol Awards

Young Adult Book of the Year
Huntress
2018 Christian Indie Awards

Gold Medal Winner
Huntress
2018 Illumination Awards

First Place Winner, Religion
Huntress
2018 IndieReader Discovery Awards

Christian Fiction Finalist

Huntress
2018 Next Generation Indie Book Awards

Alliance Award (Reader's Choice)
Warfare
2018 Realm Makers Awards

Parable Award, Finalist
Logan
2018 Realm Makers Awards

Gold Medal Winner
Huntress
2017 The Wishing Shelf Book Awards

Best Inspirational Novel
Huntress
2017 Ozarks Indie Book Festival

Best Debut Author
Julie Hall
2017 Ozarks Indie Book Festival

Second Place Winner
Huntress
2017 ReadFree.ly Indie Book of the Year

First Place Winner
Huntress
2012 Women of Faith Writing Contest

USA TODAY **Bestselling Author**
August 17, 2017 & June 21, 2018

PRAISE & REVIEWS

Filled with action, danger, romantic tension, and intrigue, Stealing Embers is absolutely addictive.

Casey L. Bond
award-winning author of *When Wishes Bleed*

With a dark, thrilling plot and beautiful, compelling characters, Stealing Embers is a fantastic take on angel lore that will keep you flipping pages long after bedtime.

Cameo Renae
USA Today bestselling author of the *Hidden Wings* series.

Packed to the brim with action, snark, angel lore, and characters you immediately fall in love with, STEALING EMBERS will enthrall fans of Cassandra Clare and Sarah J. Maas, or anyone who loves beautifully written urban fantasy with a sizzling-hot dose of romantic tension. Prepare to become addicted!

Audrey Grey
USA *Today* bestselling author of the *Kingdom of Runes* series

This delightful read was everything I wanted in a book and more. Author Julie Hall kept me turning pages far into the night, and I wanted the next book in the series the moment this one was over. Stealing Embers just may be one of the best books I've ever read. Well done!

Michele Israel Harper
award-winning editor and author of the *Beast Hunter* series

For my daughter, Ashtyn.
May you find your wings to soar.

"And when the ones who thought to overthrow the Creator were defeated, they were thrown out of Heaven and cursed to an existence they loathed."

— *BOOK OF SERAPH CHAPTER 3, VERSE 2*

"The Nephilim were on the earth in those days—and also afterward—when the sons of God went to the daughters of humans and had children by them. They were the heroes of old, men of renown."

— *BOOK OF GENESIS CHAPTER 6, VERSE 4*

1

a crash breaks the silence of the early morning. With a jolt, my eyes pop open and I'm on my feet, bag slung over my shoulder before I'm fully awake. My shoes slap the pavement beneath me as I sprint for the open end of the alley. Sparks of light flicker around the periphery of my vision.

Real or imaginary?

Casting a glance over my shoulder, I catch a garbage truck depositing a dumpster on the ground. The lid bangs against the metal side and echoes off the buildings lining the alley. The lights pulsate with each loud hit, then fade when the noise settles.

The shot of adrenaline coursing through my system leaves my heart racing, even as my mind dismisses any real threat of danger.

Slowing to a stop, I lean against the side of the building and press a hand to my chest, willing the beats to slow. *I'm safe. I'm safe. I'm safe*, I chant while practicing deep breathing.

The air nips at my heated cheeks and cools the moisture already collecting around my hairline. Closing my eyes, I focus on the sensations that ground me in reality.

The stale smell of rotten food and garbage.

Rough brick beneath my fingertips.

The fuzzy build-up and bitter tang on my teeth from my short night's sleep.

I am here, and I am awake—at least, I hope so. Opening my eyes with painstaking slowness, I silently pray the spectrum world won't fill my view.

I let out a loud sigh of relief at the graffiti-spattered wall across the alley. The ground is littered with trash and random detritus: a shoe, a discarded bike tire, the carcass of a dead rat.

This may be the first time I'm excited to see a rat in any form. Rats don't exist in the spectrum world, so the furry corpse is further confirmation I still exist in reality.

One. Two. Three. Four.

Counting my heartbeats is one way I calm myself down—a strategy for slowing the release of adrenaline into my system.

I live in fear of adrenaline rushes.

They are my main trigger to seeing the world I've been told doesn't exist. I do whatever I can to avoid them— including isolating myself, which isn't usually an issue since people are naturally uncomfortable around me. Over the years, I've honed my senses to be aware of the world around me, but I'm screwed during the few hours my body demands sleep.

If only sleeping with one eye open were possible.

I've had more instances of slipped reality in the past year than the last ten combined. One of the many negatives of homelessness is that you always live life a bit on edge. Still, that doesn't outweigh the one big, fat positive that comes from living on the Denver streets: Becoming a runaway saved me from being locked up in a psychiatric hospital.

I'll accept a wide variety of suffering to hold on to my freedom.

The first groans of an awakening city disrupt my thoughts. The beeping from the garbage truck that startled me awake stops when the driver shifts from reverse to drive and thunders on his way. Cars rumble by, their morning exhaust creating plumes of smoke in the air. Rusted metal security gates creak and clang when store owners roll them up to invite business for the day. Muffled shouts ring out from down the block and a dog's sharp bark echoes from an apartment above.

I miss the darkness already.

Pushing off the cold wall behind me, I check my hat to make sure everything is safely tucked away.

My hair grows too fast and I haven't so much as trimmed it in the last year. The strands are dirty and matted, the platinum blonde hue covered in several layers of grime. Hiding my hair has nothing to do with my insecurities and everything to do with downplaying my femininity. I don't need to make myself any more of a target than I already am.

People see me as weak.

I'm not, but making it through the day without altercations is important if I don't want to accidentally slip out of this reality.

My other option is to cut it short. It's something I've considered more than once, but I've already given up so much. I can't stomach losing something else. Instead, I'll keep it hidden.

Satisfied my head is properly covered, I tug the beanie down over my ears and plod to the corner of the building. Keeping my body pressed against the brick wall, I peek at the rousing world outside the dingy alley.

The sun is only just beginning its daily ascent. The sky holds fast to the gray and blue screen of night, but the darkness will soon be chased away by the budding light.

The corners of my mouth turn down at the evidence of the growing day.

I prefer the night. Shadows are a comfort in a way the glaring daylight will never be.

Hunger fists inside my gut at the same time my stomach lets out a pathetic grumble, reminding me it has been too long since my last meal. I don't need as much food or sleep as a normal person, but three days without a bite is stretching it a bit far, even for me.

Slinking into the alley, I consider my options.

I usually rely on a combination of dumpster diving, charity, and occasionally the odd job to feed myself. I can't afford to go to a mission—they ask too many questions and filling my belly isn't worth getting tagged as a runaway minor. Begging isn't a viable option because loitering in a public spot is too much of a risk as well.

Shelter isn't a problem . . . until winter. Things get dicey during Colorado's arctic months. Last year, I had to break into more private properties than I cared to keep track of, just to escape the frigid temperatures.

When I turn eighteen, I'll breathe easier. Becoming a legal adult means I can't get thrown back into the system—or worse. My last foster family wanted to commit me to a psychiatric hospital. To escape that fate, I need to age out. I only have to endure this degrading existence for six more months.

Leaving the city in search of a more peaceful life is the dream. Settling somewhere in the mountains would be nice. Somewhere far enough from prying eyes so there are no witnesses to my strange episodes in the spectrum world. Even better if I can build a home right into the rocks to protect me from my living nightmares.

Until then, it's safer to hide among the masses—in plain sight, but basically invisible.

Just six more months, I remind myself. The reassurance feels good, so I say it again—this time aloud.

Talking to myself has become an odd sort of comfort. People look through you when you're homeless—something I'd counted on when I ran away from my last foster family. Becoming invisible was an essential part of my survival, but what I didn't figure into my plans was exactly how dehumanizing that would feel. Chitchatting with myself reminds me that I'm still a person, albeit a strange one.

My gut twists, telling me that my most urgent need is sustenance so I can stay alert for a few more days.

I mentally run through my anemic list of possibilities. There's a grocer on 6th Avenue that throws away their expired food once a week, but that won't be for two more days. It's early, I could stop by Denver Bread and see if they need help hauling in their morning delivery of flour in exchange for a few bucks or even food. Fresh bread is delicious and hard to come by these days. People don't throw fresh loaves in the trash for vagrants like me to fish out.

There are a few downtown restaurants I could hit up. Newberry and Sassafras are close, but don't open for several more hours. Anita's opens early though. It's been . . . hmmm . . . . two weeks? That could work.

Pulling the straps of my backpack tight, I dart out onto the sidewalk at a fast jog, heading toward the greasy spoon diner twelve blocks away.

This distance is barely a warm-up for me. I can run for hours before getting winded. It's just another one of the oddities I hide from the world.

The city passes me by as I keep a steady pace. A few cars drive by, but the sidewalks are almost completely empty. It's too early for Denver to be overrun. In a few hours, pedestrians will fill the walkways, hurrying to and from work. Midday, tourists lay claim to the city's streets and sidewalks until they are flooded by commuters rushing to catch the rail or stuffing themselves into their cars to camp in stop-and-go traffic for hours.

The cycle repeats itself daily, a cylindrical juggernaut that never changes. One that I've learned to use to my advantage.

As I turn down Fifteenth Street and head toward the river. I try to remember what day it is, seventy-two percent sure it's Tuesday. That's important because Karen works Tuesdays. She's liberal with the restaurant's leftovers, so I try to only go to Anita's during her shifts.

Picking up speed, I barely take note of the buildings flying by. The skyscrapers in the business district are a blur of gray that I've never found visually appealing. Resisting the urge to close my eyes, I focus instead on the crisp morning air hitting my face. When I was younger, I used to run full speed and pretend I was flying. The longing to do so again creeps up from time to time.

My hands twitch with the desire to rip off the wool hat concealing my hair and let it stream free. My scalp itches under the mass of hair and thick yarn. I like to feel the tickle of the breeze running its fingers through my strands. The early fall chill hasn't quite set in yet, so it's too early to be wearing the tight-fitting hat, but taking it off is out of the question.

My sigh is swallowed by the wind.

Rounding another corner, I spot Anita's. The squat one-story restaurant is sandwiched between two twenty-story apartment buildings. The red Spanish-tiled roof and yellow stucco façade is out of place between the sleek buildings flanking it, but it's been a neighborhood staple for over half a century, so it isn't likely to change anytime soon.

Shaking off thoughts about my hair and replacing them with the anticipation of a hot meal, I go to the side of the building and peek through a window that gives me a partial view of the kitchen.

Wearing a pair of high-waisted skinny jeans and an Anita's t-shirt, Karen is standing in front of a wall stacked high with dry ingredients and cans. She holds a clipboard in one hand, while the pencil clutched in the other bobs through the air as she takes inventory.

The hint of a smile moves my lips when I see her.

Five months ago, Karen spotted me curled up between dumpsters behind the restaurant. With cover on three sides and an easily scaled fence in the back, it was a great sleeping spot. I must have looked pretty pathetic because she's been feeding me breakfast a couple times a month ever since. I always arrive before the restaurant opens and refuse to set foot inside the establishment. It's too easy to get cornered in public buildings. If it came down to a chase, I'd rather be outside, where my chances of escaping are significantly higher.

Knowing my quirk, Karen always brings a plate out to the alley.

She's good people, that one.

I don't stop by every week because I don't want her anticipating my visits. What if she gets overly worried about me one day? Her concern might compel her to call the authorities, not realizing how much harm that would cause me.

I appreciate her generosity, but I'm not willing to risk my freedom on the kindness of a stranger.

Watching her perform her pre-opening ritual, I gently rap on the glass that separates us, careful not to make too much noise. She raises her chin and swivels her eyes to me on the second tap. A warm smile blossoms on her face that reaches her crystal blue eyes.

I wave and stretch my smile to match hers. When she motions with her hand, I nod my understanding and go to the back door.

I don't "people" well, but my awkwardness hasn't deterred Karen yet. Whether she's pushing her unease aside, or it truly doesn't exist, I'm not sure—I'm simply grateful for it.

Leaning against the alley wall with my arms crossed, I watch the sky change colors. As the blue lightens, the shadows shorten.

I'm ready for the door when it bangs open, so I don't startle. Karen walks through backside first, her hands occupied with a tray. My eyebrows pinch together as I take in several overflowing plates as well as a glass of orange juice and a mug of coffee.

The meaty scent of maple-glazed bacon tugs at my taste buds, and my mouth waters. I'm like Pavlov's dogs when it comes to bacon; I lose complete control of my salivary glands.

When Karen moves past me I catch sight—and smell—of eggs, berries, toasted bagels with butter and jam, and hash browns as well.

This amount of food is excessive.

"Do you mind grabbing those crates and turning them over, Lizzie? I thought we could sit and have breakfast together this morning. Looks like it's going to be a beautiful day and I have some time before the other employees arrive."

Karen thinks my name is Elizabeth, and calls me Lizzie. My name isn't either of those, but giving out my real one isn't something I do anymore.

Grabbing the overturned vegetable crates, I right them so we can both sit. Karen sets the tray down on a cardboard box that hasn't been broken down yet.

I regard her and the food with a small measure of trepidation.

With glossy-black hair that hangs several inches below her shoulders, Karen is a beautiful woman. In the past, she's eaten with me a time or two, but when she did she kept her distance, knowing I was skittish. She usually stands with a shoulder leaned against the building, munching on something small while sipping coffee, as I eat leftovers from the night before. Since I only ever stop by before business hours, the cook is never in.

Leftovers are more than fine with me. I learned a long

time ago not to be picky. Not having to dumpster dive for food is a luxury I don't take for granted.

Today though, she's brought a feast—and I'm suspicious of the change. Did she make this food while I was waiting for her? Surely it would take more than a few short minutes to conjure up so many dishes.

Catching me silently eyeing the bounty, her smile kicks up a notch.

"Believe it or not, I was a cook in another life."

I suppose that's the only explanation I'm going to get. I don't welcome questions myself, so asking them in return feels hypocritical.

The crease between my eyebrows smooths as the sweet tang of pulp-filled orange juice slides down my throat. I savor the taste of the sugary goodness as if it were a sip of fine wine.

"This is too much. I couldn't eat half of this if I tried."

That's not entirely true. I may not eat often, but when I do, I can really pack it in. I usually pace myself, because a girl who eats like a linebacker tends to raise a few eyebrows.

She swats a hand through the air as if to brush away my words. "Just eat what you want and leave the rest. I felt like making sure you had a full belly today."

My smile tightens as I nod and reach for a strip of bacon, wondering if she's become a little attached to me. If that's the case, this is going to have to be my last visit to Anita's. I can't risk Karen getting used to having me around. Besides, I don't do attachments. I'm not used to them, and the few I've made over my lifetime have always broken apart in painful ways.

Nope. The only person I want to be around is myself.

I'm a loner by design. Why else would I have been dumped

on a doorstep as a baby? If my own parents hadn't wanted me, why should anyone else?

Someday I'll find a place to live where no one will bother me. Somewhere no one will judge me.

That's life goals, as far as I'm concerned.

"So, what are you up to today?"

I shrug. It's not as if I lead an exciting life. "I thought I'd stop by the Waldorf for high tea later." I wink as I chew my bit of egg to let her know I'm teasing rather than being smart with her.

"Oh, yes," she replies, playing along, "I hear their spread is absolutely divine."

"I can't imagine it holds a candle to this feast."

Is that French toast?

I've only had that dish once before. When I was about eight or nine the foster family I was living with decided to celebrate my birthday with a sugary breakfast. That was one of the better days.

Brushing aside melancholy thoughts, I bring a piece of syrup-soaked bread to my mouth.

Heaven.

"This is delish."

"Thanks." Her smile reaches her eyes and her whole face lights up. I love that about her—how one facial expression conveys so much emotion. "It was actually my grandmother's recipe."

"Mm-mmm," I mumble as I stuff my face with a third bite of the treat.

"So, I was wondering something." Karen presses her lips together as she regards me. Something about the sudden stiffness to her posture causes a rock to form in my stomach. I swallow hard and chase the food with a sip of orange juice while I wait for her to continue.

Years of intuition tell me my meal is over.

"I've never seen you without a hat. Would you mind if I ask what color your hair is?"

It's a harmless question, but a red alarm starts screaming bloody murder inside my head. My intuition has been right too many times to ignore it now.

Standing swiftly, I grab my bag and backpedal, never taking my eyes off Karen.

"Lizzie, what are you doing?" A worried line appears between her eyes as she stands too—her height rivaling my own almost-six feet—and takes a step forward. She holds her arms up in front of her, palms facing me in the universal gesture for "calm down."

Is she trying not to scare me off?

Too late for that.

"Thanks so much for the breakfast. And for everything. But I should probably get going." I don't stop my steady retreat, but she halts. That leeches some of the paranoia out of my system.

She isn't coming after me. That's good.

"Was it because I asked about your hair? You don't have to tell me, I was just—"

A crash inside the diner has both our heads swiveling to the back door.

A normal person would assume it's the cook or one of the wait staff.

A normal person wouldn't shoot an accusing glare at the person kind enough to feed her.

A normal person would smile warmly, sit down, and eat as much of the amazing breakfast as she could fit in her belly.

I'm far from a normal person.

"Emberly, this isn't—"

That one word causes my adrenaline to spike ten times stronger than my morning wake-up call.

Emberly. She knows my name. My *real* name.

2

The widening of Karen's eyes reveals she hadn't meant to say that out loud.

I should be running right now.

That's definitely what I should be doing, but bursts of lights flash along the periphery of my vision, freezing me in place.

This is bad. This is *so* bad.

"I'm sorry. It wasn't supposed to be like this. We've been searching for you for a very long time. We just weren't sure if you were the one we were looking for."

Uh-uh. No way. That's creeper talk.

Starbursts of light or not, I am out of here.

Turning so quickly my bag slaps the side of the restaurant, I take off. No holding back, a full-on sprint I never use because it draws too much attention. I can run faster than a normal person should be able to, and right now, I welcome the speed.

In a split second I'm at the front of the restaurant, but it's already too late.

I skid to a halt. The chest of a tall, broad shouldered, dark-haired man only inches in front of my nose.

Backpedaling several steps, I check over my shoulder to see Karen standing twenty feet behind me.

"She's over here," the man shouts, his deep voice booming.

It takes no time for several more people to join the giant of a man, creating a human wall in front of me.

I catalog the threat.

Eight people total. Men and women. All tall. All dark-haired.

I'm definitely not getting through them. That leaves Karen behind me. If I jump the fence in the back, I can escape through the rear alley.

"You're coming with us," says Goliath's twin.

Yeah, I think I'll pass.

Flashes of light start overtaking the central portion of my vision.

No no no no no no no!

This is not the time to slip out of reality.

"Deacon, you're scaring her. This isn't the way to do this," Karen argues.

"We don't have time to baby her like—"

Flee, instinct roars at me.

I have to get out of here.

Right. Now.

I have no idea who these people are, or what they want. But what I do know is that if I wait around any longer, I'll be a sitting duck. Stuck between this reality and the other, I'll be easy pickings for these weirdo kidnappers as I run from monsters no one else can see.

Turning, I run directly at Karen, dipping to the right at the last moment to edge around her. The movement should be too fast for a person to track, but her hand shoots out and snags my pack as I skirt her.

Dropping my arms and shoulders, I slip out of the backpack. There isn't a material possession I own that is worth sacrificing my independence for.

Jumping, I land on the fence like a squirrel, at least six feet in the air. The metal wires bite into my hands as I scramble to scale its height.

Light explodes in my vision as I drop to the ground on the other side.

"She's phasing!"

When I pop up from a crouch, my realities have merged.

No! This can't happen right now!

Structures from the real world remain, but it's as if a Technicolor screen has overlaid them.

The building to my left must be an apartment because it's bursting with light. A mix of colors pulsate around it like a giant rainbow aura. Reds and blues dominate the assortment, with sparks of yellow, green, and purple.

Currents of air move around me in tangible waves of light and sound, causing the hair on my arm to rise and a sticky-sweet aroma to tickle my nose.

I ignore all of it, because it's the dark smudges high in the lavender sky that have captured my attention.

They are the creatures of my nightmares and this distorted reality: shadow beasts.

I'm not frightened of the dark, but I am scared of them.

They're the real monsters that go bump in the night, and I have the scars to prove it.

Black splotches jerk through the air like bats, making their trajectory almost impossible to gauge.

Cover. I need it. Fast.

My feet beat the pavement as I race down the alley. I keep one eye on the beasts in the sky.

I only ever have two options when I'm attacked: find somewhere to hide, or blend in with a large group of people. The former is always the better choice, because avoiding floating blobs of color—which is how people appear to me in this reality—is tricky. Also, people can see and hear me clearly, but the shadow beasts? Conveniently invisible to the naked eye. When I'm fighting off or running from dark amorphous shadows with sharp claws that no one can see, I definitely look insane.

Since it's still early in the morning—it can't be much past six—the commuters aren't out in full force yet, so blending in with a group is not even an option.

That means I have to find one of my hidey-holes. Somewhere to lay low until the spectrum world fades.

I mentally run through the list of safe locations as I sprint. The closest is an alcove under the Platte River Bridge about eight blocks away. The white aura that encapsulates my body might as well be a beacon that reads MEALTIME to the flying creatures above, but being near running water will camouflage me. Since discovering the trick, I always have a list of places I can hide within running distance.

Bursting out of the alley at full speed, my mind focuses on reaching my destination. There is no way my human pursuers can keep up with my speed. Since there isn't a row of glowing auras waiting for me the moment I bust out of the alley, I have to assume they haven't caught up to me.

I ignore the sights and sounds vying for attention.

My path is already plotted in my mind: four blocks straight, three blocks east.

My eyes remain fixed on my course.

I eat up three blocks in only a handful of seconds. I have to hope that any people driving by didn't catch the blur darting down the street.

I'm just about to round the corner of the fourth block when a shadow drops out of the sky and lands in front of me.

Skidding to a halt to keep from colliding with it, I hear the telltale *thud* not far behind me.

Fear burns its way up my spine and explodes like a firecracker in my brain.

The monsters have found me.

The shadowy forms boxing me in are just that—formless blobs of darkness. They remind me of a moving black hole. Their edges are semi-translucent, almost like looking through shady mist. I can't see through the main part of their bodies—if that's what the darkness even is.

If this reality is like seeing the world through a sunlit kaleidoscope, these beings stand out for their absence of color. It's as if they suck the beauty of this world into themselves. Not satisfied by simply obscuring the light, they seek to devour it.

The forms on either side of me undulate and move, as if posturing. I don't know what they are or what they want, except to hurt me. My body is littered with scars from these creatures, whose sharp talons I never see, but feel slicing through my flesh.

Since no one else can see these abhorrent beasts, my foster families and social workers always thought my injuries were self-inflicted.

I learned to hide my wounds as best I could, but a particularly bad attack six months ago landed me in the hospital. I needed thirty-four stitches and two liters of blood to replenish what had been lost.

Since I had a history of similar injuries, the powers-that-be assumed I'd done something to myself. And what defense could I have given them? The leading theory was that I'd jumped out of the window of an abandoned industrial building. I suppose that would account for the cuts on my body, as well as the broken bones.

Lying in a hospital bed, I overheard my foster parents talking with my case worker about sending me to a psychiatric hospital. That was the last day I was officially a ward of the state.

Forcing the memory from my head, I scan my surroundings while the rest of the world wakes, none the wiser to the personal hell I face.

Cars zip along the street to my left. A parking garage stands to my right.

I bounce on the balls of my feet, steeped in indecision. My options aren't good, but just as the shadow beast strikes, instinct has me bolting to the right and ducking into the garage.

Finding the stairwell, I race up the steps and emerge on the upper deck of the lot. I rush to the far corner and find that over the ledge is a six-story drop to the unforgiving ground below.

Way to go, Emberly. You really stepped in it this time.

What was I thinking?

Running to the top of a garage was the worst idea ever.

Suddenly, I'm the dumb girl in a bad horror film, running into the attic when she should have raced outside.

I want to throat punch myself.

On a bad day I'm a lot of things, but dumb isn't usually one of them.

Jerking my eyes skyward, I spot several dark shapes swooping toward me. The two uglies following me have reached the top deck as well.

I've been in bad spots before, but this one may be the worst yet.

My only weapons are speed and maneuverability. Even after all these years, I have no idea how to fight these creatures. I've adopted a hide-at-all-costs philosophy when it comes to these other-world experiences.

Standing my ground, I wait for the monsters to reach me. A familiar golden shimmer zooms in front of me, leaving a trail of gold dust in its wake. I swat at the reoccurring nuisance. The flittering light appears from time to time, but since I've never figured out what it is and it doesn't seem to want to hurt me, it isn't a priority.

Refocusing my attention, I start to piece together a messy plan of action.

If I can draw the two shadow beasts away from the stairwell, I might be able to get back on the ground. I'll run into the nearest building if I have to. Who cares if I draw people's attention? This is a matter of survival.

Sweat trickles down my spine as time stretches.

A little closer, you ugly fat blobs.

As if hearing my thoughts, the shadows start toward me.

I flick my gaze upward. The ones in the sky haven't slowed their descent. It's as if the beasts on the ground and in the air are in a race to reach their prize: me.

They're going to converge on me at once. I'll be the loser that ends up a pancake beneath them.

Three. Two. One. *Now!*

When the shadow beasts are only a hair's breadth away, I dive to the right, tuck into a somersault and spring to my feet.

The ground shakes as their forms collide, but I don't glance behind me to survey the carnage or to see what is following me or how closely. Instead, I sprint for the stairs and pray I'm fast enough.

The stairwell is only feet away.

I'm going to make it!

Just as the tip of my toe passes over the threshold, something slams into me from the side, sending me flying into a nearby car.

I crash into the driver's side of a silver sedan, breaking the window and leaving an Emberly-sized dent in the door.

Landing with a thud, my forehead slaps the concrete. My view of the color-drenched world blinks in and out, but with stubborn will alone, I remain conscious.

This isn't how I'm going to go out.

I've survived seventeen torturous years with my body and freedom intact. I plan to keep myself alive for years to come.

I shove off the ground and bounce to my feet. My head's angry with that move, but I tell it to shut up.

Only two creatures still stalk me. It appears the others are battling each other. I can't be sure that's what's happening, but to my eyes, the monsters look to be viciously ramming into each other.

It would be comical if it wasn't a life-or-death situation.

The two that aren't engaged in a weird game of bumper cars come at me from the front.

Blood flows freely down the left side of my face, making it impossible to see out of that eye. Nervously, I pull my bottom lip into my mouth to chew on, only to release it with a grimace. I didn't realize it was speckled with blood as well.

Even with the massive amount of adrenaline flooding my system, my brain is sluggish. Instead of taking action, I just stand there, my feet glued to the ground.

I was wrong. This *is* the end.

I'm going to die without knowing the truth about what has hunted me my whole life.

I throw my arms up in a feeble attempt to protect myself, but look away, unable to force myself to face the end.

I'm sure any moment, my life will flash before my eyes, but rather than a montage of childhood scenes, a blinding light drops from the sky, forcing me to squeeze my lids shut.

Something lands, shaking the concrete slab under my feet.

It's only a moment before the brightness dims and my eyes pop open. Standing with his back to me is a guy in jeans and a black leather jacket, double-fisting a pair of weapons. A sword in his right hand, a gun in the other.

I'm already dead. That's the only explanation.

I can't see humans in this reality, only their strange colored auras. But I can see this guy in glaring detail. Everything from the mop of dark hair on his head down to his chunky-soled, well-worn black motorcycle boots.

I rub my eyes, managing to smear blood all over my face.

Smooth move, Emberly.

I scan the roof with my good eye. The shadow beasts are still there.

What. Is. Happening?

The guy standing between me and my attackers is a good half-foot taller than me, which puts him around six-foot-five at least. His raven black hair is longer on top than on the sides.

My perusal of his form is shoved aside when I register the faint white glow haloing his body—an exact replica of the one encasing my own.

We are somehow the same, but not knowing what makes me different, I can't say what our similarity is.

"What are you waiting for? The dinner bell?" He taunts the creatures in a deep growl.

Is he *trying* to get killed?

The silence is broken several beats later by the bark of a humorless laugh, startling me. Jerking, I smash my elbow into the car door.

Add it to the growing list of injuries for the day.

"You know I'm harder to kill than that."

My eyes scan the deck. He can't possibly be communicating with those ugly things. They don't talk. I've never once heard so much as a peep out of any of them, and I've been running from the monsters for as long as I can remember.

"I guess that means it's up to me to make the first move." The guy concludes his strange one-sided conversation by lifting the gun and shooting several rounds at the shadow beasts.

Covering my ears, I crouch during the initial volley of shots.

Ever since my second foster home, I've had an aversion to

guns. It doesn't matter that this one may have just saved my life—I still don't like them.

After another series of loud pops, the gun clatters to the ground in front of me. The acrid stench of sulfur laced with a metallic zing wafts from the barrel. It reminds me of burnt earth.

I glance up to see several of the shadows zipping toward us.

The guy mumbles something under his breath that sounds like, "This is what I live for," before the air sizzles and pops, and I'm blinded by another bright flash.

3

A roar splits the air a half-second before the brightness dims. An oversized lion towers on all fours where the guy was just standing.

I press a fist to my eyes, further smearing blood across my face. What I think just happened couldn't have really happened.

People do not just turn into animals.

The golden beast shoots forward and collides with the first dark shape it reaches, knocking it back several feet and sending both animal and shadow beast tumbling.

Several monsters join the fight. The lion's claws gleam in the daylight; sharp fangs snap, and it isn't long before the animal's coat is glistening with black liquid.

"Steel! Stand down!" a sharp voice bellows.

I'm so caught up in the battle in front of me, I missed the people swarming the top floor of the garage. There are at least twenty newcomers, all haloed in the same white glow as myself and the mystery guy who just disappeared. The group forms a semi-circle around me, pushing the shadow beasts back.

A feline growl snags my attention. I look up to see the lion jump over the line of would-be rescuers and take up a sentinel position in front of me. Shaking out its coat, the lion splatters me with a putrid mix of black blood and saliva.

Nasty.

I was already covered in my own brand of grossness, but that bath upped the "ew" factor by a million. Thank goodness I didn't have my mouth open, because the fluid on me smells like a combination of rotten eggs and butt. I have to order my gag reflex to stand down.

A man on my left turns his head to issue a command to the group. I recognize his masculine features right away.

Deacon—the man from Anita's. The would-be kidnapper.

With people and monsters both blocking the stairwell, I have nowhere to run.

"Steel, take her to the transport," Deacon barks.

The lion growls low in its throat, the sound vibrating in my own chest. The fine hairs at the nape of my neck stand on end.

"It's not a discussion. Do it. Now!"

Shaking its head in annoyance, the oversized cat turns to me. Its head alone is half the size of my torso. I move to retreat, but my back hits the driver's side door of the Emberly-dented car.

"Nice kitty," I murmur with wide eyes.

It makes a very human guffaw before rolling its teal and sapphire eyes.

There's a shock of black fur streaked through the beast's gold mane to the left of its right ear.

I'm not exactly sure what this thing is—it certainly isn't your garden-variety zoo lion—but I am sure I'm not comfortable being anywhere near it. Even if it did save my life, there's a wildness about the giant animal that makes me nervous.

Without warning, it sinks to its haunches and jerks its head in a "hop on" gesture.

I shake my head so fast I won't be surprised if I get whiplash from the motion.

No way am I climbing on that thing's back for a joy ride.

It growls low in its throat in a show of impatience.

"Listen up, buddy. I don't make a habit of climbing on strange animals."

The overgrown house cat rolls his eyes another time, proving he understands every word coming out of my mouth.

He takes a step forward, and I scramble up and over the car hood behind me. Sliding off the other side, I take off in a sloppy run.

There's another stairwell on the opposite side of the parking deck that I'm determined to reach.

Behind me, a roar morphs into a loud caw. It's like someone is jamming knitting needles into my eardrums. I stop myself from bringing my hands up to cover my ears, so I can keep pumping my arms as I run.

A wave of displaced air slams into my back a moment before I'm airborne, feet still moving as if I can run on wind.

The gusts of rushing air steal my gasp. A talon wrapped around each of my biceps keeps me suspended in air.

Sucking in a lungful, I ready myself to let out a scream, but before I can release it, we bank hard and the exclamation lodges itself in my throat.

We soar through city streets and take corners so quickly, I'm sure we're going to crash into the side of a building. Craning my neck, I confirm I'm in the clutches of a giant bird. Its wingspan alone is easily twice the length of my body.

I struggle against its hold to no avail.

I've survived my entire life completely alone in this split reality, but I've never seen anything close to what I witnessed today.

People appearing in the spectrum world with the same glowing aura as me.

Battles between the shadow beasts I've spent my whole life either hiding or running from.

Giant animals that understand English.

My head aches from more than the knocks it has taken. If I make it through this day alive, I'm going to find an underground bunker somewhere to live the rest of my life out in seclusion. Somewhere I can exist free of this terror.

I swallow a scream as we bank and swoop toward the ground. A couple more feet and my toes will skim the pavement in an industrial neighborhood I recognize. I spent several winter nights in one of the abandoned buildings here.

There isn't a single human aura in sight.

"Let me go, you overgrown turkey!" I yell at my captor.

An angry caw answers, followed by a violent shake that rattles my already jumbled brain.

When this bird lets me go, I am going to kick its feathered butt from here to next weekend.

Our speed slows and I notice a white van idling about a block ahead.

Oh gosh, it's a cliché kidnapper van.

A couple of people with pulsating white auras stand close to it. I can't make out their features beyond identifying a dark-haired male and female. The guy is leaned up against the kidnapper van, doing something on his phone. The girl is pacing.

"I'm serious!" I shout at the bird. I would bet money it can understand me, and I'm willing to annoy it into dropping me. "If you don't let me go, I'm going to hunt you down and make sure you're the centerpiece of my Thanksgiving meal! All that fat I see on you will make a juicy—ahhh!"

I'm falling.

I don't have time to release a scream before my feet connect with the unforgiving pavement several car-lengths ahead of the white van.

I try to duck into a roll, but I'm not fast enough.

I stupidly hadn't actually expected or prepared to be released when I was conducting my verbal assault on the flying brute.

My legs crumple under me right before my side slams against the asphalt. The momentum throws my legs over my head, and I end up doing several awkward rag-doll flops before I stop moving.

The back of my head cracks against the ground on the last roll.

I lay spread eagle in the middle of the road, convinced every bone in my body is broken.

My vision swims. The telltale sparks of light sputter on the edges of my eyesight before condensing in the middle and petering out, alerting me I'm back in the real world.

Everything hurts.

I'm going to skin that bird.

The sound of feet pounding against the ground grows louder as the seconds tick by.

"Steel! What were you thinking?" That musical voice is vaguely familiar and very annoyed.

"She called me a fat turkey." I hear, rather than see, the shrug in his words.

"I don't care if she called you Big Bird. You don't just drop someone from the air. She's hurt!"

A blurry face appears above me at the same time someone else blows out a harsh breath. A car engine revs in the distance.

I blink twice before Karen's concerned features register— my mind is understandably sluggish.

"Are you okay?"

That was a dumb question. Of course I'm not okay.

Another head pops into view. He's blocking the sunlight, so his features are shrouded in darkness. I squint up at him, but his face won't leave the shadows.

"She's going to be fine. You know how fast we heal. Besides, if she hadn't run from us, none of this would have happened."

"Steel," Karen snaps at the guy.

"What?" He holds up his hands, all earnest innocence. "I got her to safety, didn't I? Where's my thanks?"

What. A. Jerk.

I strain my arm muscles, fully intending to show him my favorite finger, but it hurts too much to move. I have to settle for a scathing glare that he doesn't even catch.

I don't know how he did it, but I'm pretty sure this dude shape shifted into a bird and dropped me on purpose.

"Get in the car. We'll discuss this back at the academy."

He shrugs and straightens.

Good riddance.

Karen captures my attention once again. She opens her mouth to speak but is cut-off by a surprised exclamation from Bird Boy.

"Sable, her hair!"

Sable?

Karen reaches forward and snatches a lock of my light blonde, red-tipped hair.

Somewhere along the way, I lost the hat. Not surprising when you're running for your life, getting thrown into cars, and flown through the city all before being unceremoniously dumped on the street by a giant bird.

"I didn't know if I should believe it." The words are just above a whisper, as if she's speaking to herself. She rubs the strands between her fingers.

"Could she have dyed it?" My blurred vision snaps back to the guy . . . Steel.

Moving my head, bad idea. It feels like the percussion section of a really bad high school band is banging away up there.

"We can't dye or bleach our hair," Karen responds absent-mindedly.

The guy shoves his hands in the pockets of his jeans. "I know that. But what else makes sense? Her eyes are freaky enough. This is just going to make her stand out more."

"Hey . . . you're freaky," I croak. I slam my lids shut over my very-not-weird dark blue eyes as a wave of nausea over-takes me.

"Shoot." Karen's concerned voice is back. "I'm sorry. Let's get you up."

"No. Lie here . . . and die." Unless someone is going to knock me out for good, I'm not moving.

Steel emits a short laugh.

"Come on, help me get her up. We need to get her in the car. Drake has it running."

Oh right, I'm being kidnapped. I almost forgot.

Do I even care anymore?

I think about that for a moment while footsteps shuffle around me. When hands reach under me and force me to stand, I decide that yes, I still very much care about being taken against my will.

I smother a whimper as I'm pulled to my feet. Groggily opening my lids, I concentrate on pushing energy into my right arm.

I learned to fight dirty a long time ago. Life hasn't afforded me the luxury of honor.

Almost blindly, I strike out at the blurred figure in front of me. Even more of my vision has dimmed, but I'll worry about that later.

There is a pain-filled grunt a moment before hot agony radiates down my fist and shoots down my arm.

I welcome the pain, because it means I connected solidly.

As hoped, the hands holding me fall away.

My victory is short-lived as I attempt to stumble-run away, only to find myself upside down over someone's shoulder a hot second later. I stare down at a familiar pair of worn boots from my topsy-turvy perch.

Parking garage dude is also Bird Boy, who is also Steel? I guess that means the giant lion didn't eat him after all.

Pity.

The fight has completely left me . . . and any minute, my breakfast may as well.

"Sick," I manage to whimper-whisper.

"You'd better not," Steel orders. "You already gave me a bloody nose. If you even think about throwing up on me, I'll feed you to the Fallen myself."

Who or what are the Fallen? I wonder—right before succumbing to the darkness.

4

*L*ight is the worst.

Grabbing a pillow, I shove it over my head to smother myself.

Oh, feather down. Comfy.

I snuggle into the softness, refusing to fully wake. It's like sleeping on a cloud. I like.

Wait . . . I don't have down pillows. I don't even have a bed.

Popping up with a squeak, I promptly drop several feet and land with a muffled *oof*. I'm tangled in the bedding I pulled with me and my shoulder and hip throb from breaking my fall.

"Ow."

Rubbing my bruised side, I peer up at a giant four-poster bed to my left.

"Who sleeps that far off the ground?" I mutter. "It's unnatural."

As I struggle to free myself from the bedding pretzel-twisted around my legs and torso, my mind scrambles to make sense of the situation.

Wannabe kidnappers. Getting chased by the shadow beasts. My would-be rescuer. A gigantic lion. An enormous bird. Getting dropped from the sky. A cocky jerk.

Yep, that about covers it.

Pulling a sheet off my head, I stand and suck in a lungful of fresh air.

"You must be feeling better."

I yip and spin in a circle. Karen is watching me from an oversized chair in a darkened corner of the room.

Yeah, that isn't creepy.

Standing up, she takes a few tentative steps toward me.

She looks . . . different.

Her hair waterfalls over her shoulders in sleek sheets. She's ditched the mom jeans and sneakers for black leggings and ankle boots. The artfully distressed gray t-shirt she's wearing—I'm an expert in what real distressed clothes look like—hangs off one shoulder. Her face is free of make-up except for a light dusting of blush, some mascara, and a rosy sheen on her lips.

The overall effect makes her appear ten years younger. She can't be older than her mid-thirties. I don't know how I ever thought she was middle-aged.

"Where am I?"

I scan the room, looking for something to use as a weapon. I've been taken against my will, after all.

The room looks like a fancy hotel suite. A glass vase is the most threatening object I can find. In a pinch, I can work with that.

I'm scrappy.

Karen sighs and indicates the bed. "Why don't you sit down? It's been a long day."

Crossing my arms, I jut my hip to the side and stare her down. She's right, it *has* been a long day.

"Why don't you tell me what's going on, *Karen?*" I practically spit the name, which I'm beginning to doubt is real.

"Right. Okay then. Fair enough." Bringing a hand to her face, she pinches the bridge of her nose. "First off, my name isn't Karen, it's Sable."

"And where am I . . . Sable?"

"We're in the Rockies, about three hours from Denver. Glenwood Springs. It's an old mining town. We brought you to one of our academies. As you've probably worked out, I'm not a waitress. I'm actually the headmistress of this institution —Seraph Academy. This is a safe place for people like you. People like us."

I cock an eyebrow. "What do you mean, 'people like us'?"

Karen—Sable—gestures to the bed again. I continue to glare and she sighs when it becomes clear I'm not planning on moving.

"People with the blood of angels. Everyone here—"

"The blood of angels?" I rear back. My foot tangles in the forgotten bedding balled on the floor and I go down hard.

Stepping over the mess, Sable offers me a hand up. When I'm on my own two feet, she continues. "Nephilim to be exact."

"Nef-a-what?"

"Nephilim. Everyone here is descended from the union of a human woman and an angel of darkness."

"Wait . . . you're telling me my father is an angel? Or, an

angel of darkness?" The phrase feels awkward and clunky. "What even is that?"

"You ready to take a seat yet?" Sable asks as she crosses her arms over her chest.

I nod.

Yep. I think it's time to do that. Sitting sounds fantastic right now.

Wide-eyed and attentive, I drop my butt onto the soft bedding and gesture for her to continue.

Sable shakes her head and silky hair brushes over her shoulders. "The original couplings of disgraced angels and humans was just the start of our lines. It's very unlikely your father was a fallen angel—those we simply call Fallen. The original hybrids were born several millennia ago. We haven't heard of a child of a Fallen and a human woman in over two thousand years. Those of us that exist today are descendants of the original hybrids."

She takes a seat next to me, the bed dipping slightly with her added weight. "There are academies like this one smattered all over the globe. Our young come here to learn and train until they are old enough to fight on their own. We've brought you to one of the safest locations for our kind. For your protection, and also to learn about who you are and what you can do.

"There's quite a bit to tell you, actually. It's going to take a considerable amount of time to get you caught up to speed, but for now you need to know that there is a war going on. One fought in the spiritual and mortal realms between angels of light, and angels of dark—the Fallen.

"Whether you knew it or not, you were born into this

conflict, but you are not alone. Everyone here at Seraph Academy is like you—an angel-born child."

My head still hurts. That was a massive information dump. Bringing a hand to my forehead, I scrub my palm down my face. If I hadn't been accused of it so many times myself, I would have called her out as insane or a liar.

Could her story be just unbelievable enough to be true?

And . . . a war? I have a hard enough time getting through the day. I don't need to be dragged into what appears to be an ancient grudge match between good and evil.

"So, you want me to believe I'm not . . . human?" That last word was a little hard to push out. I never felt as if I fit in, but not human? That's a stretch.

"Exactly."

"And that a fallen angel is lurking somewhere in my family tree?"

"Yes."

I count to sixty as Sable and I stare at each other. I'm waiting for her to break. To yell "Just kidding!" or start crazy-laughing. But it never happens. She doesn't so much as flinch, and it starts to make me nervous.

"I'm going to be honest. I have no idea how to react to all this."

"I can only imagine." Sable's expressive eyes soften and she lays a comforting hand on my shoulder. "Most of our children grow up knowing exactly what they are. It's very rare for a Nephilim child to be raised by non-angel-born. Your life up until this point must have been very challenging . . . as well as confusing."

I bark out a humorless laugh. She has no idea.

"I'm going to be straight with you."

After all her deception, I should hope so. I tilt my head, waiting for her to continue.

"You've been on our radar for years now. We just didn't realize you were one of us. There are a very small percentage of humans who can see through the veil into the spirit realm. We have a division dedicated to identifying these individuals and monitoring them, if only loosely. We rarely interfere with human lives, and only intercede when we think they're a danger to themselves or others."

Hold on a second.

"You've . . . known about me? And you let everyone believe I was crazy? You let *me* believe I was crazy? That's messed up."

I scooch away from her until my shoulder touches the headboard and I can't go any farther. I'm sure the look on my face is filled with disgust. Sable glances at the empty space between us then lifts her gaze to meet mine.

"Most humans come to their own conclusions about their visions, so we let them believe whatever they need to believe. It may seem cruel, but to bring them fully into our world would be much more dangerous. Up until very recently, we assumed you were one of these humans."

"Maybe I am?" My life may be a confusing mess, but I think I'd rather be a messed up human than a Neph-a-whatever.

"You can't be." She shakes her head, her waterfall hair rippling slightly with the movement. "Humans can't jump worlds the way you do. At most, they can see glimpses."

"If you've known about me for years, why reveal yourself now?"

Shifting, Sable brings her leg up to rest on the bed so she can face me. "When you ran away, it triggered a review by one of our investigators. When she looked into your files a bit more deeply, the episodes you'd been having didn't add up. Humans can only see into the spirit realm—they can't interact with it. The reports of your injuries were consistent with wounds our own warriors would get.

"Students at this academy, even potential ones, are ultimately my responsibility. Someone reported you sleeping behind Anita's. You fit the description of the girl we were looking for, so I was sent in to build a rapport with you. Without diving too deeply into things, I can tell you that you are a bit of an enigma to us. You were very careful with what information you shared with me. I imagine you had to learn to be cautious. When I couldn't find any definitive answers, we decided to pull you in anyway. It wasn't until you phased that we knew with certainty you were one of us."

There's that word again. *Phased.* What exactly does that mean?

"I'm confused," I admit.

Her smile doesn't reach her eyes. "Like I said, I can only imagine what you're going through. But I want to assure you that you belong here. You belong with us. You're never going to be alone again."

Her words, meant to assure, have the opposite effect. My palms grow sticky and my heart rate picks up.

To belong.

To find a place among others.

To not feel so alone, day after day.

Those used to be my deepest desires, but years of hardship and rejection have beaten the longing out of me. The craving is gone.

I've worked my whole life to be content alone. That's all I

want anymore—to be left alone. To live my life on my own terms.

I won't rely on anyone else. People always leave. They always let you down.

The darkness that prowls the spectrum world aren't the only creatures I avoid. People can cut just as deeply as the shadow beasts' sharpened claws.

"Am I a prisoner?"

Sable's perfect brow pinches and her lips pucker. "A prisoner? Of course not. We only want to help."

"Then why did you kidnap me?"

She looks confused and . . . disappointed? Uncrossing her arms, she leans forward and steeples her hands under her chin.

"We didn't kidnap you. We're bringing you into the fold. We brought you to a safe haven."

"I was fine on my own until you and your muscle showed up. I didn't ask to be *saved*." She flinches when I spit the word "saved" at her. That's a low blow, but I don't care. "If I'm not a prisoner, I'd like to go."

Seconds tick by as Sable and I face off. Finally, she leans back and regards me warily.

"Where would you go? Back to living on the streets?"

I pop my jaw before answering.

"Yeah, if I have to."

"It's not safe for you to—"

"Says you. But you're trying to pull me into a war! There's nothing safe about that."

"You're already part of the conflict, even if you didn't realize it. We don't even know how you've stayed alive for this long on your own. It was only a matter of time—"

"Like I said, I was doing fine before you and your friends showed up."

Sable presses her lips together, clearly frustrated that I keep cutting her off. "I know you believe that, but there's more out there than you realize." She sucks in a deep breath and lets it out slowly, regarding me the whole time. "How about this—I'll make you a deal."

I narrow my eyes. It's in my nature to be suspicious of deals.

"What kind of deal?"

"You stay here for six months, until your eighteenth birthday—" She holds up a hand when I open my mouth to protest. "You stay here for that long. Not a single day less. Let us teach you about our world. All the strange things out there. How your power works. How to use it—"

"Wait, I have a power?" If that's true, it's several shades of awesome.

"And when you turn eighteen," she continues without acknowledging me, "you can go wherever you want."

"How do you know when my birthday is?" I ask. A note stating the date of my birth and my name, and a yellow baby blanket were the only two things I was left with after someone abandoned me on the steps of a fire station sixteen and a half years ago. The note is currently tucked away in a social worker's file cabinet. The blanket is most likely molding in a pile of landfill debris. I don't expect to see either of them again.

"We've seen your files."

"I'll bet that was an interesting read." I suck my bottom lip into my mouth and saw my teeth back and forth. "What's the catch?"

"No catch. The only thing you will have lost is a few months. But what you'll have gained—besides steady meals and a place to sleep—is the knowledge you've been robbed of all your life. I understand you don't really know me, and you don't know the others at all, but I can promise we only want to help you."

I turn her words over in my mind. The years have taught me to be naturally wary of people, but having a place to stay is a pretty big bonus. This bed is amazing. And if what she says is true and there are other people like me—whether this angel thing is a hoax or not—it'll be good to know more about the crazy that is my life.

On the other hand, this might be some sort of cult that wants to sacrifice me to some pagan god.

Oh gosh, why did I think that?

A shiver runs down my spine.

As long as I can rule out the cult thing, the smartest move would be to learn as much as possible and then hightail it out of here the second I turn eighteen.

If I take this deal, then for the next six months I'll be fed, get decent sleep, and hopefully learn how to properly protect myself. After all, the group who fought the shadow beasts held their own. And I'm seventy-six percent sure one of them is a shape shifter of some sort.

Ohhhh . . . what if I could do that?

"So, start by telling me about these magical powers."

A slow smile overtakes Sable's face. Her eyes sparkle with warmth and she holds out a hand.

"Bathe first. After we get some food in you, I'll sit down and answer whatever questions you have."

Bringing a hand up to my head, I wince when I touch my

crunchy hair. It's been a little too long since I've had a decent shower.

I'll accept her terms. Get cleaned, get fed, and get answers. I can live with that.

Taking her outstretched hand, I pump it twice.

"Welcome to Seraph Academy. I think you're going to like it here."

5

So. Many. People.

After taking an elevator several floors down—apparently half this academy is underground—we only make it two steps into the giant windowless room before a sea of dark-haired, light-eyed faces snap in our direction.

Or rather, my direction. Sable isn't the oddity.

I feel each set of eyes on me like a brand.

This is one of my nightmares come to life. Having spent my life keeping to the shadows, the attention of an entire room of teenagers makes my skin crawl.

It's so quiet, I can hear my own ragged breathing. Heat seeps up my neck and overtakes my face.

"It's just a cafeteria," Sable reminds me with a hand on my shoulder.

"Why are they all staring?" I whisper-yell.

Lifting her eyes, she regards the room as if for the first time.

She's not fooling me. There's no way she didn't notice the

shift when we entered. I heard the ruckus through the closed door. Now, all I can hear is their collective hive-mind working.

Oh no—it *is* a cult.

That's why they all look the same. They're going to flip when they figure out I can't dye my hair to match theirs.

Where are the closest exits? Time to put my running skills to good use.

"Okay, everyone. You've looked your fill." Sable's raised voice jolts me out of my rabbit trail thoughts. "You're making your new classmate uncomfortable."

My breathing starts to slow a bit. Maybe this won't be as bad as I thought.

I rub my heated palms against the material of the borrowed baggy jeans then tug at the hem of my oversized t-shirt. My underarms start to moisten.

Great, I'm going to start stinking soon.

"You'll all have time to introduce yourselves later."

Nope, back to panic mode.

Closest exit is the one we just entered through.

Pivoting on a heel, I rush back the way we came. Sable's surprised "Emberly, wait!" doesn't stop me from busting through the doors.

Experiment over. I'd rather sleep on the ground than be forced to interact with a group that large.

Sable's hurried steps catch up to me before I reach the turn in the hallway. She jumps in front of me with her hands raised.

"What's going on? Where are you going?"

I point a finger in the direction I just fled. "Nope. No way. I'm not doing that."

Her eyebrows knit together in confusion. When I try to step around her, she moves with me, blocking my path.

"Hold on a second. I promise it won't always be like that. You're just new."

"I can't dye my hair," I blurt.

"Um, we don't expect you to?" The statement hangs in the air as a question. A clear sign my abruptness derailed her.

I rub my forehead. Darn headache.

"There's no way I'm going to turn into a clone for you. So it's probably best we just part ways now. I'm sure you'll find another young girl to fill . . . ah . . . whatever sort of thing you've got going on here. Okay?"

Sable's eyes grow a fraction before she bursts out laughing. A melodic sound that, given my current state of unease, is entirely vexing. I tap a foot while I wait for her to compose herself.

"I'm so sorry," she finally says, "I'm not laughing at you."

I have a hard time believing that.

"It's just that I've gotten so used to it, it doesn't even register with me anymore. I realize everyone looks the same at first glance, but I can assure you that's not the case. I can also assure you that quite a few of the students would love to change their hair color if they could, but we can't dye or lighten our hair. The color we're born with is the color we keep throughout our lives."

My breath catches. My hair is the same way. Down to the freaky tinted ends that don't match the top.

"I can see by your face that that news is either incredibly surprising to you, or very familiar."

I absently run a hand through my long—recently cleaned —hair. During my shower, months of built-up grime had swirled down the drain. It's back to its light color with bright red tips.

"I can't dye mine either. I tried so many times when I was younger, but it all just washed out."

"I figured as much. That's a quality unique to our race."

She says that like we're a completely different species. Oh gosh—maybe we are?

Stuffing the thought away for later, I stick to the subject at hand.

"Why is mine so different, though? Everyone in there has dark hair. And I have this." I hold a chunk up between us to emphasize my point. The blonde parts practically glow under the overhead lights.

A few beats pass before Sable answers. "Truth is, we're not exactly sure. You are somewhat of an anomaly in that regard, but we will do our best to help figure it out. At the end of the day though, it's just hair."

"It's also a highly visible feature that sets me apart from every single person in that very large, very crowded room."

She nods, understanding in her eyes. "I get that I'm asking you to step outside your comfort zone here, but I truly believe this is for the best. That this is for *your* best. Will you please just give it a chance?"

I turn to look down the hall. The noise from the cafeteria has started up again, as if I'd never been there. Or perhaps they're all talking about me now. The strange girl with the odd hair.

"I have an idea. If I leave for a moment, will you promise not to run?"

That's a promise I don't want to keep. Sable notices my hesitation.

"Trust me, please?"

I reluctantly nod.

Sable hurries down the hall and through the dreaded doors. She's only gone a few minutes before she's pushing back through them, a teenage girl on her heels.

"She's right over here. Thanks for coming out."

"No problem," the girl says with her eyes—her very light blue eyes—glued on me. When she and Sable reach me, she just stares. In all fairness, I'm having a hard time not doing the same.

Her hair is a beautiful dark mass of curls that springs from her head and bounces a hand-length past her shoulders. Her eyes are crystal blue, bordering on silver. And her brown skin has cool, rose undertones that complement and enhance her features.

She's one of the most beautiful people I've ever met, but the novelty of seeing such light eyes contrasted against her other features makes it hard not to stare.

I grimace, realizing how long I've been gawking at her. She waits for me to look my fill with a soft smile on her face.

"Emberly, this is Ash. I thought it might be easier for you to get your feel around the other students if you were with one."

"That was really thoughtful of you, Sable," I say in a small voice. I'm half-ashamed I reacted to Ash like everyone in the room had done to me, and half-embarrassed that it's so obvious how socially awkward I am.

"Hi, Emberly. It's so nice to meet you." Ash waves at me. "I'd love to help you grab dinner if you're up for it. I heard you whacked your head pretty hard. It must have been bad. It takes quite a lot to knock us out like that."

She'd used the word "us" like I'm already part of the group. I'm not sure if I like that or not.

Reaching up, I finger the knot on the back of my head.

"Several hits, in fact," I confess with a smile loaded with chagrin.

She winces in sympathy. "Ouch."

"Yeah, that about sums it up."

"You interested in trying to make another go of it?" She indicates the cafeteria behind her with a hitch of her thumb. "I promise there are a lot of really nice people in there."

I glance at Sable. She's wearing a giant smile.

I restrain an eye roll. This was an obvious set-up that's going to work in her favor.

Giving Ash a tentative smile, I force myself to nod. "Sure."

She does a little jump thing and claps her hands together. "I can't wait to introduce—oof."

Did Sable just elbow her?

"Ah, I mean, I'd love to show you how to get dinner." Her smile is a little crooked when she calms down.

"I'm glad that's settled. I'm going to let you have a quiet meal with Ash. I'll find you after dinner and explain a little more about how things run around here."

"Wait!" I say loudly as Sable starts backing away from us. "A hat."

"I'm sorry, what?" She cocks her head at me.

Apparently my verbal skills are a lot rustier than I realized.

"A hat. Is there one around I can use to hide my hair? A dark one if possible."

Sable's eyes soften. "I hardly think that's necessary in this —" She stops herself mid-sentence and nods after a momentary pause. "Sure. If you girls can just give me a few minutes, I'll see what I can find."

She hurries down the hall and disappears around the corner. Only then do I turn to Ash.

"Girl, are you crazy?"

"Um, excuse me?" Oh no, what have I done this time?

"If I had hair like yours, I'd be flaunting it however I could." She tosses her hair, stopping to fluff it and wave at imaginary admirers. It's ridiculous enough that a genuine smile breaks out on my face.

"I'm not really into standing out in a crowd."

Her smile is sad enough to be knowing. "Yeah, I can respect that. Hopefully in time you'll be comfortable enough here not to worry about it anymore. And if not, hey, you can start a hat trend. Goodness knows we could use a little more fashion up in this place."

It's an olive branch I'm happy to receive. I hope my smile conveys my thanks, because words fail me.

"Here we go," Sable calls as she rushes toward us. She extends a dark blue baseball hat with a Denver Broncos logo on it.

Denver, really? So over that city.

I hold in a groan because it's better than nothing, and I truly appreciate the effort she's gone to.

"I know it's probably not exactly what you were hoping for, but it's all I could find. We can order some hats if you decide that's what you want."

I won't be able to twist the length of my hair under it, but it's something. I can knot my hair into a low bun so it's not as obvious.

"Thanks." Accepting the hat, I quickly adjust the back—it

was obviously worn by a guy—and slip it on, pulling it low over my forehead.

Ash throws me a reassuring smile before grabbing my hand and hauling me to the cafeteria doors. She stops right before the entrance and levels me with a stare.

"It's time to be brave," she declares, and pushes them open.

6

*T*he gawking factor isn't quite as bad this time around, but it's still there. Ash hauls me through a maze of tables to a long counter at the back of the cafeteria. Stacks of food are laid out over the surface of the countertop, creating the most lavish buffet I've ever seen.

The aroma of fresh baked breads and sliced roast beef makes my stomach growl, even though I've already eaten today. I spy bowls of fruit and platters of hamburgers, French fries, green beans, even full roasted chickens you can pull from. This feast would rival the best Thanksgiving meal.

With wonder and a dab of disbelief, I turn to Ash. She's grabbed a couple plastic trays from the pile in front of the counter, and slides them on a metal railing attached to the ledge. Catching my look, she hitches and dips a shoulder.

"What can I say? We're a species of big eaters."

No doubt.

Just then, a prickle of awareness causes the fine hairs at the back of my neck to stand on edge. For a moment, I'd forgotten about the academy students at my back. Even covered with a hat and wound into a bun, my blonde hair is on full display.

I dip my head and keep my eyes downcast as I shuffle along next to Ash, answering questions about which foods I like—which is basically any and everything—whenever she asks.

I trick myself into thinking that if I don't look around, no one will stare.

After she piles my plate with as much food as it can hold, Ash steers me toward a round table. As I settle into my seat, I glance up long enough to notice the faces of several other students seated around me. Their curious gazes make me uncomfortable. Keeping my eyes fixed on the plate in front of me, I check to make sure no hair has escaped the tight bun at my nape.

Shrinking as best as I can, I try to make myself a smaller target. I have a strong desire to squirm in my seat, but movement will only attract more attention.

It's impossible not to notice the rest of the room buzzing with conversation while our table is a black hole of silence. Picking at my food, I pretend not to notice.

"So, I was thinking," Ash starts. "It's better if we just rip off the Band-Aid."

Oh gosh. What is she doing?

"Everyone, this is Emberly. She's obviously new and I'm sure is super excited to answer any and all of your questions. Also, in case you haven't noticed, under that super stylish hat she has a mane full of platinum blonde and red hair. Yes, I know you're all jealous, but it's better if you just get over it because she's a really cool girl and you're all gonna want to be friends with her."

No. She didn't just say all that.

I let out a low groan and duck my head. Heat rises up my neck and takes up permanent residence on my cheeks.

"Emberly." Ash nudges me with her elbow, and I have to stop myself from jabbing her in the nose. "Let me introduce you to my friends."

I *think* the sound that comes out of my mouth resembles grumbled agreement. At least that's what I'm going for.

Forcing myself to raise my eyes, I glance at the people sitting to the right, left, and in front of me. Various expressions of amusement light their faces as I regard them.

Guess they're used to Ash's brash personality.

Unfortunately, I'm not.

Ash goes around the table, rattling off names.

Kenna, the girl sitting to my right, wiggles her fingers at me in greeting. Her mahogany-colored hair is slicked back into a trendy bob, the edges razor cut in a straight line right at chin level. Her green eyes resemble a prairie field in springtime, the slight bronze color of her skin making them pop and giving her a slightly otherworldly look.

The girl next to her is Hadley. When she's introduced, she adjusts the tortoise-shell glasses sitting on the bridge of her nose.

"They're not prescription," she explains. "We all have perfect eyesight. I just like the look of them." Her smile is on the shy side, and she clears her throat before brushing a lock of her charcoal-colored wavy hair behind her ear.

I like her.

Sterling and Greyson, the two dudes at our table who are sitting across from me, nod when their names are announced.

I promptly forget which is which. They look too much alike with their matching dark hair—only a shade above black, and long enough to curl at the ends. They both sport square jawlines and blue-green eyes.

"Greyson and Sterling are twins," Ash announces. I continue to regard them from underneath the bill of my hat. The longer I stare, the more I can tell them apart. There's an obvious resemblance, but they can't be identical. Something a lot like déjà vu tickles my brain, but I brush it away.

"We're all tenth-years," one of the brothers explains. "Even Sterling here, although you wouldn't know it from his maturity level."

Okay, so you must be Greyson.

I bob my head as if I know what he's talking about.

"Hey! Low blow, bro." Sterling scowls at his brother and tosses a wadded napkin at Greyson's face. Greyson deflects the projectile easily and continues.

"Tenth-year is the equivalent to human twelfth grade . . . at least here in the States. But unfortunately, we all still have three years left at Seraph Academy. We don't graduate until we're twenty."

"Well, that sucks." The words fly out of my mouth without thought. I hear Ash chuckle next to me. Hadley's and Kenna's eyebrows shoot up and Sterling covers his reaction with a cough.

Greyson simply shrugs as if he doesn't have an opinion either way. "You get more freedoms and participate in ops your last few years, so it's not so bad."

Two extra years of high school is not my idea of a good time. No way am I sticking around for that. I want to figure out how my supposed powers work, get a grasp on how to survive in both the real and spectrum worlds, then get the heck out of Dodge.

"Stop boring her with academy factoids, Grey. Besides, there's something else we all want to know." Sterling hunches his large body forward, a court-jester grin on his face. "Did you really think you were being kidnapped?"

"Sterling," Ash warns.

"What?" His eyes widen with feigned innocence.

"Oh, wipe that look off your face. It's not becoming on you." Ash launches a French fry at his head.

Catching it easily, he pops it in his mouth. "Yum. Thanks, Ash. You're a doll."

Ash's eyes turn toward the ceiling before she angles her body in my direction. "Ignore him. You don't have to answer that."

Easy for her to say. She doesn't have five sets of eyes boring holes into her.

My cheeks heat under their regard. The curse of being fair-skinned is I can never hide my embarrassment.

"Um." I swallow to wet my throat . . . and to stall.

"Kind of? Everyone came at me at once. I mean . . ." Shoot, why is talking to people so hard? "I was carried off by a big fat turkey-bird at one point. The thing even dropped me from the sky. So, yeah. I thought I was being abducted."

I finish on a shrug, not sure what else to say. I don't bother pointing out that technically, I *was* kidnapped. No one asked my permission to whisk me away to their fancy academy.

After a beat, Sterling turns to his brother. Their rapid-fire exchange goes completely over my head.

"It must have been, right?"

"Who else would have pulled something like that?" Greyson responds with a smirk.

"Oh man, I'll bet Deacon is still chewing him out."

"Not like that's ever bothered him before."

"Very true. I still would have liked to be a fly on that wall."

"If only we could shift into something that small."

"So true, man."

"I'm sorry," I interrupt, surprising myself. "Are you saying you know who the bird boy is?"

Twin smirks grow on their faces.

"Yeah. The fat turkey was our brother, Steel."

I definitely remember that name. That's the a-hole who called me a freak.

I don't bother concealing my reaction and it's only a tick before both brothers break out in a fit of laughter. I can't really blame them. If I had to guess, I'd say I look like I've eaten something particularly gross.

"Is that who you saw?" Greyson points to the left.

I scan the cafeteria until I spot a guy who looks vaguely familiar. He has the same jawline as the twins sitting across from me, but he appears a bit older than them. Similar dark hair, but shorter on the sides and a shade darker—the black reminds me of a raven's feather. His full lips twist into a side smirk as he listens to someone talking on the other side of his table.

Squinting my eyes and with a head tilt, I keep filing away information about the guy.

He's slouched comfortably in the almost-too-small chair, with his arm lazily draped along the back of the seat of the beautiful girl beside him. Dark brown hair the color of chestnuts hangs in loose curls down to her waist. Her face is the perfect heart-shape. Even from my spot, I catalogue her delicate nose and large green eyes framed by thick lashes.

Laughing, she brings her hand to rest on Steel's bicep in a gesture of familiarity.

The gesture prickles my annoyance even when I know it shouldn't.

"That may have been him," I confess, forcing my attention to my own table.

"Oh, man!" Sterling slaps the table. "This is the best day ever. Not only has she dubbed him a fat turkey, but she broke his nose and can't even remember what he looks like. I'm going to hold this over him forever."

It's a miracle all the commotion hasn't drawn the gaze of the whole cafeteria. As it is, several of the closest tables have stopped their conversations to cast curious glances our way.

I am not going to survive with this bunch.

How many people would notice if I slid under the table and hid?

Hiding is my thing. I'm good at hiding.

"You're right," Greyson adds, looking as if he's enjoying this—whatever *this* is—as much as his brother. "This ought to deflate his ego a bit."

To my absolute horror, Sterling starts waving his arms in the air and shouts above the chatter. "Yo, Steel. Looks like you don't have a perfect record anymore."

A teal-blue gaze swings to our table and lands on Sterling before sliding over to me. The girl at his side continues to talk even though she no longer has his attention.

I try to look away—I swear I try—but can't.

"Grey, this is classic." Sterling is standing up now and pointing at his older brother. "Does he have a black eye?"

It's hard to tell from so far away, but it does look like the skin under Steel's right eye is slightly discolored by a greenish-yellow hue. I remember the punch I threw before I was hauled over his shoulder. I can't muster up the strength to feel sorry for it though. In fact, I'm glad I clocked him instead of Sable.

"You punched him?" Ash's voice is full of awe. I break eye contact with Steel to answer.

"He was trying to kidnap me."

Howls of laughter start from the brothers again and I roll my eyes.

"I wasn't trying to kidnap you. I was rescuing you from the Fallen."

A zing of awareness shoots up my spine when the words are uttered in the familiar deep timbre. I may not have recognized his face, but his voice certainly left an impression.

Greyson and Sterling laugh so hard, their faces turn red and blotchy. Not a great look on either of them. Sterling's eyes have even started to water.

Well, these two are obviously useless.

Kenna and Hadley stare slack-jawed at a point above my head—presumably where Steel is standing. Their eyes take on a bug-like quality and if I'm not mistaken, a few stars float in them as well.

After a beat, Hadley's gaze moves to me before she looks down at her plate like it holds the answers to the universe.

Kenna keeps staring at Steel with those otherworldly eyes of hers.

Is that drool?

She hasn't spoken a word since I joined the table. Maybe she's mute?

Ash is the only reasonable one. The grimace on her face conveys her apologies.

Bringing a hand to my face, I pinch my nose. The back of my neck is hot—I imagine it's because Steel is trying to burn a hole there with his gaze.

I slowly twist in my seat and find myself facing his broad, t-shirt covered chest.

Yikes, maybe this guy is older than I thought? There's just so *much* of him.

"Listen, I didn't mean to offend you or anything . . ." Of their own volition, my eyes travel up the remainder of his chest and connect with blue fire.

Oh man, big mistake.

The intensity in his stare freezes the words on my tongue. And I just . . . sit there . . . gawking at him.

And he just . . . stands there . . . staring back.

The cafeteria has suddenly gotten uncomfortably muggy and suspiciously quiet. I'd bet money that I'm once again the star of the evening, but I'm too overwhelmed to check.

Why isn't he saying anything?

Why is he just staring at me like this? Like he doesn't notice or care about anyone else in the room.

It's incredibly unnerving. I wish he would stop.

"I . . . ah . . . there were . . . um." Words stutter out of my mouth in an incomprehensible mess.

I'm seriously considering crawling under the table when an alarm sounds loud enough to jolt me almost out of my seat. The lights in the cafeteria pulse red.

What's happening?

Gasps echo throughout the room. A recorded voice blares above the alarm. It repeats the words "level one breach" over and over.

I can only hear the sound of chairs scraping over linoleum as students jump up and scatter in some sort of organized chaos.

Ash grabs my arm and tries to pull me to my feet. My confusion makes me sluggish to respond.

Hadley and Kenna have already disappeared. Greyson and Sterling round the table and stand by their brother. And Steel . . . he towers above me, eyes unfocused and head tilted at a forty-five degree angle, as if listening for something. What he can possibly hear over the alarm, recorded voice, and pounding of feet as people run from the room, I have no idea.

"Emberly, come on." Ash's eyes are wide and wild. I don't like that look one bit. Panic is already crawling up my gut.

Steel's voice cuts through my anxiety. "Grey. Sterl. Don't even think about phasing."

Phasing?

"Don't give us this big brother crap," Sterling shoots back.

"I'm not arguing with you two. I outrank you in age and class. You'll follow orders like you've been trained."

At Steel's barked command, Sterling clamps his mouth shut. If he were Superman, lasers would be incinerating Steel right about now. Grey doesn't look much happier.

Wiping a hand down his face, Steel tries to soften the blow. "Listen, you need to help get Newbie to one of the bunkers. She has no idea where to go. Then find yours and make sure Blaze and Aurora are there. But I'm not kidding, don't phase."

"Yeah, sure mom," Sterling grumbles under his breath, but not quietly enough to go unnoticed.

"Let's go, girls." Greyson jerks his chin toward the exit, seemingly unconcerned with speed.

"Get out!" Steel suddenly yells. "They're here."

In a flash of light, Steel disappears. I gasp as the two remaining brothers and Ash herd me toward the exit.

"Show off," Sterling mutters.

"Where did he go? Is he all right?"

What the heck is going on right now?

"Steel knows how to take care of himself."

Their somewhat blasé attitude to the obviously tense situation does nothing to calm me. In fact, my heartbeat ramps up and I can feel my adrenaline spike.

Multicolored lights explode around the outside rim of my vision.

There'll be no stopping my slipped reality now.

Just hold on a little longer, Emberly. Maybe you can find somewhere safe to hide.

I make the mistake of glancing behind me before we leave. Color bursts, and from one blink to the next, I slip into the spectrum world.

The hands that had been propelling me forward fall away. The ringing of the alarm fades, but snippets of broken conversation reach my ears. It sounds as if people are talking very far away from me.

"Where is—?"

"—she partial phased, because that—"

"—see her, but I can't hold on—"

"What should we—"

Confusion circles me until my gaze lands on a very large,

very golden, very familiar lion posturing in the middle of the room.

His fur stands on end and a low growl emanates from his chest. I spot the same shock of black hair slicing through his mane.

Steel. As sure as I am of my own name, I know it has to be him.

The gold beast starts to prowl back and forth and my heart jumps into my throat. A pale, emaciated man crouches on the ground just beyond the lion.

Shrouded in a mist of darkness, he scurries like an insect, his movements jerky but swift. The man's dark hair reaches his shoulders and if I had to guess, I'd say it hasn't been washed in months. Chunks of it hang in limp, greasy dreads that obscure most of his face.

Through the strands, his eyes glow ice blue. His blood-leeched lips are pulled back from his mouth and reveal elongated eyeteeth that come to a point.

The man—or rather creature—hisses at Steel, who returns the warning with a low, bone-shaking growl.

Is that a vampire? First shape shifters and now vampires? What else exists that I don't know about?

I'd moved forward, only realizing it when Steel's growl causes me to jerk back and knock over a chair. The sharp sound echoes in the nearly empty room.

The vampire-man's head swivels in my direction. His pink tongue darts out, licking along his top lip before caressing both canine teeth.

I'm going to be sick.

The creature jolts toward me with inhuman speed. My eyes only see a blur of motion.

Steel's jaws clamp down on his leg and he drops to the ground with a shriek a mere five feet in front of me.

Backpedaling, I ram into something hard. Hands lock on my shoulders and I strike out at whatever is restraining me.

"Yo, calm down. We got you," Ash whispers. "We need to get out of here now."

"Yeah, preferably before Steel notices we phased." Sterling pipes up from my other side. Greyson was there as well.

I stop fighting when I realize it's Ash and the twins behind me, all ringed in a soft white aura, just like mine. Further confirmation of our shared otherness.

"What *is* that thing?" Morbid curiosity overrides my sense of self-preservation—not something that happens often.

"It's a Forsaken. We really do need to get out of here," Greyson answers.

"We can't just leave that thing with Steel." I cut my eyes to the twin. Surely he would agree with me.

A moment later, Steel throws the carcass of the vampire, or whatever it is, across the room. The body hits the wall with a sickening crunch.

"I think he's got it covered," Greyson replies dryly.

Sterling moves in front of me and bounces on the balls of his feet, clearly longing to get in on the fight.

"Don't even think about it, man." Greyson points a finger at his brother, his brow pulled low.

"Yeah. Yeah, I know. Okay, let's beat feet outta here."

We're almost out the doors when an unhinged laugh pierces the air. Even the spectrum world hates the sound. Angry waves of light vibrate off the walls.

"Yes, run you disgusting little hybrids. We like the chase as much as the hunt."

Ice splashes through my veins as we shove through the cafeteria doors. The voice turns into a barbaric shriek that's cut off by a sharp crack.

Oh, gosh. Oh, gosh. Oh, gosh. Do not look back, Emberly.

For once, I listen to myself.

We're only halfway down the hall when the cafeteria doors open and slam against the wall.

My nerves are so frayed, I hardly jump at the new intrusion.

A low growl causes Greyson to skid to a halt.

Ash bumps into him, I slam into her, and Sterling stumbles into me.

I whirl around the moment Sterling's weight eases off my back.

"Oh, sh—" Sterling grumbles under his breath as he stares at the lion form of his brother.

Steel explodes like a firecracker in a flash of white light. I'm in awe as the light particles put themselves into the shape of a man before pulsating one final time to reveal a very angry Steel.

"What were you thinking?" He stomps down the hall and gets in Sterling's face.

Greyson appears and lays a hand on his older brother's shoulder. "Cool down, man. We were just trying to protect the new girl."

Great, they've already forgotten my name.

Steel's glower turns on me. His eyebrows are black angry slashes that punctuate the blue fire burning in his eyes.

I concede a step, but refuse to give him the satisfaction of lowering my gaze in submission.

"Are you trying to get yourself killed? Or worse?"

Wait. What?

"Only a complete idiot would phase with no defenses with a Forsaken in the room." His gaze sweeps my body and the curl of his lip tells me I'm found wanting.

Surprisingly, that stings.

"You're what, sixteen? You can't be old enough to have gone through training yet."

"I'm seventeen. But what the heck does that matter? I've been taking care of myself for long enough to know I don't need you."

His dark brows shoot up, but so do mine.

He isn't the only one surprised by that little outburst. In a fight or flight scenario, I'm usually a flight kinda girl. I survived this long by blending in, hiding in the shadows. Being bold isn't usually my style.

Steel barely gets his mouth open to respond when Sterling cuts him off. "She's half-phased. We couldn't get her out any other way."

"Half-phased?" he asks in disbelief.

"He's serious," Greyson adds. "We can see her on the mortal plane, but she's only experiencing the spirit realm. There wasn't anything else we could do."

Steel's angry glare swings back to me. I force myself not to cower. I'd dealt with bullies before. Steel's nothing new.

"Phase back," he orders.

I blink at him, a crease forming between my brows. "Sure, just as soon as you tell me what that means and teach me how to do it."

A very human growl vibrates in Steel's chest and he shoves a hand in his hair.

Ash steps in front of me, her head of corkscrew curls

almost completely blocking my view of the fuming man-child in front of me.

"Give her a break, man. All this stuff is new to her. And besides, we shouldn't be arguing about this right now. We've got to get to a bunker."

The breath Steel releases blows some of Ash's curls. Reaching around her, he grabs my upper arm, hauling me out from her protection.

"Whoa. What is your problem?" I shake free of his hold, but his attention is locked on his brothers.

"I'll make sure she gets somewhere safe. You guys phase back. Just go straight to Blaze and Aurora's group to make sure they made it, and stay there."

When Sterling opens his mouth to argue, Greyson slaps a hand over it and pulls him back. "We'll meet up with you when this is over."

Greyson and Sterling disappear into thin air and I shake my head, not used to seeing other people vanish like that.

Ash shifts her weight from foot to foot as she chews her lip, her eyes bouncing back and forth between me and Steel.

"You sure you got her?" she asks.

Steel barks a humorless laugh. "You really worried I won't be able to take care of her?"

"Conceited much?" I scoff.

Ash's mouth quirks in a half-smile.

"I'll find you when the threat has been eliminated, okay?" Her eyes beg me to agree.

I don't have much of a choice. Besides, it seems that whatever is going on, it's safer for her not to be in the spectrum world. I may have just met her, but I don't want her to get hurt.

I answer her with a tight nod.

With that, she disappears too.

Looking down his nose at me, Steel turns on a heel and stalks down the hall. "Keep up," he throws over his shoulder without slowing.

This is going to be interesting.

7

$\mathscr{I}$ start going cross-eyed the longer I tag along behind Steel. The underground part of the academy is more extensive than I'd realized; my sense of direction is thoroughly jumbled. Without a guide, I'd probably roam the maze of hallways indefinitely.

We haven't run into any other people yet, but the echoed shouts and screams that lash at my ears are enough to make me jumpy.

With a shake of my head, I shatter my unease. I don't have room for frivolous emotions right now.

Fear gets you dead.

My mind's eye conjures an unwelcome vision of the color-blanched Forsaken. Pointed teeth bared in an inhuman hiss. Greasy hair hanging in limp clumps. Stick-like fingers bent and ready to claw its enemy.

It's only a moment's distraction, but long enough for me to miss that Steel's stopped moving. I throw my hands up as I plow right into him and elbow myself in the gut. The air whooshes out of my lungs with a harsh *oof*.

Steel's body barely sways forward on contact.

To keep from tripping, my arms latch around his waist. My face is smooshed between his shoulder blades. Tipping up my gaze, I find Steel peering at me over his shoulder. One eyebrow is raised.

Snapping my arms wide, I scurry back several steps. My cheeks flood with heat as he turns.

"Sorry." Unsure what to do with my hands, I busy them in my hair, rechecking that my hat is still in place. "I didn't notice that you stopped."

Obviously.

I should eye-roll myself. I won't blame him if he does.

Instead, his cocked eyebrow ratchets up and the corner of his mouth tips ever so slightly. Several seconds pass—an awkward and long several seconds—and we just stare at each other. Then, as if remembering himself, his lips flatline and his face hardens to granite.

A chill zips down my spine when the change occurs.

"Wonderful. You're clumsy, too." Even his voice has morphed into a mocking lilt.

Not usually, I want to spit out, but bite my tongue to keep quiet. I haven't survived all these years by not being able to swallow my words.

As if reading my thoughts and finding them amusing, his lips twist into a cruel smirk. My stomach knots with the unsatisfied craving to punch the look off his face. My fists clench and I force my eyes away from him in order to stop scanning his body for vulnerable places to land a blow.

"Why did we stop?" I push out through clenched teeth.

I never react this strongly to people I don't know. I perfected the ability to let insults and slights roll off me years ago. It's a necessity when you're constantly the target of school bullies.

"I heard—" A scream tears through his words. As one, our heads snap in the direction of the cry. It came from down the intersecting hallway, and we give chase.

As we round the corner, a body punches through the wall in front of us, sending drywall flying. Dust, splintered wood, and chunks of concrete explode everywhere as the person slams into the opposite wall and crumples to the ground.

I'm frozen in place. Steel takes off to check on the hunched figure.

"Powers, on the left flank! Guardians, on the right! Dominions, to the front!"

A shouted command carried through the newly created hole cracks through my shock and frees my limbs. I rush to where Steel is bent over the figure.

Blood pours out of the man's nose and trickles from his left ear as Steel holds two fingers to his neck. I think I see his chest moving, but my attention is stolen by a shriek loud enough to split the air. A fresh wave of fear-induced adrenaline is released into my body.

Steel rises and starts toward the danger. Spurred by panic, I catch his arm in a firm grip as he brushes past me.

His body vibrates with barely contained violence. I don't trick myself into believing he was stayed by my strength alone. I get the impression that if Steel's mind is set on a course, only an act of God can stop him.

"What?" he barks.

The fierceness of his gaze causes my insides to clench. Even in his human form, he's a force when angered.

Glancing at the prone figure on the floor, I grasp for an excuse that doesn't reveal my own cowardice.

"You're just going to leave him like this?" My words are clipped with annoyance. Annoyance at myself for my spine-lessness, rather than the cavalier way he dismissed the injured man—but that's not something he needs to know.

"Mark is alive. He's safer out here than he would be in there." He jerks his chin to the room beyond the jagged opening Mark's body created. Dark-haired men and women stand in lines, shoulder-to-shoulder, around an unseen threat.

And oh my gosh, some of them have feathered wings.

Steel rips out of my grasp, upsetting my equilibrium. I stumble a few steps. My feet tangle and my body tilts toward the hole.

With a squeak, my shoulder slams into the wall and I pitch through the opening. I throw my hands out to catch myself, but before I connect with the floor, bands of steel wrap around my middle and my body jerks to a halt. Then I'm yanked up and set on my feet.

With my back settled against a warm chest, I suppress a shiver.

"You're going to have to work on your coordination if you want to stay alive." Steel's breath fans over my cheek, causing the hairs at my nape to stand at attention. His arms melt away from my stomach and he steps away before my muddled brain figures out I should pull free.

"Steel! Emberly! What in the world are you doing here?" Sable stands to our left.

Her once-perfect hair is a dark nest on one side. A small

cut leaks blood from her brow that trickles down the side of her face and over a bruise that has already started to swell on her jaw. Her unkempt appearance rattles me almost as much as the shrieks of the creature the hoard of Nephilim warriors are battling.

Her eyes dart between the two of us.

"You should both be in a bunker." Her gaze lifts over my shoulder to land on Steel. "You know the protocol. I know you think you can take on the world. But we have our emergency plans in place for exactly this reason. I don't want—"

"One entered the cafeteria as everyone was fleeing." Steel's words are filled with frustration. "I dispatched it, but the newbie here accidentally phased and doesn't know how to phase back."

Sable's surprised gaze cuts to my face.

I hunch in on myself. What did they expect? Up until a few hours ago I had no idea there were people in the world like me, let alone how and why I can see the things I do.

I'm still waiting to find out if I can do magic.

"Right." Sable nods, accepting Steel's explanation. "Take Emberly to the above-ground bunker. If she can't phase back, that's the safest place for her."

"Sable, you know I could help. If I shift—"

"No. We don't know that they aren't here for her."

I straighten my spine.

They think these creatures might be here for me? Why? What could I have done to draw their attention? I've never even seen one of them before.

"You need to get her hidden, and you need to do it right now," Sable continues. "We'll come collect you when we've eliminated the threat."

Steel shoves a hand in his raven hair and fists it. The teal in his eyes seems extra bright.

Are his eyes . . . glowing?

Neat trick.

With a muttered curse, he releases his hold on his hair and drops his arm. "Fine."

Grabbing my hand, he tugs me into the hallway.

I snap my teeth at him. The next time he jerks me around, I'm going to bite his hand.

If I don't get some concrete answers soon, I'm so out of here. Yeah, the streets weren't a safe place, but I never encountered ugly, unwashed vampire things before being kidnapped for "my safety."

"Steel," Sable calls right before we disappeared from view, "who was it?"

Who was what?

My eyes cut to Steel. His lips are pressed into a firm line. "Gabe."

Sable lifts a hand to her lips, and with sad eyes she gives a curt nod before turning away.

With another tug, Steel rushes us away from the battle.

8

"*Y*ou want me to put what in where?"

A small gap yawns in the side of the mountain. It can't be more than two feet in diameter. Steel's instructions were clear enough, but I don't want to believe him. Thankfully, I don't suffer from claustrophobia, but still. Wriggling into a tiny hole in the ground isn't my idea of a good time.

Pressing both palms to his eyes, Steel groans. "Do you have to make everything so difficult?"

Crossing my arms, I glare. I'm not saying anything until he acknowledges me.

When his arms drop and he takes in my stance, he immediately returns his hands to his eyes.

"Will you please just get in?" After scrubbing his face, he gestures to the hole.

"This can't seriously be the best place to hide."

"It's bigger inside . . . slightly. Veins of natural springs run through these mountains, which will help hide you from view. The alluvium between the rocks will disguise your smell."

Resisting the urge to sniff myself, I heave a sigh and drop to my knees. Gingerly putting my head, shoulders and arms in the cramped space, I shuffle forward until most of my body is in the opening. I'm forced to duck my head until my chin is almost skimming the ground.

"Any day now," Steel calls from behind. His voice echoes throughout the black abyss.

Biting back a sharp reply, I keep army crawling. The sharp rocks and loose pebbles grind against my forearms.

After a couple minutes of shuffling, I only make it a handful of body lengths forward, but the air has chilled considerably. Goose bumps pebble on my arms. I stare into the black void before me and suddenly don't want to continue.

Like, *really* don't want to keep going down this rabbit hole.

Hands shove my backside and I yelp.

"Keep going," Steel's stern voice orders.

"Hey, boundaries, dude."

"That's a luxury we don't have right now." A quiet chuckle follows his words. "Just wait until we get to the cavern."

"What?" I crane my neck to try to see him on the ground behind me, but we are so deep into the hole that the darkness conceals his body.

"Do you need another nudge?"

Gritting my teeth, I resume squirming. This is seriously messed up.

Several long minutes later, I notice the tunnel widens enough that I can finally crawl on my hands and knees rather than having to keep wriggling forward on my belly—that is, if I bow my head.

How Steel is making it through this tunnel is beyond me. The guy is not small.

"We're almost there," he calls.

"Great," I mutter under my breath.

I make it another body length forward and am able to stretch my neck without hitting my head.

"Finally. I can crawl like a normal—ow!"

My face slams into an uneven stone wall. I sit on my haunches and check my nose, glad to find it isn't bleeding.

Steel crowds me from behind, shuffling around in the pitch black. I think he's turning his body and sitting, but without my sight I'm not sure. I'm certainly not going to feel around to find out.

"Sit. We're here."

"Here?"

"Yeah, this is the glorious cavern where we get to wait out the siege. Impressed?"

My head moves on a swivel in a vain attempt to take in our surroundings. "I might be if I could see anything."

"Trust me, you wouldn't even then." He blows out a breath that kisses my right cheek. Shocked by his nearness, I rear back and bang into another of the mini-cavern's walls.

"Ouch!" My spine throbs from the impact.

"Sit down already." Steel's fingers wrap around my bicep and when he yanks, I tumble into his lap.

"Not on me," he complains.

I'm a hot mess of limbs. I try to scramble off him but end up elbowing him in the throat instead.

That wasn't on purpose, but consider it payment for pulling on me again.

The gruff noise he makes when I knee him in the midsection only makes me smile.

"Stop! Just stop moving already."

I freeze with a knee pressed to the dirt beside his hip, the other leg thrown over his, and a hand on each of his shoulders.

Blindness does nothing to dim the intimacy of the moment.

"I can't just stay like this." My body is sore from the crazy crawl into this foxhole and my legs have started to shake.

Bending my head, I suck in a frustrated breath of air, then instantly regret it.

Rather than the cool dirt-scented musk from the caves, Steel's masculine aroma fills my lungs.

Sweat, cheap dude shampoo, and the faint echo of detergent.

I want to be grossed out by the typical guy odor, but I'm not . . . and that irks me.

I don't let myself take another hit of his smell.

"Here, do this."

Warm hands guide my bent leg to the side and turn my body so my back is pressed against the wall perpendicular to where Steel sits. Drawing my hands from his shoulders, I place them against the dirt floor and ease my body down. Now fully seated, my legs are squished up against my chest so tightly it's hard to breathe.

I'm not about to complain.

"You're not claustrophobic, are you?"

I wheeze out a laugh. "Isn't that," half-breath, "something you should have," another half-breath, "asked me before?"

I yelp when my legs are pulled forward and draped across him. Without room to straighten, everything from ankle to mid-thigh is pushed against Steel's chest. He's forced to wrap his arms around my lower body in an awkward embrace.

This is so much worse than before.

I squirm and wiggle, trying to free myself, when his arms clamp around my legs, pressing them even more firmly against him.

When I stop my silent struggle, resigned to be pretzeled in this tiny space with a stranger, his upper body shifts against my legs. It might have been a shrug.

"It wouldn't have mattered. We were coming in here whether you were scared or not."

Is he not going to say anything about half my body being curled on his lap?

Great, denial it is.

We fall into an uncomfortable silence. Between our breaths and the dripping sound from some nearby water source, our lack of conversation is deafening.

I try to ignore Steel, but the places our bodies touch itch with awareness. Heat from his arms sears my skin through my jeans. My muscles are tense from holding still. An uncomfortable ache from holding the same position permeates my body.

And darn it! I can't stop sucking in his stupid boy-smell.

The slow passage of time is making it worse.

"What is phasing?"

Might as well try to distract myself.

"You really don't know anything, do you?"

Without being able to see his expression, I can't be sure he isn't insulting me, but his tone is filled with curiosity rather than mockery. Even so, I fight back a sharp reply and remind myself people have said much worse to me.

"I wasn't raised like you," I remind him. "I've been forced to make assumptions about the spectrum world based only on my own experiences."

"Spectrum world?"

I lift a shoulder in a half-shrug before remembering he can't see me.

"It's just what I call the otherworldly place only we can see. The place with the monsters."

Several moments of silence slip by while Steel takes in my words. When he speaks, I finally get a few of the answers I've been so desperate for.

"I suppose that makes sense. It's as good a name as any. We call it the spirit realm, by the way. Phasing is when we pass from one realm to the next. The mortal realm is where humans live. The spirit realm is where the Fallen exist—the beings you consider monsters. They were angels that got booted out of heaven. Nephilim—that's us—can toggle between both realms. The Fallen can't."

When I'm sucked into the spectrum world, my body always remains rooted in reality, even as it exists in the other realm as well. My erratic behavior was the main reason why I bounced to so many foster homes. Was it different for them?

"What do you mean by 'pass from one realm to the next'?"

Steel shifts his body and readjusts my legs. I pretend not to notice, which isn't hard in the dark.

"When we phase, our bodies disappear from one realm and appear in the other. In the mortal world, we are very similar to humans. We have increased strength and speed, don't need as much sustenance or sleep, but aside from that, we blend in with the rest of humanity. It's not until we phase into the spirit realm that our celestial powers manifest."

Powers. Yes. Now it's getting interesting.

"So, you can't turn into an animal in the real world?"

"No, I can only do that in the spirit realm."

"But I don't disappear when I phase. And I don't think I have any special powers."

It's quiet for a moment. I wouldn't mind being able to see his face right about now. Any expression will give me a small clue as to what he's thinking.

"Several things about you are a mystery," he finally admits.

I never liked being different. For years it had been a secret dream of mine to find a place I truly belonged. I gave up that dream the moment I ran away. Even as I tried to convince myself it didn't matter, the truth is that to discover there's a place I belong, but to still be an anomaly, is devastating.

Sable was wrong. The more I learn about this group, the more obvious it becomes how different I am.

I shake the melancholy off once again.

"Can everyone shape shift?"

"Only Nephilim descended from cherubim can shape shift. And even then, they can usually only turn into one of the forms. Lion, eagle, or bull. Other angel lines have different powers."

My mind reels. There are different types of Nephilim . . . different types of angels? There are several different powers. And hold up—some Nephilim turned into bulls? I really hope that doesn't turn out to be my specialty. With so many questions floating around my head, I have to pick a starting point.

"But you're different. You can shift into two: a lion and an eagle." It's a statement rather than a question. I've seen it for myself.

"Three. I can shift into all three."

"Why? What does that mean?"

Steel's sigh brushes against my head and stirs the fine hairs that frame my face. "Do you have to ask so many questions?"

"Why are you being cagey?"

"Why are you being annoying?" he shoots back.

"Part of my charm."

"Right." I don't have to be able to see to know an eye roll accompanied his clipped response.

"What's the big deal? I'm just trying to figure out how all this works. Is it something embarrassing? Do the other students make fun of you for turning into a bull?" I don't really care all that much, but since he said I was being annoying, a very immature part of me bubbles up and urges me to continue poking the sleeping bear.

"Oh, and what happens to your clothes when you shift?"

"Are you serious?"

"Yeah, of course I am. In books, shifters are always tearing through their clothes and reappearing in human form naked. That doesn't seem to happen to you."

"Read a lot of shifter romances about naked dudes, do you?"

Do not answer that, Emberly. Divert conversation immediately.

"It's okay, you don't have to talk to me about shifting. I understand that we all have our insecurities. I hadn't realized this was one of yours, but I get it. I wouldn't want anyone to know I turn into a giant cow either. I won't ask again."

"I don't turn into a cow," he grinds out. "I turn into a bull."

Question successfully ducked. Point: me.

"Oh, my bad. But is there really much of a difference?"

My voice drips with fake innocence. I have to bite my lip to keep from laughing out loud. I'm suddenly thankful no light has penetrated our hidey-hole, or Steel would see the amusement splashed across my face.

Steel shifts and his presence invades my space.

I yelp as my legs are tossed to the side and I slide down the wall until I'm half-laying half-sitting on the packed dirt ground.

Steel hovers above me, his arms supported on the ground and wall on either side of me.

Once again, I'm struck by how intimate the lack of sight makes our interactions.

I'm caged in. His scent surrounds me. His breath fans my skin.

Something a little like fright and a lot like something else I'm not familiar with blooms inside my chest.

Whatever it is, I hate it.

Steel speaks slowly, enunciating each word. Branding them in my mind. "What it means, little angel-born, is that I am a very powerful Nephilim and you should not mess with me."

Even though he can't see, I nod in the darkness.

Okay Steel, message received.

9

*B*y the time someone comes to tell us the campus is clear, I've calmed down enough to phase back into the real world, but the lower half of my body has gone numb. After Steel's little intimidation power-play, we lapsed into an uncomfortable silence. My legs were once again folded against my chest rather than more comfortably spread across him. I wasn't about to let Steel know how awkward the position was for me. He'd probably find joy in my pain.

When the signal comes—a slight flicker of light and a noise that sounds an awful lot like an owl—Steel starts crawling without a word.

Don't worry about me, it's cool. I'll just bump around until I find the opening.

My limbs protest when I order them to move, and I bite back a pain-filled noise. Needle pricks run up and down my legs as the blood flow returns to normal. Gritting my teeth, I feel around until I find the opening and follow Steel's lead.

Eventually, a stream of light filters through the tunnel and my eyes begin to pick up a few details.

Steel stops and words fly out of my mouth without forethought. "Is this when I get to shove your butt?"

His head jerks around. In the cramped space and low light, I make out the narrowing of his eyes before he faces forward and resumes crawling.

"Grump," I mutter under my breath.

I shouldn't have said anything at all because the next moment, I'm choking on the cloud of dust he kicked in my face. His low chuckle at my hacking cough tells me it wasn't an accident.

In my head, I call him every unflattering name I can think of, but hold my tongue. I don't relish another dirt bath.

Some hand gestures behind his back will have to suffice.

At the end of the crawl-shuffle, someone reaches down a hand to help me up. The strong grasp pulls me free of the tight space and into the early morning light.

I blink against the rising sun, my eyes watering at the brightness. Streaks of orange paint the sky from the east and set the red brick and terracotta façade of Seraph Academy aglow.

This is the first solid look I've gotten of the aboveground portion of the academy. I was unconscious when I arrived yesterday, and the building had been shrouded in darkness last night when Steel and I ran for cover.

The structure rises six stories into the air. Two wings extend on each side, giving the academy a u-shaped configuration with a manicured lawn in the middle.

My gaze bounces over each of the architectural elements. The elaborate Gothic building boasts turrets on every corner of the roof, stone carved balconies along each window on the upper three floors, and intricate carvings that run up and down the stone walls. I can't decide if it reminds me more of a fairy-tale palace or medieval fortress.

I rub at the grit in my eyes and cringe at my dingy appearance. So much for the fresh change of clothes they provided me.

Touching my head, I realize I've lost the blue baseball cap Sable gave me. It may be back in the hole we just slithered out of, or on the floor in the academy sublevel somewhere.

I brush my long hair—now covered in cave dirt—over my shoulders.

Looks like I'm scheduled for two showers in a twenty-four-hour period. That's practically unheard of for me.

"Glad to see you're unharmed."

Sable has two dark-haired adults with her. A man and a woman. Teachers perhaps?

All three of them look like they've been in a tussle—hair every which way, some torn clothes, superficial scratches and bruises—but I don't see any serious injuries.

I spot Steel's retreating form over Sable's right shoulder as he stalks to the main entrance of the academy. Two small figures, a boy and a girl, burst out of the oversized front doors and run at my reluctant bodyguard.

They're both roughly the same height, landing somewhere between Steel's chest and midsection. The girl has stick-straight black hair that reaches almost to her waist. The little boy sports a haircut and color that mirrors Steel's. If pressed, I'd guess they're only eight or nine, but I'm certainly not an expert at determining children's ages.

When the little ones reach Steel, he bends over and scoops

them up, holding one in each arm. They squeal in excitement. Their muffled noises reach my ears—two animated voices followed by one deep baritone—but they are too far away to be heard clearly.

Steel marches them inside without a backward glance; the door slams shut behind him with a bang. It's not as if I expected anything special from him, but at least checking to make sure I'd made it out of that hellhole would have been nice.

Blowing out a frustrated puff of air, I turn my attention to Sable.

"So . . . ah . . . everything safe now?" I'd love it if someone would fill me in on what, exactly, is going on. "No more of those . . . you know . . ." I bend my fingers to look like claws and imitate the hissing sounds the creatures made—the ones they call Forsaken.

The woman behind Sable lets out a light laugh and the man coughs into his hand, a smile on his face.

I lift a shoulder in a half shrug. It wasn't a bad impression.

Sable's lips curl into a fleeting smile that flatlines a beat later. When she speaks, it's as if the trickle of humor never touched her.

"Yes, the Forsaken have been eliminated and we've done a sweep of the academy. Our tech team is checking our perimeter security system to figure out how they made it into the building without detection. An alarm should have been triggered the moment they crossed onto the grounds, not when they were already in the sub-levels. The rest of the students are in lock-down in the dorms, but once we're cleared by tech, the restrictions will be lifted."

"Lock-down? What about those two kids I just saw with Steel?"

The man behind Sable scoffs, then cracks his neck. "There's only so much we can do to control *that* family."

The woman beside him nods her agreement.

Interesting.

"Emberly." Sable grabs my attention when she lays what I believe is supposed to be a comforting hand on my shoulder. I stare at it as she goes on. "I want to assure you this is highly unusual."

I can't help the snort of disbelief that escapes me. This is the second attack in the last twenty-four-hours. When I was on my own, I went months—if I was extra careful—without slipping into the spectrum world. I maneuver out of her grasp. A crease appears between her eyes as her brow pinches.

"I'm serious. It's been several decades since a Forsaken has entered the academy. Any of our academies."

"So I'm just lucky then?" There isn't any bite to my words, only grim resignation. I rub my eyes again as exhaustion hits me like a tidal wave.

Deep down, I'd hoped this would be a safe place for me. All the running, hiding, and scraping by day-to-day was getting old. Being able to live, even for a short while, without having my guard up all day, every day, sounded like heaven. But it may not be in the cards for me.

When I glance up, Sable's pretty face is somber. Her lips are pulled down in a frown and her eyes strain, the start of fine lines visible at their outer corners.

"Every one of our academies is heavily warded—meaning we have an invisible shield protecting the grounds that Forsaken and Fallen can't pass through, at least not without suffering severe injuries. The barrier burns them like the sun's light. We'll figure out what's going on. And until then, this is still the safest spot for you."

"I don't know."

I chew on my lower lip. I don't want to be an ungrateful jerk, but come on. Ugly vampires? Hard pass on meeting one of those again. A wave of doubt crashes over me.

"My life may not have been fun, but from what I've seen in the last twenty-four hours, anonymity may have been safer."

"One more chance. Give us some time to equip you with the knowledge you need to unlock your abilities. Right now, that's all I'm asking."

What she wants from me, really for me, isn't unreasonable. I just . . .

I suck in a lungful of air, holding it in my chest for several beats before releasing it. I'm going to give in, again.

I don't like the thought of depending on anyone else, but knowing more about where I come from and the creatures that want to hurt me is the smart move.

Straightening my spine, I give her a firm nod.

She releases a breath and a smile blossoms on her face.

"Great." She gestures to the people behind her I'd all but forgotten about. "This is Seth," the man nods at me in greeting, "and Angelica."

A small laugh slips free and I slap a hand over my mouth.

Whoops.

Angelica, a tall woman who appears to be in her mid-twenties, grins and waves me off.

"Happens every time I'm introduced," she says. "My mom wasn't very creative."

"Hi." I wave at Angelica and Seth with a small smile of my own.

"Angelica will be catching you up on our history, and Seth is going to be your combat instructor."

"Combat?"

"Think of it as the Neph equivalent to PE."

Remembering the organized way these people fought, I highly doubt it's going to resemble any gym class I've ever been in, but I bob my head politely anyway.

"All right." Sable gestures for me to walk with her. "Let's get you settled," she continues after I fall into step beside her. "Regular classes start back up this afternoon, but you'll have your first class tomorrow. Get some rest today; you'll need your strength."

I don't like the sound of that, but follow her anyway. For better or worse, I've chosen my fate. Only time will tell if I've chosen poorly or not.

10

"Oh my gosh, I'm so glad you're okay!"

Ash slams into me seconds after I walk into the dorm room. The air punches from my lungs from her exuberant greeting.

"Can't . . . breathe," I choke out.

Her arms drop as she steps back. Her cheeks darken to an umber glow.

"Whoops, sorry about that. I was just so worried!" Her eyes sweep me from head to toe. "Why are you so disgusting?"

I choke on nothing and it turns into a crazed-sounding laugh.

"Geez, I'm sorry again. I just mean . . . you're really dirty."

When I step farther into the room, I'm careful not to brush up against anything. She's not wrong. I'm covered in a fine layer of dirt, among other things.

Is that a cobweb clinging to my calf? Yuck.

"Yeah, that'll happen when you're crawling around in a gopher tunnel."

Ash tilts her head. Her curls fall over her left shoulder. "Come again?"

"Steel forced me into some hole in the side of the mountain, and we had to wait in a poor excuse for a cave until it was safe to come out. It seriously stank."

Actually, Steel smelled rather good.

Traitorous thoughts. I tell myself to shut up.

Ash winces. "That's awful. That hideout is only meant for a single person."

"Pfft. I can understand why."

I won't be surprised if my legs are riddled with bruises under my jeans.

"Here, use the bathroom to get cleaned up. You can change into some of my clothes." She steps back to assess me. "I think we're probably about the same size. Hard to tell with all that extra fabric. Did you ask to be put in men's clothes?"

Maybe . . . but she doesn't need to know that.

Buzzing around the room, she opens and closes drawers in a whirlwind as she grabs everything I'll need to shed my nasty attire. She herds me into a bathroom on the far side of the room.

"We all have private bathrooms. It's really nice." Setting the clothes down on the clean counter, she shows me where the towels and shower essentials are kept. When finished, she leans against the sink cabinet.

"Does this mean you're rooming with me?"

I suck my bottom lip between my teeth. Sable waited until we were almost to Ash's room to explain I'd be rooming with her. What if Ash doesn't want a roommate? She probably appreciates having a whole room to herself. This conversation is on the verge of getting awkward.

"Um, I'm sure I could talk to Sable about putting me somewhere else. I don't want to intrude."

"Are you kidding? No way! I'd love to share with you. I've always felt a little left out because I didn't have a roomie," she confesses.

"Seriously?"

"Absolutely!" Straightening from her perch, she turns on a heel and heads into the bedroom. "I can't wait to start online shopping. You're going to need a full wardrobe."

Shopping. Er . . . that's not really my thing.

"Don't worry," she says, mistaking the reason for my hesitation. "Seraph will pay for everything. The Nephilim's long life makes accumulating wealth easy. We're invested all over the world."

"Oh, ah. Good to know?" I can't imagine not having to worry about money.

With a wiggle of her eyebrows and a shoulder shimmy, she shuts the door.

I make quick work of getting the shower going and jump in. Breathing in the steamy air, I lean my head against the tiled wall. The tension drains from my shoulders. This shower is somehow even better than the last. Red, chalky dirt runs off my body like dried blood, turning the water a gross rusty color before it finally runs clear. I use some of Ash's shampoo and conditioner and hope she doesn't mind. The shower stall fills with the scent of warm vanilla and jasmine.

Heaven.

Guilt for my lengthy shower settles on my shoulders when the water begins to cool, but I rarely have the opportunity to indulge in hot showers. Most of my bathing over the last year has involved paper towel wipe-downs in gas station bathrooms.

I cringe thinking about all that time I went without proper personal hygiene. I'd mostly gotten used to my constant state of unclean, but looking back, I'm not sure I could do it again.

I struggle to fully regret taking advantage of the simple luxury as I step out of the shower. I sure hope Ash doesn't need to wash up right after me.

After patting my hair with one of the towels Ash gave me, I leave it down to air dry and pull on a pair of borrowed soft gray leggings and a loose-fitting rose colored sweater. The large neck of the sweater is so wide it drops off one shoulder, but I'm used to that. Baggy clothes that hide my form are sorta my thing.

What I'm not used to are the pants that cling to every curve of my body from ankle to waist.

I fidget with the clothes for a few minutes before leaving the bathroom. At least the thin sweater is long enough to cover my butt.

Entering the room, I spot Ash sitting cross-legged on her bed with a book full of strange symbols laying open in front of her.

"What's that?" I ask, trying in vain to get the sweater to cling to both shoulders rather than just one.

"It's my copy of The Book of Seraph. Have you heard of it?"

I shake my head.

"It's like our version of the Bible, except it's not a religious text. More like a history of our species. Just wait until you have to start studying this tome. The struggle is real."

"Oh." Is there a proper response to that? Chit-chatting isn't my strong suit. "That stinks."

Yeah, that sounded almost normal.

"Don't worry . . ." Lifting her head, Ash's words taper off and her eyes grow large. "Hey, look at you. You were hiding a teenage girl under all those layers after all."

She laughs at her own joke as I shift uncomfortably. Ash's amusement thins to a stop when I don't respond. I must look constipated or something because her eyes soften in pity.

"Hey, I'm sorry. I wasn't trying to make fun of you. I only meant that you look nice. More like . . . yourself. It doesn't seem like you're hiding anymore."

"I usually dress not to get noticed."

"No more of that, okay? You're with your own now."

"Am I?" I ask, subconsciously playing with a damp strand of my long blonde and red hair—the very thing that makes me doubt how much I actually belong in this group of angel hybrids.

"I know I said this before, but that hair of yours is wicked cool. It just grows like that, huh?"

Bouncing to her feet, Ash circles me like a shark.

Boundaries are going to be an issue with her, I can tell.

"For as long as I can remember. It was one of the things that always made my foster families uncomfortable. Well—the hair, the mysterious injuries, the insistence that monsters were after me, and that people turned into bursts of color sometimes. I suppose considering everything, the hair was the least of the oddities."

Ash snorts a short chuckle. "Yeah, ya think?"

I shift my weight, at a loss for words.

"How are you holding up? It's been an eventful couple of days for you."

I'm thankful for the subject change. Thinking about all the families I was placed in and removed from . . . well, it's a sore subject for me.

"Is it always this exciting?"

"Ha, not even close. We run lockdown drills all the time, but that's the first time in the six years I've been going here that I actually used one of the safe rooms. All those teenage bodies in a small space." She fans a hand in front of her face. "Nasty. I thought I was going to pass out from the stench of B.O. and farts."

I wrinkle my nose, imagining the horror.

But something else she said stands out to me. Sable wasn't lying about the frequency of attacks on the academy after all.

So why did it have to happen the first day I arrived? Was it just a coincidence? Do I even believe in those?

"Those things that attacked us . . . I have no words." Picturing the fanged creature that Steel fought, I only just manage not to shudder.

"You've never seen a Forsaken?"

"Never."

Ash blows out a breath, causing the wispy curls framing her face to dance. "Girl, you must have a protective bubble around you. Or a guardian angel warding off evil. Avoiding the Fallen for so long is one thing, but the Forsaken hunt in the mortal world *and* the spirit realm. They're like supernatural bloodhounds when it comes to smelling out lone Nephilim. Our numbers keep them away from the academy, but getting attacked out in the rest of the world is pretty commonplace for our kind. It's part of the reason why we get sent to an academy so young. Safety in numbers is a real thing for us."

She stares at me like she expects an explanation as to how I didn't know Forsaken existed. She's going to be waiting for a while, because heck if I know the answer to that.

"It's a good thing you're here with us now. Thank the Creator you made it this long on your own."

"The Creator? Like . . . God? Is He . . . real?"

I've always wondered.

"Oh yeah, girl. He's real for sure. The Bible is no joke. We just happen to have a bit more information about Him and the supernatural world than the rest of the populace. It can be fun being in the know. Until it's not."

I don't know. Being oblivious but safe sounds better than joining some paranormal circle of trust. But even so, I can't seem to stop the questions.

"So the Forsaken. They're like . . . vampires or something?" I can't believe those words just came out of my mouth. The world was definitely a safer place when I woke up yesterday morning—which isn't saying much, considering how hard it's been to survive on my own.

I scrub my fingers over my forehead as a throbbing ache begins to pound a steady cadence in my head. My body may be stronger than the average person's—and now I know why —but it still has limits. I'm flirting with overload.

Ash shakes her head.

"They are and aren't. Vampires are a myth, but the Forsaken are what inspired the legends. They can't walk in the daylight and they do sometimes drink blood."

So. Creepy.

"Are they another type of species then? Are they . . . born?"

"No, not exactly." She worries her bottom lip. I can feel that whatever answer is coming, it's bad.

"I can handle it," I assure her.

"Well, you see, the Forsaken were once . . . us."

Nope. Wasn't expecting that.

"More precisely, the Forsaken are Nephilim possessed by the Fallen. Once a Fallen possesses a Nephilim, they change into those things you saw today. The Forsaken. They become the vessels for evil to walk the Earth."

A chill skates down my spine. When Sable asked Steel who it was that attacked us, and he said Gabe . . . Did I watch Steel fight—and kill—someone he used to know?

The mixed feelings come fast and hot: A flash of pity for Steel, who might have been facing off against a friend. A sharp pang of concern when I realize the ties that bind this seemingly happy family of angel-borns together are broken easily enough. And finally horror. I could become that . . . *thing*. Any of us could. "Can the possessed Nephilim be saved?"

Ash's lips pull down in a frown. "No. Once overtaken, the Nephilim is lost. The only way to destroy the Fallen inside is to kill the vessel."

What have I gotten myself into?

"This must be a lot to process," Ash surmises, correctly reading my body language. "You probably feel a little like Alice, having fallen down the rabbit hole into a topsy-turvy world."

I croak out a broken laugh and Ash leans forward, grasping my cold hand in her warm ones. "But I'm glad you're here. I don't know how you managed to survive alone, but I promise you sooner or later they would have found you. They hunt us."

Her hands squeeze mine for emphasis. "The Fallen created us as a way to walk in the mortal realm, never believing we'd fight back. But we did, and we still do. We fight against the fate they planned for us every day. We fight to protect the world from their evil."

I don't even know how to respond. My mind is a whirling mess. Suddenly, my enemy is even more formidable than I realized.

In my wildest dreams, I wouldn't have been able to imagine any of this. My life goals were to stay alive and live in peace.

I'm not sure how I feel about all of this—the Nephilim, Fallen, Forsaken, or even Seraph Academy—except that it scares me. Within a single day, my whole existence has flipped upside down.

"You're not alone anymore. We stick together. We have each other's backs. And we hunt the hunters."

11

$\mathcal{I}$ pick a desk in the rear left corner of the classroom. It's a normal room, nothing fancy. Six rows of desks, eight desks in each row. Teacher's desk angled in front of a large chalkboard. A wall of books behind me. Windows line the right side of the room and overlook the lawn's pristine checkerboard stripes.

I arrived to class ten minutes early, mostly to make sure I could choose a seat as close to the door as possible. Strategic seating is one of my quirks. I have to be sitting in the very back of the class. Under no circumstances can anyone sit behind me. Over the years, I've been tormented by too many students to trust my backside to anyone for an entire period.

My other rule is that whatever side the door is on, that's where I have to be. Being close to the door means being able to make a quick exit. Lingering in classrooms has only ever painted a bigger target on me.

Rolling my number-two pencil between my fingers, I fidget in my borrowed clothes. Ash's stretchy jeans cling to every inch of my skin. The top I'm wearing is a simple blue graphic tee, but only hangs to my hips and stretches across my chest and stomach in a way I'm wholly unfamiliar with.

I miss my men's extra-large tees.

Baggy enough to hide my form and long enough to cover my butt—not that there was ever much to see back there since I prefer wearing men's or women's pants several sizes too big.

As I pull the shirt away from my chest, the door opens.

Jerking my head in its direction, I watch a female student enter then stumble a step when she spots me. She doesn't even try to hide the curiosity that washes over her face as she makes her way to the front.

Slanting my head down, a strand of red-tipped platinum hair flops in front of my eyes. I quickly twist it up in my bun and force myself to pretend I'm the only person in this small classroom.

This is just like every other school I've attended. People gawk until they get used to me. Then, if I'm lucky, I become invisible.

I refuse to lift my head when the door slams open again and the noise from the hall filters through the opening, along with what I assume are several more students. People will be more apt to ignore me if I keep my gaze down and avoid making eye contact.

I've had years to perfect my moves.

"Emberly! Whatcha doing at the back of the class?"

Or maybe not.

Sterling sits on the desktop in front of me and perches his black-sneakered feet on the attached chair. His head tilts to the left and a smirk turns up the corners of his mouth as he regards me.

I will not squirm.

"Maybe she's trying to fly under the radar. Ever considered that, brother?" Greyson scolds his twin as he settles into a desk next to me.

"Why would she want to do that? She's the new academy celebrity. I'd be capitalizing on that social status and streaking through the girl's dorm." Sterling looks genuinely confused.

I scrub a hand down my face while the brothers continue their conversation.

"Of course you would." I can practically hear Greyson's eye roll. "But not everyone is like you, Sterling." And then he mutters under his breath, "Thank goodness for that."

A quiet laugh slips past my lips. "So true."

"Ah, she speaks. Phew!" Sliding off the desktop, Sterling flops into the seat. "We were worried our brother might have frightened you back into your shell."

Bristling at that comment, I raise my head to stare between them, annoyed because Sterling's offhand joke is rather close to the truth.

"Your brother is an overgrown man-child with an identity crisis. He doesn't scare me."

"You sure about that?"

My heart jumps to my throat as Steel's deep voice slaps against the back of my head.

I fight my instinct to slouch and return my eyes to the desktop. Instead, I glare at Sterling as he mumbles "busted" behind his hand and shakes with laughter.

He so saw Steel coming.

I need to make some new friends. These brothers are bad for my health.

Feigning nonchalance, I shrug without turning to look at

the eldest brother. "What's there to be frightened of? You turn into a few overgrown animals. So what? That can't be the most impressive thing happening at this school."

Steel's hands wrap around my seat back. His knuckles graze my shoulder blades and I straighten to avoid the contact. When he talks, his breath feathers across my neck, causing my blush to deepen.

"Whatever you need to tell yourself," he whispers in my ear.

The next instant he brushes by me, stopping briefly to give Greyson some weird, guy handshake, and flick Sterling—who's bent over laughing—on the forehead.

Without a backward glance, he takes a seat on the opposite side of the room near the front. It would have been difficult for him to sit any farther away, but that's fine with me.

Leaning forward, I swat Sterling with the back of my hand.

"What was that for?" he asks as he rubs the sore spot.

"You couldn't have warned me he was standing there?"

He snorts a short laugh. "And why would I have done that?"

Shaking my head, I turn to Greyson. "You need some new family members."

"Don't I know it," he agrees.

"Whatever happened to family loyalty, bro?"

"What's he even doing in this class? He's not our year," I press Greyson, ignoring Sterling.

"Not all academy classes are split by grade. This is one we all have to take to graduate, so there are several different years in here. Steel was trying to get away without taking it at all, but it backfired on him. Now he's stuck with us."

My eyes sweep the classroom, taking in the mix of students spread across several age groups. My gaze lands on Steel's back then tracks to the girl sitting in front of him. Unless I'm mistaken, that's the same girl he was seated next to in the cafeteria yesterday. A girlfriend maybe?

The auburn-haired beauty is twisted in her seat to face Steel. She's leaning forward as if she needs to eliminate the small space between them in order to hear him.

Pfft. Like it's anywhere near loud enough in this room to have to do that.

"Look, Grey. She's at it again."

Huh? Who's at what?

Greyson sighs. "If he'd just be clear with her, he wouldn't have to put up with it anymore."

They must be talking about Steel. Maybe not a girlfriend after all. At least not yet. Or perhaps not anymore?

"Put up with it? Ha. Are you blind, man?" Sterling gestures to Steel and the girl laughing at something he just said. "Does he look *bothered* to you?"

Steel is slouched down in his chair with an arm thrown over the back. His legs stretch in front of him—one under the girl's chair and the other lazily resting in the aisle. At first glance, he's the picture of ease, but as I examine him more intently, he rolls his neck as if stretching a kink out and his shoulders look a little tense. But maybe I'm reading something into the situation that isn't there.

"Yeah, maybe you're right," Greyson reluctantly offers.

"More like *maybe* he's keeping his options open. Besides, if I had a chick as smokin' as Nova all over me, I wouldn't be in a rush to shut that down either."

I shift, suddenly uncomfortable in my seat.

I don't know why Sterling's observations are bothering me, but they definitely are.

Why should I care one way or another who Steel is paying attention to? It's not like I want him to be a jerk to everyone since he's one to me.

Okay, that's a lie.

It bothers me that he's capable of being charming, but chooses not to even try with me. What's his problem?

"Sterling, come on." Greyson gestures to me as if the topic of conversation is too delicate for my ears. I raise a brow to say *seriously?*

Like this conversation is anywhere near as crude as the ones I've overheard before. A side effect of being invisible is that people tended to talk in front of me all the time, forgetting that just because I'm quiet, it doesn't mean I'm deaf.

"Seriously, man. You need to develop a filter."

"What would be the fun in that?" Sterling answers with a straight face.

I bark out a laugh. He does have a point.

Unable to help myself, my gaze drifts to Steel and Nova.

I have no idea what they're talking about, but when Steel lifts his hand and points a thumb in our direction, turning his head so he can glance over his shoulder, I have a bad feeling I've just become the conversation's hot topic.

It's all but confirmed a moment later when another mountain-sized guy goes over to talk to Steel and the chick's gaze cuts to mine and narrows. She glares a couple long seconds before returning her attention to both guys.

That was bizarre.

"Uh-oh, Emberly. You might want to start sharpening your claws."

"Huh?" Startled, I turn confused eyes on Sterling.

"I can't believe I'm saying this, but he's right." Greyson itches his eyebrow. "You don't want to get on her bad side. She's vicious."

They can't be serious.

What does this Nova girl have to be mad at me about? It's not like I'm after her man. That's laughable. The only thing I want to do with Steel is stay far away from him.

I tell them as much.

"Well, everyone knows you guys spent a night together. And in a very *very* tight space." Sterling wiggles his eyebrows suggestively.

"You mean the longest, most uncomfortable night of my life? There's no way people are talking about that."

"Once again I hate to agree with my brother—"

"That's cold, man!"

"—but he's right. As much as I'd like to tell you we are, this school isn't above spreading petty gossip. We are part human, after all. You'd be surprised by what gets around. And Nova can get rather . . . territorial."

"Yeah, that girl can be straight-up diabolical."

I let out a low groan.

The last thing I need is an enemy. And Steel is not someone I'm willing to fight over. She can have him. In fact, I hope she will. If she keeps his attention off me, I won't have to deal with him anymore.

"And here I thought you were all supposed to be the good guys."

"Oh, we're still the good guys," Greyson says. "But no matter what fancy name they give this academy, it's still high school."

12

Sable looks up from the paperwork in front of her when I shuffle into her office. Wearing a tailored cream blouse, she's seated behind a sturdy mahogany desk. The midday sun shines through the window and haloes her head like a real angel. Her long straight hair brushes the desktop as she waits for me to settle.

Setting my borrowed messenger bag down, I take a seat in a leather chair across from her. Leaning forward, she steeples her hands.

"How has your first day of classes gone so far?"

Not knowing exactly how to answer, I purse my lips and fidget. "Good?"

"Is that an answer or a question?" Her light laugh sets me at ease and some of the tension in my back abates.

"A little bit of both, I guess. The classes have been good. I don't think it'll be too hard to catch up, even with my break this past year. Starting a new school has never been my favorite thing."

Understatement of the century.

Sable nods as if she understands completely. "I'm glad your morning classes aren't too overwhelming. And starting a new school must be hard. I hope the other students are welcoming."

She stops talking and stares. There was a question buried in that statement.

"Oh, um, yeah. They've been very nice."

"Good." A smile overtakes her face. "As you might have already realized from your schedule, the first part of your day is rather conventional. All the normal classes similar to the ones at your other schools, I'm sure. For you and the other upper class students, the second half of the day will consist of training and learning about your skills. In your case, that will involve an hour a day with me while I catch you up on the history of our race and we try to uncover more about your angel-line."

I nod. I noticed all this when I got my schedule early this morning and went over it with Ash. I have gym with her after tutoring with Sable. She said to be prepared for "weird-ness," whatever that means—apparently it isn't a normal gym class.

I'm trying not to psych myself out.

"So." Sable clasps her hands and stands. "Let me find some-thing to start with." Skirting her desk, she pauses in front of a floor-to-ceiling bookshelf. Her fingers dance over the spines as she searches. "Ah, here we go."

Pulling out what has to be the largest book on the planet, she plops it in front of me and returns to her seat.

The leather on the book is dry and cracked. There are no words on the cover, but an intricate symbol of interlocking swirls and slashes lies in the middle. It reminds me of the book Ash was studying yesterday.

I brush my fingers over the embossed symbol and a spark pricks the tip of my index finger—like static electricity. Yanking my hand back, I rub my thumb over the pad of my finger.

"What happened?" Sable asks.

I continue to rub the shocked digit. The electric sensation is still there.

I don't like it.

"It shocked me."

"That's . . . odd. Leather doesn't usually carry a static charge." Pulling a note pad out from her desk, she writes something down. Catching me trying to take a peek, she smiles and explains. "All Nephilim are descended from certain lines. Certain types of angels, if you will. Even if two Nephilim from opposite lines have children, the children will always inherit one of the parent's angelic genes, not both. One of our goals, especially since we don't know who your parents are, is to determine what line you're from. So, from time to time I'll probably ask you some pretty bizarre questions. That's just me trying to figure it out. Once we know, we'll be able to train you in the skills you should already be developing."

Considering my conversation with Steel, that makes sense.

"Do you have an idea which line I'm descended from yet?"

"I'm afraid not. Many things about you are an enigma to us right now."

An unexpected wave of sadness envelops my heart. It shouldn't. Her answer is what I expected.

Seeing my disappointment, Sable reaches forward and

covers my hand. "Don't worry. We'll get this figured out. This is a good place to start. Let me explain the basics of angelic hierarchy. Who knows? Maybe something will resonate and help us unravel your mystery."

"I'd like that."

By the end of our hour together, Sable has wheeled out a white board and drawn me a diagram.

"So there are three different groupings of angels, and three different kinds in each?" I ask.

"Right, but the groups are called *spheres*. Each of the nine different Nephilim academies spread out over the world are named after a different line of angels. Each type of angel performs different services, and their abilities help them accomplish their tasks. If I flip the board over, do you think you'll remember what the different spheres are and their primary purpose?"

"I can try."

Sable turns the white board over so I can't see her writing anymore. The names of the different types of angels float in my head as I try to recall everything she's told me.

"The first sphere includes the seraphim, cherubim, and thrones. They guard the throne of God. I think."

With both parents being cherubim, Steel and his siblings belong to this grouping.

"Very good. And thrones can manipulate and build the wards by pulling on energy contained in the natural spring water running throughout the cracks and fissures below us. Every academy is built above natural springs for this purpose. And there are no seraphim Nephilim. Do you remember why?"

"Because none of the seraphim rebelled against God, so they weren't cast down to Earth."

"That's right. Keep going."

"The angels in the second sphere are the dominions, virtues, and powers." I'm the most shaky on the duties of this sphere. "They . . . govern things?"

I believe Ash is part of this sphere. Maybe a dominion? I could be wrong about that though.

"You're not alone in that confusion. This is the most elusive grouping of celestial beings. Their job is to regulate the duties of the lower angels as well as govern the laws of our universe. They make sure everything is acting the way it should, from gravity keeping the planets in orbit, to the grass growing under our feet. The Nephilim descended from this sphere have some unique abilities."

"They're all unique to me."

Sable smiles and checks her watch. "We'll get to those abilities in a different session, we're almost out of time today. But how about that last group?"

"Right, the third sphere includes rules, archangels, and angels. Which isn't at all confusing because we refer to all of them as angels." The corner of my mouth quirks up before I continue. "They are the guides, protectors, and messengers to humankind."

"Exactly. Great job. We can pick this up tomorrow. I don't want you to be late." She checks her watch again and grimaces. "Or rather, later than you already are to combat training. Do you know where to find the gym?"

"Yep, sure do."

The gym is on one of the subfloors beneath the academy. I haven't been down there since the attack. I'm not frightened, but I'm not exactly excited about being entombed in the earth again either.

"What about this?" I ask, pointing to the large leather-bound book still resting on her desk. We haven't touched it yet.

"Oh right! Why don't you go ahead and borrow it? You won't be able to read it just yet, but it will be useful in time."

My fingers hover over the cover once again, but I don't allow them to connect with the symbols.

"What are these?" I ask, pointing at the scrolls embossed in the aged leather.

"The language of the celestials. Angelic writings. This is The Book of Seraph. Essentially, a history of our species. We'll start studying from this later in the week. Once you have a general understanding of the markings, instinct will kick in and you'll be able to read it in no time."

I hesitate a few moments before gingerly grasping the ancient tome. Setting it in my messenger bag, I heft the satchel over my shoulders.

Sable settles in behind her desk and gives me a short wave goodbye as I slip out of her office.

My steps echo off the empty hallway as I walk to the elevator. Classes have already started, which means I'm going to be interrupting the session when I show up late.

Great, more people staring at me.

Hitching my bag farther up on my shoulder, I round a corner. Since I'm looking down—which is my habit in public—I almost run right into another student. We both skid to a halt, just in time.

After taking several quick steps back, I lift my head,

prepared to apologize. The words stick in my throat like bugs on flypaper.

The smile on Nova's face doesn't match the cold look in her eyes.

"If you looked up, it would help you see where you're going."

There's just enough honey in her voice for someone to confuse her words for good-natured ribbing.

I'm not convinced. I've run across numerous "Novas" in my life. Every school has at least one.

I can't stop myself from giving her a quick once-over. Except for the artfully messy braid banded across the top of her head like a headband, her hair is down in flowing waves the color of burnt autumn leaves. The ends brush the space between her shoulder and elbow. She's wearing a tight pink tank with the word *princess* written in sequins. Her short jean skirt is wholly inappropriate for a fall mountain day, but leaves an expanse of toned leg on display—no doubt exactly what she intended.

Her feet are covered in what have to be at least four-inch, pencil-thin red heels, bringing her already tall stature well above six feet. She's towering over me in my cute flats. At almost six feet myself, that rarely happens.

Is this a joke? She couldn't be more cliché right now. Well, maybe if she was in a tiny cheerleading uniform—but a shirt that says *princess*? I can't make this stuff up.

"Thanks, I'll remember that," I say flatly while trying to sidestep her. As I move to my left, she leans to her right, blocking my path.

I sigh.

The elevator is just beyond her. I can see the doors. Do we really have to play this game?

"It's Emberly, right?"

Yep, I guess the games have begun.

"That's right." I grasp the strap of my borrowed book bag with both hands and wait for her to get to whatever catty point she's leading up to.

"I heard about your first day here, when the Forsaken attacked. That must have been pretty upsetting." Again, her voice carries all the right tones to convey sympathy, but her slightly narrowed eyes tell a different story.

Why does every girl think they need to stake their claim on a guy? Are they really so insecure that they have to figuratively pee a circle around a man to keep him out of the clutches of another woman?

As if that crap even works.

And if that *was* what you had to do to keep someone interested, why would you want him to begin with? Is it so hard to wait for a guy who won't be swayed by a pretty face?

I'm thinking too deeply about this. Time to wrap up this little tête-à-tête.

"Yeah, it was a shock for sure. Glad no one was seriously hurt."

She nods her agreement. "It's a good thing Steel was around. With you not being able to phase properly and all. Him being there to save you—and for the second time—what a stroke of luck. I can't even imagine what it would be like to not be able to do something as simple as phase correctly. That's something children learn before going off to primary school."

Well, that was a lovely zinger.

I stand quietly, deciding just to wait her out. Her lips, eyes, and brow pinch in annoyance when she realizes I'm not going to take a big ol' bite of the bait she dangled in front of me.

Interesting. This girl likes her prey to either fight back or start running. She wants to make sure her words hit their target.

This time my eyes narrow.

"You should really be working on those elementary skills, at least. Next time Steel may not be around, or may not be interested in saving you when—"

"Listen." I don't know what it is that prompted me to talk when I've held my tongue so many times before. Maybe it's just exhaustion over repeatedly biting back my words? At some point, silence stops being the easy way out.

"Let me be crystal clear with you. I'm not interested in Steel—like *at all*. I find him incredibly frustrating and quite frankly, a bully. He's all yours, I promise. I'll happily stay away from him. And not because you want me to, but because I'm not interested in being anywhere near him. Is that good? Are we done here?"

Oh lookie, she's speechless.

Nova gawks at me as if I've sprouted wings of fire and set the hallway ablaze. Her eyes are no longer narrowed slits of suspicion, but rather round orbs filled with shock. She actually takes a half-step back. The heel of her ridiculously high stiletto clacks against the floor.

I can't help the short laugh that bursts from my chest. This girl is not used to people talking to her like that.

Capitalizing on her surprise, I step around her and stride to the elevators—not checking over my shoulder once. That last part was the hardest. I've been attacked from behind on too many occasions.

I jam my finger against the down button three more times than necessary and pray the elevator will show up soon.

She's only going to stay in her shocked stupor for so long.

"Hey, wait up."

Leaning my head back, I groan up at the ceiling.

Why me? Why is it always me?

With a *ding*, the doors slide open and I jump into the cab, not bothering to acknowledge Nova as her heels clip-clop their way toward me.

The doors close slowly and I grin.

Maybe if you weren't wearing such ridiculous shoes, you'd have gotten here faster.

Just as the doors are about to come together, a manicured hand shoots between them.

No!

Since their sensors have been triggered, the doors open again to reveal one pissed off Nephilim girl.

"Did you not hear me calling?"

"Do you really want the answer to that?"

Her eyes flare as she stomps into the elevator with me.

Why didn't I just keep my mouth shut and swallow her insults? Now I'm going to have—

"I like you."

Say what?

"Huh?"

Crossing her arms, she cocks her head before leaning against the metal wall of the elevator. "You don't take any crap. That's ballsy. I like it."

It's my turn to gawk at her as we descend. Have I stepped into an alternate universe?

I'm still staring at her, mouth gaping, when we jerk to a stop and the doors slide open.

Nova saunters out of the elevator with natural confidence and takes three runway steps before noticing I'm not accompanying her. Casting a glance over her shoulder, she rolls her eyes.

"Seriously, close your mouth. You look like a trout."

My jaw snaps shut. Well, then.

"And hurry up. I was sent to fetch you. They thought you'd gotten lost and needed a babysitter. I'm only so patient . . . even with people I like."

I scurry to catch up as she sashays down the hall, leading the way to the gym—wholly confused as to what exactly just happened. Because if I didn't know better, I'd say I made another friend.

This place is weird.

13

*N*ova points me in the direction of the locker room and gives me a brief rundown of where to find my training clothes. I'm still in a state of shock, so I do a lot of nodding before she walks off. She throws up a hand on the way out and says she hopes I don't break my neck. I'm sixty-two percent sure she's being sincere.

Exiting the locker room, I spot Ash waving at me from the other side of the gym. Her hair is pulled into a mop of dark curls that bounces with her movements.

We're dressed similarly in a pair of black spandex shorts and a matching tank—an obvious combat class uniform. These are by far my least favorite academy attire. I don't care if every other girl is wearing the same thing, I still have the urge to hold my hands over my butt when I walk.

I begin navigating toward Ash, trying not to get distracted as I weave through the cavernous space—but it's impossible.

The gym is easily the largest room in the compound,

which is impressive since it's located underground. The ceiling stretches four floors above my head. The floor space is divided into six different zones. About twenty students are in each of the zones, with anywhere from one to four teachers overseeing and instructing.

I walk through the middle of the room, three zones on each side. To my left is an area that looks most like a normal gym. People climbing ropes, playing basketball, running laps, and working out on weight machines.

My gaze skates over the activities I categorize as normal and pauses on the students training on the right. They spar with broadswords and ancient-looking weapons I don't know the names for. They run through a complex obstacle course while popping in and out of the spirit realm, disappearing at seemingly random points and appearing at others. Most bizarre of all is a cage set up in the far corner.

The students inside wear helmets with visors covering their eyes. A metal arm with several hinged joints hangs from the ceiling and clamps around their middles. Students bounce through the air with the help of the metal arm. They kick, punch, and swing imaginary weapons.

Maybe it's some sort of high-tech virtual reality?

I'm still rubbernecking when I plop down on the mat next to Ash.

"Please explain." I point at the cage.

"It's a simulation. Each person's Nephilim skills are loaded into the program, and they train by fighting computer-generated Fallen and Forsaken. Wild, right?"

"That's one way to describe it."

"Ladies, you ready to start or should we give you a few more minutes?"

Oh, gosh. I close my eyes and duck behind Ash.

"Sorry, Seth."

The instructor nods once then addresses the class.

"As you all know, we had a scare this past week. For some of you, this was the closest you've ever gotten to a Forsaken. You're the fortunate ones. For the rest of us, this experience was all too familiar. Whatever your experience with the Forsaken has been so far, the thing we all have in common is that it won't be our last confrontation."

Nope, don't like the sound of that. Fighting gross Fallen-possessed vampire-creatures is not on my life goals list.

"What that means for your time here is that we're going to be stepping up training. We're going to be pushing your comfort zone to propel you to the next level." He claps his hands together. "Today, we start with some sparring. Emberly, come on up here. We need to assess your level."

Oh, no. No, no, no, noooo. He did not just say my name.

Oh, crap. But he did. Crap, crap, crappity-crap.

Where to hide?

Ash nudges me with her elbow. Her eyes say *what's the problem?* and mine silently reply, *what isn't?*

My cheeks burn as I push off the mat and make my way up to the front. My eyes remain laser-focused on the spongy black mat beneath my feet rather than any of the students.

"Where would you like me to go?"

Please say a room with no witnesses.

"Hold up here for a second. Let me grab a sparring partner."

Ticking my eyes up from the ground, I watch Seth jog a few feet away and cup his hands in front of his mouth.

"Yo, Steel."

Oh, no. Oh, no. Oh, no.

This is not happening.

Steel's wailing on a punching bag hanging in the section next to ours. He glances up when his name is called. His eyes connect with mine before sliding over to Seth, who waves him over.

"What's up, man?" Using his forearm, Steel wipes at the sweat beaded on his brow. His knuckles are red from pounding on the punching bag. Don't normal people wear protective gear for that kind of activity? I snap my gaze to the ground before I have a chance to ogle any more of him.

"Mind if I borrow you for a minute? I need to assess Emberly's skill set."

Just say no, dude. You know neither one of us wants to do this.

There's an awkward pause before Steel replies.

"Sure."

Why me?

Seth positions us within a circle on the black mat. It's probably about fifteen feet wide. My eyes stay glued to the floor. The collective stare of the class burns into my side, and Steel's gaze blisters my front.

"Go get 'em, Em!" Ash shouts.

"Yeah, show my big brother who's boss!"

Awesome, Sterling's in this class too. Which means Greyson is probably going to have a front row seat to my humiliation as well.

Ignoring the jeers, Seth steps in front of me. "Alright Emberly, Steel is going to come at you. Just do your best to protect yourself."

I nod, still not lifting my gaze.

Seth's feet disappear from view. I shift my weight back and forth and fold my arms across my chest. Hunching my shoulders, I try to make myself as small as possible.

I wish I had the power to melt into the floor. I can't believe they're making me—

A boulder slams into my stomach, knocking me off my feet and punching the air out of my lungs. In a flash, I'm on my back, blinking at the overhead lighting and wondering what the heck just happened.

Wasn't I just standing?

I squint at a figure above me until he leans over, blocking the light shining in my eyes. Steel's blue-black hair brushes his forehead as he watches me gasp for air. Without a word, he offers me a hand up. I roll to my side, ignoring the help, and push myself into a standing position. Something dark flashes in his aquamarine eyes before he slants his gaze away.

That was a cheap shot.

This time, I keep my eyes glued to Steel—but it doesn't make a difference.

Faster than my sight can track, he snaps his leg out and I'm once again on the ground, gasping for air. I lay there—my body aching in places I didn't even know existed—for several long seconds.

With knit brows, Seth joins Steel and speaks to him in hushed tones. Steel nods and shrugs before their heads swivel toward me.

I'm on my feet by the time Seth makes it to me.

"You okay to keep going?" he asks.

I jerk my chin in a curt nod.

"Nephilim all have natural fighting instincts. I'm trying to engage yours to assess where your strengths are, but I don't want you injured in the process." He tries to find my eyes, but my gaze is focused on my opponent. "Steel isn't going to knock you off your feet this time. Just do what you can to defend yourself. See if you can get in a shot."

Interesting. I should pick up reading angelic language *and* combat skills quickly. I don't hate that thought. There are worse things to have a natural aptitude for.

When I don't respond, Seth steps out of view.

Steel saunters forward, his steps deceptively casual.

I'm not sure what he has in mind, but I'm beyond wary.

He cocks his head to the side, narrowing his eyes as he regards me.

An uncomfortable itch of awareness beckons me to hide, but I stand my ground.

A cruel smile quirks the corner of his lips.

He's laughing at me.

I launch my body at his. I'm a mass of flailing arms and clumsy legs as I go at him in an uncoordinated attack. My mind isn't calculating strategic places to land blows, or which limb can do the most damage. Instead, I'm a whirling kaleidoscope of emotions.

Fury and embarrassment dance together in my chest as I shoot out my appendages in sloppy, easily-deflected blows.

Steel isn't doing anything but dodging and blocking my hits.

I'm tiring and he hasn't even thrown a single punch.

My anger doubles, making my movements even more uncoordinated.

Losing my footing, I stumble a few steps when Steel

dodges an ill-aimed kick. After regaining my balance, I twist to face him and snarl my displeasure.

His eyes widen at the inhuman noise that leaves my throat, but a moment later his lips curl at the corners in an annoying smirk I want to slap off his face.

"All right, Steel. Stop playing with her," Seth yells.

Steel's smile kicks up a notch.

Oh, you find this funny, do you buddy?

The grin doesn't leave his face as he lifts his arms in a fighter's stance and beckons me forward with his hand, *Matrix*-style.

I charge him, putting my weight into the punch I plan to land on his perfectly symmetrical face. But when I swing, his head is no longer where it's supposed to be.

I register his outstretched arm too late to stop my momentum and run straight into it . . . with my throat.

Steel barely budges when he clotheslines me. Inertia keeps my lower body moving forward even as my upper body is forced back. I'm airborne for a second before my body slams into the padded floor for the third time.

I grab my neck and gasp for air.

Did he break my trachea? Am I dying?

Black dots swim in my vision as I fight for air.

I'm dying and nobody cares. Why isn't anyone helping me?

Finally, a trickle of sweet air reaches my lungs. I want to suck it down in greedy gulps, but my body won't cooperate. Each inhalation burns my throat.

Turning my head, I catch my classmates' mixed expressions. They vary from horrified to amused. A grimace is frozen on Sterling's face. Ash regards me with sad eyes, a hand covering her mouth. A few of the guys in the back row are openly laughing.

Walking over to Steel, Seth lays his hand good-naturedly on his shoulder, then glances over at me with worried eyes. After shaking his head, Seth pats Steel on the back in the universal gesture for "job well done."

With a single wave, Steel cracks his knuckles and saunters toward the punching bag in the neighboring zone.

No way is it ending like this.

I get that I don't have their fancy training. I understand that I've only just found out the truth of who I am, and they've all been raised to embrace their heritage.

But none of that means I'm weak.

None of that means I'm somehow less than the rest of them.

I may not have the technique, but I'm scrappy.

I don't remember standing up. I don't know how I reach Steel, but I'm fully aware when I jump on his back and hang on like a spider monkey.

Steel falters under my weight—after all, I'm not a small girl—tipping forward and stumbling a few steps before catching himself.

"Get off!"

You're not the boss of me, you brute.

Steel's arms swing back, and he tries to grab my clothes to rip me off him.

I'm not having it.

Tightening my legs around his middle, I sink both hands into his hair, fisting the strands. Using all my strength and weight I pull, forcing his head back and throwing him off-balance.

Is it a sophisticated move?

Nope.

Do I care?

Not at all.

With a roar, Steel's giant body tips back.

Timber!

No amount of core strength is going to keep him upright with my full weight tugging him down and his neck bent at such an unnatural angle.

I hold tight as we go down. I manage to swing my body to the side before I'm crushed beneath his bulk.

My left leg and arm are trapped under a stunned Steel, but I don't let that stop my assault.

Using what leverage I have, I pummel Steel's chest with my right hand. I only get a few solid hits in before he recovers from the shock of being bested.

Those few moments are glorious.

With the fluidity of a born hunter, Steel flips me onto my back and tries to subdue me with his entire form.

Not happening.

I use my whole body and every bit of strength I have to attack. Whatever I can move becomes a weapon. My nails and teeth are daggers, my arms and legs battering rams.

Rearing up under him like a person possessed, I try to throw him off. I wiggle, buck, hit, and kick as if my life depends on it.

Steel growls curses under his breath as he struggles to subdue the beast I've morphed into.

I noticed the sheen of sweat coating his face with a healthy bit of satisfaction.

After some fumbling on his part, his hands capture my

wrists and hold them tight. Then he rears back, pulling my upper body off the mat before slamming me down.

My brain rattles around in my skull, but the fight in me doesn't abate.

"Cut it out!" he roars.

Several angry slashes on his face leak blood.

Good, I've left a mark.

His body shifts above me as he traps my arms over my head.

I smile to myself. Perfect alignment.

Focusing all my energy on my leg, I jam my knee up into the junction between Steel's legs.

His body freezes.

No cup? Tsk tsk, Angel Boy.

I watch with satisfaction as his face turns red and he slumps onto me with a groan.

Shoving his weight off, I lumber to my feet. It's only then I notice how incredibly silent the gym has become.

Scanning the area, I realize all surrounding activity has stopped. The other Nephilim—teachers as well as students—watched our display.

My classmates are on their feet. Most of the guys are grimacing, their faces a picture of sympathetic agony as they watch Steel roll around on the floor. Some even have their hands cupped over their fronts, protecting themselves from a phantom attack.

The girls' faces are a mix of satisfied smirks, wide eyes, and gaping mouths.

I curl my shoulders forward out of habit and bring a hand to my head to scratch an imaginary itch.

My hair is a mess. Half of it has fallen out of the ponytail and the other half is ratted like a raccoon has been nesting up there for the winter.

I thought I was embarrassed before. That was nothing.

The weight of a hundred pairs of eyes causes me to shrink into myself even more.

Why are they all staring? Is it really that surprising someone dared to defy the mighty Steel? Or have these supremely sheltered angel kids never seen someone fight dirty?

Certainly, they've all seen a girl knee a guy in the family jewels before.

Is it admirable?

Not really.

But this isn't an eighteenth-century duel, and "honor" isn't the watch-word I care about. I get that this is training, but the real world is life or death. A real survivor will use every skill she has in her wheelhouse—even the unsavory ones.

Steel's low groans turn into coughs.

He stumbles to his feet, his face still red as he stands with his hands on his knees doing some sort of breathing thing that sounds an awful lot like Lamaze.

I roll my eyes.

Tilting his head, he catches my gaze. Fury churns like molten lava in his eyes.

"What . . . was that?" he spits at me.

I thought there was hate in his glare before. I was wrong. What was certainly no more than cold indifference has transformed to hellfire burning in his eyes.

I walk toward him with a paper-thin façade of calm masking my true emotions.

Pausing briefly before brushing past him to get to the locker room, I put as much ice into my words as I can muster.

"That's how I survived on my own."

I march through the throng of Nephilim, who give me a wide berth. I don't allow myself to steal a glance over my shoulder to catch Steel's reaction. After all, no one ever got where they were going by looking back.

14

"You're insane if you think I'm going in there after what happened this afternoon."

Ash stands in front of me with crossed arms, hip jutting to the side, determined to stare me down.

Pfft, like that's going to intimidate me. I'm waiting at least a week before I show my face again.

"You have to eat."

"You know I don't. I ate yesterday. It won't be another three days before I start to get hunger pains. Nice try though."

Because of our strange eating habits, the academy only serves one meal a day. Our school days are extra-long as well, because we only require a few hours of sleep a night. I have a lot less free time than I'm used to. I don't really mind, but right now, I'm not eager to mix and mingle.

Why didn't I just let Steel humiliate me instead of going all She-Hulk in front of the entire upper class?

Squeezing my eyes shut, I scrub a hand across my face.

The heat of embarrassment from my stunt earlier still hasn't faded.

"Emberly!" Ash stomps a foot. Dropping my hand, I hold back a smile. I'm more than content to stay on my bed right now. It isn't the four-poster beaut I woke up in a couple of days ago, but it's still one of the most comfortable beds I've ever slept in.

"It's not that I don't want to spend time with you, it's just—"

A sharp *bang* interrupts me.

"Yo, Ash! Emberly! Let's go!" Sterling yells through the door.

A smile blooms on Ash's face. Her expression makes me decidedly uncomfortable.

"Have a nice meal," I say.

"Come on in, Sterling."

The door swings open to reveal Sterling and Greyson. Sterling has a hand covering his eyes and the other outstretched in front of him to feel his way forward.

"Everyone decent in here?" he yells unnecessarily.

Greyson stands a few steps behind him, shaking his head.

"No, don't look," Ash drolls flatly. "Emberly and I are mud wrestling and need some privacy."

"What?" Sterling wrenches his hand away from his eyes and scans the room. "Hey, you aren't mud wrestling. You're not even in bikinis. That's false advertising." There's a definite pout in his voice.

I laugh so hard I have to put a hand down on the bed to keep myself from tipping over.

Ash shakes her head. "In what world would we be doing

that in our room? In what world would we ever do that at all?"

"In my world obviously," Sterling grumps.

"Out of my way, you gorilla." Greyson shoves Sterling forward and pushes past him.

"Not too bright, but still pretty to look at." Ash tilts her head like she's considering Sterling.

"You're not wrong," I agree. Sterling plops on the bed beside me and throws an arm over my shoulder.

"What are you doing?" I try shrugging off his arm, but he adjusts it to stay put.

"You said you thought I was hot. I'm simply making your unspoken dream come true." He bounces his brow up and down.

I blink at him and cock my head, not even sure how to address that. He's a real piece of work.

"I see I've left you speechless." Sterling snuggles closer.

Pulling his arm off my shoulders, I return it to his lap and give it a pat. "You keep telling yourself that."

"Oh, I will."

I'm not used to this level of harmless flirting, but there is something decidedly humorous about it.

"Okay, time to leave the pretty girl alone, Sterling."

Sterling frowns at his brother's chastisement, but rolls off the bed and onto his feet.

"You're right." At least he rebounds quickly. "Too much attention will go to her head."

"All right, enough of that. You're going to make me sick," Ash says.

"Am I not lavishing you with enough attention, babe?"

Sterling sidles up to Ash, who just shoves him away with a snort.

"Moving on, I need your help. Emberly is refusing to come to dinner because of what happened during training today. She's embarrassed."

"Ash! Seriously?" These halflings need to learn how to filter themselves. It's like an epidemic. She lifts her hands, palms up, as if to say, *What? It's true.*

I glance over at the guys. They have their hands cupped in front of themselves. "Are you kidding me right now? See," I point at them, "that's exactly why I'm not going."

Greyson recovers first. "Actually, it was rather epic. I think you may end up earning legendary status around here. You should enjoy your fifteen minutes of fame. Not very many people can get the best of our brother."

I shake my head.

No way, no how am I facing the general angel-born populace.

"Emberly, I have a very serious question for you," Sterling starts.

"Somehow I doubt that."

He goes on as if I haven't spoken. "Are you ever planning to, or will you ever, knee me in the junk?"

"No, of course not!"

"That's all I needed to hear."

The next moment I'm tossed over Sterling's shoulder like a sack of potatoes and carried down the hall.

"Sterling!" I screech, "Put me down right now!"

"No can do. You need to keep up your strength. Can't go skipping any meals. You'll waste away to nothing."

I beat on Sterling's back to no avail. Before I know it, we're in the elevator, headed down to the cafeteria. Ash and Greyson are up against the far wall, trying to avoid my flailing limbs.

"You're all dead!"

The elevator dings and the doors open. I stop struggling when, under Sterling's arm, I see the dining hall filled with people staring at us.

This day just keeps getting worse.

"If I let you down, will you agree to have dinner with us? And not retaliate against me?"

I don't want to agree to either of those things. But I also don't want to be carried into the cafeteria with my butt in the air.

"Fine," I grit out.

Sterling slowly lowers me to the floor. Regardless of any promise, I slug him in the shoulder before walking through the crowd.

He deserved it.

People part for me like the waters of the Red Sea.

"Ouch," I hear Sterling complain behind me, "you have an arm, girl."

I shake my head and keep walking, doing my best to ignore the eyes that follow me. Ash catches up with me at the buffet line and offers a weak, apologetic smile. "Don't hate me?"

Who am I kidding, I can't stay mad at her. She's my first true friend. For that I will always be grateful. The girl can get away with murder now because I'll be there to help her hide the body.

"I don't," I confess. "I'm just really uncomfortable with all this attention."

I let my eyes stray to the round tables peppered throughout the room and I know it's not my imagination. Students scattered throughout the space are stealing glances at me while talking to their friends. I can't hear them, but I can imagine what they're saying. It's what people always say about me.

Look at her. Isn't she a freak?

Why doesn't she look like us?

Did you see what she did today?

A spot between my shoulder blades tingles and burns. I curl my shoulders forward to alleviate the pain.

I grab a plate and pile food on it, hardly paying attention to what I'm grabbing. My gaze stays glued to Ash's feet as she picks a table. It's not long before a few people slide into seats next to and across from me. Assuming it's Greyson and Sterling, I don't bother lifting my head. Instead I concentrate on slicing a thick steak into small pieces.

It's several minutes before I realize an unnatural quiet has bubbled over our table. Lifting my gaze, I check on the issue. Greyson and Sterling sit across from me with matching looks of confusion, brows pinched and mouths twisted to the side.

"Have you two never seen a beautiful girl or something? Gawk much?"

I yelp at the voice next to me.

Sitting to my right with her arms and legs crossed, staring bullets at the gaping brothers, is Nova. A quick glance at Ash reveals she's observing Nova with narrowed eyes of distrust.

"Nova, what . . . ah . . . are your friends not here yet?" I don't know what else to say. It's weird she's sitting with us, and from the twins' and Ash's reactions, I know I'm not the only one who thinks so.

Nova turns to me with a perfectly plucked eyebrow raised in a graceful arc. "I saw your little show in the gym this afternoon."

Oh great, she's here to rip into me for kneeing Steel. Maybe she's worried the trauma to his baby-making organs is going to screw up her plans for their perfect two-point-five kids.

"Oh, um . . ." Is she expecting me to respond to that?

She lifts the corner of her mouth and turns to the food in front of her.

"Oh good, Tweedle-Dee and Tweedle-Dum have finally figured out how to eat."

"Super original," Sterling says around a mouthful of food.

"I thought so," she replies.

What is happening here?

"Are you not mad about today?" I want to suck the words in the moment they emerge. Why can't I just keep my mouth shut?

She laughs. And not just a polite giggle, but a full-body laugh. After slapping the table a couple of times, she pulls herself together.

"Are you kidding? Now I know you weren't lying to me earlier. If you had any interest in Steel, there's no way you'd have put him down like that. And if you were looking for a way to ostracize yourself from him, well . . . congratulations. I doubt he's ever going to come within ten feet of you again."

I blink at her, sure my mouth is hanging open.

She chuckles again and spears a green bean with her fork.

"No, we're cool," she says before putting the vegetable in her mouth and chewing.

Well, then.

I look to Ash. When she meets my gaze, she shrugs. I return the gesture and finally start eating.

I guess this means I've made another friend . . . and that I'm right. This place really is weird.

15

The next several weeks fly by. Long days of classes and training are broken up by sleeping, eating, and spending time with my new friends. I still struggle to wrap my brain around that concept—having friends—but I find having people to hang out with is . . . nice. Even Nova joins us for meals from time to time, and although it freaks me out a bit, I'm warming to her snarky sense of humor.

Nova was right about Steel: he gives me a wide berth and acts like I don't exist. His attitude might offend me if I wasn't already used to that kind of treatment. I've had years of experience being ignored and bullied. If I have to choose between the two, I'll take the former over the latter any day of the week.

But even so, if I'm honest with myself, Steel's indifference does nag at a hidden part of myself. Like an annoying splinter I can't dislodge. It's irritating and starting to fester.

It doesn't help that we run into each other all the time. We have several of the same classes, I'm friends with his brothers, and then there are the random encounters—the times I round a corner to find him on the other side, or when I slip outside to walk the grounds alone and he has the same idea. Sometimes we've even asked to be excused from different classes at the same time and accidentally meet in the hallway.

And with each chance encounter, Steel reacts to me the same way—with cool indifference.

But that's good . . . isn't it?

A heavy weight drops on my shoulders and shakes me from my thoughts.

"You ready for an exciting trip into town?" Sterling uses an arm slung around my shoulders to steer us toward the oversized van parked in front of the academy.

Twice a month the school arranges for interested students to visit Glenwood Springs. The small mountain town boasts three restaurants, one ice cream store, and a smattering of quirky shops geared toward the tourists who visit the town for its thermal spas.

It's not exactly a bustling metropolis, but when you've been cooped up on the same few acres of land for long enough, a trip anywhere is a welcome break.

"I'm ready for a little fresh air."

"We live in the mountains. All we have up here is fresh air."

Good point.

I open my mouth to answer when the roar of a revving engine cuts me off. I jerk my head toward the noise. Greyson strolls toward us as Steel peals past the front gates on his chrome motorcycle.

Only twelfth-year students are allowed to have their own transportation on campus. Steel's ride is by far the flashiest vehicle here.

"Oh, now I see what you mean."

"Huh?"

There's a familiar twinkle in his eye when I shoot him a perplexed stare. I'm instantly leery. "You need a little break from a certain someone you're doing your best not to notice."

"What in the world are you talking about?"

Sterling's smile ramps up.

"You don't need to play coy with me. Lesser females have fallen captive to his charms. Our family genes are quite irresistible." He punctuates his comment with his signature brow wiggle.

He really is a flirt.

"I don't disagree," Greyson adds, joining us at the side of the van. "Our family members are known to have a certain dark allure, but what is my brother trying to convince you of this time?"

"Nothing. Absolutely nothing." I climb in the vehicle to the sound of Sterling's laughter and sit down in a vacant seat next to Ash.

"You keep telling yourself that, Em. But for what it's worth, I think he's working just as hard for it to be 'nothing' too."

Ash arches a questioning eyebrow. I shake my head once. Sterling loves to stir up trouble, something Ash is so accustomed to that she doesn't press me for more information. Leaning against the headrest, I wait for the rest of the students to settle. Hopefully by the time we arrive downtown, Sterling will have moved on.

"So you're saying Sable still doesn't know which sphere you're descended from?"

"Right," I answer, before taking a sip of my creamy hot chocolate.

Yum. Just the right balance of whipped cream and chocolate.

The sweet liquid slides down my throat, heating my insides. I haven't tasted the decadent drink in ages. We're crammed into a little café with worn blonde hardwood floors, exposed brick, and white-washed walls. The décor is a smidge heavy on hipster vibes, but they know how to make a heavenly cup of cocoa.

Indulging in small luxuries such as this helps me feel human again after my six-month stint of homelessness—or at least, half-human.

"She must have an idea." Greyson rolls his empty coffee cup between his hands absentmindedly.

"Sable's best guess is that I'm an angel descendent since I keep getting stuck in a half-phase. Since we don't know who my parents are, one theory is that they were part of an unaccounted for angel line."

"Oh man, that blows."

Ash punches Sterling in the gut . . . hard. An "oof" leaves his mouth along with a spray of caramel macchiato.

"Don't listen to Sterling. He's an idiot."

"Hey!"

Ash silences him with a look.

I wave them off. "It doesn't really matter."

"Are you kidding?" Sterling starts, but after a side glance at Ash, he waits to continue until he moves his seat out of striking distance. "You may not be able to do anything cool."

"Oh right, like I'm going to cry over not being able to turn into a cow."

"I do not turn into a cow!"

I cover my smile by taking another sip of chocolatey heaven. Sterling is a cherub, like his brother, but doesn't know which, if any, shifting abilities he's inherited yet. I'm crossing my fingers that he only turns into a bull.

Truthfully, learning I'm most likely descended from an angel line—the weakest of all the celestial beings—is a disappointment. Not because I'm embarrassed about not having an awesome power, but because I most likely won't be able to defend myself as well as the other Nephilim. Apparently, the angel line was annihilated over a thousand years ago because they weren't able to defend themselves against the Fallen or Forsaken as well as the other angel-borns. If my parents were angel Nephilim, that means the line isn't extinct—which according to Sable is not only exciting but a huge discovery for our race. But that also means I'm from a line they know the least about and there-fore, they don't know how to teach me about my skills. Learning as much as I can about how to stay alive is para-mount if I'm going to leave the academy when I turn eighteen.

A buried part of me also mourns yet another dead-end where my family history is concerned. Sable has spent the last few weeks looking into every Nephilim disappearance, contacting other academies across the globe, and even going so far as to meet with the Council of Elders—a group of super-duper-old Neph that everyone defers to for disputes, or when the world is on the brink of destruction. But even they don't know who my parents were.

A feeling of emptiness sits heavy on my soul from the lack of answers.

I just want to know where I belong.

"Since everyone thinks all the Nephilim descended from plain ol' angels were wiped out ages ago," I continue, "one theory is that a few survived in hiding. That's the best guess at the moment. Might be the cause of my ah . . . unique hair color. Watered down genes."

Greyson observes me thoughtfully. "Watered down genes? But Nephilim can only reproduce with other Nephilim. They actually think your parents were human?"

I lift my hands. Given what I now know about Nephilim, it seems unlikely to me as well.

"It's as good a guess as any," Ash chimes in. "Maybe Emberly's line of Nephilim could always make magic Neph babies with humans and the Council never knew? Maybe that's how they blended in and survived? The truth is, no one really knows right now."

"Magic Neph babies?" Greyson shoots Ash an amused look.

"Hey, Emberly here is definitely magical. You've all seen her train by now."

Greyson and Sterling both wince, no doubt remembering the damage I inflicted on their brother. I'm pretty sure Steel was walking funny for a full week after our fight. I look back on that week with fondness. But Ash has a point: That initial sparring nightmare aside, I've been killing this combat stuff.

It's almost as if this training was hand-tailored just for me. I pick up defensive and offensive strikes after the first try and my form is always flawless. Even weapons training is coming along well. No doubt it has something to do with the celestial blood running through my veins, but I'm not complaining. I'll take the extra leg-up in any area I can. Especially considering my phasing is still sporadic and no special abilities appear when I do make it to the spectrum world.

I'm playing a serious game of catch-up and am thankful for any advantage I can get.

"How are your sessions with Sable going?" Greyson asks.

Oy, that's another sore spot. Sable has started teaching me to read angelic symbols. I usually leave her office with a headache from all the over-thinking.

"It's a lot of information to take in."

"Yeah, I'll bet."

"Angelic language is hard." I press my fingers to my temples and groan.

Sterling jumps out of his seat, surprising us all. His eyes are glued to the smart phone in his hand. "Doc Holliday's Saloon for dinner. Let's roll."

He makes a beeline for the exit without waiting to make sure we follow—but that's Sterling, always searching for the next party.

"Hey, wait a minute. You guys said you'd go to Luna's with me after we stopped for coffee. I wanna find a new pair of jeans and look at the dresses." Ash whines as we dump our trash and leave the café.

Sterling's already halfway down the block when Greyson turns to Ash with a grimace.

"It's okay, Grey. I'll hang with Ash. We'll catch up with you guys in a bit."

A thankful smile breaks out across his face. "Thanks, Em."

"Hey, don't look so relieved!"

Lifting his hands in front of him, Greyson walks backward

in the direction his brother took. "I don't know what you mean," he yells from several store fronts away, before spinning and jogging to catch up with Sterling.

Lacing my arm through Ash's, I tug her in the opposite direction. "Come on, let's go before it closes."

The evenings come all too quickly in the mountains. The sky is currently streaked with oranges and pinks that are quickly fading into purple. It'll be fully dark in no time.

Entering the boutique clothing store several blocks off the main drag, Ash makes a beeline to the dress section. She's a serious shopper. Never having had more than the essentials, I don't understand her need for so many different outfits. I realize a girlie part of me is probably underdeveloped, but I don't care.

"Oh, Emberly, look at this dress!" Ash shouts from the other side of the store, gaining the attention of the shopkeeper as well as a few of the other patrons. "You would look fab in this!"

I rush to her side for no other reason than to shut her up. The attention makes me itch.

Ash holds out a small, dark blue piece of fabric.

"That's a top."

"No, it's a dress."

I tilt my head to the side. "No way does that cover all the important bits."

"It stretches. Look!" She pulls the fabric and to her credit, it lengthens. I'm still not convinced. "I promise. Here." She shoves the dress in my face, forcing me to grab the hanger. "Try it on. It's going to look amazing with your hair."

I shoot her a droll look. "I'm going to look like an American flag."

"Will not. Try it on!" She claps her hands excitedly.

I hang the minuscule dress back on the rack. "No thanks."

"Please?"

"I would never wear something like this."

"Who cares? Come on, if for no other reason than to prove me wrong."

I'm about to refuse again, but Ash starts to jump up and down, chanting "Try it" over and over again. I duck into a dressing room to get away from her.

Pushy friend. But friend, nonetheless.

Five minutes later, I turn to the mirror. Technically Ash is right—this is in fact a dress, but there is no way I'll ever wear it in public.

The blue stretchy fabric clings to me from bust to mid-thigh. Two bands of fabric wrap around my upper arms right below my shoulders. I look like I'm ready to go clubbing.

"Ash," I call. "This dress is ridiculous."

It's quiet on the other side of the door.

"Ash?"

I stick my head out of the fitting room, not seeing her anywhere. Hunching my shoulders, I tiptoe out of the room and hear her talking to someone on the other side of the wall.

Ah, she must be asking the salesperson for something.

"I can't believe you talked me into—" The words freeze on my tongue the moment I round the corner to find Ash standing with Nova and Steel. Three sets of eyes swing in my direction.

Shoot.

Steel's gaze sweeps me from head to toe and back again.

I should be running to the changing room. Why am I not doing that?

Steel's eyes harden when they connect with mine, but not quickly enough for me to miss the frisson of heat they contain.

I cross my arms over my chest to hide myself and backpedal.

"Dang, girl!" Ash gushes before I can escape. "I was right. You know how to wear that!" She appraises me with a smug look.

Nova's gaze bounces between me and Steel, a small frown marring her perfect face.

"I'm out of here. See you at Doc's, Nova."

Turning on a heel, Steel stomps out of the store. Nova watches his retreating form with a furrowed brow. Sparing us a distracted wave, she follows in his wake.

"You have to get that."

My attention snaps to Ash. "Are you crazy? Why would I?"

She's obviously affronted. "Are you kidding? If I looked that amazing in anything I'd be wearing it twenty-four-seven." Ash strikes a pose. "Oh, *this* old thing? I just threw it on to be comfortable."

Laughing at her antics will only encourage her, so I wrestle my face into an approximation of grim fortitude.

"Never gonna happen," I call as I retreat to the safety of the changing room.

Ash knocks on the door right as I struggle out of the material. It doesn't seem to want to let me go. "Hey, wanna hand me that dress? I'll hang it back up."

When I'm finally free, I toss it over the door to her. Good riddance.

"Hey, my drink just hit me. You know how fast tea works

STEALING EMBERS | 151

its way through my system. I don't think I can hold it for long."

TMI, Ash.

"Mind if I head to Doc's ahead of you? I'll save you a seat."

"Um."

"Thanks. You're the best."

I hear the pitter-patter of Ash's feet scurrying away before I can fully answer.

Did she seriously just leave me here? The only reason I came to this store was for her, and she didn't even try anything on herself.

I dress quickly, but by the time I leave the dressing room Ash has disappeared.

"You have got to be kidding me."

"Hey, your friend forgot her receipt." A middle-aged woman waves a white slip of paper at me from behind the front counter. Taking the receipt from her with a half-smile, I look it over as I push through the front doors. There is a single purchase listed for a blue dress.

"Ash," I groan and fold the paper, shoving it and my hands in my pockets. That explains why she was in such a rush. I never would have let her buy that dress and she knew it.

Hunching my shoulders, I start down the street. The crisp air nips at my cheeks and coats my throat with each inhale. The angel-blood running through my veins keeps the harsh sting of the chilled temperatures at bay.

The sun has set and streetlights are few and far between in this part of town. Shadows have always been my friend, so I don't mind.

My feet crunch over the icy snow still lingering on the sidewalk. Each step echoes in the deserted street. The deadened night is so soothing to me that I don't notice when the first few streetlights flicker.

I don't notice when the nocturnal sounds of the mountains go silent.

I don't notice that I'm the only person walking down the sidewalk in either direction—and I don't notice the form hiding in the darkness, tracking my movements as I pass.

I don't notice anything I should, and by the time I do, it's too late.

16

a chill skates up my spine a split second before the figure steps out of the darkness. Roughly ten feet away, he isn't exactly in my space, but the way he stands—unmoving in the middle of the sidewalk—brings me up short.

Shrouded in shadows, his downward-tilted head of inky hair and tall stature are the first things I notice. I can see better than any human at night, but it's as if darkness clings to the stranger, undulating like a pulsating wave of mist around him.

This isn't natural.

"Ember-ly," a female voice sings.

I whip around to find a woman on the sidewalk behind me. She's beautiful, with midnight hair hanging loose around her shoulders. Her arms are crossed in front of her and a trail of mist slithers in, out, around and up her legs.

My internal alarm was tripped the second the man stepped onto the sidewalk in front of me, but now it's blaring.

I don't know who these people are, but I know I need to get out of here.

"You're a hard one to catch alone," she purrs.

I sink into a defensive position, angling my body to keep both threats in sight. The man takes a step closer. A sliver of moonlight lights the contours of his face, revealing an Adonis with midnight eyes.

"How adorable. They taught her some of their moves." The woman speaks over my head to the man. His lips turn up in a smile. Despite his beauty, it makes me think of the Joker from Batman—maniacal and more than slightly unhinged.

"What do you want?" I spit at the pair, my eyes volleying between the two as they continue to take measured steps forward, closing the space between us.

My fight-or-flight instinct has kicked into high gear and I'm already planning my escape.

There's an alley down the street that will take me to the main road. I just have to make it across the street and down a few houses. This isn't a bustling metropolis, but a screaming girl running down the road will still make a scene.

"What do we want, brother?"

"How about we leave that a mystery for now?" he replies.

I'm only half-listening. They're close enough that some of the mist circling them disengages and reaches for me.

Nope, not letting that stuff touch me.

I take off for the opening between the buildings. Starbursts of color pop in my vision as I run. My heart sinks. If I phase, I'll be vulnerable in the real world as well as the spectrum world.

I will myself not to phase, and for a moment it works. The lights dancing at the corners of my sight disappear.

Without checking behind me, I reach the alley and change my trajectory. Skidding around the corner, my boots scrabble for traction on a patch of black ice. Regaining my footing, I cast a glance behind me. There's no sign of the dark-haired stalkers and Main Street is only a block away.

I'm going to make it.

I'm slammed up against a wall before I have time to experience a rush of relief. The back of my head strikes the brick with a sickening thud.

My vision blurs before clearing. When it does, a third stranger is revealed. His face is only inches from mine.

Why can't I breathe?

I raise my fingers to my neck to find a hand circling my windpipe.

I claw at his grip as the stranger tilts his head and regards me with narrowed black eyes.

The bursts of colors that indicate I'm about to half-phase are back, exploding not only on the periphery, but throughout my vision.

The panic can't be held back this time. It blows over me like a torrent of wind, erasing my captor from view even as I remain pinned to the wall.

From one blink to the next, I go from a darkened alley to a world flooded in a dark rainbow of purples and blues.

Beautiful yet deadly.

Sucking in a half-breath, I continue to struggle against the now-phantom hold on my throat. Desperately, I kick out with my legs as the pressure increases, but my wild strikes find no purchase.

My sight begins to fade. Lack of oxygen is going to force me to pass out.

"Playing with your prey again, Ronove?" The raven-haired female's voice echoes in the alley. The spectrum world reacts violently to the melodious sounds, like a stone thrown in the water; angry ripples in the air zig-zag and spread before dissipating.

The pressure at my neck blocking my airflow lessens as a figure materializes in front of me.

I hack and gasp as the creature holding me captive—a monster with the likeness of a man—glares at me.

"I find this task tedious." The creature hisses the words between elongated fangs.

"Even so, we're not supposed to damage the merchandise . . . much."

The unnamed female appears over the shoulder of my Forsaken captor, Ronove. Her long hair drapes across her shoulders in matted dreads. Her skin is bleached of color. Her eyes are not only dark, but the area that should be white is blackened as well. It's like looking into someone's eye sockets.

Clothes dangle off her emaciated frame as she lays a hand on the back of the ugly beast in front of me.

How is this possible?

I just saw these people in the real world. They weren't Forsaken—they were beautiful. But the stench wafting from them, as well as the physical characteristics of a corpse, prove they're Forsaken and not human. They smell like they're rotting from the inside out.

"How?" The creature in front of me chuckles. I must have spoken part of that out loud. "Oh my pet, you have much to learn."

Gross.

"I am not your pet." My voice is scratchy.

A half-smile lifts his cracked lips. Nasty.

"We shall see."

"Are you sure this is the right one?" The other male appears at the mouth of the alley. Also a Forsaken. "She hasn't even fully phased." He tilts his head as he studies me. "I think she may be defective."

Great, even monsters think I'm substandard.

"Shut it, Aamon," the female barks.

Aamon leans against the wall, watching the show.

It's only then I realize these Forsaken aren't quite the wild beasts that attacked the academy last month. Yes, they're scary, fanged, and seriously lacking in personal hygiene, but they possess a measure of intelligence and restraint the other creatures didn't.

If the Forsaken last month were rabid beasts, these three are . . . intelligent beasts? Beasts to be sure, but of a different breed.

The one that holds me captive, Ronove, shoves his free hand—er, claw—into my shoulder. His sharpened nails bite into my flesh, and he squeezes until the skin breaks. A trickle of warm blood leaks down my arm.

He rips the fabric from my shoulder to wrist—coat and sweater both—until the wound is exposed.

My struggle ramps up as he brings his face closer and . . .

Oh gosh, I'm gonna be sick.

. . . licks the blood from my skin.

He leans back and closes his eyes, slurping the excess blood from his pale lips.

A shiver of revulsion wracks my frame.

"It's her. I can taste it on—"

A low growl cuts off his words.

In unison, my three captors' heads snap up and to the right. The synchronized motion reminds me of puppets connected to the same strings. In another situation, I would have found it humorous, but considering the gravity of my predicament, it isn't funny at all.

I twist my neck as far to the right as possible, and relief floods my system.

A massive golden lion with a black-streaked mane paws at the ground. The hair on his back stands on end as another deep growl rips from his throat.

Steel has arrived.

17

*R*onove was frightening before, but Steel's threatening growl releases his inner monster. The Forsaken in front of me transforms into a true creature of darkness. His fangs descend even farther, almost touching the bottom of his chin. His fingers curl around my shoulder, punching sharpened claws into my flesh again, releasing new rivers of blood.

I swallow the pain-filled scream that bubbles in my throat and dig deep for my scrappy skills.

Using my free and uninjured arm, I throat-punch Ronove.

With a piercing howl, the monster uses the claws still embedded in my flesh to toss me away from him—straight into a brick wall.

My back cracks against the hard surface, and I slide into a crumpled heap.

I'm keenly aware of my heart thudding twice before I collect my wits. Scrambling to my hands and knees, Steel's angry roar and the Forsakens' furious shrieks ricochet off the narrow alley walls.

Steel plows into Ronove and they roll in a flurry of paws, claws, and snapping jaws.

Aamon joins the fight, making it two against one.

"That one is strong," yells the female. "Don't kill him. We can use him too."

Wait, what?

As far as I know, the Forsaken only have two uses for the Nephilim: wear them like a skin suit, or eat them.

I'm not letting Steel—or myself—be used for either of those purposes.

Jamming my flight instinct deep down into a sealed box, I push to my feet, ready to even the numbers. I'm about to rush into the middle of the battle when the female Forsaken jumps in front of me.

"Oh no. You won't be going anywhere except with us. Time for a little lights-out for you." Her lips peel back in a grotesque smile that reminds me of a re-animated corpse.

I run at her only to find myself flat on the ground with only a vague idea of how I got there.

"That was rather pathetic. Why don't you just stay down while the grown-ups work things out?"

She examines her curved claws as if she's checking her nails for chipped paint. She doesn't even spare me a glance with her soulless eyes.

Behind her, Steel continues his assault on Ronove and Aamon.

His pelt is splattered with his own red blood as well as the Forsakens' black ichor. With a burst of speed, Ronove climbs on Steel's back and bites his muscled shoulder.

Three-inch incisors sink into Steel's hide just as he's shaking Aamon's body back and forth by the forearm. Raising his giant lion head, he roars; Aamon's body drops, then flops around on the ground like a dying fish.

The female who so easily put me down spares a glance over her shoulder.

She frowns, her twisted features pulling at her gaunt face as she watches Steel swipe a paw at the creature on his back, flinging Ronove against the brick wall. Steel then catches Aamon by the leg as he's crawling away. Yanking him back, his giant paw swings and hits Aamon across the face, shredding the skin and tearing out half his throat.

A gurgled shriek wheezes out of the injured Forsaken before Steel lowers a claw toward his head, separating it from his body with one powerful stroke.

Impressive.

The female screams in outrage. I press my hands over my ears as the piercing sound hammers nails into my eardrums. The shockwaves pound in my head and vibrate the air as both remaining Forsaken dive at Steel.

Sitting stunned on the icy ground, I'm all but forgotten.

The battle in front of me is a jumble of sounds, blurred limbs, and bloody claws. The Forsaken are even more savage than Steel in his animal form. The earsplitting screeches of anger from the unholy creatures mix with Steel's mighty roars, distorting the spectrum world around the group as if they are fighting in a bowl of murky water.

Steel's furious bellows fill the alley before he's suddenly cut off.

When the air clears, Steel—in human form—lies unconscious on the dirt-caked asphalt. A growing puddle of red liquid stains the ground beneath his head.

The Forsaken stand above him, panting, crimson blood dripping from their claws and mouths.

No. Steel has to be faking.

The Forsaken are vicious, but Steel is trained. Steel is unbeatable.

Or at least I thought so.

Lying on the ground with his eyes closed, he looks painfully vulnerable.

"We'll take this one, too." Ronove reaches down and grabs Steel under the arms. "If for no other reason than he pissed me off. Get the girl, Lilith. It's time to go."

Terror churns in my gut, but when Ronove hefts Steel's body over his shoulder, a wave of acute anger washes over me, leaving no room for fear.

Springing to my feet, I rush Ronove, completely ignoring the body blocking my way.

Razor sharp talons claw at my clothes and flesh, but I barely register the pain as I rip from their grasp.

I'm on Ronove in an instant, yanking Steel's limp body away from him.

The unexpectedness of my actions is probably the only reason why I'm able to wrestle the unconscious Neph away from the Forsaken.

With my arms wrapped around his middle, I drag Steel to the mouth of the alley. Dropping him unceremoniously on the ground, I take up position in front of him, making my intentions clear.

"We're not going anywhere."

Ronove's lips peel back in a snarl, giving me a nice good look at his red-stained fangs. Rage cyclones up from my gut and spreads throughout my body.

That's Steel's blood dripping from the monster's mouth—and he is going to pay.

18

*A*s if sharing one mind, the two monsters rush me simultaneously.

I'm ready for them. I've been training for this moment and I'm sure—

Oof.

Nope. I was wrong. So not ready yet.

I'm exactly where I was when I faced off against Lilith the first time: laying on the ground with the wind knocked out of me, staring at the spectrum world's purple night sky.

"What a nuisance. Are you sure we can't kill her?" Clumps of Lilith's stringy hair cover half her chalky face.

Good. That means I only have to see half her ugly.

"You know we can't. Now shut up and get her under control already. I've had enough of this night." Ronove leans down to collect Steel.

"No," I cough, pain stabbing my side. The sharp ache is familiar—must be a few broken or cracked ribs.

Flipping over, I shove to my hands and knees. I know I've already lost, but something deep inside refuses to relent.

"What is she doing?"

I ignore Ronove's disgusted sneer and labor to my feet. Lilith watches me with a tilted head.

"I think she still wants to fight back."

"The challenge is so pathetic, it isn't even amusing anymore."

Ouch.

"Shut . . . your . . . face," I huff out.

These comebacks are as weak as I am.

Ignoring me, Ronove throws Steel over his shoulder, and I snap. Completely shedding my sense of self-preservation, I launch myself at Ronove a second time, clawing to get at Steel even as the Forsaken holds me off with only one arm.

I might as well be a chipmunk going up against a giant for all the damage I'm inflicting—which is to say, none at all.

"Just kill the male," Lilith says from somewhere behind me. "She obviously has an attachment to him and it's just—"

"NO!"

A bubble of heat forms in my chest and detonates, shooting blazing fire throughout my limbs and outward in a blast that hits the Forsaken, propelling them into the air. Their bodies smash against the rough alley wall like a Mack truck, but they recover quickly, each landing in a crouch.

I must have held onto Steel, because his body is sprawled at my feet.

Waves of white light—much brighter than the usual Nephilim glow—pulsate off me.

The Forsaken hiss at me with fingers bent and claws

extended. Hatred drips from their black eyes. They'll come at me any moment now.

The searing heat is still building in my chest and dancing uncomfortably across my skin. It weaves and curls around my torso, skating up and down my arms and legs like a fiery caress.

"What was that?" Ronove casts a glance at his companion.

"She must have a weapon hidden."

Stepping in front of Steel once again, I firm my resolve. He may have a serious attitude problem and he probably hates me for no good reason, but I'm not going to let these two monsters harm a hair on his head.

Heat lashes my skin as a flurry of possessiveness overtakes me. A single word rumbles up from deep in my chest.

"Mine."

Whoa.

No, not mine. I don't want Steel. I simply want to keep him safe at this particular moment in time.

He's definitely not *mine*. Not now. Not ever. I will happily hand him off to Nova or whoever else wants to tolerate the arrogant male.

As if a different being lives inside me, the urge to stomp my foot and disagree with myself rides me hard. Gritting my teeth, I push back against the compulsion and focus on the hideous creatures across from me.

"Take her down. The other might make a nice trophy, but we don't have time for this. We'll dispose of him after she's out. This mission has already been too much trouble."

With a barely perceptible nod, both Forsaken charge.

Lilith slashes with her claws, forcing me to duck and roll out of the way, popping up several feet from Steel's prone form. It's just enough room to allow the beasts to circle me. But I don't mind because it means their attention is on me instead of Steel.

I shuffle a few steps back to put even more distance between them and Steel, but still keep his body in my line of sight.

Ronove dives; I spin to the right, bringing my leg up in a roundhouse kick that's supposed to land across his face.

It would have, if he weren't so stinkin' supernaturally fast.

Failing to connect with my target causes me to lose my balance and stumble a step before regaining it. That's all the distraction the creatures need. They collide with my body and we fall in a tangle of limbs.

Lilith wraps her legs around my torso and her arms around my neck, and squeezes. Ronove delivers a quick jab to my face.

A blast of pain explodes on my right cheekbone—I see stars.

The bands of arms around my neck tightens as Lilith tries to cut off my air supply, hoping I'll blackout. If I let that happen, it's over. I won't be able to defend myself, let alone Steel.

The heat that has wrapped itself around me like a boa constrictor whirls across my skin in a frenzy, mimicking my frantic thoughts. The glow emanating from my body throbs. A low beat resonates in my head, shaking my eardrums as the pace and volume increase.

Lilith curses.

Ronove's next punch lands in my gut and leaves me gasping.

I buck, trying to loosen the Forsaken's hold on me, but my strength wanes along with my air supply.

My struggles turn sloppy and weak.

"I've got her," Lilith snarls. "She'll be out any moment. Dispose of the boy."

I looked to the left.

Blackness threatens the edges of my vision, but I spot Steel flip onto his stomach and struggle to his hands and knees. He shakes his head, completely unaware of Ronove's intentions.

I try to yell out a warning, but it comes out as a pathetic wheeze.

Ronove stalks Steel like the practiced predator he is. His nails are elongated daggers waiting to bite into Steel's flesh.

No! Mine!

My back bows with a renewed effort to escape.

As Ronove lifts his hand to deal Steel a killing blow, the heat surging through my body races to my chest and surges, as if a million volts of electricity have been forced into my heart.

My scream drowns out the noise around me as my body arches.

My muscles contract painfully. My body lifts into the air, hair blowing around my head in a tornado of movement.

I'm on fire.

At least, that's what it feels like.

My skin melts beneath an unstoppable inferno.

The agony spreads from my chest to my arms and legs, then up my neck and onto my face before wrapping around my body to consume it whole.

Golden light engulfs my vision.

Something sharp punches out my back, forcing muscle, tendons, and tissue to rip and reform.

I gasp in a dry breath of boiling air as the new part of me arches.

A phantom limb that's been contorted and concealed for too long straightens in a pleasure- and pain-filled stretch.

My feet touch the ground and the golden light dims, allowing me to see the alleyway once more.

The world around me is bathed in the light shooting off me. The two Forsaken are cowering against the brick wall across from me. And one very confused Nephilim stands to their left.

Steel takes a determined step toward me. His hair is ruffled, his clothes covered in dirt and wet from the ice and snow, his hands balled into fists. Even without a weapon, he's a fierce sight to behold. With golden light kissing his features, he reminds me of a modern-day Adonis, dressed in a Henley and dark washed jeans.

"It's you." His whispered words are filled with awe and float to me on a rippling band of light.

I begin to ask what he means, but I catch a sliver of move-ment to my left and turn my head in time to see both Forsaken disappear around the bend of the building.

Instinct says to follow them, but when I take a step in their direction it's thwarted by the body of a six-foot-five, raven-haired angel-born.

"They're going to—" My words die a quick death on my tongue when Steel's hand brushes a tangle of hair away from my cheek. The small contact causes a tremor to work its way through his body.

He closes his eyes and steps into me.

I retreat a step.

"Finally," he breathes, dipping his head to gently rub the tip of his nose up the column of my neck before his lips just barely brush my earlobe.

It's my turn to shiver.

What is he doing? my mind screams. *And do I care?* it whispers as an afterthought.

Shaking my head out of a confused fog, I take another shaky step back.

Yes, I do care. The boy must have hit his head harder than I thought.

"Listen, Steel, we don't have time for this. You're not yourself right now."

I bring my hands up to push him back. He's invading my space—big time.

When I reach forward to give him a shove, he grabs hold of my wrists and uses my momentum to bring me closer.

The guy has moves, that's for sure.

One look in his eyes and I can tell he's not all there. His lids are lowered to half-mast and his gaze sweeps lazily over my features.

Steel takes another step forward, forcing my capitulation until he's maneuvered me against the rough bricks. A foreign sensation zips along my spine, as if something heavy is fused to each vertebrae, weighing me down. I don't have a chance to investigate because Steel's head is dipping again and I have nowhere to move within the cage of his body.

I freeze, wholly unprepared for the situation. That gives Steel the perfect opportunity to dive in and take what he wants.

A shudder racks my frame the moment Steel's lips connect with mine.

He's . . . kissing me?

The soft press of his mouth to my tightly sealed lips, and the way he's coaxing them to soften with a languorous, persistent pressure seems to suggest that yes, he is indeed kissing me. But I just stand there with my arms hanging lamely at my sides, eyes wide open.

I'm not kissing him back.

I've never been kissed before. When would I have had the opportunity, considering that up until moving to the academy, everyone I met either gave me a wide berth or tried to make my life a living hell?

I have no idea what to do. I'm not prepared for a moment like this at all.

Jerking back, I bonk my head against the brick wall. The movement severs the connection with Steel.

If he was surprised, he doesn't let on. A ghost of a smile curls the corner of his mouth, and he cups my face with his rough hand.

Calluses aren't supposed to feel good, are they?

I resist the urge to rub my cheek against him. What is he doing to me?

"Listen, I don't think—"

"Good, don't think," he cuts in before his head descends again.

He swallows my gasp of surprise and increases the pressure on my lips.

This time my eyes slide close without permission and my hands find their way to his chest.

And suddenly, I'm kissing him back.

19

I'm easily lost in a barrage of sensations. My lips brush against his to the beat of my frantic heartbeat.

Steel makes a noise deep in his chest. Twining his other arm around my waist, he pulls me more fully to him. In that moment I lose my grip on any sort of reality that doesn't include him and the way he's holding me, the way he tastes on my tongue, the way I melt under his touch.

The part of myself that laid claim to his defenseless form rushes to the surface and rejoices.

"Mine."

The word whispers from my lips on an airy breath, but it's enough to break whatever spell he's under. Steel's body tenses beneath my hands. His grip on my waist dissolves and his hand slides off my face.

My eyes blink open slowly—resentful of whatever caused the disruption—and catch the panicked expression on Steel's face. His eyes are stretched so wide I see the white around his irises. His brow and nose scrunch as if he smells something off-putting.

Ripping himself away from me, he stumbles back several steps—his usual gracefulness nowhere to be found.

His head swivels to take in our surroundings. It's almost as if he's just now realizing where he is.

"Wh-what were we doing?"

A rush of heat darkens my cheeks. Isn't it obvious what we were doing? No way I'm going to walk him through it.

Steel shoves a hand in his hair, agitation rolling off him in waves.

"What happened?"

He can't be serious. A sickly knot of unease churns in my gut, like a snake coiling in on itself.

"The . . . Forsaken?" I offer as a question rather than an explanation.

Scrubbing a hand down his face, he turns his confused eyes on me.

"Wasn't a dream," he mutters. The agony on his face is punctuated by the hand he fists in his hair. "I thought . . ."

What does he think?

My brain is still muddled from that mega kiss and the craziness of the Forsaken attack.

One of those events is definitively more important than the other, yet my mind keeps snagging on the former when it tries to focus on the latter.

Steel and I stand on opposite sides of the alley, staring at each other.

I watch as he lifts a hand and wipes his mouth—and with that simple action, my heart cracks.

I didn't think Steel had the power to hurt me, but I was wrong.

Tucking the broken pieces of myself away, I square my shoulders, intent on getting back to the real world.

"I don't need this. Especially not from you."

Head held high in mock indifference, I march away from him. At least that was the plan, but I only make it half a step before my body pitches backward.

I twist and catch myself against the wall. Craning my neck to the left, I finally take note of the foreign weight anchored to each side of my spine. A flash of gold catches my eye.

"What the—?"

Blinking, I take in the full expanse of the gleaming wings attached to my back. Made up of rows of shiny gold feathers, they drape behind me like a cape, the tips brushing the ground. The span of the wings must be at least six feet in each direction.

Taking a deep breath and relying on instinct, I stretch the new appendages, experimenting with their mobility. The wings flare to my left and right—they obey my mental commands to expand and fold like any other part of my body. Like any underused limb, they protest. The burn of the movement eventually gives way to a satisfying release.

Curving them around my body, I inspect the feathers with a sense of wonder. The whole plume is colored a shimmering golden hue, but the last couple inches of it—the part that comes to a point—looks like it may actually be made of gold.

I certainly don't dismiss the thought. They're heavy enough to be part metal. I can feel them anchored along my spine. It's a mystery how I didn't notice the weight before now.

"I sprouted wings?"

"That doesn't seem to be all."

Steel's voice hits me like a slap. I'd momentarily forgotten his presence. The sting of his rejection rises up on the heels of his words. I cast a glare in his direction before taking stock of myself. The wounds the Forsaken inflicted have completely healed. And also . . .

So. Much. Gold.

My body is drenched in it. Instead of a sweater and coat, I'm fastened into a golden breastplate. It wraps around my torso and cinches in the back like a corset. I give it a knock and it clangs like a metal sheath.

Circling my left wrist is a gold bangle. When I fist my hand, spikes protrude from the bracelet. A cuff, also gold, hugs my right bicep. Four gilded bolts are stuck to it, tips facing down.

My legs are encased in some golden leather-like pants. They are pliable, lightweight, and buttery soft.

Fastened around each thigh is another scrolling cuff. A small crossbow is attached to my left leg, and a twelve-inch dagger to my right.

I'm armed and ready for battle—that is, if I'm planning to fight in a LARPing war.

"Why in the world am I dressed like a medieval superhero?"

His brow furrows and he shakes his head, most likely clearing his mind. He winces with the movement, touching his fingers to his head. They come away red. Wiping the blood on his jeans, he refocuses on me once again.

"If I had to guess, I'd say you finally fully phased, and jumped right to the metamorphous stage of your development. I've never seen a Nephilim turn into . . . whatever it is you are now. It's just more evidence that you're most likely descended from an angel line. Perhaps all your ancestors phased like this?"

Ha! Perhaps my ancestors weren't so wimpy after all.

Steel presses a hand to the cut again and squeezes his eyes shut. The injury is on the right side of his head, underneath his hairline. Since I can't see it, I'm not sure how bad it is. It must have been some hit though, since it knocked him out.

Opening his eyes, his stare is part-glazed, part-pained. Tendrils of concern dig their way into my hardened heart.

"We need to get out of here and get back to the academy. Find Sable or another instructor and let them know what happened."

"Let's phase back and find the other students."

"I still don't know how to phase on command." It's physically painful to admit.

Steel's lips press together in a hard line. He'd forgotten about that. He looks to the sky, studying the waves of deep blues and purples before coming to some conclusion with a jerky nod.

"All right, I'll shift into an eagle and fly us back. The academy's sensors will be tripped when we arrive." Steel rolls his shoulders, preparing for his transformation.

"Wait!" I hold a hand up and rush to his side. The bulk at my back makes the quick movements awkward and the extra weight makes stopping short a problem. I almost barrel into him. He catches me and wraps his fingers around my upper arms, keeping them there while I wobble.

How embarrassing.

I tug out of his grasp the moment I stop teetering.

Looking anywhere but his eyes, I provide an explanation for my sudden action. "You were just knocked unconscious and it looks like you may fall over again at any moment. You can't shift, let alone fly us up a mountain."

Several uncomfortably silent moments pass before I allow myself to look directly at Steel. He regards me with a slight tilt of the head. His eyes skip over my face, taking in everything at once.

I don't like that look. It's as if he sees something I don't. It gives me an itchy feeling that makes me want to shake out of my skin.

Clearing my throat, I back away from him. The wings pull on my back, giving me an idea.

Giving them a few test pumps, a smile spreads on my face.

"I have an idea."

"No way." Steel's clipped words do nothing to dampen my mood.

"You know what they say. One set of wings is as good as the next."

"Nobody says that."

"Well they should. I just need to figure out how exactly to work these things." Using more force and quicker motions, I'm able to catch enough air to pull myself off the ground about a foot.

"Not gonna happen. You have no idea how to fly with those."

I'm only half paying attention to him while I focus on trying to keep myself aloft. This is hard work. Beads of sweat form along my brow, my energy resources are almost completely tapped, but I'm determined.

"Just give me a few minutes. I'll figure it out."

Crossing his arms over his chest, he shoots me a droll look. "Let's say you do figure out how to get yourself more than a foot off the ground. How do you think you're going to get us both up to the academy?"

I stop flapping and let myself float down to the pavement. "Um, I could hold you?"

Maybe I haven't thought this through.

"Oh yeah?" Steel marches forward and plants himself directly in front of me. I try not to breathe in his spicy scent, but it's impossible.

"Go ahead. Pick me up then," he challenges and lifts his arms.

Fine. He has a point.

Even if I could fly us both, I don't want to have to be pressed up against him the whole flight.

Steel drops his arms and pins me with a look. "We're sitting ducks in this alley—pun intended."

"I do not look like a duck."

He cocks one of his eyebrows. "If the feathers fit."

Jerk.

"Oh, whatever. You're just trying to be smart."

"That's not something I have to try at, sweetheart, I just am."

Eye roll. Could he be more arrogant?

"Listen—"

A drumbeat of pounding footsteps brings me up short. Steel's head jerks to the left, his gaze glues to the alley's entrance.

I grab the dagger at my leg. The weapon easily peels off the metal cuff when my fingers wrap around the smooth leather hilt.

Steel shifts so his body is blocking mine.

"I've got this. Stay back," he commands.

I snort.

Bending my knees, I jump and give my wings a mighty flap. Launching myself over Steel, I land several feet in front of him with an ease that I can't begin to explain—but I'm not complaining.

"No. *I've* got this."

Slipping into a defensive position, my blood buzzes with an influx of adrenaline.

"Round two," I whisper.

20

"*C*heck the alleys, guys!"

Wait. I know that voice.

A half-second later Sterling careens around the corner. Catching sight of me, he skids to a halt.

"Whoa, Emberly!" His eyes skate up and down my body. "That's a good look."

"Um, thanks?"

Steel moves from behind me. "Hey, I'm here too, in case you care."

"Nope. No one really cares, bro," Sterling responds, never taking his eyes off me.

"Any sign of them?" Greyson calls from somewhere out of sight.

"Over here," Sterling bellows, still gawking.

I cross my arms over my chest and shake out my new appendages.

"Are those real?" Sterling's eyes go perfectly round. "Wicked cool."

Another person clears the opening of the alleyway and slams on the breaks.

"Emberly?" Greyson gapes at me.

My gosh, has no one ever seen a Nephilim dressed completely in gold armor with metal-tipped wings before?

"Yep, it's me. I have wings. Look, I can even do tricks." I flap twice to levitate off the ground before dropping to the asphalt. "No, I don't know how it happened. No, I don't know what it means. Yes, I'm a little freaked out. Any questions? No? Great. Let's accept this and move on."

Greyson gives his head a hard shake. "Yeah, of course. We can talk about all that later. First off, are you guys okay?" His concerned gaze bounces from Steel to me.

"Oh, yeah." Sterling moves closer, giving me another once-over. "We will definitely be talking about this later. Think your outfit will manifest in the mortal realm too?"

I tip my head skyward. Sterling could not be a bigger flirt. At least I'm finally getting used to it.

"Back. Off," Steel warns and steps into his brother's space.

Sterling's brows shoot up at the same time as his hands. "Whoa there, bro."

When Steel's face doesn't lose its hardness, Sterling retreats. Only then do Steel's hackles flatten and the air loses its crackle of tension.

Canting his head to the side, Sterling studies his older sibling. "So, it's going to be like that, is it?"

"Stop that thought immediately," Steel bites out. "You're way off the mark with this one."

"Am I?" A smile creeps across Sterling's face. He looks as content as a cat who caught a mouse.

Greyson steps between his siblings. "Sterling, stop antagonizing Steel," he orders. "And Steel, tone down your vibe, will ya? We need to get your head injury checked out."

Oh, right!

"He was knocked unconscious for a while."

Steel's narrowed eyes snap toward me with a clear warning.

"What?" I shrug, "It's the truth. Get over yourself already. You're not invincible."

He scoffs at me. "I'm about as close to it as you'll ever see."

"Conceited much?"

"It's not conceit if it's true." He throws open his arms. "This is just me stating facts."

I bare my teeth. I'm too far past annoyed for a simple eye roll.

"Yeah, you're not God's gift to mankind."

"In fact, that's exactly what I am." With a smarmy smile he adds, "Womankind as well."

"You disgust me."

"I highly doubt that's the emotion you feel when you think of me."

"Guys?" I barely register Greyson's voice past the blood pounding in my ears.

"How would you know *anything* about how I feel?"

I don't even attempt to conceal the venom in my voice. Instead I shoot the words at him like bullets. Steel returns my lob with slitted eyes.

"How could I not know *everything*? You wear your emotions like an open bottle of cheap perfume. I couldn't escape the fumes if I wanted to."

"At least I have emotions," I spit at him. "You sure you have a beating heart in that chest?" I can't stop the purge now.

"Nothing gets through that hardened shell, does it? And if anyone gets close, you shove them away. Shove—ha, that's too mild of a word. It's more like you punch and kick them until they run screaming in the other direction. But who cares if you hurt someone, right? As long as you can stay protected on your island of one, the ends justify the means. What was it exactly that turned you into an emotional zombie?"

"Emberly!"

Ash?

I'm so caught up in my rant, I ignored the spectrum world around me, choosing instead to hyper-focus on the object of my frustration. My friend's voice snaps me out of the red haze of anger.

I find myself standing in front of Steel, chest heaving, my finger shoved up against his chest.

When did I do that?

Turning my head, I see Ash and Nova now standing with Greyson and Sterling. Matching looks of shocked horror are splashed across their faces.

I've gone too far. Stepped over some line I didn't know existed.

Taking a physical step back, I drop my hand to my side.

Steel glares daggers at me, and I can't say I blame him.

"That. Was. Awesome! Way to put my big bro in his place, Em."

"Do you ever shut up?" Greyson sighs.

"What are you talking about?" Sterling directs an injured look at his twin. It's fleeting and most likely not sincere. "You just got a full five minutes of silence from me. That was like watching a younger Steel pull a girl's pigtails on the playground and then getting slapped with a mud pie in return. Priceless, man."

Steel stomps forward and grabs the nape of his brother's neck, forcing him to hunch over. "Shut it, Sterling."

"Why does everyone keep telling me to stop talking?" Sterling tugs out of Steel's hold, only to have his arm twisted behind his back. "Ow, ow! All right, uncle, uncle! I call uncle!"

"We need to get back to the academy." Steel talks over Sterling's protests and starts down the alley, his brother still in tow.

An impressive task—Sterling isn't a small guy.

"Why aren't we phasing back?" Greyson asks with his eyes trained on the place his brothers disappeared. A furrow mars his brow.

I rub my forehead. A headache is brewing. "Because of me. I'm stuck . . . again. We should get going."

I start forward, but come up short when a fiery brunette steps in my path.

"What is going on right now?" Ash demands. "Why are you dressed like that? And when did you get wings?" Her voice gets progressively more shrill as she continues.

"The short answer is, I don't know."

Ash sucks in a deep breath through her nose and plops her hands on her hips. She narrows her eyes, not buying that answer.

"Trust me, the long answer is just an explanation of why I don't know." My headache morphs from a painful throb to a burst of heat. I wince. "Can we get back to the academy and talk about it there? I'm sure Sable is going to want a step-by-step breakdown and it would be great not to have to repeat the story over and over again."

The anger drains out of Ash, but it's replaced by an injured look. Heated agony stabs my forehead. I'm not thinking clearly. "Ash, I'm sorry. I think I just need to get somewhere safe and sit down or something." Her form swims in my vision and I blink to clear it.

Are my eyes watering?

"I just . . ." Ash's hands are clasped together under her chin. Her lower lip trembles and she sucks in a full breath of air. "It was my fault you were out here alone. I never would have forgiven myself if something happened to you. I'm so—"

I sink to a knee when a bolt of pain cuts from my head down the back of my spine.

"Emberly!" Ash shouts. Her voice is a muffled exclamation to my ears as the roar of an unseen blaze drowns out the world around me.

I squeeze my eyes shut as fire leaps and tangles behind my lids.

I'm being roasted alive.

Ash yells for help. Her panicked shouts barely register over the flames charring me from the inside out.

I'm dying. I have to be. There is no way to be in this much pain and survive.

But I don't want to die—I want to live. So I fight against the pain. Forcing my lids open, I catch blurred forms running toward me. They zap in and out of focus like a staticky television screen.

Another wave of heat engulfs me and my neck tips back; my mouth opens in a silent scream as my sight fills with the spectrum world's night sky—the beauty a sharp contrast to the agony rippling throughout my body.

"Her eyes," someone gasps. I'm beyond being able to identify a speaker at this point.

Someone grabs my face and forces my attention back to Earth. The hands that press against my cheeks cool the inferno wherever they touch.

I press into the caress as my vision clears. Sapphire-rimmed teal eyes draw my attention even as pain continues to roll over my body from the neck down. I grasp for any bit of relief I can get and vaguely realize I'm not actually on fire.

"Deep breaths. In and out." Steel's face is serious, but not unkind.

"The pain," I wheeze out on a labored breath. He can't possibly understand what I'm going through.

His thumb wipes a tear that's escaped from my eye. "It will pass. I promise."

Despite everything, I believe him.

I suck in a searing gulp of air and bend forward. Folding as much of myself into his cool embrace as possible, I allow Steel to comfort me.

My body shakes with the force of the battle raging inside. The scorching heat makes a desperate attempt to overtake me, opposed only by the cool touch of fingertips on my face and arms.

My wings curve forward, cocooning both of us.

"It's almost over."

I hang onto Steel's whispered words like the lifeline they are.

Liquid magma drenches each of my vertebrae and races up my golden wings. I spread them wide to protect Steel from their fiery embrace, but a moment later they compress tight against my spine on their own accord.

I cry out as a seam splits in my back and my wings fold into myself.

With one final flash of light, the world is washed white before returning to normal. The inferno leaves my body in a rush, sweet relief taking its place.

I've phased back into the real world. The ordeal leaves me a panting, sweaty mass of muscle, bone and flesh sagged in Steel's arms. I try to push away from him, but my shaky limbs won't cooperate.

"Is she all right?" Ash's face appears over Steel's shoulder. I have a tough time focusing. My eyes blink lazily and refuse to stay open despite my harshest commands.

"I think so." Steel's words rumble through his chest to my own.

I think it's time for a nap.

My head lolls.

Definitely naptime.

"Emberly." A very rude someone jars me awake. "Do not fall asleep right now."

"Not the boss of me." I blow a half-hearted raspberry.

"She's even feisty when she's only half-aware. I like that."

"Shut up, Sterling."

"Let's get her back to the academy." Oh . . . Nova. Great idea. My bed at the academy is amazing. "Steel, maybe let one of your brothers take her? You *are* still injured."

"No, I'm fine. I can handle her." I'm hefted into the air. "The rest of you keep watch. Those Forsaken are still on the loose."

Wait, Steel is carrying me? No thank you. I can walk on my own. Come on body, time to come back online.

I squirm in Steel's hold. My eyes only flutter open a few

times, but I catch the tightening of his jaw. Looks like he's grinding his teeth.

"Will you stop wiggling already? I'll drop you if you don't."

"Let. Down." Why is it so hard to form words?

"Hey." Ash gives my upper arm a reassuring squeeze. "Just sit tight, okay? We're going to get you back and figure out what's going on."

I pry my lids open using stubborn will alone. My head bobs along with Steel's strides. Trying to focus makes me slightly nauseated.

"Never speak of this again." I force the words out.

"Of your transformation?" she asks.

"No," I flop my head to the side and knock it against Steel's chest. "Him. Carry."

A bubble of laughter rolls up from her chest and bursts free. "No promises there."

Great.

I let my eyes slide shut and body relax. Might as well enjoy the ride. I'm going to be paying for it later.

21

*S*able's office feels smaller with seven bodies crammed into it. Nova is perched on the window seat, sitting with her arms and legs crossed. She leans against the sill, checking her nail polish for chips. She's the picture of boredom.

Greyson and Sterling are propped against the built-in bookshelves behind me. I haven't turned to look at them since entering the room, but every once in a while I hear a book crash to the floor. My money is on Sterling.

Ash flanks my left side like a silent sentinel. Her hand drops to my shoulder and gives it a light squeeze when I recount the more intense parts of the story, but besides that she remains silent.

I'm seated in one of the two chairs across from Sable's desk. I squeezed a mini-nap in while Steel carried me back to the academy, and now I can actually keep my eyes open. My energy seems to be returning exponentially—I almost feel normal again.

Steel is spread out in the other chair. His head is tipped back as he studies the ceiling.

Sable is seated behind her desk, her hands steepled under her chin as she listens. Aside from a few clarifying questions, she lets me relay the story in its entirety—well, most of it anyway. There are a few choice details about Steel and myself I'm not going to be retelling to anyone. Ever.

"So, that's pretty much the whole of it," I finish. I glance at Steel to see if he wants to add anything, but he's still scrutinizing something on the ceiling.

It's completely quiet for a full minute before Sable speaks. "So, you completed your metamorphosis early. And the pain you experienced when you phased back—that shouldn't happen again. The first time you phase back after metamorphosis is known to be particularly grueling."

"That's what I was thinking," Steel adds.

Grueling?

I suppose that's one way to put it. That is if you consider feeling like your skin is being burned off and limbs are melting from the inside out to be *grueling*.

"I'm going to have to alert the Council of Elders."

The room erupts.

Ash leans on the desk and yells at Sable. Greyson and Sterling abandon their posts behind me and surge forward. They alternate between arguing with each other and shouting over Ash. Nova fidgets on the window seat, but even she looks alarmed. Her eyes are wide and bounce between the shouting forms in the room.

Sable does her best to calm my friends down, but so far it isn't making much of a difference.

Only Steel seems mostly unaffected by the news, his gaze introspective. I can't get a read on him.

I'm simply confused.

I'm not sure what a metamorphosis is, or why it caused me to sprout wings. I've heard mention of the Council before, but I'm not sure what the fuss is all about.

"Enough!" Sable bellows, shooting to her feet. "You all know there are rules we live by. We report to a governing body, like any other group. We can't just go around doing whatever we want without repercussions."

"But Sable," Ash argues, "you know what they'll do to her."

Whoa, don't like the sound of that.

"What will they do to me?"

"They'll send you away," Greyson answers.

"Or experiment on you," Sterling adds.

"What? Are you messing with me?"

"Sterling." Sable pinches the bridge of her nose. "You know that's not true."

Sterling rounds to the side of the desk. "We don't know that. They just might. She's already an anomaly. Who's to say the Elders won't want to open her up to see how she ticks?"

I jump up so quickly, the heavy desk chair falls to the ground. I dart toward the doorway, my flight instinct having kicked in big time.

I'm not letting anyone cut me open.

Steel jolts from his seat and bars my exit. I skid to a halt only a few inches from his wide chest.

Whipping my head around, I search for another escape route.

Nova catches me eyeing the window and slowly shakes her head. "Don't even think about it."

But that's exactly what I'm doing. We're on the fourth floor. The drop will hurt, but I don't think it'll kill me.

I sprint for the window, the only other escape route in this small room. A ring of arms bands around me and I'm lifted off the ground.

"Let me go, Steel," I growl through clenched teeth. Spectrum world lights start to twinkle in my periphery.

Steel drops me in the chair. "Calm down. No one is going to dissect you."

"We don't know that for—"

"Sterling." The rumble in Steel's voice broadcasts a clear warning to his brother, and Sterling snaps his mouth shut. "Maybe this room is a little crowded for this conversation. Don't you think, Sable?"

Sable eyes the room before agreeing. "Steel's right, everyone out but him and Emberly. I need to ask them a few more questions anyway."

Ash, Greyson, and Sterling begin to argue over each other again and Sable saws her jaw back and forth, frustration clearly written in every one of her movements.

Nova jumps down from the ledge and saunters to the door without a word, casting a worried glance between me and Steel before slipping out of the room. I check Steel's reaction from the side of my eye, but find him watching me rather than his kinda-girlfriend. I'm not expecting that, and a rush of heat infuses my cheeks.

Looking away, I dip my head to allow my hair to form a veil between us.

The door bangs open and two small people come barreling through.

"Steel!" squeals a petite little girl with straight black hair to her waist. She launches herself into his lap and throws her arms around his shoulders, burying her face in his neck. Steel wraps an arm around her and rubs circles on her back.

A young boy is hot on her heels. He bounces on the balls of his feet in front of Greyson and Sterling.

"Is it true?" he asks, wiggling excitedly. "We heard that Steel put the smack-down on a couple of Forsaken." He grinds his little fist into the open palm of his other hand. "I'll bet he took down like eight of them at the same time, right? Was he in lion form? Or maybe the eagle? Probably not the bull because I know he's sensitive about that form. Mom said not to bring it up because—"

"Blaze," Steel groans, the small girl still clinging to his neck, "that's enough."

Is that a bit of color tinting Steel's cheeks?

Shifting my eyes to Greyson and Sterling, I can tell they're fighting off smiles.

"But Steel," Blaze whines, "I was just sayin' what Mom told me."

"I know, bud. But now's not the time, okay?"

Blaze's face falls in the perfect expression of young disappointment, but he nods at his big brother.

"Are you all right? When we heard I was so scared for you."

The little pixie in Steel's arms finally raises her face. She is adorable. Her round, sky-blue eyes shimmer with unshed tears, her porcelain skin is completely unblemished, and her lips are rounded in the perfect cupid's bow. She's going to be breathtaking when she grows up.

Both she and her brother looked young. First-year students probably.

Brushing the hair away from her face, Steel answers, "I'm

fine, Aurora. You know nothing can hurt your big brother. I'm made of steel after all."

Aurora giggles at the awful joke.

It's difficult not to melt just a little watching Steel interact with his youngest siblings. This is a side of him I've never seen. He obviously cares about them a lot.

"How did you two hear about any of this?" Greyson asks.

Aurora turns her large doll-like eyes on her twin. Blaze bobs his head, avoiding eye contact with anyone in the room, and nudges a book on the ground with his foot. "People are talkin'. You know, because you carried the one with the white fire hair in earlier."

Blaze points to me but keeps his eyes glued to the floor.

White fire hair? I've been called worse.

"And we might have maybe sorta listened at the door just a little bit."

Sterling presses his lips together, the corners turn up. Lifting a hand, he cups it over his mouth. Greyson groans and Steel just lifts his eyes skyward and shakes his head.

"Are you a princess?" a soft voice asks. Aurora's clear eyes are fastened on me.

"Me? Um, no?" That wasn't supposed to be a question.

"Are you sure?" Her stare is unnerving, and I squirm in my seat. It's an innocent question from a little girl, but it still bothers me. Princesses have never eaten out of dumpsters or slept in public parks; they host banquets and sleep on a thousand mattresses in plush palaces. Princesses aren't orphaned, anti-social loners; they know exactly who their parents are and have armies of people who love and adore them. Princesses aren't left to fend for themselves in a savage world; they are protected and cherished.

I'm as far from a princess as any girl can get.

"Yeah, I'm sure." I quirk a half-smile because she looks so disappointed in my answer. "There's nothing special about me."

She shakes her head. Wispy strands of blue-black hair float in the air around her face. "No, that's not true. The air around you sparkles. You're very special!"

I blink at Aurora and then cut Steel a look. Sparkles?

He's watching me with a thoughtful expression that hardens after a moment. "Grey, Sterling, can you get these two back to their rooms? It's late."

Sterling heaves out a frustrated breath, realizing staying in the office isn't a battle he's going to win. "Sure. Come on munchkins, looks like you still need your big bros to tuck you in."

Aurora slides off Steel's lap and claps her hands together in glee. At the same time, Blaze lets out a moan, a scowl pinching his features. "I'm not a baby," he argues. "You don't have to bring me back to my room."

Greyson leads the two to the door, Sterling bringing up the rear. "Oh, we know you're capable of getting to your room, squirt. We just think you're sneaky enough to find a new hiding place instead of heading there."

A mischievous smile breaks out on Blaze's face. His brother has him pegged. He must have given his parents a few gray hairs already. A clump of dark locks falls into his eyes and he swipes it away, winking at me as he exits the room.

"Did you see that? Is he trying to flirt with me?" I ask Sterling as he passes by.

"What can I say? He takes after his big brother." Sterling

throws me a matching wink as he follows the group out the door. Aurora's excited voice can be heard down the corridor.

"Grey-Grey, wait until you see the new nail polish Mom sent me. It would look great with your complexion."

Ash and I both snort a laugh before the door fully closes.

"I'm afraid I have to ask you to leave as well," Sable says to Ash. She holds up a hand to stop Ash's complaints. "We both know she's going to tell you everything when she gets back to your dorm anyway. Please just let me deal with the issue between the two of them."

"You promise not to send her away?"

"I'm not sending Emberly anywhere. She's welcome to stay here for as long as she likes."

Ash crosses her arms over her chest. Her eyebrows arch. "But what if the Elders demand it?"

"We'll cross that bridge if we come to it."

Ash doesn't appear completely satisfied but nods anyway. "I'll wait up for you, okay? I'm sure it's going to be all right."

"Sure." How can she say everything is going to be all right when she's obviously concerned I'm going to get dragged out of the academy by this so-called Council of Elders?

When the door clicks shut, only the three of us remain. Steel's attention is fastened on Sable.

"You know what they're going to want. They're going to expect her to fight."

22

*L*eather creaks as Sable leans back in her chair. Her arms are folded in front of her and her head is tipped back.

What's up there that everyone finds so interesting? I don't see anything but white ceiling paint.

"I wish you were wrong, Steel, but I can't say that you are." Pushing out a lungful of air, she sits forward and reaches for the phone on her desk. "I need to call Deacon."

"Wait." I cover the receiver with my hand. "Before anything else happens tonight, someone needs to explain to me what a metamorphosis is. Am I going to turn into a butterfly or something? And why everyone is so freaked out about the Council of Elders? Are they a group of old angel-borns who wear long gray robes and chant over a special stick or something?"

"Chant over a stick? Really?"

I swat at Steel without looking in his direction. "How in the world am I supposed to know what your Elders do? I didn't even know they existed before coming here." Popping my jaw, I slouch in my seat.

"That's fair." Sable says. "Metamorphosis is the final stage in a Nephilim's development. You know that new powers are only ever manifested in us once a year—on our birthdays."

But it's not my birthday.

"Our young adults usually go through a phase where stronger powers develop. It typically starts on their eighteenth birthday and ends on their twentieth. That's why our students don't graduate until they're twenty."

"Are you saying I'm going through Neph puberty right now? Because that's a whole bag of unfair."

"I suppose you can think of it that way. Different side effects though. You don't need to worry about hormonal surges and acne. And from the looks of it, it seems you may have just blasted through the whole stage. I can't imagine you have any more abilities that will develop. Not to mention how soon it happened."

"Has anyone else ever gone through it early?" I chew my bottom lip, unsure what I want her answer to be. Sable's eyes slide to Steel.

Oh, great.

"It happens occasionally. Steel here started on his seventeenth birthday and recently finished the last phase when he turned nineteen. That's why he's been going out on some missions. Technically speaking, he could have graduated early and left the academy on assignment somewhere."

I twist to Steel. His jaw is set and his eyes are fixed forward.

"Well, why haven't you left then?" I ask.

He grinds his teeth together, clenches then releases his

fists. He's not going to answer me.

Sable clears her throat. "The more pressing matter is that it's not your birthday."

Exactly.

"Starting and even perhaps completing metamorphosis early isn't particularly alarming. The fact that it happened at a seemingly random time is. Can you tell me again what happened right before your wings appeared?"

"Well, um, the Forsaken said they were going to kill Steel and I just kind of reacted."

"Hmm, interesting."

"You don't think it has anything to do with him." I point my thumb at the silent jerk next to me.

"Probably not, but it's a possibility. I'm afraid to say that there's still a tremendous amount of mystery surrounding you. I wish I had more answers, I really do. The best I can do right now is educate and train you to the best of my abilities, and try to help you navigate all of this."

I let my head thump back against the chair and squeeze my eyes shut. "There's just so much I don't know. Being a woman of mystery might sound exciting, but it's darn inconvenient in an angel-born world."

Sable's gaze is sympathetic when I lift my head. "So, about this Council."

"Right, they're a little easier to explain. The Council is made up of the oldest Nephilim in each line. So there are seven Elders, one from each line of Nephilim in existence."

"There's no seraph or angel Elder then, right?"

"Correct. A chair on the Council only opens up if someone dies. Then the next oldest takes their place."

"What if they don't want to be an Elder? Or what if they

stink at leading?"

"It doesn't matter. They get the position whether they want it or not, whether they've earned it or not."

Well, that seems like a disaster waiting to happen.

"What's so special about this group? I'm assuming they aren't just figureheads."

"The Elders can control your life if they feel like it." Steel finally speaks up. "It's in every Neph's best interest to fly under the radar as long as possible. At least if they value their freedom. Too bad for you, I guess."

"Insensitive much? Gosh, do you even know how to fake compassion?"

Steel leans toward me, bringing his face parallel to my own. Sucking in a whiff of Steel-laced air, my mind goes a little fuzzy.

Mmmm, yummy. I give my head a minute but sharp shake. *No, gross, Emberly. Man sweat and Irish Spring are not delicious.*

"Compassion won't do you any favors in this world, Em." He's close enough that his warm breath kisses the side of my face. So distracting. "What I offer is far more useful."

Settling back, he notches his chin at Sable, indicating she can continue.

My brain snaps to attention.

What he offers. What's that exactly? Sarcasm and a healthy dose of humiliation?

I can't believe some part of me claimed him as "mine." Even if it was a buried part of my subconscious that did it, it was still wrong. If Steel had his way, I'd be rocking myself in a corner somewhere, afraid of my own shadow.

"That's a bit dramatic, Steel, don't you think?" Sable laughs lightly, probably trying to cut the tension in the room.

It doesn't work.

Steel just lifts a shoulder as if to say, "believe what you want, but I know I'm right." Sable's laughter peters out and she clears her throat.

"The Elders make sure our rules are being enforced, and on very rare occasions they add a rule or amend one. The current governing system was set up millennia ago, back when the first angel-born revolted against the Fallen. The only way our race was able to escape slavery was by banding together. Each line has an equal say and an equal vote. But yes, they also assign some of our kind to certain tasks."

I suck my bottom lip into my mouth and release it with a pop. "Why was everyone so against you contacting them?"

"Because the Council's word is final."

"They'll own you," Steel adds.

"But none of your young friends have ever had direct contact with them," Sable continues, ignoring Steel completely. "I think it's very likely the Council would agree that keeping you in our academy and continuing to let you learn and train would be for the best." She inhales a deep breath and holds it for a beat, then releases it in a heavy rush. "Yes, I'm sure that's the conclusion they'll reach."

"Right. And I'm the Easter Bunny," Steel mocks.

"Steel, that's enough." She sets hard eyes on him and miracles do exist, because Steel closes his mouth. "It's late. Nothing has to be decided today. I'm going to call Deacon and discuss this matter with him. You're both excused."

"But I want to decide what happens to me. Not you. Not some group of super old dudes I've never met. This is my life."

Reaching forward, Sable places her hand over mine. I yank it back. I won't let my emotions manipulate my good sense.

"Nothing will be done tonight, I promise. You've had an extremely trying day, and you need rest. None of us are invincible."

I eye her skeptically. "You won't call the Council?"

She shakes her head. "No. I'm just going to fill Deacon in on the new development. I'll circle back with you tomorrow."

Nodding, I rise from the chair. I'm beat.

"Okay, then. I guess I'll see you tomorrow."

I head for the exit, ignoring Steel at my back.

"Emberly," Sable calls. I stop and glance over my shoulder. "You did well. I'm proud of you."

I duck my head to hide the warmth that rushes to my face. I can't help the glow her quiet praise creates in me. This is the first time anyone has ever said they were proud of something I did. Usually it's quite the opposite. I've grown up thinking I can't do anything right, and that staying hidden is the best way to stay out of trouble.

"Thanks," I answer, my voice just above a whisper as I leave.

My mind is running over the evening's events when my arm is grabbed and I'm swung around.

I'm shoved into the wall. Steel's large frame boxes me in. A zing of awareness and annoyance races from my head down to my toes.

My body is such a traitor.

"What do you think you're doing?" I shove at his chest. The big oaf doesn't move. His hands are planted on the wall on either side of my head. I'm so surrounded by large Neph-body that the shine from the overhead lights doesn't reach me.

"We already had a personal space convo, Steel. Get out of

my bubble."

"You need to stay away from my family. Every one of them. I don't want to see you hanging out with Greyson or Sterling anymore. And I certainly don't want to see you talking to Aurora or Blaze."

Anger fizzes in my gut like acid. It foams up from my stomach and settles in my chest.

Steel is trying to tell me who I can be friends with. More than that, he's trying to control who I even interact with.

I am livid. And I hate to admit it, but I'm extremely hurt as well.

"I don't know where you get off thinking—"

Steel crowds me, his chest almost touching mine. The thin layer of air between us is charged with mutual resentment.

"They are my family, and I will do anything—*anything*—to protect them. And right now that means keeping them away from you, because you are dangerous."

"Dangerous?" I want to rear back, but I don't have anywhere to go.

"For whatever reason you have a bullseye painted on your back, and until it's gone, I don't want you around my brothers or sister."

"News flash. I couldn't care less what you want." I'm so worked up I'm practically panting. I briefly consider kneeing him, but dismiss the idea. That is a literal low blow and I'm not interested in sinking to that level . . . again.

Steel glares lasers at me, his teal eyes taking on an unnatural glow. "I'm not joking around here. This isn't a game."

I push against his chest, but he still doesn't move. Time to flip this intimidation tactic on its head.

Rising up on the balls of my feet, I bring my face close to

his. Nudging off the wall, I step right into him. Rather than shoving him away, I place my hands on his shoulders. Leaning impossibly closer, I tip my head back so I'm looking directly into his eyes. I lick my lips and watch Steel's eyes drop and his pupils dilate.

"Oh, I know this isn't a game." I hope I know what I'm doing. This is playing with fire, but if anyone deserves to be burned, it's Steel. "Your brothers can make decisions for themselves. I'm not going to purposely ignore them just because you want me to."

Steel jerks his head back at my words. Perfect.

"But I'll tell you what I *will* do."

His eyes narrow. Smart boy.

His gaze drips downward as I slide a hand off his shoulder and down his chest. "I will tell you to go to Hell and do whatever I want."

"If you think—"

I don't let him finish as I thrust my forearm up and into his throat.

We are in such close proximity that he doesn't have time to stop me, even though his eyes widen a split second before my arm connects with his Adam's apple.

Coughing, he stumbles back, clutching his throat.

I glide away from the wall and head toward my room.

I took damaging his package off the table, but throat punches are still fair game.

I throw one final word of advice over my shoulder before slipping around the corner. Steel's still getting his breathing under control.

"Stop getting in my face. You'll only get hurt. Like you said, I'm dangerous."

23

"What. A. Jerk!"

The door slams behind me with enough force to rattle Ash's angel figurines on our bookshelf. She jack-knifes up in bed, fully clothed, but she'd obviously been asleep.

"What? Who? Yeah, huge jerk. Wait. Huh?" Rubbing sleep out of her eyes, she blinks up at me in confusion.

Plopping down on my bed in a huff, I brush my fingers back and forth over the soft cotton comforter. It's probably a million thread count. One thing this academy isn't lacking is money. Maybe the supple material will soothe the jagged edges of my sour attitude.

"I'm really sorry. I shouldn't have stormed in here like that. You should go back to sleep." The words come out sharp and biting, a far cry from the sincere apology I'm going for.

"What, no!" Swinging her legs over the bed, Ash faces me with an expectant look. "What happened after I left?"

"Not much."

I swat at my pillow in an effort to vent my lingering frustration, before flopping back on the bed. I tick off the events on my fingers.

"Sable explained metamorphosis and the Council of the Elders. Steel tried to put the fear of God in me. Sable is going to update Deacon on events and get back with me in the morning. Oh," I wave an agitated hand in the air, "and Steel ordered me to stop being friends with his brothers and to never have contact with Blaze and Aurora again."

Ash gapes at me. "No, he didn't."

"Oh, yes he did. The stunt he pulled earlier this evening was bad enough, but this is a new low."

My heart pinches. Steel tried to snuff out the glimmer of hope that I could make some real friends. My instincts were right—I shouldn't have gotten attached to anyone. I've let my guard down in the last few weeks. Shouldn't I know better by now?

Shame on me.

"What exactly did he say? Maybe you misunderstood him?" Ash scooches forward until she's sitting on the edge of her mattress. "Wait, what did he pull earlier?"

Oh, shoot.

"Oh, that was nothing." Ash's eyes miss nothing as I sit up and slide toward my headboard until my back is pressed up against it. Squirming, I fluff the pillow before settling in.

Gosh, can I act more guilty?

It's not like kissing is a crime, but reminding myself of that doesn't erase the vestige of deceit from my conscience.

Ash's scrutiny weighs heavy on me.

"In a nutshell, Steel said that since the Forsaken had it out for me, I was dangerous. He thinks associating with me will get one of his family members hurt."

It's a preposterous concern. I shove out a harsh chortle.

But seeds of doubt begin to burrow like termites in my mind. They eat through the flimsy barrier I constructed to protect myself, take root in the deepest depths of my subconscious and make me question the situation.

What if he's right?

I wrap my arms around myself. What may appear to be a posture of defiance is really one of self-comfort. Having lived a life deprived of physical consolation from others, my crossed arms deliver my version of a hug.

My overworked mind throbs, firing pulses of denial in regular intervals. But what if I *am* putting his loved ones in harm's way?

Steel is one of the most powerful Nephilim at Seraph Academy, and tonight almost spelled his doom. If something like that happens again when one of his siblings is with me, the conflict could be deadly.

I'm used to facing dangers and protecting myself, but to be responsible for another life... a bolt of terror spears my heart.

Until this moment, I haven't slowed down enough to consider Steel may have a point.

"What's that look for?" Ash asks. "I don't like it."

"I guess it's just . . ." I gnaw on my lower lip, my teeth sawing back and forth. Indecision rides me hard as premature guilt opens its mouth wide, ready to swallow me whole. If anyone ever got hurt because of me, I'd never forgive myself. "When I think about it, he does sort of have a point."

Why can't I be one of those people who doesn't care? Considering I grew up without a soul watching out for my best interests, I should be programmed to stay focused on number one.

Why can't my inner workings be as hard and unfeeling as the shell I project?

Ash uncrosses her legs and travels the short distance to my bed. Settling gently at the foot, she waits until she knows she has my attention.

"No, he doesn't. Battling the Forsaken—that's something we all have to face someday. It's part of our purpose, divinely etched into our DNA. The Fallen may have created us to aid them, but our instincts to fight against evil won out. Steel just has more trauma than most of us."

Pulling my knees to my chest, I dangle my arms over them. "You mean because he's going on missions already?"

Ash shakes her head, her curls bounce against her cheeks and shoulders. Reaching up, she winds her hair into a top knot, securing it with an elastic band.

"No, Steel had a twin sister, Silver. She—"

"Wait, you're telling me all the kids in that family are twins?"

Ash itches her brow. "Yeah, it's kind of a Durand family thing. They always have kids in pairs. I don't know all the details—it was about six or seven years ago now— but it happened when Steel's family was on vacation in the Swiss Alps. Steel and Silver went missing one night. I've heard there was a blizzard, but maybe that was an exaggeration. Either way, search parties didn't find them that night. The next day Steel returned. Silver never did."

"Did she . . . die?"

"That, or worse. They never found her body. From what I've heard, Steel was half frozen when he found his way back.

He couldn't remember anything. Silver could have easily been buried in the snow somewhere. Parts of the mountains in that area never thaw, and even though we're hardy, we can still freeze to death.

"I don't think Steel ever talks about it, but considering he's already lost one family member—a twin at that—it makes sense why he's so protective of the rest. Even fanatically so. I don't know him well, but I get the impression he takes his role as the oldest sibling very seriously."

That's an understatement. He doesn't just play the role of big brother, but protector as well.

I release a breath and settle against the headboard again.

"How long ago did you say this was?"

"I don't remember exactly. I transferred into this academy in my sixth-year—that's like eighth grade in a human school—so I wasn't around when it happened. I think he wasn't much older than Blaze and Aurora though."

To experience such a traumatic loss so young, I can't even imagine all the ways in which that shaped Steel.

"Every once in a while Greyson or Sterling mentions something about Silver, but it doesn't happen often. I never thought it was my place to pry."

A handful of seconds pass while I try to process this information. I'm not sure I can . . . at least not fully in one night.

"From what I've gathered, Silver was the heart of their family. They all adored her. I think Steel used to be a lot more lighthearted than he is now."

I run a hand through my hair, grimacing at the feel of grease. How quickly I've become accustomed to cleanliness.

"That's a horrible thing to happen to anyone, but at such a

young age, and to have been with her on that mountain . . ." I let my words hang in the air.

Steel's attitude toward me is beginning to make a bit more sense now. It's easy to stay angry at someone for being a jerk, when you think it's simply for the sake of being a jerk. It's much harder when you realize they have layers—that there are probably reasons for the way they are and the things they do.

Squeezing my eyes shut, I press my palms against them until white stars dance behind closed lids.

"What am I going to do, Ash?"

Her gentle hand squeezes my knee before she slides from my bed. "I didn't tell you that so you'd stop being friends with Greyson and Sterling. I don't think you should let Steel's fears get in your way. Like I said before, monsters and dangers are a part of our reality, and Steel needs to come to terms with that on his own. He can't put a protective shell around everyone he loves."

A protective shell. I wouldn't be surprised if that was something he'd tried.

"I just wanted you to know where he was coming from so you don't take it personally. Just because we're part angel, doesn't mean we're perfect, ya know?"

I huff out a half-laugh. "Yeah, that's for sure."

She glides to the bathroom, but turns back before closing the door.

"Don't let him get to you, okay? I think you've spent most of your life with people telling you you're less-than, or not worthy somehow. But, that's a lie. You are worthy of friendship, and loyalty, and love. You're worthy of all the good things life has to offer. You're building true friendships here—

don't let them go easily. You, probably more than any of us, know how special they are."

My throat clogs with emotion, so I simply nod and offer as much of a smile as I can muster. It's not much, but it's enough for Ash.

The moment she disappears from view, I allow the moisture prickling at the back of my eyes to seep through.

She's right: I've spent a lifetime with people who belittled my very existence. Friendship is a precious gift I've been denied, and I'm the last person who should take it for granted. But knowing what Steel has already lost, can I knowingly endanger one of his loved ones simply to chase after something I desire?

And if I do, doesn't that make me the monster in the end?

24

I poke at the gravy-drenched chicken breast on my plate. It's probably cold by now, which is a shame. I happen to like chicken and I'm not in the habit of passing up free food. But who can eat while they're being watched?

Not this girl.

At my last school I used to take my lunch down to the basement to escape the prying eyes of my fellow students. It was always dank and smelled like mold and sometimes dead rodents, but for a moment of peace I'd pay that price.

Disappearing acts have always been my specialty. I wanted to pull one tonight, or skip dinner altogether, but Ash is a bossy little thing and won't hear of it.

"I promise, no one is staring."

I lob my drill sergeant a miffed look, one laced with as much annoyance as I can infuse into my features. I only have to twist my neck a quarter notch to the right or left to catch at least six sets of eyes covertly stealing peeks at me.

Blaze and Aurora aren't the only two who caught wind of

what happened over the weekend. I'm the freaky new girl all over again.

Academy students murmur behind their hands. Their whispered conversations itch my eardrums. Their glances weigh heavy on my back, burning through my clothes like hot coals and singeing the skin underneath.

The worst was during PE, when Seth tried to get me to phase. I managed to blink into the spectrum world a few times, but no magic wings or gilded armor appeared. When I returned to the real world, the students' faces were stained with disappointment. I was tempted to ask if they wanted a refund on their tickets, because they were obviously counting on me being the day's entertainment.

"Just ignore them, Em. They'll find something new to talk about in a day or two."

Fisting my knife, I stab my chicken and then hurl a pointed look at Sterling. I'm pretty sure he took bets on whether or not I would transform during training.

I point my empty fork at him. "Nothing out of you."

He has the good sense to press his lips together and tuck his chin. Greyson breaks out in a boisterous round of laughter.

"I told you not to use Emberly's experience to further your gambling addiction, bro. You brought her wrath upon yourself."

Half of Sterling's mouth lifts but his cheeks darken. "Naw. I'm too charming. Emberly could never hate a face as pretty as mine."

Unfortunately, he's not wrong—he is annoyingly impossible to hate.

What am I going to do with him? What am I going to do with his entire family?

I can use this betting thing as an excuse to put distance between myself and the middle Durand twins. The pretext would be flimsy, but I can use it to drive a wedge between us.

An ache pulses in my chest, and I scrub at the spot.

I'm still torn up inside about what to do about Steel's siblings. I can—and will—easily stay away from Blaze and Aurora. I don't want them mixed up in anything that might hold a hint of danger. Steel and I are of one mind there.

But Greyson and Sterling are a different story. In the few short weeks I've known them, they've become like the brothers I never had—the ones I would have wished for if I'd known what I was missing.

Greyson reaches over. The pad of his index finger runs a path between my eyes and down the bridge of my nose. "Why the frown, pretty girl? Don't you know if you keep your eyebrows pinched like that, they may stay that way?"

"Oh, um . . ."

What can I tell him?

"Don't mind Sterling. He can't help himself. He's barely housebroken." A spot warms in my belly and a light chuckle escapes. Greyson always has entertaining excuses for his brother's antics.

"I heard that!" Sterling shouts from the other side of the table, giving his brother the stink eye.

"I know." Greyson's attention flicks in his direction before returning to my face.

"No, it's fine. I mean, it's annoying, but that's not really—"

A screeching noise followed by a body dropping down next to me jerks my attention away from Greyson. When I twist in the opposite direction, it's to see Steel's large frame lounging in the chair to my right. His beefy arms are draped over the seatback and he's staring right at me.

I blink twice.

"What are you doing?" I ask.

"Eating dinner." Reaching across me, Steel grabs my discarded fork and pokes a limp piece of asparagus on my plate before bringing it to his mouth.

I snarl at him and snatch my fork back. "Do not touch my food. I. Will. Cut. You."

He lifts a shoulder in an unconcerned shrug and risks his life a second time by swiping a fry off my plate. I snag it out of his hand before it can reach his lips.

"You're asking to be shivved, you know that, right?"

He sneers and eyes my chicken. I scoot the plate further away, resting one arm between him and my food, and clutching my fork like a dagger in my hand. I dare him with my eyes to try and steal something else.

You don't mess with a former homeless chick's food.

A cleared voice has me casting a quick glance to the other side of the table before rubber-banding back to Steel.

"Um, hey Steel." Ash's voice carries a heavy hint of tentativeness. "You need something?"

"Yeah." He snorts. "I need to make sure your pal Emberly here doesn't get us all killed."

A gasp gets stuck in my throat. Did he really just say that?

A gargled cough comes from my left and I turn in time to watch milk dribble out of Greyson's nose. Across from me Sterling is laughing so hard he starts to choke on the half chewed food in his mouth. In no time both twins are red faced and hacking.

"What is happening right now?" Nova's words mirror my internal thoughts as she sets her tray down to the right of Steel. I have a hard time seeing her around his bulk.

When no one answers, she leans forward and shoots me a look.

"Honestly, I have no idea. You know him better than I do." I tip my head toward Steel to let her know which brother I'm referring to. It's the only body part I'm willing to move since I'm still hunched over my plate with my fork in the defensive position.

The noises from Grey and Sterling die down.

"Oh, man. That burned," Greyson gripes and blows his nose one last time. "Steel's being weird," he finally announces by way of explanation.

"I am not." Steel grabs a handful of fries off Nova's plate and starts popping them in his mouth, talking in between chews. "Emberly is currently a monster magnet. She refused to stay away from you two." He gestures to his brothers with a couple limp fries. "So, I'm gonna have to babysit her until we figure out what the Forsaken and Fallen want with her."

There's a beat of silence before the whole table explodes— that is everyone except me. I'm processing what he said, and the repercussions.

He's taking it upon himself to shadow me? I don't like the sound of that one bit. There isn't any stretch of the imagination where Steel and I exist peacefully in the same space. This has disaster written all over it. And it's not like he can be with me twenty-four-seven. What exactly is going through his head right now?

"Whoa, man. That is not cool." Sterling's complaint zaps me back to the here-and-now. His face has almost returned to its regular color after his near-asphyxiation. "You don't think Grey and I can take care of ourselves? Or Emberly if it came down to it?"

"We may not have morphed yet, but that doesn't mean we're defenseless," Greyson adds.

"What do you mean, 'babysit'?" Nova asks.

Ash closes out the peanut gallery comments with, "Have you even asked Emberly how she feels about this?"

Steel looks utterly unphased by the havoc he just created. He munches on another one of Nova's fries and I have the errant thought that she'd better move her plate away if she wants to eat any of her dinner.

"I never said you were defenseless," Steel addresses his brothers. "And what's to ask about?" he answers Ash. "This is life or death. I'm hardly concerned with her wants."

Ash's mouth gapes open.

"You realize how much of a brute you're being right now?" I ask Steel.

"Does it look like I care?"

Well, then.

I sit back in my seat and cross my arms. "So, what's your plan, then? You aiming on sleeping on the floor by my bed? Following me to the bathroom? Sitting behind me during classes?"

He tips his head in my direction. "If I have to."

"Wait a second. Let's not get hasty." Nova's face is pinched. "If you feel like Emberly needs extra protection, I'm sure Sable can assign some people to help. Some *female* people."

Steel's hand zips toward my food, and I lurch forward. The fry is past his lips before I can grab it this time. I consider trying to fish it out of his mouth, but dismiss the thought. He'd probably bite my finger off.

"Already talked with Sable," Steel says around the food. "She doesn't think Emberly needs watching here at the academy. I disagree."

"What? You went to Sable behind my back and tried to get me a bodyguard?" My face heats and for once it's not from embarrassment. My food becomes a secondary thought as I squeeze my right hand into a fist so tightly the nails bite into my palm. "You had no right."

Steel's face hardens and his eyes deaden. The transformation from nonchalant to austere is so complete, a heavy knot twists in my stomach and I subconsciously lean back a fraction. When he speaks his voice is only a breath above a whisper, but he may as well be shouting at me. "When it comes to protecting my family, I have every right. There isn't an act I won't commit and a level I won't sink to in order to make sure they are safe. You'd do well to remember that."

He doesn't make a move toward me, but it feels like his hands wrap around my throat and squeeze. It takes me a beat to swallow a gulp of air.

"Hey, what's going on over there?" Ash asks. Her gaze boomerangs to me before resting back on Steel.

Steel levels me with one final, chilling look before veiling his emotions under a pretense of levity. "It's all good. We were just getting some facts cleared up. Anyone have any extra fries?"

Looking down I notice all of mine are missing, but in that moment, I no longer care.

Tipping forward, I face-plant into my pillow. Screaming into the soft cushion releases some of my frustration, but not nearly enough.

Steel. Is. Everywhere.

After a very uncomfortable meal, I escaped the cafeteria only to have him dog my steps. He followed me to the library, the science room, and to the gym for my evening workout.

Leaning against the wall, he watched my every move. I stumbled my way through box jumps and burpees, tweaked my lower back during barbell deadlifts, and almost tripped over my own shoelaces during my cool-down run.

I couldn't shake him until I entered the girls' locker room to shower and change. And the only reason he didn't park himself in front of my shower stall is because one of the instructors caught him trying to go in after me and refused him access.

I had to slip out the locker room's faculty exit and tiptoe through the hallways to get to my room unaccompanied.

Dude is tenacious.

A soft click sounds to the right and I flop my head to the side. Ash, dressed for bed, fills the bathroom doorway. Warm steam trickles out from behind her, embracing her in a vanilla and coconut scented cloud.

Her body wash smells amazing—I may have used it a time or two. Fingers crossed she doesn't mind.

It's a moment before she looks up from rubbing the last bit of her peach-colored lotion into her arm. The pigment disappears, leaving a shimmery coating to her skin. I know when she spots me because her eyes flare. Rushing over, she plops down on my bed, making it bounce beneath us.

"Dinner was intense."

I groan and snatch my pillow, ready to jam it over my head, when there's a knock on the door. Ash and I trade a glance before she shrugs and jumps up to answer it. Her strides eat up the distance too soon and I smother my face into the bedding once again. I'm not in the mood to face anyone.

"What do you want?" Her voice sparks like flint. Ash may have been sympathetic to Steel last night, but after his little show in the cafeteria, she's not having it.

I smile into the pillow. Atta girl.

"I'm here for Emberly. We need to talk."

My jaw tightens and I have to order it to relax before I shove off the bed and cross to the open doorway.

"Yeah, we do," I agree. It's only been a few hours, but I've already had enough of this song and dance.

Grasping my bent arm beneath the elbow, he draws me into the hallway. "Let's have a little alone time, shall we?"

"I think I've had enough alone time with you to last me a lifetime."

Ash clears her throat behind me. Twisting, I see her standing with hands on hips, brows raised, a million questions written all over her face. I need to get this over with.

"I'll be right back."

"If you say so." She retreats into our dorm room and gently —and slowly—shuts the door.

When the door clicks shut, I round on my nemesis, all geared up to lay into him. His long body is casually leaned against the wall, one shoulder propped against the hard surface and his feet crossed at the ankles.

His chin is tilted down as he flips a switchblade in his hand. His lids lift but not his head as he studies me from behind the fall of dark hair that curtains his eyes. One side of his mouth lifts in a sinful twist as I stand there, drinking him in.

Is there anything more attractive than a guy who knows he's good-looking?

Wait, no—not attractive. Annoying. Anything more *annoying.*

I stomp over to him. The sound of my sneakers slapping against the polished tile with each step smacks some sense into me.

My hands cut through the air even before words explode from my mouth. "This is not going to work."

Flipping his blade closed, Steel tucks it in his pocket. "I need your class schedule."

"What?"

"Your. Class. Schedule." He enunciates each word. "And nice slip you just gave me, by the way. I'll have to keep a closer eye on you."

If he keeps any closer eye on me he'll be watching me shower—and there's no way I'm letting that happen.

I press my fingers into my eye sockets until I see bursts of white light. "I'm not giving you my class schedule."

I hear him push off the wall and drop my hands from my face. He advances toward me, his movements feline in their fluidity. It makes me feel like prey.

Stopping with only a foot of space between us, he cocks his head and narrows his eyes.

"If you don't give me your class schedule, I'll make good on my threat to sleep in your room."

Two sharp raps on the door behind me are followed by

Ash yelling, "You won't be sleeping in our room unless you don't mind losing one of your dangly bits."

I can't help the laugh that springs from my chest. I think I have a girl-crush on my roommate.

Steel glances at the door above my head and bares his teeth before zeroing in on me. "Just make this easy on the both of us and tell me what your second and fourth period classes are so I can prepare."

"Easy on the both of us?" The laugh that shoots out of me is forced and full of disbelief. "What would be easy on the both of us is if you just left me alone. You don't need to do this."

Scrubbing a hand down his face, Steel shows the first real signs of weariness. He cracks his neck and heaves a sigh. "Listen, I'll try not to be so invasive, okay? But you're wrong; I do have to do this."

My gaze flits over his face, taking in the dark smudges under his eyes, the clumps of hair falling over his forehead, and the pronounced worry lines between his eyebrows and stemming from the corners of his eyes.

I don't understand what makes Steel tick, but I do believe that he believes this is something he has to do.

Placing two fingers on each of my temples, I massage in circles. A headache is going to hit me any minute now. Steel has that effect on me. I don't have the energy or desire to fight him anymore tonight. I just want him gone so I can sleep.

"History and math."

Pulling his bottom lip into his mouth, he bites down on the flesh and nods once. "See you in the morning."

As I watch him turn and start down the hall, I think about the end of our dinner this evening. Greyson and Sterling wouldn't look his way, Ash glared daggers at him, and Nova barely ate any of her meal. This stunt of his, however justified he thinks it may be, is already causing some ugly waves.

"Steel." He stops when I call and turns his head. I can only make out the side of his face. "This isn't going to make you any friends, you know? You're only pushing the people closest to you away."

It's several heartbeats before he responds. "Not having friends isn't the worst thing that can happen in our world."

As he rounds the corner and disappears from view, I can't help but agree.

25

*T*he rubbernecking is worse than the day before. Hunching my shoulders, I focus on the shiny marble floors and put one foot in front of the other, moving at a brisk clip.

Would pretending I'm not suffocating under the heavy weight of everyone's regard make the trek between classes more bearable?

Nope. It does not.

"This is awful," I side-whisper to Ash, ducking my head even further and digging my chin into my sternum.

"It will blow over. I promise."

My knuckles whiten as I grip the stack of textbooks plastered to my chest. "How quickly?"

Yesterday was bad, but today has brought me to a new level of Hell. Not only have the stares and whispers increased, but I also have a six-and-a-half-foot Neph "shadow" today. Steel has escorted me to and from every class this morning. That alone is bad enough, but he insists on following about ten feet behind—his idea of being nonintrusive, I guess, but really it's just awkward.

I don't need to turn to know he's there right now. I feel his eyes on me like a fiery brand. I itch to escape.

A large body side-checks me before looping an arm around my neck. I swerve to the left before being yanked back. "Hey there, sis! Welcome to the family."

"Sterling, what are you talking about?" I'd dig my fingers into my temples if my arms weren't filled with books.

"Now that you're with my brother, we're practically related." He bends over and matches my five-ten height. "Between you and me, I like having a hot sister."

I free an arm to shove the giant man-child away. "Ew. That's gross. You're not supposed to think your sister is hot."

He wags his eyebrows at me.

"But that's beside the point. What's this about me and Steel?"

"Oh, I see you haven't heard that juicy rumor yet." He slants his head to check over his shoulder before continuing. There's a flash of anger in his eyes that I've never seen from the jovial twin before. Fallout from Steel's actions, no doubt. Sterling and Greyson are not happy with their older brother at the moment. If he wasn't currently making my life so difficult, I may have been able to drum up some sympathy for him, but as the situation stands, I'm fresh outta f—

"Apparently the fine angel-borns in this institution think stalking is a sign of true love."

"What?" I squeak.

"Personally, I think it's that sparkly vampire dude's fault. That relationship was messed up. But for some reason chicks got it in their heads that codependency was hot."

Oh no. No no no no! That is the last thing I want circulating this academy.

"Real smooth, Sterling." Greyson appears next to his brother. The look he lobs Sterling is full of warning. "Stop trying to regale her with your *Twilight* epiphanies. Nobody wants to hear them."

I halt in the middle of the busy hallway. My friends pause a few steps ahead and turn back when they realize I'm not keeping pace with them.

"I am not dating Steel Durand!" I shout.

A blanket of silence presses down on the hallway. Heat blisters my cheeks.

Ash, Greyson, and Sterling regard me with identical grimaces.

That was stupid. They know I'm not dating Steel. My mini-tantrum will likely create even more buzz among my classmates.

"Let's go. We have a date," a voice rumbles from behind.

"Excuse me?"

Steel rounds me and then plants himself in my path. One eyebrow is arched and there is the smallest hint of a smirk dancing across his lips.

There's no way he didn't hear my outburst. And he finds it . . . funny?

This is so far from funny.

"In Sable's office. Did you forget?"

Shoot, I had forgotten. Sable caught up with me yesterday and said we'd be meeting with her and Deacon this morning. I didn't realize Steel would be there though.

"Shall we?" Steel motions me forward. I feel the gazes of my classmates as they scurry past us.

Straightening my spine, I power-walk all the way to Sable's office, leaving Ash and the twins in the hallway and not bothering to check if Steel is following—I already know he is.

When I reach her office door, Steel's hand shoots out and grasps the knob, turning and opening it before I have a chance to do it for myself. I stop myself from thanking him and stomp right on by, flopping into the first of the two chairs in front of her desk.

Steel shuts the door and calmly takes the seat to my right. Sable looks up, her eyes volleying between the two of us for several seconds before she speaks.

"Good, you're both here." There's an open book in front of her that she closes and sets to the side.

"Why is he here?" I hitch a thumb in Steel's direction. He quirks a half-smile and settles into his seat, legs stretched out to the side of Sable's desk, arms on the rests on either side of him. One would think he's a spoiled prince lounging on a throne instead of seated in a cracked leather side chair. Smug pleasure practically radiates off him.

Sable cocks her head and folds her hands in front of her before leaning back. "There are several reasons he is part of this meeting. A very important one being he was the only witness we have to the incident a few nights ago."

The door clicks open to reveal a giant of a man, clad in dark jeans and a black biker jacket. He's wearing aviator glasses and moves like a predator—all stealth and strength. He must be somewhere around six-seven, which is tall even by Nephilim standards.

His hair is shorn on the sides and a few inches longer on

top. The cut reminds me of a more conservative version of Steel's.

I've seen this man before. At Anita's, the day the Nephilim found me.

Sable rises from her seat and crosses the office and extends her hand to the giant. "Deacon, thanks for joining us."

Ah, right. Deacon.

After returning her greeting, Deacon removes his glasses and turns toward me. Light blue eyes consider me before his icy gaze narrows. Something about his inspection chills me.

"I remember this one. She was a runner." Refocusing his attention on Steel, he notches his chin in a standard guy greeting. "Steel, nice to see you again."

"You too, man." Cutting a glance at Steel, I notice he's retracted his legs and is sitting straighter.

Interesting. This is someone Steel either respects or wants to impress.

Deacon crosses his arms over his chest, making his biceps grow to the size of tree trunks. It's impossible not to notice.

One look at Sable proves I'm not the only one who's taken note. There's a slight flush to her cheeks. Blinking rapidly, she clears her throat and takes her seat once again.

I suppress a snicker.

"The students just arrived, so I haven't updated them yet."

"Does Steel really need to be here? This truly doesn't have much to do with him." I slouch in my seat like a petulant child. When did I turn into this person?

"I would have thought considering your relationship, you'd want him here."

"Excuse me?"

Oh no, this rumor better not have spread to the faculty as well.

"Now that you two are an item, I mean."

"Steel," I shriek before launching myself at him. I'm going to scratch his eyeballs out with my blunt nails and watch rivers of blood stream down his face.

But I never get close enough to claw at him. I'm barely on my feet before I'm lifted off them and carried across the room. I'm deposited on the ground next to Deacon, his giant body a wall of flesh between me and my prey.

"What's going on?" Sable is on her feet. The question is directed at Steel.

He shrugs. "Hormones?"

"You're dead!"

Deacon holds one tree trunk arm out in front of me, thwarting my attack yet again.

Scanning the room, I spot a purple geode sitting on Sable's desk. It's on top of a stack of papers and roughly the size of a softball.

Snatching it up, I chuck it at Steel's head. He palms it out of the air right before it connects with his nose.

Pity. He could use a facial flaw to deflate that giant ego of his.

"Emberly!" Sable's gasp jolts me back into reality. "What has gotten into you?"

Deacon turns his head and lifts a dark eyebrow. "Nice arm."

I point an accusatory finger at Steel. "The entire academy thinks we're dating."

"And you're not?" Sable asks.

I throw my arms in the air, my body vibrating in fury. "Why would people believe that? What about Nova?"

"Nova?" Steel perks up. "What does this have to do with her?" He looks genuinely perplexed.

"Because you're with *her*, not me."

Steel purses his lips like he just sucked on a lemon. "Nova and I aren't dating. She's just a friend."

My body freezes as I wrack my brain, trying to remember if anyone ever explicitly told me they were together. I never sought clarification. Had I assumed the nature of Steel and Nova's relationship this whole time? I shake my head. I couldn't have invented it all. I'd bet my golden wings that Nova's feelings for Steel go deeper than friendship. Steel doesn't strike me as clueless. I must be missing some pieces of the story.

Deacon steps in front of me again. His large body blocks my view of Steel and snaps me out of it.

Sable inclines her head toward Steel. "Okay, now that we have the Nova situation cleared up, let's talk about this rumor. Is that something you started?" Disapproval is written all over her face.

I peek around Deacon's frame. Steel shifts uncomfortably and slouches deeper into his chair.

"Hey, don't look at me like that. This isn't my fault. I didn't say anything."

"Well somehow the students got the impression you two are an item. It circulated rather quickly, I might add. Explain."

Steel stares stone-faced at her for a full thirty seconds before confessing. "It's because I've been shadowing her the last day, all right? People just got the wrong idea. I didn't start the rumors."

"You've been doing what?" Sable moves back a step, and her mouth falls open. The look on her face can only be described as dumbstruck. "We already had this conversation. I told you she's safe on school grounds."

"She's a walking disaster waiting to happen." Steel rakes a hand through his hair. His cool veneer is cracking. "I need to stay close to her to make sure no one else gets caught in the crossfire whenever the next monster comes after her. It's been the Forsaken so far. What if the next time it's an army of Fallen?"

"I think you're getting a little ahead of yourself there." Sable lifts her gaze skyward and pinches the bridge of her nose.

"It's not an awful idea," Deacon chimes in, his voice a low rumble.

"Excuse me?" I gape at his back.

Craning his neck, he gives me another once-over. "Are you cooled down yet? It would be nice to be able to address everyone in this room at the same time."

Pressing my lips together, I offer him a curt nod. He gestures with his hand to the unoccupied chair. I gingerly grasp the armrest and move it farther away from Steel before sitting.

"Deacon, I have to agree with Emberly. Putting her in a position where she has to fake a relationship with Steel is not okay for so many reasons."

"That's not what I mean. I'm just saying," Deacon goes on, "that Steel sticking close to Emberly while at the academy isn't a bad idea. He can act as her bodyguard while on the grounds. And I could use his help during her supplemental training as well."

I scoff. As if I need Steel to protect me.

Wait—supplemental training?

"Hmm." To my horror, Sable appears to be second-guessing her earlier decision as she lowers herself into her seat.

"Supplemental training?" Steel's words echo my unspoken question.

"Right." Sable steeples her hands, refocusing on us. "Deacon and I discussed the situation and decided that since you've only ever morphed the one time, Emberly, it's not imperative that we alert the Council just yet."

Sweet.

"However, we are interested in getting you phasing on command and exploring what's happening with you further. We don't yet know what the Forsaken want from you, but we think figuring out some of your secrets is imperative to staying a step ahead of them."

Not sure I'm liking where this is going.

"For the foreseeable future, when Deacon isn't out on a mission, you'll be training directly with him. We're hoping the one-on-one attention will help you get caught up. And under supervision, we'll find more answers."

I eye Deacon. He's standing next to Sable, but I'd somehow missed the movement. He was by the door a moment ago. His face looks like it's cut from stone for all the emotion it reveals.

I briefly wonder how old he is. If he were human, I'd say early thirties, but being an angel-born, it's anyone's guess.

"And you want me to help?" Steel asks.

"I think we should give it a try," Deacon confirms. "You were there the first time she morphed—maybe we can duplicate some of the elements to help her do it again. And if you're sparring with her part of the time, that will give me a different vantage point to critique."

I tilt my head in Steel's direction. "You really want to take a chance sparring with me again?"

He clenches his jaw and lifts his top lip in an animalistic snarl. I grin, showcasing as many teeth as possible.

"I'm not sure what you two have going on—" Deacon says.

"Nothing, there is absolutely nothing going on between us." Haven't we already established that?

"—but you need to put it aside. I know you're still getting used to our world, but you are in a very serious position right now. Forsaken very rarely target a particular angel-born. There's something going on here, and if we don't figure it out soon, it could mean very bad things for you."

I squirm in my seat, unwilling to meet Deacon's milky-blue stare.

Sable leaves her seat and starts for her door, a clear indication our meeting is over. "All right then, it's settled. Steel will continue to stick close to Emberly and also help with her training sessions."

"W-wait." I scramble to my feet. "What about the rumors?"

Sable and Deacon exchange a look.

"Steel, take care of it," Sable orders.

"Me?" Steel eyes Sable as if she's grown a second head. "I told you I didn't start them."

Her hands land on her hips. Uh-oh. He's about to get laid into. "That may be true, but I also know that you could have stopped them from ever circulating in the first place. You can wipe that innocent look off your face. I'm sure you had an idea this could happen when you decided to implement your half-cocked plan."

The leather seat next to me squeaks as Steel shifts uncom-fortably. He doesn't deny her accusations. "So then you want the entire academy to know you've put a bodyguard on Emberly?"

"Not particularly, but it's better than the alternative." Sable pauses, taking time to pin us both with a guilt-inducing stare before continuing. "Can't you two just learn to be friends? That would solve a lot of issues."

Steel and I exchange a wary look. I want to argue against friendship, but after Deacon's mini-lecture, my resistance feels petty.

Steel pushes out of his seat. "Yeah, Sable. We can work on being civil."

That wasn't exactly agreeing to what Sable asked, but I'm not going to point out the difference.

"Head to the gym after your morning classes. Training starts today."

Steel answers Deacon with a curt nod. His face is blank of emotions, but his hands are fisted at his sides.

What has him worked up this time?

"I'll wait for you in the hall," he tells me before pushing through Sable's door. The hallway beyond is now clear of students.

My lips pull into a frown as I watch the door shut behind him. I don't know if the sinking feeling in my gut is from feeling so out of control, or induced by Steel. Whatever the reason, I think I may have to get used to it.

26

The rattan sticks smack against each other in quick succession.

Crack, crack. Crack, crack.

The vibration from each impact sends a wave up my arm that leaves my hand throbbing.

The frosty bite in the air doesn't help. My body is equal parts fatigued and frozen. Some parts of me drip with sweat, while other parts feel near frostbitten.

The negative-degree temperature and snow flurries bite at my exposed skin. Mountain air freezes the moisture in my nostrils with every inhalation, and melts it on the exhale. The conditions aren't affecting Steel in the least. His attacks are furious and don't abate, so I'm fighting with a constant ache in both wrists and jiggly arms.

If he can't make it through my defenses, his strategy is to force me to drop my weapons.

I'm not going to let that happen.

Gritting my teeth, I ignore the sting from the sweat pouring into my eyes and order my limbs to keep functioning.

I've been told the angel-born have reserves of energy available to us, but right now I feel as weak as a full-fledged human.

Seeing a small opening in Steel's defense, I deliver a front kick to his side. Sticking with my strengths, I follow it up with a roundhouse kick to his hand, which causes one of his rattan sticks to go flying through the air.

"Good, Emberly!" Deacon yells from somewhere out of view.

My sparring stick swipes for Steel's head as he dives to the right, sending a tornado of crystallized snowflakes into the air.

Swinging around, I see him bounce to his feet just out of striking range.

He grasps his remaining rattan with both hands and slowly cracks his neck.

Trepidation whispers over my skin, causing the fine hairs on my arms to stand on end. His icy glare doesn't help matters. My instincts scream at me to run for cover, but I force myself to stand my ground.

Besides, the barren mountain terrain around us doesn't offer many hiding places. A natural arena of snow-covered red and orange rocks surrounds us. Deacon stands on an outcropping, observing us from above.

The whole thing has an outdated gladiator-ish feel— including the murder-y look on Steel's face.

The next instant, his weapon whistles through the air toward my mid-section.

Jumping back, I bring my rattan sticks down to block the

assault.

He returns my block with a counterstrike to my bicep.

I gasp at the pain that explodes in my arm, but manage to keep a hold on my stick as I backpedal.

That's going to leave a nasty bruise.

"Don't retreat! You'll give your opponent the advantage."

I'll tell you where to shove your advantage, Deacon.

Steel comes at me with a series of attacks so speedy that even with two weapons to his one, I can't keep up.

Every fourth hit lands on my body somewhere. My movements become sloppy as panic sets in. Shimmers of light appear in my peripheral vision.

Steel raises his rattan above his head and swings it down toward me.

I lift my weapons to block, but already know they'll make a flimsy shield.

The lights that had teased my vision now swim in front of my eyes; rather than fight the transformation, I embrace it, seeing a chance to escape.

I slam my lids shut. When I reopen them, I'm standing in the color-drenched spectrum world with my arms still raised above me.

No Steel in sight.

Sagging with relief, I take the opportunity to catch my breath. I've barely filled my lungs with a full breath of air before Steel appears before me.

"You didn't think it would be that easy, did you?" he taunts.

"Honestly, I kind of hoped it would be."

Instead of continuing our banter, he lets his rattan stick do the talking.

It isn't long before I'm backed underneath a rock formation—stone trapping me above, below, and at my back.

My ankle rolls when I step on some loose stones and I drop to my knees, one hand releasing my weapon to catch myself.

Rookie mistake.

The grin on Steel's face as he stands tall above me grates on my nerves.

"Do you yield, or do you want me to knock you out . . . again?"

Yielding would be the smart thing to do—the reasonable course of action. But as I glare up at Steel, I can't make the words slip past my lips.

His smile broadens. "Suit yourself."

I chuck my remaining rattan at his head with a warrior's cry.

Ducking out of the way, the weapon smashes into stone above our heads and shatters into pieces.

Steel's gaze swings to me. "Impressive."

I snarl.

A rumble of amusement bursts from Steel's chest.

So glad he's finding this humorous.

The thunder of his laughter continues as I rise. I open my mouth to speak when a trickle of pebbles lands on Steel's head. Our faces crane upward as the trickle becomes a waterfall of rocks and stone dust.

A building sense of dread keeps me paralyzed as a fissure cuts across the boulder above our heads.

Steel grabs my shoulders, swings me around and chucks me out from underneath the rock cavity. I land on my right side with a grunt.

Snapping my gaze up, I watch as the cropping of rock

above Steel slams into the ground, burying him beneath them.

I'm on my feet and sprinting toward Steel even as loose rocks continue to fall.

A sudden ball of fire sparks and then blasts from my chest, racing from its point of detonation to the tips of each of my fingers and toes.

Hot coals burn down my spine and my wings rip free from their enclosures.

Reaching the spot Steel is buried, I stretch my hands out and blast an energized ball of fire at the largest stone, shattering it to dust.

Whoa, how'd I do that?

Figure it out later, my mind screams. *Find Steel first.*

With the largest piece of the downfall removed, I dig through the rest of the rubble with my bare hands.

I uncover one boot-clad foot first.

Oh gosh, please let it be connected to the rest of him.

I scoop through the mess with shaky hands until I unearth him to the knees.

Crawling over to where his head should be—my heavy, metal-tipped wings make the movement awkward—I start digging again.

The back of his head appears first and I claw my way through the dirt and rocks until I grip the material of his shirt. Pulling upward, I drag his body free of the debris. Taking as much care as possible, I lay him down and roll him face-up.

His normally midnight hair is rusty with crushed rock and his face is streaked with red dirt mixed with blood. His skin has a nightmarish pallor under all the grime.

Parts of his clothes are torn, but most are still intact.

I run my hands over him from head to toe and down each limb. I don't think anything is broken.

Despite being buried underneath hundreds of pounds of rock, Steel seems relatively unscathed. The cuts I find bleed, but don't look deep. One on his side is seeping blood through his shirt, and so I lift up the hem to investigate.

There's a jagged four-inch wound right under his rib cage, but no organs are pouring out of the cut, so that has to be a good sign.

Bending forward, I lift his shirt higher and tilt my head for a better angle.

"Have you looked your fill yet?"

With a squawk, I jerk away from Steel.

Losing my balance, I tip over onto my butt. My wings flare wide, sending pebbles and red dust swirling around us.

We both start coughing from inhaling mouthfuls of the dirty air.

"I'm not sure there's a right answer to that question," I force out between hacks.

"What happened?" Twisting my torso, I see Deacon jump down from his perch and race to us. Looks like someone finally decided to phase into the spectrum world with us.

The spectrum sky is a pale pink with a lazy river of orange running through it. Delicate snowflakes of frosty purple start falling from the sky by the time he joins us.

Deacon bends over to help Steel to his feet.

Once he is vertical again, Steel brushes a hand through his hair to shake out some of the dust as a few lingering coughs leave his chest. Gingerly moving his limbs, he checks for injuries.

"I'm a bit banged up, but I think it's all superficial."

"What happened?" Deacon repeats, trading looks between us when I join them on more even ground.

My wings are so long, the ends brush the earth. I hike them up as best I can to keep them clean. Why that matters, I don't know.

"Rockslide? Avalanche? I'm not sure what you call it. There used to be a jutting ledge right there." I indicate the spot I'd dragged Steel from. "The boulder just cracked and then buried Steel."

Deacon's eyes appraise the mess. "What boulder?"

Steel's curious eyes take in the rock pile, no doubt noticing it's mostly comprised of stones the size of our heads or smaller.

"Oh, right." I bring a hand to my forehead and itch along my hairline, bringing my cuffed bicep into view. Looking down, I realize I'm in my full golden garb and armed to the teeth.

I suppose that makes sense. It's what happened the last time I sprouted wings.

"I kinda . . . blew up the boulder that fell."

Deacon's gaze swivels and narrows on me. "Blew up?"

"Yeah, I shot a fire ball or something out of my hand and poof, the rock sorta disintegrated." Whipping my hands up, I hold them palms-up. "And before you ask, I have no idea how I did that." I swipe a hand up and down in front of me, gesturing to all my gilded greatness. "Or this."

"You look like you did before."

Steel's body isn't quite angled toward me, but he's not quite turned away either. His gaze is lasered in on something over my shoulder, but when I sneak a peek behind me, I don't see anything all that interesting.

Purple snowflakes are starting to gather in Steel's and Deacon's hair, and it's only then I realize I'm not cold at all.

Reaching up, I pat my own head to find it wet rather than snow-dusted.

Strange.

"But you did manage to morph, that's good news." Deacon studies me with the detached eye of a teacher. "I can't say I've ever seen anything like this. As you know, some Nephilim do manifest wings in the spirit realm when they reach full maturity, but I've never seen any like yours. And the armor that morphs with you . . ." He lets the sentence drop as he walks a slow circle around me.

Well, this is awkward.

"I think Steel triggered the morph," he concludes.

"What? What would Steel have to do with this?"

Deacon stops circling me and plants his hands on his hips. "I'm not saying it was Steel, himself. I mean that you needed to help him. It was the same before. Maybe your urge to protect is the key, or at least part of it."

"Oh, yeah, that could be it."

He's not wrong. The first time it happened, the Forsaken were about to kill Steel. This time, I was terrified Steel was dying under the weight of those rocks and boulders.

My transformation wasn't premeditated either time; I simply reacted. In that way, my phasing is similar—I'm most likely to slip into the spectrum world while under duress.

"All right, let's get you both back. Steel needs to get checked out, and I need to have a talk with Sable."

"Um . . ." I shake out my wings, still getting used to their weight. "Small problem."

27

*T*he sun's bloated orange belly sits on the horizon as the three of us trudge back to the academy. Citrus streaks dash through the sky behind the western range. A dark bruise of clouds rolls in from the east, ready to swallow the last bit of the day's light.

Steel stomps forward, reminding me of the darkness above. The powder-covered ground muffles his footfalls, but I'm surprised I can't feel the aftershocks of each impact. He's that agitated.

It took close to an hour for me to phase out of the spectrum world.

Deacon encouraged Steel to leave several times—his wounds needed tending—but he refused. I have no idea why. I may have been able to phase sooner if he hadn't been distracting me. By the end of the first half-hour, the fresh blood that had stained Steel's clothes and trickled down his face was dried and congealed.

Saying he was a morbid sight wasn't an overstatement.

He'd spent most of that torturous hour pacing, muttering under his breath and putting pressure on his side-wound.

Hovering makes me self-conscious.

Deacon was trying to get me to meditate on the mortal realm—hoping visualization would help me gain control over phasing—when Steel stalked over and sandwiched my face between his palms and ordered me to morph back.

Annoyingly enough, my body obeyed.

The change was blessedly free of pain this time. Heat swept over my form, melting my wings away, but the discomfort was muted. For that, I was thankful.

The moment we phased, Steel snatched his hands back and hoofed it toward the academy. Deacon observed the exchange with a keen eye and stoic silence. After a minute, he pounded after Steel and gestured for me to follow.

We've received the silent treatment from Steel the whole walk back. Which I can't say isn't nice, but if anyone is allowed to be aggravated, it should be me. Needing Steel for anything is degrading. Both times I morphed, he's had to help me return to the real world—a fact I hate deep into the depths of my soul.

Skirting the last hill, the rear of the academy comes into view.

"Steel, head to the med wing," Deacon orders.

Steel throws up a hand to let Deacon know he's heard him and plods ahead, his strides quickly eating up the space between him and the school's side entrance. The wooden door creaks when he shoulders it open and disappears without a backward glance.

"I need to talk with Sable," Deacon explains before following in Steel's wake.

Thank goodness.

My bones ache and my muscles shake from fatigue and leftover adrenaline. All I want is to find my pillow, kiss it, and sleep for a couple of days.

Rounding the corner of the mammoth building, I plot a course for the main entrance. It isn't until I'm standing at the bottom of the front steps that I notice a figure. She's curled in on herself, her head bent over something and leaning against the pillar that supports the archway.

Nova hasn't seen me yet, and for that I'm glad. It gives me a beat to collect my thoughts.

She's been a ghost the last few days; when I've spotted her, she's disappeared again before I could reach her. If I was lucky, I'd catch the withering glare she'd lob my way before she vanished.

I want to believe her absence is coincidental, but I know better. Something is off.

I study Nova as I scale the stairs, forcing one foot in front of the other. I long to talk to her as much as I dread it. Since the day two weeks ago that Steel announced his intention to watch over me, there has been a wall between us. Until I find out exactly why, I'm never going to be able to kick it down.

Her feet are resting on the top step and she's hunched over a book or a pad of paper in her lap. The pencil in her hand drifts in lazy arches, making me think she might be drawing. Her hair is twisted up in a messy knot at the top of her head. Her fingers and the bridge of her nose are smudged with black, and she wears plain black leggings and a muted blue puffy coat that hides most of her curves.

Not her usual posh style, but she doesn't look bad, she

looks . . . comfortable. I'm pretty sure it's impossible for Nova to look anything less than crazy gorgeous at all times.

I'm three steps below her when she lifts her head and our eyes connect. Her green cat-eyes widen before they narrow to slits.

The crack from her pencil breaking in half echoes off the academy's exterior walls and slaps me in the face.

Tipping whatever she was writing to her chest, she rises in a liquid motion and shifts away.

"Wait. Please."

Nova's hand pauses against the door. Her fingers curl against the grain as if she's holding herself back from clawing at it . . . or maybe she's imagining it's me.

"Nova, let me . . ."

Let me what, explain? How can I explain when I don't truly understand the issue? Maybe she simply needs reassurance that there's nothing going on between me and Steel?

I finally worked up the nerve to ask Ash what the deal was between Nova and Steel, but her knowledge of their relationship was murky. Sterling was zero help—just recited some platitudes about the "heart wanting what it wants" and "fighting for love." I'd really like those five minutes of my life back.

Only Greyson gave me any real insight into the situation. Steel and Nova have been close for years. He thinks they had something on-again, off-again a few years back, but as far as he knows nothing has been officially "on" for a while. It's common knowledge that Nova is into Steel, but Greyson made a point to mention that Steel isn't the type to broadcast his personal business, so the true nature of their relationship is anyone's guess.

It sounds like a complicated situation to me, but I'm stunted when it comes to things like romance and relationships. Heck, basic social skills are a challenge for me most days. It feels like I'm going into this whole situation with Nova with one arm tied behind my back.

After several tense moments, Nova does an about-face and plants her fists on her hips, a thin notebook still clenched in her right hand. Her left hip juts to the side as her chin tips up. The stance is signature "Nova", but her usual fire doesn't reach her eyes. Behind the bravado, she looks worn out. "What do you want?"

"I want . . . to make sure you're okay?" That wasn't supposed to be a question.

"I'm peachy. Thanks." Every word is drenched in sarcasm.

I have to crane my neck to maintain eye contact. Standing a few stairs below her, Nova now has at least a foot and a half of height on me. She's at the perfect level to kick me in the face and send me tumbling down the hard and unforgiving marble steps.

I shift to the right and ascend to the top landing—just in case.

"Nova, I'm not sure exactly what's going on here," I admit honestly. "But I'd like to make it right."

"Would you now?"

Isn't that just what I said? "Um, yes?"

"And how exactly do you intend to do that?"

Good question. I'm too new to friendship to understand all the rules. Be honest, but not brutally so. Be sincere, but don't let yourself be taken advantage of. Be accepting, but don't be afraid to call someone out on their crap.

"Um. Are you upset about Steel?"

Her eyes flare and the fire that was absent from her gaze just moments before sparks to life. I want to tiptoe into this topic, but there's not a great way to tackle the issue that doesn't involve bluntness.

"There's nothing going on between me and Steel. You know that Sable is making him hang around me. I'm pretty sure he's at the point where he'd walk away from guard duty if he could. It's wearing on both of us."

If all this angst is stemming from her anxiety over Steel's feelings toward her, I feel doubly bad for her. I'm not a relationship specialist by any stretch of the imagination, but whatever she has going on with Steel doesn't seem healthy. Whether he is ignoring her feelings willfully, or due to ignorance doesn't really matter. The point is the ambiguity in their relationship is causing her pain. I want better for her. If I was in her situation, I'd want better for myself as well.

"You're unbelievable. Do you know that?"

"Um." That was not meant as a compliment.

"Gosh." With a humorless laugh and a shake of her head, she pirouettes back toward the door, ready to push it open. "Not everything in the world is about you."

Wait . . . huh? Jerking back a step, I teeter on the top stair before righting myself and lurching forward. I snatch Nova's designer coat-clad arm and whirl her around. "Nova, I'm sorry I don't understand what—"

She rips out of my grasp. "You're right, you don't understand. Because *you're* not the one who's been made a fool of. That would be *me*." She points a finger at her chest and her lower lip wobbles before she bites down on it.

Is that a tear, or is frosty air making her eyes water?

"I'm . . . I'm sorry."

"You're sorry? That's just great. That makes everything better." She crosses her arms over her chest and her lids flutter, but no moisture leaks from them. "I'm sure that will make all the whispered gossip about how I keep throwing myself at Steel disappear. And I'm sure that will make people just forget about how desperate—" The words catch in her throat until she clears it. "How desperate I've looked trying to get his attention."

My heart aches. Nova isn't truly angry at me, she's angry at herself. I don't know what I can do for her. I can't reverse time and undo her actions. Regret is an emotion that sits heavily on even the strongest of us.

"No one thinks you're desperate."

She purses her lips and shoots me a stare that says she doesn't believe that. Reassurance isn't what she needs right now, but what else can I give her?

"What can I do?"

She's silent for several heartbeats before speaking. The guarded way she looks at me is laced with vulnerability. "You know what you can do for me? You can be honest with yourself. Burying the truth isn't helping anyone."

Wait . . . I thought this wasn't about me.

"I'm not blind." Genuine hurt is splashed across her face. I hate that I did something to cause that emotion. "I can see there's something between the two of you."

"Mutual dislike and distrust?"

"Very funny." Annoyance slides back over her features, wiping away any vestige of vulnerability.

"I wasn't trying to be," I grumble under my breath.

Nova arches a perfectly plucked eyebrow. "You can't

honestly tell me you don't feel anything for Steel. That there isn't any part of you that wants to call him your own."

I open my mouth to answer and the memory of the spectrum world appears. Some part of me does consider Steel "mine." It's a part I'm trying to extinguish, but it's still there.

Shoot, maybe I haven't been truthful about my feelings. But even if there are twinges of emotion toward Steel, who says I have to act on them? Last time I checked, free will was still a thing.

I suck my bottom lip into my mouth, wracking my brain to figure out a way to explain a situation that I don't fully comprehend myself.

Nova scoffs, not waiting for me to work out my internal thoughts. "Yeah, that's what I thought."

"It's not as simple as you're making—"

The doors behind Nova fly open and Ash spills out. Her eyes are as wild as a frightened filly's as she takes both of us in. "Have you seen the twins?"

"Greyson and Sterling? Not since second period." Has something happened to the brothers?

"No, Blaze and Aurora. They're missing."

"What do you mean, they're missing?" Nova demands, instant concern tweaking her features.

"Yeah, what she said," I add.

"No one has seen them since mid-day. They never showed up to their classes in the afternoon. The teachers thought they were messing around in one of the academy bunkers—apparently they think it's funny to hide in them—but they've all been checked."

"Well, they have to be somewhere around here, right? They wouldn't have left the building, would they?"

"Ha." Nova's laugh is devoid of any real humor. "You obviously don't know the youngest Durand twins very well. Those two can find trouble anywhere."

"It may be nothing, but the eastern wards are down. They may have fallen by accident, but considering that . . ." Ash digs a hand in her hair. "It just doesn't look good."

The eastern wards? That's the direction Deacon, Steel, and I just came from.

"We were just out that way. We didn't notice anything unusual. Has anyone searched the grounds yet?" Evening has succumbed to full night. Light halos the academy, but beyond the glow, darkness reigns. "Could they have phased? Maybe they're hiding in the other realm?"

Searching both the mortal realm and the spectrum world will take twice as long. But if they did phase, someone could walk right by them without noticing. It's like being invisible.

"That's actually where most everyone is already searching. Considering the recent Forsaken attacks, everybody is a bit more concerned than normal."

A crash on the other side of the doors causes me to start. Ash and Nova both whirl in the direction of the noise, arms raised and ready for a fight.

"I don't care if I'm injured," a voice bellows from behind closed doors. "I'm going to find them."

So, Steel knows about the younger twins.

The doors burst open and slam against the exterior wall of the academy. Steel marches through the opening, tugging on a clean shirt, Greyson and Sable hot on his heels.

I backpedal several feet to get out of their way.

"Steel, get back to the med wing immediately," Sable demands, but he stomps down the steps without heeding her.

His face and arms are wiped clean of the mess of rock and blood from our sparring session, but I caught a glimpse of his unbandaged wound when he pulled the long-sleeved shirt over his head.

Greyson lays a hand on Sable's arm. "I'll go with him. He'll be all right."

"He doesn't even know where to start looking. Not to mention he's going to die of exposure if he goes out like that. If he'd just take a few moments—"

"No!" Steel pivots and charges back up the steps, getting in Sable's face. "A few moments was probably all it took for someone to snatch them. They could be—" I must have made a sound because Steel's head snaps in my direction.

"You." He points a damning finger at me and I shrink back. Rage sheds off him in palpable waves. "This is your fault."

"Me? What did I do?"

"Existing is enough."

Something pierces my chest and I glance down, sure I'll find a sharp object protruding from my heart and my lifeblood spilling to the ground. I'm confused to discover I'm unscathed.

"The Forsaken are here for you. I knew it was only a matter of time before someone got caught up in your mess. I knew it!"

"Steel. Enough!" Greyson shoulders his brother to the side and comes to stand in front of me. "He doesn't mean it. He's just scared."

"I knew this would happen," Steel spits before storming down the steps and into the night.

"Steel, wait!" Greyson shouts and races after his brother.

Sable watches them leave with her fingers pressed against her lips.

"Emberly, I'm so sorry." She starts to apologize, but I hold up my hand to stop her flow of words.

Turning from her, I walk woodenly to the open doorway.

"I'll come with you," Ash offers, but I wave her off.

"No, it's important everyone look for the twins right now. I'll help once I've changed into something warmer."

I have to skirt Nova to escape. Her gaze bounces between me and the black night, her mind most likely trying to make sense of the events that just unfolded. Someone who cares for me wouldn't have spoken to me like Steel just did.

I ache for her to know the truth, but it will come out soon enough. I'm only just barely holding pieces of myself together and need some privacy to superglue my fragmented soul.

Without a backward glance, I tuck tail and jog to my shared dorm room. Finding a book bag, I cram a pair of jeans, two sweaters, and some essential toiletries into it.

That's enough. I've lived on less.

Shedding my training clothes, I don the warmest outfit within arm's reach. It ends up being the only pair of jeans I have that don't have holes in them—Ash only purchased one pair of those online—and an itchy wool sweater.

Grabbing an insulated coat out of our shared closet, I set out with two goals: find the youngest Durand twins, then leave Seraph Academy for good.

28

The snow isn't merely dusting the ground, instead, a thick blanket of white covers the terrain.

My feet sink into the softness as I slog on. Without the ability to phase properly, I'm relegated to the mortal realm to search for Blaze and Aurora.

The vast majority of students and teachers are searching in the spirit realm. Unsanctioned phasing isn't allowed for first-year students, but apparently sneaking off to the spectrum world is one of the twins' favorite pastimes.

What has everyone worried today is that they've been gone for so long. In the past, the twins' disappearing acts have flown under the radar because they weren't caught until they were already back. The very fact that it's so obvious they're missing is what has everyone concerned.

That, paired with the dual attacks from the Forsaken this month, of course.

Glacial winds slap my face as I plod through the mountain

wilderness. I hike my shoulders up around my ears, refusing to let the elements deter me.

I search for Blaze and Aurora for over forty-five minutes—the last fifteen without any evidence of human life besides the footprints I leave in the snow. Between the wind and the fresh fall, those markers are starting to disappear as well.

Stopping, I turn my back to the wind, letting the heavy pack I carry buffer some of the gusts. With only the full moon to guide me and snow falling heavily now, it's hard to see more than a few feet in each direction.

The moon's light is mostly obscured by the storm clouds. My enhanced eyesight doesn't help much.

Cupping my hands around my mouth, I shout. "Aurora! Blaze!"

The sound is swallowed by the abyss.

I hold my breath and strain my ears to pick up any sound, but can't hear anything past the howling wind.

I was traversing east, toward the breach Ash mentioned. But setting out on foot by myself is beginning to feel foolish.

Inside my boots, my toes went numb five minutes ago. I have to keep my hands jammed in the pockets of my coat because I didn't grab any gloves before fleeing the academy. The strands of my hair, damp from snow, are starting to freeze, creating hair icicles.

Nausea roils in my gut.

If I'm this frozen after less than an hour, and with a decent amount of cold weather protection, the twins could very well be popsicles by now.

What would keep them from returning to the warmth and safety of the academy?

As much as I want to believe they're simply playing a bad

joke on everyone, I can't. To willingly remain out in this weather, they have to be hurt or trapped somewhere.

Or worse.

Guilt froths up from my core and overflows.

Logically, I know it isn't my fault if the Forsaken have captured the siblings. I have no idea why the dark creatures are after me and it's not as if I ordered them to snatch anyone. I hate that Steel is blaming me for the academy's current monster issues.

And yet, part of me agrees with him.

If it turns out this hunt for the twins really is a mission to rescue them from those creatures, I have no doubt Steel will lay the blame at my feet. Of course, I was ignorant of the threat, but he can make the argument that I had a hand in these sinister events, even if it was unintentional. And I'm not even sure I'd blame him anymore.

The dark thoughts steel my resolve to leave after the twins are found. Things will go back to normal for everyone, and that's for the best.

My eyes burn and mist. I tell myself it's just a reaction to the sting of frozen air.

Okay, Emberly, suck it up. You're going to keep searching until the twins are safe, or your nose falls off from frostbite. Whichever comes first.

You're going to stop feeling bad for yourself and do what you need to do. You've been on your own before—you can certainly do it again. Going back to your own life will be safer for you and everyone else.

My pep talk keeps me lumbering forward. I pause every five minutes or so to call out the twins' names, but am only ever answered by the elements. It's not long before I reach the timberline and the evergreens and aspen trees disappear, opening up to a sprawling white tundra.

My trek becomes somewhat of an uphill climb, and I bat around the idea of turning back. After all, I'm not doing much more than aimlessly wandering the mountainside, hoping I'll stumble across the missing children.

My plan was ill-conceived, at best, but my pride—and real fear for the twins—won't allow me to give up.

The freezing temperature paired with my exhaustion must be playing tricks on me, because the next time I scan the area, I catch a glimpse of a trail of . . . glitter?

Is that . . . fairy dust?

I blink, certain the moonlight is bouncing off the snow at a weird angle, but then the streak of sparkles appears again before curving around a bend and vanishing.

I don't have the thought *not* to follow the strange light, but I should.

Is there something mesmerizing about the shimmer I'm helpless to resist? Has the numbing cold frozen a few brain cells too many? Or is it just a bout of poorly timed curiosity?

Whatever the reason, I don't stop to ponder my motivations as I stumble after the bizarre light.

My feet sink into the deep snow all the way up to my knees, and my eyes water from the sting of crystals that strike my face. A gust of wind pushes against me, as if warning me from going further.

When this is over, I'm going to have to seriously consider moving somewhere tropical. The freezing mountain temperatures, mounds of snow, and unrelenting gales are really getting old.

I reach the bend in the mountain face where the fairy dust

disappeared. Taking a deep breath of mountain air, I peek around the corner.

A vertical rock wall and about twenty-four inches of a crumbly footpath are the only things there—that is, besides the straight drop down.

Don't do it, Emberly. Don't even think of it.

I chew on my lip while my survival instincts fight with my protective instincts. The latter are ones I didn't know I had until recently, but turns out they are strong. Only a crazy person would step out on that ledge to follow something they *might* have seen. But there may be two children waiting for rescue on the other end of that trail.

I already know which appeal will win, but it takes a few moments to gather the courage to step out on the narrow ledge.

Edging forward, I hug the rock wall—literally—and move one inch at a time.

The bottom drops out of my belly when a blast of wind pummels the rock face, sending my hair blowing in all directions.

My heart pumps the blood through my veins so quickly, the tips of my ears warm.

Bits of stone and dirt dribble down on me from above. The rough rock bites into the pads of my fingers and cheek as I smoosh them against the lifeless mountainside and wait for the gust to pass.

I may be made of tougher stuff than the average person, but I'm not immortal. At least, not completely.

This is a stupid idea. This is the king of stupid ideas. You're an idiot of the highest order, I silently berate myself as I shuffle along the path.

There's a good chance that by now the twins have been found. They're probably warming up in the academy, regaling the students with the tale of their adventure while the teachers try to decide on a solid punishment for them.

Yet here I am, practically scaling the side of a mountain, pursuing Tinker Bell with only a trail of fairy dust to guide me.

My foot slips on a patch of frozen ice and I fall to a knee. Loose stones barrel down into the dark abyss below me and my stomach heaves into my throat.

I need to turn back. This is too treacherous. One powerful gust and I'll be engulfed by the harrowing pit of darkness below.

I carefully adjust my body in the other direction, planning to trek back the way I came, when a glimmer of light dances in front of my face.

Jerking back, I slam my uncovered head on the wall of rock and ice hard enough to scramble my brains. An instant headache blooms from the point of impact. Its fingers grip my skull and squeeze.

Reaching back, I prod the injury, wincing when I come in direct contact with the tender area. My fingers come back wet with crimson blood.

Great, just what I need. A head wound while free-climbing a mountain in the middle of a growing blizzard on an ill-conceived rescue attempt.

I am a genius.

Just then, the metallic sparks zoom in front of me another time. They loop and soar and spin. The effect against the backdrop of falling snow is dizzying, and I squeeze my eyelids shut.

"All right, I get it. I can see you. Enough already."

Slowly opening my eyes, I find a ball of flickering lights about the size of my fist hovering in the air several feet away.

Its sparks quiver and shoot in all directions, like a Fourth of July sparkler. Crystal flakes whip in a vortex around the little ball of light, but it doesn't move.

It's like the thing is staring at me. It's beginning to creep me out.

"I'm just gonna head back that way." I jab a thumb behind me and shift, ready to get the heck out of Dodge.

The ball flies right at me, vibrating in front of my face.

With a squeak, I fall back on my butt. One of my legs skids along the path and dangles over the edge.

I wrench it back, contorting my body so that it is fully resting on solid ground.

The sparkler flutters in jerky motions, its color changing from metallics to an angry red.

The little thing is obviously agitated.

Picking myself—and my dignity—off the ground, I start to edge in the direction I'd been going and the little sprite, or whatever it is, seems to calm down. Flying in front of me, it lights and guides the way. Every so often, it jets out ahead of me, then comes back to make sure I'm still following.

Its mannerisms remind me of a family dog in one of my old foster homes. He behaved similarly when he wanted you to follow him. The light even bounces, reminding me of the dog bounding through a field.

"Is Timmy stuck in a well, girl?" I ask.

The spark, which flickers red before returning to its white-golden color, ignores my question and continues leading me farther from safety.

Eventually the narrow path along the cliff's edge just disappears. There's nowhere else to go except up or down.

Down is a straight drop who knows how far. I can't see the ground in the moonlight.

Up is a severely sloped climb I'd only attempt with the right gear and a safety line.

"All right, little dude." The spark is zipping around me in an obvious attempt to keep me moving. "This is the end of the line."

I'm shuffling backward, determined to ignore the sparkler this time, when it swings around my body and nudges my butt.

"Whoa."

The thing is corporeal.

Swatting at it with my hand when it comes back for another shove is useless. The little gnat is speedy—and strong. It drives me forward a half-foot and I almost lose my balance.

"Cut it out! You're going to make me fall!"

It zips around me and rests on the perfect handhold only a foot out onto the cliff.

This little guy actually wants me to scale a mountain . . . in the middle of the night . . . during a snowstorm . . . in boots!

It drops down about five feet and rests on another small ledge—somewhere I can place my foot. Then it flies into the air and circles my head.

My head throbs. I open and close my fists a few times to make sure my hands are still working. Without gloves, I lost feeling in them ages ago. I really hope I make it out of this situation with all my appendages—even the minor ones.

"Oh, I just followed some fairy dust up a mountain." I place my hand on the hold I've been shown. "No big deal. I wasn't doing anything important so I figured, 'Hey, why not? I haven't had a life-threatening event in a few days.'"

Taking in a deep breath of crisp air, I shift my weight onto the foothold and pray I don't plummet.

"What now?" I ask the flying nuisance.

For the next ten minutes, the little light bounces from spot to spot on the mountainside, showing me exactly where to put my hands and feet. Eventually, we reach a plateau. I throw my body on it and lay my forehead to the snowy ground.

Have I ever been so excited to be laying on the frozen earth before?

I think not.

My limbs are jelly.

How I managed to make that climb without accidentally phasing is a mystery. My body shakes with the aftereffects of the adrenaline rush.

When I get my breathing under control, I crawl toward the rock wall. The plateau is shaped like a triangle with stone shooting up on two sides, and a scary drop straight down on the short end. It's like someone cut a pie-slice out of the mountainside.

Shuffling forward on my hands and knees, I tip my head up and squint into the night sky.

Just how high do these cliffs ascend?

My hand lands on something chilled and a little squishy— that is, compared to the rock beneath me.

A lump is blanketed in a fresh layer of snow in front of me. When I brush some of the loose snow away, a hand is revealed.

Yelping, I fall back on my butt. Luckily, that part of me is half frozen, so I hardly feel the bite of the unforgiving ground beneath me.

There is a person buried under there.

A dead one from the looks of it.

I can't detect any movement from the mound that indicates the person is breathing.

Working up the courage to take a closer look, I notice that only about an inch of snow covers the body, so it can't have been here long.

I don't know what to do.

Would ignoring it make me a horrible person?

The annoying sparkler swoops in and flits over the lump, hopping up and down on various parts of the body.

I swat it like a fly. Its actions seem disrespectful.

The little nuisance doesn't appear to have liked that and rings my head like a pixie on Red Bull before zooming back and forth over the frozen person.

"You have *got* to be kidding me. You want me to touch it?"

The sparkle stops on what I assume is the head and doesn't move.

Is it trying to stare me down?

"This day just keeps getting worse," I grumble as I creep forward.

Grimacing, I stretch out a shaky hand and wipe some of the snow away, revealing an expansive upper back and broad shoulders.

Definitely a guy.

Don't think too hard about it, I coach myself as I continue to dust the flakes off the body.

I leave the head until last. He's facedown and I'm more than a little worried his face went *splat* when he fell, which won't leave much for anyone to identify . . . and will be super disgusting.

Nephilim or not, crushed faces are not something my stomach is equipped to handle.

Stalling, I let my eyes sweep the poor dude.

This guy might be an angel-born. He definitely has the build. Clad in only dark jeans and a long-sleeved shirt, he isn't wearing a coat. Who would wander the Rockies in the winter without proper gear?

My gaze drifts to his feet. The furthest point from his buried head, and my pulse starts to drum triple-time.

Oh, no.

Shooting forward, I clear the whiteness away from the person's head. The icicle-encrusted head of black hair is exactly what I don't want to find.

Grabbing his large shoulders, I heave the body over and look down onto Steel's frozen face.

29

Steel's face is a sickly shade of bluish-white. His eyelids are closed, his lashes frozen into spikes.

I press one of my icy hands to my mouth and the other against my middle to hold myself together and the screams in. A bead of moisture slips from my eye and slides halfway down my face before freezing on my cheek.

I have to check to make sure he's actually dead . . . but I don't want to.

The stupid glitter bug is back and this time it actually pulls my hair, jerking me forward and over onto Steel's cold body.

It's like laying across a giant ice cube. The chill from his glacial flesh seeps into mine.

Squeezing my hands between us, I push off him. My weight forces the air from his chest, which escapes his nostrils and mouth as white mist and is accompanied by a low moan before he falls silent again.

That was because I pressed on him, right? Fresh corpses still make noises, don't they?

I'm not sure. Everything I know about death is limited to the few *C.S.I.* episodes I've watched.

I know dead bodies can fart, so maybe they can fake breathe too?

Bending forward, I place my hands back on Steel's chest and heave. His body rocks from the chest compression and another breath of foggy air seeps out of his mouth.

Leaning over him, I place two fingers on his throat and search for a pulse. Not feeling anything, I tilt my head and press my ear to his chest.

I think I hear a sluggish thump.

Snapping up, I search the area.

If Steel is still alive, he isn't going to be for much longer. It will be a miracle if his heart is still pumping. Maybe somehow the hypothermia has kept him alive?

I can't see all the way to the back corner of the precipice, but at the very least, back there we'll be protected from the wind.

Snatching Steel's arms, I drag him away from the cliff's edge and toward the area where the moonlight doesn't penetrate.

Blinking, I will my Neph-sight to kick-in and adjust to the low light.

It's so dark.

And so cold.

A shudder wracks my frame.

Rubbing my shoulder against the wall for direction, I haul Steel's body back into the cradle of the mountain.

Stumbling when the wall falls away, I drop Steel's heavy weight, but remain standing.

"What the . . ."

The darkness blinds me, so I use my hands to feel the shape of the stone structure I've toppled into.

As far as I can tell, it is a small cave about eight or nine feet in diameter. It's a giant ice cream scoop hole in the mountain.

My stomach rumbles, reminding me I haven't eaten since the day before. Ignoring the physical discomfort, I pat the ground, searching for Steel. I find one of his arms and tug him into the enclosure.

Now that we're somewhat sheltered from the elements, I sink to my knees.

Steel is still deathly cold. He needs to be warmed up, but I have no idea how. I don't have anything with me to start a fire. And even if I did, there's nothing except dirt and stone in this hovel. I have no kindling or wood to light.

The flying sparkle drifts into the cave with us. Its brightness reflects off the smooth stone walls, and for that I'm grateful.

Starting at his arms, I peel Steel's ice-crusted shirt off and lay it flat on the ground. Hopefully the Colorado air will dry it out a bit now that we are protected from the snowfall. Maybe I can get that sparkly thing to heat it up?

Turning back to Steel, I swallow a gasp. His chest is an expanse of blue-tinted, polished marble, the wound he sustained during our sparring session only a thin white line on his whiter chest. If I didn't hear his lethargic heartbeats myself, I would swear I'm looking at a corpse.

Tugging my bag off my back, I pull the meager amount of clothes out. They'll never fit him, but at least they aren't wet or frozen like Steel's clothes currently are.

I yank the largest of the two sweaters over his head and fit one beefy arm in it. He's too broad to get any more of it on him. I tug the excess material as far as possible over his chest, but it only covers one of his pecs. I wrestle his other arm into the second sweater and drape the loose fabric over his exposed skin.

Focusing on the task keeps my mind from dipping into a dark place. Seeing Steel so vulnerable and perhaps close to death causes panic to churn and boil in my belly. But I have to hold it together. His life is on the line.

Sitting back on my heels, I survey my handiwork.

Steel looks ridiculous with the fuzzy pink and gray fabric laying haphazardly over him—but so what? At least most of his flesh is covered.

Now for the lower half.

Without thinking too deeply about it, I undo his jeans and slide them off along with his socks and shoes, placing the garments on the ground next to his shirt.

Keeping my eyes fixed on my task, I stretch a dry pair of my socks over his giant feet. No way am I getting my spare jeans up his legs.

I shake out the thin blanket I had rolled up in my pack and lay it over his waist and legs.

"Why do you have to be so stinkin' big?"

His feet poke out from the bottom of the covering.

I twist my fingers together and saw my teeth over my bottom lip. The wind screams and forces a handful of flakes into our sanctuary. The flying sparkler swoops down and hovers over Steel's body, surveying my sloppy efforts. It stops in front of my face, as if asking for an explanation.

"What else am I supposed to do?"

The little imp flies around me and shoves me forward. I

270 | JULIE HALL

land sprawled on top of the frozen Neph. The pads of my fingers connect with bits of exposed flesh.

Shoot. Body heat. That's Wilderness Survival 101.

Grumbling, I shift off Steel. Wadding the last bit of my clothing—an extra pair of jeans—into a ball, I lift Steel's head and shove the pants under him. Climbing back on his prone form, I wrap my arms around his shoulders and coil my legs in-between his and do my best not to notice which bits of me are lined up with his.

"If you live through this, you owe me big time. By my count, this is the third time I've saved your life. I'm going to start a tab for you."

The light flits around the cave for a few minutes before settling on the ground on top of Steel's discarded clothes, and then it dims.

"Mood lighting. Awesome."

The dryness of my tone would be stronger if my teeth weren't chattering. Cozying up to a frozen Steel is like trying to warm an ice sculpture.

My cheek rests half on my pink angora sweater, and half on his chilly skin.

His heart continues its sluggish cadence. It's the only assurance I have that he hasn't passed yet.

I will it to keep working.

Closing my eyes, I try to pretend I'm somewhere else. Somewhere toasty warm. The shudders that wrack my body make the illusion particularly hard to conjure.

How did I find myself in this position? Aren't I smarter than this?

I survived the harsh world for over seventeen years without a soul truly looking out for me. I used to think I was street smart, but listening to my teeth chatter while I'm trying to warm up an unconscious half-human, while trapped on a deserted mountain, makes me second guess that assumption.

"Follow Tinker Bell on a free climb. Yeah, seemed like a good idea at the time."

The twinkly ball of light vibrates and glows red before dimming out again.

"Touchy, are we?" I ask.

It darkens even more, dipping our temporary shelter in shadows.

That's fine with me. I thrive in the shadows.

My lids slip closed, exhaustion or hypothermia forcing them shut. At the moment, I don't really care which one it is, since it causes my muscles to relax and the tremors shaking my body to abate.

The skin beneath my cheek isn't warm, but it also isn't as cold anymore.

As my mind starts to wander, I allow it to reach for the darkness. Maybe when consciousness returns to me, I'll discover this has all been a nightmare.

That is as good of an explanation for this predicament as any other.

Just before I'm engulfed by sweet oblivion, I send up a silent plea for the half-dead man beneath me.

I may not like him, but some part of me is strangely protective of him. There is a connection between us neither of us wants to acknowledge, but a buried part of me knows I'd never recover from his loss.

"Mmmmm," I cuddle into the warm rock beneath me and ignore the crick in my neck because the heat is delicious.

Something jabs me between the ribs and I twitch away from it. With closed lids, I reach a hand down to massage the sore spot, only to find myself poked on the other side.

"Ouch!"

Curling on my side, I slip off my perch and bounce on the uneven ground. The blow shocks me fully awake.

Snapping my eyelids open, I see my reflection in a pair of teal-colored orbs.

"What happened?" Steel's sleep-soaked voice rumbles.

A breath catches in my throat.

"You're alive. I mean, you're awake."

I curl to a sitting position.

Using his arms for support, Steel slowly rolls the top part of his frame so he is sitting as well. He grits his teeth and squeezes his eyes shut, depriving me of that lovely Caribbean ocean blue.

"Yeah, I'm awake . . . and alive."

With his eyes still squeezed shut, he cranes his neck from side to side. The cracking vertebrae echo off the enclosed space around us. Bringing a hand to his head, he itches the back of it before opening a lid and eyeing the pink sweater wrapped around his bicep. "What am I wearing?"

Folding my arms over my chest, I lift an eyebrow. "Angora. It's very warm. You should be grateful I grabbed that one instead of the cotton knit."

Baring his upper teeth at me, he lets me know he's not amused. A look of disgust washes over his face as he surveys the rest of his body from his chest down to his toes.

"Did you take my pants off? Am I wearing your socks?"

It's obvious I did and he is, so I don't answer.

Cocking his head, he levels me a look of disbelief.

"You undressed me and tried to put your clothes on me?"

"You were a human icicle when I found you. I thought you were dead. Besides," I wave an unconcerned hand through the air, "everyone knows you have to get out of wet clothes to warm up."

"Is that also why you were just snuggled up on my chest?" The smile curling his lips is wicked. "To warm me up?"

"Of course! Why else would I be laying on top of you?"

His full grin speaks volumes.

"You wish, dude. You're a grade-A jerk. The only reason I climbed on you was because it was life or death."

"You're saying you climbed on top of me because you would have died if you hadn't?"

"Stop twisting my words . . . and being gross."

I struggle to my feet and then cast a glance around the enclosure, looking for my tiny sparkling friend. Light trickles in from the cave opening, so it must be morning. The little sparkle pixie is nowhere to be found.

Weird.

Steel lets out a series of pain-filled grunts and groans behind me.

Checking over my shoulder, I see that he's managed to lumber to his feet. He is casing the ground—probably looking for his clothes—as he holds the small blanket around his waist. It covers even less of him while he's standing, showcasing his bare shins and ankles.

I face forward to laugh into my hand. I choose to ignore the rustling behind me, assuming Steel is struggling into his own clothes.

"How did you get here anyway? Besides being frozen, I didn't see any injuries."

The cave gets uncomfortably quiet. I'm about to spin around when Steel's question brings me up short.

"Just how closely did you check me over?" The deep timbre of his voice is filled with suggestion.

"Steel," I warn as I slide a hand into my hair. It gets stuck halfway down its length. Yuck, I really need a shower. "Just answer the question."

A pair of lazy snowflakes dance in the air outside the opening of the cave. The morning air smells fresh, like pine trees. I hope it isn't still snowing.

"At least they're dry."

Huh?

Irritated, I spin. Steel is yanking his shirt over his chest. He'd already tugged on his jeans.

My clothes and the blanket lay haphazardly on the ground at his feet. I bend and collect the items, shaking them out before rolling and cramming them back in my bag.

"How did we both get here?" Steel demands.

"That's exactly what I wanted to know."

Lifting my chin, I shoot Steel a glare hot enough to melt metal. It's lost on him though. His gaze is far away.

After almost a minute, he blows out a frustrated breath of air and gruffly replies, "I'm not sure."

"You're not sure?"

Straightening my legs, I stretch to my full height. In the close quarters, I'm forced to tilt my head upward to search his face.

"You must have fallen at least a hundred feet, maybe more.

You're saying you don't remember how you ended up on top of a mountain? You don't remember how you almost died?"

"Stop being so dramatic. We're hard to kill."

A spark of panic fizzles high in my belly. "Someone was trying to kill you?"

He waves his hand through the air. "Figure of speech. So, what happened to you?"

"I followed a sparkling light. I tripped on your mostly frozen and completely snow covered body and dragged you in here."

"You followed what?"

"A floating twinkle light. I thought it was leading me to Blaze and Aurora. I was pretty bummed when I ran into you instead."

Steel twitches when I mention his siblings; his back goes ramrod straight and his fingers curl into fists.

"Right, I have to get out of here."

He marches past me and out of the cave. I blink after him before coming to my senses.

"Steel, wait up." Reaching forward, my fingers wrap around his shoulder. He dislodges me with a sharp jerk.

"Stay out of this. You've done enough."

The knife he stuck in me yesterday twists. The pain causes me to fumble a step before righting myself.

He's being a prick and I know it. But knowing that doesn't stop the internal bleeding.

"Why do you keep treating me like the enemy?"

We reach the spot where I found him, not that it's easy to tell. The wind and snow covered the tracks I made the night before.

Steel's head angles back and he examines the cliffs jutting upward.

"Listen, it's nothing personal." He tosses the comment over his shoulder as he moves toward the edge of the plateau.

"Excuse me?" I mirror his steps, resentful of how flippantly he is treating his dagger-filled words. "How could it not be personal? You've blamed me for everything bad that's happened since you kidnapped me and dragged me to Seraph Academy. You've belittled me, treated me like garbage, and taken every opportunity you can to tell me I don't belong with the other Nephilim. Tell me how any of that isn't personal."

I see a flicker of regret twitch across his face when he shifts in my direction, but then he turns back to his task— whatever that may be.

"It's just the way it has to be."

My feet plant and my eyes track his movements as he slowly walks the perimeter of the plateau.

That's really all I'm going to get out of him?

It's just the way it has to be?

Am I of so little value as a person?

I press myself back into the shadows. Their dark arms are always there, waiting to comfort me. It's where I belong. Hidden from view. Watching from the shade.

"I found it."

"Found what?"

"Our way out of here."

30

*R*eaching a shaky hand up, I grasp the last handhold. My leg muscles bunch as I heft myself up and over the crest, flopping face-first onto safe ground.

My limbs, now reduced to Jell-O, burn with exertion.

My lungs heave air in and out, stirring the fresh powder stacked on the ground.

Super-charged muscles or not, that climb was challenging.

With a grunt, I hear rather than see Steel reach the top. He isn't breathing like an overused racehorse, like I am, but scaling a few-hundred-foot vertical cliff can't have been easy for him, considering his bulk.

"Remind me why you didn't just phase and then fly up here in your Big Bird form?" I flip over, the bulge of my pack making the position uncomfortable.

Steel stands on the edge of the overlook, feet shoulder-width apart, arms at his sides, and scans the surrounding area.

"Why didn't you?" he throws back. The acid of his words doesn't melt his icy tone.

"Pfft. Like that needs an explanation. I couldn't."

"Well, there you have it." He grumbles as he stomps past me.

I clamber to my feet and chase after him.

Everything is white up here, except the sky. Last night's snowstorm cleared the clouds, making way for the perfect bluebird day. Another time, I might appreciate the beauty of the powder-covered mountain range yawning before us. But with the possibility that Blaze and Aurora are still missing, my insides clench with apprehension.

"You can't phase?" Painful pinpricks jab at my heart, encouraging the beats to surge.

Steel's shoulders hitch up around his ears. His back muscles contract under his long-sleeved Henley, which is currently plastered to parts of him by sweat.

His non-answer is answer enough.

"Why not? And since when?"

Steel's lips remain sealed.

Why does it always have to be one of two ways with him? Either he's saying things I don't want to hear, or he's not talking when I want answers.

Lurching forward, I snatch his forearm.

Steel releases a frustrated growl and lifts his captured arm in the air, almost taking me with it. I relinquish my hold and straighten my spine, needing every inch of my height to stand up to him.

"And while you're at it, you can clue me in on where we're going. Should we start digging for your sister and brother in all this fresh snow? Because in case you haven't noticed, they aren't here." I fling both my arms wide. My words bounce off the peaks around us and echo into nothing. "There's nothing here!"

"You are such a pain in my—"

"Steel," I warn. "Don't even start with me. Just answer the questions."

Heated air pours out of his nostrils like an angry cartoon bull. It curls in the air around his face before evaporating. I half expect him to transform into his bull form at any moment. I take a half-step back, just in case. I don't want to get squished under the girth of a Steel-cow.

For a long minute, I'm sure he's going to shove past me and continue his random search in the frozen wasteland. Instead, he bites his bottom lip in a move that's all aggression before pulling the abused flesh into his mouth to suck away the sting. His gaze ticks away from me to land on the horizon.

"I've been trying to phase since the moment I regained consciousness. I haven't been able to . . . and I don't know why." It's like the words have to be dragged out of him, kicking and screaming.

"What about this morning is different?" I wonder aloud. "Wait, you were going to phase when I was sleeping on top of you? Were you going to just dump me on the ground and be on your way?"

Popping his jaw, Steel grabs the back of his neck with both hands and looks skyward. "Is that really what's important here?"

"Okay, fine. Not important . . . you turd." I can't help but sneak the insult in at the end. "And you have no idea why things are different this morning?"

"Maybe even since last night. But I can't remember, so . . ."

As Steel's words taper off, his molars grind together. I wince at the noise. It's almost as bad as nails on a chalkboard.

Admitting flaws, even ones out of his control, isn't in Steel's nature. I imagine confessing them to me, in particular, is even more painful. I try not to enjoy his discomfort too much.

"What was the last thing you remember from yesterday?"

Yesterday. Yuck. That was a bad day. Don't want to visit those memories myself. They carry a bundle of hurt.

I tell myself the sting I feel inside is from the cold. It's an easy lie to believe.

A gust of wind picks up some of the snow and whips it in a tornado around us. Winter's chilly breath blows against my neck. After pulling the sleeves of my puffy jacket down to cover my hands, I cross my arms over my chest. It helps keep me warm.

"The last thing I remember was . . ." Steel scours his fingers against his forehead as if he can scrub the memories back into existence. "Getting into a fight with Grey over," his gaze clicks over to me before dropping to the ground, "a disagreement. And shifting—"

Steel snaps his head up and zeroes in on something over my shoulder.

Twisting, I search for whatever has grabbed his attention. There isn't anything there except snow, ice, and rock.

"What?"

"I shifted into an eagle. I was tracking something from above. Maybe I didn't fall after all." With that he takes off, using Nephilim speed to his advantage. The snow is up to our knees in some places, but Steel's pace never slows.

My bag beats against my back as I struggle to keep up.

Coming to an abrupt stop, Steel becomes an immovable statue—a dark slash against the white backdrop.

A strangled sound squeezes its way out my throat a moment before I face-plant into Steel's solid back. "I think I just broke my face on your shoulder blade. Do you have metal plates back here instead of muscles?"

My fingers rise to inspect my sore cheekbone. That may swell. Maybe I should put a handful of snow on it?

"Steel, do you realize I smashed right into . . .?" My words trail off when I finally look at Steel's face. His alien-blue eyes are focused on something in the distance, his expression so stone-still, it reminds me of how I found him the night before.

A horrible shudder, borne from more than the icy air, dances through me.

Rather than speak, I search for whatever has so thoroughly captured his attention. I have to drop my line of sight before I notice anything.

Deep, deep, *deep* in the valley, a cabin is tucked between the folds of two mammoth mountains. A thin tendril of smoke snakes out of the small dwelling's chimney.

Thank goodness for that or I wouldn't have seen it. As it is, I can only make out some of the green tin roof and brown log siding—and that's using every bit of my Neph sight.

My first thought is that it's built to blend into nature, but that isn't unusual for this part of the country. Lots of homes are built using natural elements and the colors of the Colorado countryside. Besides being located in a remote area, there doesn't seem to be anything particularly noteworthy about the discovery of the cabin, but Steel is fixated on it.

"It's probably just a local."

My words are heavy with sympathy. I'm worried Steel is

hanging all his hopes on that one small cabin. There are lots of people who choose to live in the backcountry, away from the general public.

It doesn't make sense for Blaze and Aurora to be there. If they went out on their own, how could they have found the cabin? And if they've been taken—as we all fear—won't the kidnappers be long gone by now?

"Perhaps we should—"

"That's what I saw last night." His jaw is set. His attention hasn't shifted from the cabin, as if he'll be able to see through the walls by sheer force of his will.

"I thought you didn't remember anything?"

"I remember that cabin. Blaze and Aurora are there."

Squinting, I shift my focus back and forth from the unassuming cabin to Steel's profile.

I have doubts. Big ones. But what are the chances Steel is going to listen to me?

"If they're really there, maybe we should go back and get some help," I offer tentatively, rubbing my hands together for warmth and to cover nerves. "If someone really has taken them, it's probably going to be a bigger fight to get them back than the two of us are prepared for."

Twisting toward me, Steel enters my space.

"Yes, by all means. Go back, Emberly. Get help. I'd love that." He throws a heavy arm in the air that falls back to his thigh with a slap. "Mind giving me directions? Because I made a straight line as a bird flies. But I'm sure you were keeping track of your route during the blizzard."

Dang it. He's right.

I know the general direction I need to head—I think—but don't know exactly where to go. It's not as if there are marked roads out here. Only obstacles stand between us and the academy. Mountains, trees, streams, snow, rock, ice, and wildlife.

"We're at least ten miles from the academy. I know how I got here. Mind telling me how you did it?"

"I . . ."

I have no idea. Ten miles. How did I hike that far without realizing it?

Not to mention scaling a mountainside in the dark during a winter storm. The whole thing seems impossible, and that's after I experienced it firsthand.

Steel gives me a wide berth as I mentally run over the events of the night before.

He marches ahead, a man on a mission.

"Steel—" I start after him.

"We can't get back the way we came, so there's only one path from here anyway." He doesn't break his stride or turn his head to talk to me. "Your only options at this point are to freeze or follow me."

"Let's just take another moment to think this through."

"Do what you want. I really don't care." The bite in his words brings me up short. "But I'm going down there."

31

*I*t doesn't take long for Steel's large form to disappear. The mountain begins to slope downward a few hundred feet away and once he reaches that point, his broad shoulders bob below the white line of separation and I can no longer see him.

I stand where he left me for a long while.

Numb.

Vaguely, I wonder if I stay here long enough, will my legs grow roots and plant into the soil buried beneath the layers of snow? A part of me secretly hopes they would. It would be a relief to know that the curse of my life—always running from someone, or watching them leave me—would be at an end.

If my own parents didn't stick around, why do I think anyone else will?

I tell myself it doesn't matter what Steel says or does, but it's a lie. Somewhere along the way, I started to care—an affliction he obviously doesn't suffer from as well. He easily dismissed me and walked away without a backward glance. He's not concerned if I make it back to safety. He all but told me it would be impossible, and then just left.

The wind at the peak picks up and throws chunks of my hair every which way. Its chilly fingers absorb whatever warmth my body creates and carts it off.

That's fine. I want my skin to mimic the cold inside.

Steel may have reached the valley below, but I can't tell. The evergreens surrounding the cabin are too thick for me to see anything between them.

Besides, I don't want to wonder about someone who regards me as little more than a nuisance on a good day, and trash that should be disposed of on a bad one.

Squeezing my lids tight, I command my mind to blank— for my subconscious to go somewhere else.

Anywhere else.

To travel to the dark place inside that is so deep, so far away from this world that nothing real matters. Because when nothing matters, there's no way to get hurt.

I'm just entering my Zen-zone when brightness flashes behind my eyelids. My eyes instinctually open.

The flying glitter-bomb is back, weaving drunken circles in front of my face. I bat the annoying creature away.

"I don't want anything to do with you or your crazy plans."

The sparkles spitting from the little entity take on a reddish hue, and it circles my head, dive-bombing me every few rounds.

"Cut it out!" I shout, ducking and weaving out of the demented creature's way.

Getting behind me, it whirls like a tornado, spinning right

for me. I dive out of the way, only to watch it jerk and circle back at me.

It zips back and forth, once again reminding me of an impatient puppy on a leash.

"I'm familiar with that move. I'm not following you this time. I don't care who's lying unconscious." I brush loose snow off my legs and shake the white specks out of my hair, then get to my feet. Swiveling in the opposite direction, I take off.

I only make it several steps before I'm jerked off my feet . . . by my hair.

"Ow!"

I pitch backward into the snow.

In a fluid motion, I stand again and start chasing the sparkler down the steep mountain, screaming obscenities at it the entire way.

"You psychotic pixie! You'd better pray you're only a figment of my imagination or I'm going to trap you in a mason jar and use you as a flashlight."

The stupid thing keeps zipping out of my grasp. Reaching down, I grab a handful of snow and chuck it at the flying light —and miss it by a mile.

"Or better yet! I'm going to pin your wings to a bug board and leave you in the science lab!"

The light stops mid-flight and hovers twenty feet in front of me.

I use every bit of that space to try to brake, as I slide down the slippery slope, grabbing for purchase the entire time. A small evergreen finally stops my momentum. Or maybe it's the top of a big tree. I'm not sure.

The little sparkler grows into a baseball sized mini-sun. Its edges blaze red, its center blinding yellow. It's now a pulsating orb of aggression.

Oh, shoot. I took that too far.

I crab-walk backward to put space between myself and the fiery creature. My arms sink into snow that is well past my elbows and my feet slip out from underneath me.

Double shoot.

"Okay, Tinker Bell. How about we both simmer down a bit? You know I'd never actually trap or tack you to anything, right? We're buds, aren't we? Friends don't pin other friends to things. Or, ya know, fry them with magic glitter dust. That's not something you can do, is it?"

The red and yellow ball drops to the snow and returns to its smaller, less threatening size. It also changes back to its buttery gold color.

My fingers unclench as my breathing evens out.

Note to self: Do not piss off Tinker Bell.

Beyond the creature, the tree line slashes a hunter green border against the sharp white topography. Without realizing it, I traversed down the top quarter of the mountain.

The slope behind me is steep. It would take the better part of the day to get back up to the top.

I hang my head in resignation. Lifting my hand in the air, I wave it around like a dead fish.

"Okay, you win. Lead the way."

The light leads me down the rest of the mountain, zigzagging me back and forth so I don't have to free-climb to reach the valley. The sun hangs heavy in the western sky by the time the ground levels out and the timberline begins.

Without hesitation, the sparking brightness flies right into the forest. With a heavy sigh and my head tipped skyward, I follow the creature into the woods.

Eventually, we come upon a set of fresh footprints that I hope are Steel's. When that happens, my guide disappears into the foliage and doesn't come back.

Steel has a significant head start on me, but I don't know what else to do but follow the breadcrumbs. After the first hour of walking, I lose feeling in my fingers and toes and hope they're all still attached. I'm beginning to wonder if there will be permanent damage if I keep this freezing and thawing out routine up.

I stop once to drink the remainder of the water I put in my pack and eat one of the granola bars. If I don't find shelter soon, I'm going to be in trouble. Angel-born aren't impervious to injury or the elements, it just takes us longer to succumb to them.

My body is already showing signs of wear and tear.

Trudging through the forest, the snow isn't quite as deep as on the mountain slopes. A lot of the crystal flakes are caught on the tree's piney branches, weighing them down so they bow under the heavy loads. Every few minutes a clump of wet slush falls from a tree, hitting the covered ground with a *plop*. Besides that soft sound and my labored breathing, the woods are silent.

As the day grows old, I feel every degree drop in temperature. Jeans are a horrible material to wear in the cold, and my legs join my hands and feet in numbness.

I've always had such a good sense of self-preservation, but

the moment I set out on this quest to find the young Durand twins, it's as if I chucked all sense out the window. If only I could return to that moment when I made the hasty decision to trek after the missing kids. I'd . . .

I'd what?

I'd probably make the same decisions, even knowing where it landed me. Maybe I just would have walked in a different direction? But then I wouldn't have stumbled across a half-frozen Steel.

It's a conundrum that occupies my bored and sluggish mind as I plow forward.

Hours tick by slowly. I convince myself I've missed the cabin—there's no way it was this deep into the trees. I fell, tripped, and slipped down the mountain quickly, but this trek through the forest is never-ending.

I'm so tired. Maybe I'll take a short break?

I sit on the ground, my teeth chattering and every inch of my body vibrating to generate heat. I resist the urge to lean up against a tree. The wells around the bases of the trunks are deep; it will be like being sucked into quicksand if I try to rest in one. The ground will swallow me whole.

Snow-covered branches and a purple-and-blue bruised sky come into view.

Curious . . . when did I lay down?

The ground is heating up, I'm sure of it. My teeth stop banging together and a delicious warmth melts my frozen bones.

My lids droop and take an eternity to flop back open.

I'm sure if I close them for a bit, it won't be an issue. Nothing bad ever happens when someone falls asleep in the snow in below-freezing temperatures, right?

The lure of rest wraps me in its embrace and pulls me under.

I sigh. Finally warm. Finally safe.

As I sink into darkness, my thoughts are smudged and fuzzy.

I try to care, but I just don't.

32

*W*hack.

"Get up."

"Ash, are you kidding me right now?"

I snuggle back into the bed, dragging the cotton sheets over my head, keeping my eyes sealed shut. It's a crime to leave the softness of this amazing bed.

Whack. whack.

The pillow doesn't hurt, but it's supremely annoying.

"Ash! I'm going to flush your tea collection!"

Throwing the covers off, I come up swinging, only to wave my arms through empty air.

My breath catches as I soak in my surroundings. The stacked log wall beyond the foot of the bed is utterly unfamiliar. My eyes trace the line of the rounded planks of timber to a small gray stone fireplace. The bare mantel is a lacquered slice of tree. A red-framed print of llamas in a field hangs above it.

Weird.

Four split logs are set in a tee-pee against each other in the hearth, fire licking up and down the crackling kindling. A mound of firewood sits in a neat pile on the worn red-stained hardwood to the left of the fireplace.

"Finally." Steel's deep voice sounding over my left shoulder gives me a start.

Not Ash after all.

He drops a white-cased pillow on my lap and walks to the kitchenette on the opposite side of the one-room cabin. Steam spits out of the spout of a teapot resting on the stove.

Taking a rag, he grabs the handle and pours the boiling water into two mugs. The tag of a teabag flops over each rim.

"What happened?"

I cringe when the words leave my mouth. I sound like a damsel in distress, prone to fainting spells—but my mind is a foggy mess.

"Found you lying in the snow, half-buried and mostly frozen." His head inclines toward me so I can see his profile. A shadow of a smile curls the corner of his lips. "I guess this means we're even."

I remember sloshing through the knee-deep snow in the tree-rich valley as I followed a pair of footprints I hoped were his. I also remembered the cold that burrowed through my clothes and latched onto my bones. The last frost-laced memory of the journey is me laying on the ground and thinking a nap was a phenomenal idea.

I moan, pressing my palms against my eye sockets.

"I must have had hypothermia. Sleeping seemed like a good idea at the time."

Gosh, sometimes I'm really stupid.

I slide my legs out from under the covers and drape them

over the side of the single bed, only to yelp and shove the lower half of myself back under the blankets.

"Where are my pants?" I squeak.

"Oh yeah." He's turned away from me, but even an idiot can hear the humor laced in his words. "We're even about that as well."

Seeing my jeans folded over a crooked wooden chair not far from the foot of my bed, I throw an angry look in Steel's direction. Too bad he's not looking.

Since he's busy in the kitchenette, I take the opportunity to make a grab for the discarded garment and then dive back under the sheets.

Squirming under the covers, I punch each leg into the appropriate holes in the fabric. When I'm done I peek out to find Steel standing in front of me, holding out a steaming cup of tea.

Grasping the warm mug between my hands, I breathe in. It smells like Christmas. Cinnamon, nutmeg, and a hint of orange. My favorite.

"I found some honey to sweeten it, but there isn't much else here."

Scrunching my nose, I bare my teeth at him. This doesn't mean he's forgiven for the pants trick. Unimpressed, he settles into a high-backed chair behind a two-seater wood table several feet away. There is definitely a lumber theme going on in this place.

He stretches his legs to the side of the table. His oversized form dwarfs the cabin that only holds the one twin bed I'm sitting on, a bistro table and two chairs, and a loveseat situated in front of the fireplace.

Steel sips his drink, his body angled toward the fire instead of me. I take a moment to trace his profile with my eyes. A chunk of his blue-black hair rests against his forehead and brushes his brow. The straight line of his nose is only broken by the smallest of bumps at the bridge. His full lips create a double ridge, the bottom bump slightly larger than the top. The cut of his jaw is an almost-perfect ninety-degree angle from his chin to the lobe of his ear.

He really is beautiful. That is, when he's not talking.

Turning my attention back to my hands, I blow over the surface of the spicy drink before taking a tentative sip. The liquid slides down my throat, heating a path to my stomach.

Despite the fire, the cabin air is still chilled with winter's bite. Wrapping my free arm around myself, I watch the butterscotch-colored tea swirl.

"How did you find me?" I finally ask.

The sound that emerges from Steel is a bit like a laugh, but off. "I imagine the same way you found me." Lifting my gaze, I find his pinned on me. "Flying sparkly creature. A bit of an attitude. Sound familiar?"

Ahh . . . "Tinker Bell."

Steel's eyebrows arch. "Seriously? What if it's a dude?"

"What if it's a figment of our imaginations?"

He tips his chin in concession and then takes a slow drink from his steaming mug as he continues to regard me over the lip.

"I knew you were following me. Once I found the cabin, I was on my way back for you anyway when *Tinker Bell* helped me locate you faster." A softness leaks into Steel's gaze that I know I'm not imagining. It's a bit like a layer of his armor has melted away. I wonder if he realizes it? He's not the type to let anyone see his soft underbelly, most of all me. Which means it's probably unintentional. "I know what I said before was . . . harsh. I was frantic to find Blaze and Aurora. I *am* frantic. But I'd never . . . or at least you should know . . ." He squeezes his lips together, obviously frustrated he can't find the right words.

"I wouldn't actually let anything happen to you." He finally shoves the words out, breaking eye contact and looking everywhere but at me.

Maybe he's suffering from a head injury? That's a definite possibility.

I clear my throat for no other reason than to break the tension. "How long have I been out?"

Steel rolls the ceramic between his hands as he looks to the front door. "About ten hours. I found you some time in the middle of the night." His attention swerves back to me. "I got tired of waiting for you to wake up."

Standing in one fluid motion, he strides a few steps to the kitchen sink and places his cup in it.

"So you decided the best way to rouse me would be to hit me repeatedly with a pillow?"

The muscles beneath his shirt bunch as he grabs the edge of the sink and casts a glance over his shoulder. "It worked, didn't it?"

I force a short burst of air from my lungs in a mock laugh. "What, you didn't want to kiss me awake?"

Rotating, he leans back against the counter, arms crossed over his chest. A slow smile spreads across his face. "How do you know I didn't try that first?"

It's not until my fingers brush my lips that I realize I've raised my hand. Snapping it down, I clear my throat. An unwanted blush creeps up my cheeks.

I hate it when he messes with me.

"Right." I play it cool as I place my half-empty mug of tea down on a tiny one-drawer nightstand, paying unnecessary attention to its woodgrain surface. "Did you find anything before you found me? Any sign of Blaze or Aurora?"

Flint sparks in Steel's teal eyes and his face hardens, draining the levity from his expression. Beams of sunlight shine through the hazy half-window above the sink behind Steel's head—but shadows block my view of most of his face when he tips his chin down. Moving with the speed and stealth of a panther, he's at the rickety front door within a half-second and shoving on a pair of clunky snow boots.

"Finish your tea and grab your stuff. We have to go." His voice drops an octave and warns against disagreement.

"Wait, what? Now? We?"

Sliding off the bed, I search the rust-stained floor for my boots while Steel thrusts his arms through the sleeves of an ugly brown hunting coat I'm positive I've never seen before—

I'd have remembered something that fugly.

Finding my footwear under the bed, I bounce on one leg and then the other as I struggle into each boot.

"Hurry up." Steel's impatient command irks me, and I straighten my spine. So much for whatever moment we may have been having. King Jackass is back.

"Hold on a second. You can take two minutes to explain to me what's going on here."

I'm well acquainted with the aggravated look that pinches his features. He shoves a frustrated hand in his hair, fisting the strands before letting his arm drop heavily to his side. His eyes dart to the window and then back to me.

"Fine. Come here." He strides forward and pulls a wrinkled

piece of paper out of his pocket. Dropping it on the table, he smooths it out and jerks his chin in my direction as if to ask, *what are you still doing standing over there?*

I move so I'm standing beside him, looking down at the aged paper. It's browning and torn around the edges; if I had to guess, I'd say it was torn from a larger drawing. The crinkles on the paper distort the aerial view of the mountain range it depicts. The highest peaks are represented by blobs of white surrounded by green.

"What exactly am I looking at here?"

"It's a piece of a topographical map of this area."

"Yes, I figured the map part out, but how do you know it's of this area?" Turning my head, I watch Steel closely. His gaze sweeps back and forth over the piece of map that can't have been bigger than the size of my spread hand. "There isn't any writing."

"I can read a map."

"This could be any part of the Rockies. It could be a different mountain range all together. Are you planning on using this to get back to Seraph?"

"I flew over this area—I know it's where we are. But even if I didn't, look at this."

I lean over to see the exact spot Steel points to. At the tip of his finger is a dot of red, not much larger than the head of a pin. Easy to miss.

"This is where we are," he announces before sliding his finger over a couple of inches and indicating another spot on the map with another pinprick of red. "And this is where Blaze and Aurora were taken. And we're going to go get them."

33

Steel's hunched shoulders bob up and down with every step he takes. I stopped trying to figure out exactly where we're going an hour ago. Steel is convinced the ripped piece of map he discovered crumpled on the floor is a message from Blaze or Aurora.

I'm not so sure.

It's a stretch to believe that they found a map, ripped off the exact piece of it that showed where they were and where they were going to be, or even that they'd known the plans of the people who'd taken them. And that's also assuming they were kidnapped at all—which we still aren't sure about.

My only comfort is that since Steel and I have both been gone for a couple of days, the academy is probably searching for us now too.

My boredom leaves me counting snowflakes that dribble through the thick canopy above and land on Steel's dark head. I'm on flake number forty-three when he breaks his silence.

"What made you think to bring the pack? Were you planning on getting lost?"

Steel has hardly spoken to me in the last two hours, which was also about the time we left the rustic comfort of the tiny cabin. When I'd pointed out there weren't any footprints in the snow, he'd only grunted and mumbled something about the storm and fresh snowfall and set off without a backward glance.

The bag he asked about lies heavy against my back. I shift the straps before answering him. He's going to find out sooner or later . . . or we're going to freeze to death. Either way, there's not a reason to keep my intentions hidden.

Paying special attention to placing my feet in the prints Steel leaves, I answer him.

"After we find Blaze and Aurora, I'm gonna take off. I was just getting a head start on the packing."

The sound of crunching snow under Steel's heavy footfalls ceases. Pulling up short, I lift my eyes in time to see him twist. A scowl covers his face.

"You're leaving Seraph Academy?"

"Yes."

"Where are you going?"

He takes a step closer, and I don't like the proximity. His fists open and close, and I get the feeling he's stopping himself from reaching out and shaking me.

"Emberly . . ." There's a warning in his voice.

"I don't know, Steel. I'll figure it out. I always do."

Uncomfortable with the conversation, as well as Steel's intensity level, I brush past him, but only make it a few feet before he stops me. The straps of my bag dig into my shoulders when Steel pulls on it. He just as suddenly lets go again.

"Whoa!" I stagger a few steps before righting myself and then rounding on him. "Geez! What is your problem?"

"My problem?" He takes a menacing step forward, forcing me to back down. "My problem is that my sister and brother have most likely been kidnapped by Forsaken, or worse. Your problem is that you have a death wish."

"Death wish? What are you talking about?" I throw my hands in the air.

"Leaving the protection of the Nephilim would be suicide."

"Now who's being dramatic?" I spit at him. "I'm not trying to get myself killed. I'm just trying to get away from you!"

"There are smarter ways to go about that than running away." Steel's top lip curls. The sneer on his face drips with disgust.

Spinning, I march off, uncaring if I'm heading in the right direction.

"I cannot even believe we're having this argument," I yell over my shoulder. "You've been trying to get rid of me since practically the moment you flew me off that parking garage. You should finally be satisfied, not berating me."

Catching up to me, he grabs hold of my bicep and twists me around. I rip from his grasp.

"Stop doing that!" I demand.

He pushes a hand through his snow-speckled hair, melting the flakes caught in the strands.

"Yeah, I want separation between you and my family. You're a danger magnet. I *have* to protect them." An edge of desperation coats his words.

"My point exactly. You should be thrilled. I'll finally be out of your hair. This is just what you wanted."

"I don't want you to get yourself killed, either!" he roars at me.

I blink up at Steel, who is once again in my personal space, almost toe to toe with me. His breathing is elevated and his pupils are blown out.

"What is going on right now?"

I'm honestly perplexed as to why he is so agitated. This is what he wanted. He hasn't been subtle about his desires. He's been pushing me toward the academy front door for weeks now. I didn't anticipate this reaction at all. I expected a moody "It's about time" from him, not this emotionally charged beast panting in front of me.

"Why are you acting like this? This makes zero sense."

"Just . . . ask for a transfer or something. There are other Neph academies all over the world. Choose one of those. I can't handle thinking of you that exposed." Steel's words come out in an explosive rush and with an intensity that gives me pause. He seems wrecked, but for the life of me I don't understand why.

In contrast to the anxiety pouring from Steel, I speak my truth slowly, a soothing note attached to each syllable I utter. Instinct poking me to handle this situation delicately.

"I can handle being alone. It's been that way my whole life."

"Well, *I* can't handle it anymore."

A strong hand wraps around the back of my head and tugs me forward. Steel's frost-chilled lips cover mine. His cinnamon taste and all-male musk cocoon me in a Steel-only bubble. I have a foggy notion that I shouldn't find dude sweat so appealing, but goodness help me, I do.

In a split second, the deepest thoughts my brain produces are things like *whoa* and *yum*.

Steel's mouth moves over mine with just the right amount of sweetness laced with passion. There can't have ever been a more perfect kiss than the one we are currently sharing.

I may not be experienced at this kissing thing, but I know enough to know he does it well—or rather, *we* do.

He swallows the tiny noises that bubble up in my throat, sounds I don't even understand.

It's like he has a sense about when I'm going to come to my senses because the pressure changes a moment before I'm about to break free from the delicious mind-fog his touch creates.

He drags me back under, every time—and I can't muster the will to care.

For these moments in time, I exist in a Steel-centered world.

His taste, touch, and smell are the only senses my body registers. The cold is no longer a factor as blood pumps double-time through my veins.

His tongue traces the seam of my mouth, and I tip my head back farther, granting him entrance. His hand tightens against my rib cage.

It feels like a claiming.

I want it to be one.

Plop. A cold pile of slush lands on our heads and slides down our faces, forcing us apart. The wet snow—it must have fallen from an overhanging branch—sneaks into the back of my coat and traces frozen fingers of ice down my spine.

The Steel-only bubble bursts and the rest of the world rushes in. And not only the crisp snap of the frosty air on my skin or the pine smell in the air, but the very real memories of how Steel has treated me. The harsh words. The cold shoulder. The way his actions and words have cut me over and over again until I felt lower than low. Even the look on Nova's face the last time I saw her.

I lurch away from him, a hand held up in front of me to ward him off.

It looks like he's debating going back in for round two.

"No! You do *not* get to do that."

My breath comes out in short pants. My body's betrayal stings my pride.

I may be embarrassingly inexperienced with guys, but I have enough self-respect to know that I shouldn't lip-lock with someone who treats me like Steel does. Heartache and low self-esteem are the only outcomes of our toxicity. Loneliness isn't a good enough excuse. Behavior like this will only drag my self-worth to a new low. Realizing that makes my animosity ramp to a new high.

"You don't get to do that!" I screech again. The hand suspended in the air between us shakes.

The volume of my words—that or the crazy-eye I'm no doubt sporting—penetrates Steel's lust-soaked brain. He stops looking at me like I'm a tasty piece of cake and takes a step back.

Something akin to pain washes over his face as his boot sinks into the soft snow. He lifts a hand to rub his forehead, only to drop it a moment later and give his head a violent shake.

"It's the dream. I've been half out of my mind ever since I started having it. I can't get it out of my head."

"A dream? You're blaming your erratic behavior on some nighttime hallucination?" I intend for my words to pack more of a punch, but the curveball Steel just let loose has weakened my resolve. What could his dreams have to do with me?

Fine lines grow at the corners of his eyes and his forehead is ridged with worry lines.

"I didn't know." His pleadings make no sense.

"Didn't know what?"

My tremors have stopped, but they seem to have transferred to Steel. His hand shakes as he shoves it back into his thick hair and fists the strands so tightly the skin pulls at his forehead.

I have an urge to soothe him, but I bury it.

"I didn't know she was you until that first time. Until you morphed, I thought they were only dreams."

Whoa.

"You had a dream . . . about me?" The words leave my mouth on a whisper. I'm not sure I want the answer to that question.

"No." His eyes blink shut. "I didn't have a dream, I'm *having* dreams. And they won't go away. And every time I have another, I feel compelled . . ."

I hang on his every word, involuntarily moving a step closer. The wind picks up and hits me like a wave, snapping me out of the trance.

"I don't think I understand. Compelled to do what?"

"It's like I'm bound to you, against my will."

His hands reach forward, but he stops himself and stares down at them as if they don't belong to him anymore before letting them drop to his sides.

"I don't have room for this in my life. I can't—I won't—let this get in the way of my obligation to my family. I already let them down once. I won't do it again."

I stare up at him, reeling from these new revelations, wholly unsure of my feelings on the matter. Unsure of his as well.

Taking a deep breath, Steel fixes his emotional armor back in place. It's like watching the life drain out of his body while something else—something false—takes its place. Like he's a cyborg rather than a living, breathing, feeling person.

"Listen, I never wanted you to know about them, okay? Let's just forget I said anything."

A short laugh bursts from me.

"You want me to forget you're having dreams about me that are so potent you think they're overpowering your will? Yeah, I don't think so, buddy. You should have told me about this a long time ago. I could have helped you figure them out."

"Let's go. We're wasting daylight."

And just like that, Steel shuts down on me.

Turning, he stomps into the forest. And a buried part of me is glad. That part of me knows I'm not ready to deal with all the layers that make up Steel.

A stoic Steel, I've learned to handle. A vulnerable one . . . no, I don't truly want that. Because I know a Steel that pricks my heart will cause it to bleed out.

34

*S*teel is the most infuriating, most annoying, most contradictory person to ever walk this earth—human, non-human, and half-human included.

Okay, yeah. I can admit I don't really want to delve into his inner workings, but a bit of conversation won't kill him. Or better yet, maybe we can talk about how we are probably just walking in circles and not getting any closer to finding the younger twins.

He trudges forward like the machine he is, one foot in front of the other, pace never wavering. Meanwhile, my semi-frozen limbs started to make me trip and stumble two hours ago.

Evening comes early in the mountains, and even more so in the winter; the dwindling light has me seriously concerned. If we hope to survive the night, we need to find shelter. And soon.

I'd tried to bring up the topic several times in the past

thirty minutes, but Steel only ever responds with a grunt or non-verbal wave. As if I'm a peasant he can dismiss.

The man is insufferable and probably going to be the death of us. Which is almost humorous considering how he reacted to the idea of me leaving the supposed safety of the academy.

Maybe he just wants me to die on his terms?

"Stop."

Steel's clear command brings me up short. I don't like how quickly I snap to attention from just a word uttered from his lips. My mouth pinches like I sucked on something sour.

Nope, don't like that one bit.

I don't say anything—a silent rebellion I'm hoping gets under Steel's skin.

"Look." Another one-word command.

My fingers curl inward, nails cutting into my flesh.

There's a flicker of light in the direction he wants me to look. I squint, using every ounce of my angel-born eyesight to make out what lies in the distance.

"What is it you think we're looking at?"

Steel's eyes are laser-focused on that one spot.

"It could be them."

I soften my voice. Steel is hanging a lot on the notion that one of his siblings left a secret message for him. "Or it could be someone living in the mountains. Maybe we even managed to make it to a small town in the area? It may not be them at all."

At some point I laid a hand on his bicep without realizing it. He looks down at my fingers and then lifts an icy-aqua glare to my face. I pull my hand back as if burned.

But that's Steel, isn't it? Icy cold, or burning hot. There

never seems to be a middle ground for the two of us. We only operate in extremes.

"We should check it out."

"Sure."

What else is there to say? We're headed in that direction whether I agree with the decision or not.

If we're fortunate, we may come across someplace with a phone. We can call Seraph Academy and get picked up.

I still hold hope that the twins were found a few days ago and this whole jaunt has been for naught. I'd like nothing better than to find that they've been safely tucked in their beds at the academy while we froze in the forested wilderness.

As we draw closer to the flickering light, the trees thin. Through them, I can make out the base of a shear rock face. Night is almost upon us, so the details of the stone wall are smudged.

Like a lot of the mountains in the Rockies, I can see the stacked layers of rock and sediment, as well as veins of minerals running diagonally throughout the cliff. But the colors and the details in the stone are hidden in shadow.

Even though sparsely distributed, the trees grow right up to the base where stone juts up from the earth. We pause several hundred feet away and do our best to hide behind the thin trunks of some aspen trees.

The light we're stalking is a lantern hung on a metal peg above the entrance of an old mine shaft. Not at all what I expected or hoped it would be.

From what I can tell, it's an old oil lantern. A lamp like that would need to be refilled to keep light burning, meaning there must be someone—or something—nearby.

I'm about to ask Steel what he wants to do when the

trickle of voices reaches my ears. It isn't until two figures emerge from the hole in the mountain—carrying flashlights and, unlike me, decked out in weather-appropriate apparel—that I can decipher any words.

My fingers press into smooth white bark as I strain to pick-up their conversation.

"This had better work."

"I'm over this assignment already. If that white-and-red-haired freak doesn't show up soon, I'm just going to kill them and say they died in an accident."

White-and-red-haired freak . . . that must be me.

"I'd think twice before I did that, if I were you. This order came straight from the top."

"If it were up to me, I just would have smashed her on the head and taken her. I don't know how Ronove screwed up so badly. She's just one girl."

Ronove. Shoot. Yep, they're definitely talking about me.

Steel has clearly made the same connection. Tension is etched over his face and his fingers white-knuckle the bark.

He stands behind the tree closest to me, but that's still fifteen or twenty feet away. His shoulder width is easily three times that of the skinny aspen he hides behind, so he has to twist to the side to cover more of himself.

We're both sitting ducks.

"Let's just get this sweep over with. A few more days of babysitting and I'm sure they'll abandon this plan."

"Guess she wasn't as attached to the shape-shifter as they thought. Maybe their intel is going bad?"

"Let's hope not. I'm dying for a fresh kill."

The Forsaken separate, each walking the line of the cliff's base in opposite directions. I assume they're going to loop around and search the forest eventually, so we are officially on a clock. These trees won't hide us from prying eyes.

Once the Forsaken are out of sight, Steel appears at my side.

"They're in there."

I nod. "Yeah, I figured that as well. And . . ." This next part is hard to get out. Not because of my pride, but because it hurts that it's true—that those two innocents were taken because of me. It's a horror I don't want to let myself believe, but it can't be denied.

"I'm so sorry." I flick my gaze to the ground, unable to look Steel in the eyes when I admit it. "You were right. Blaze and Aurora were taken because of me."

Eons pass before Steel speaks.

"Let's not focus on that right now. Let's just figure out how we're going to get them out and to safety."

"Where do we start?"

Our plan is flimsy at best, but we don't have much of a choice. After going through what we both know about the situation—which admittedly isn't a lot—and facing the reality of our situation—we may not make it a full night in the elements, and the twins don't have the time for us to go back and look for help—our strategy is basically to rush into the main shaft and deal with problems as they come up.

It's a horrible plan, and we both know it.

There's a solid chance we won't make it through the night. I feel it deep down in my bones.

What we are doing is basically a suicide mission. But what choice do we have?

I never really considered I'd go down like this, especially since I hadn't known the evils that truly existed in the world. So considering that, I'm handling my demise fairly maturely. I manage to only hyperventilate when Steel's back is turned.

"You're sure you can't phase?" I ask for the third time.

His only response is an annoyed glare shot over his shoulder like a bullet. His inability to phase is still a mystery. I haven't been able to phase either, but that's not unusual for me.

I would feel a lot better going into this dark tunnel in the spectrum world, flanked by Steel's lion form.

Steel gives me the all clear sign, and we sprint toward the mine entrance.

My heart is beating so fast the blood rushing through my veins feels supercharged. This is the time I should be seeing bursts of color, but the world is conspicuously steady. I don't even know where to start on trying to guess what's keeping us from the spectrum world.

When we make it to the mine opening, and the world is pitched in darkness, I let out a relieved sigh. Something about breaking that invisible barrier allows me to relax. Although it shouldn't. We are in more immediate danger here than outside, but I feel less exposed in the shadows.

Without speaking, we shuffle along the tunnel.

The dirt crunches beneath my feet, earning me a warning glare from my companion. Wordlessly, he shows me how to cut down the noise by walking heel to toe. After that, the only thing I can hear is my own breathing, and the faint whistle of air blowing outside the tunnel entrance.

No sound comes up from the path in front of us, and that concerns me. If there are Forsaken here, wouldn't their voices travel in the rocky tunnel?

My concern balloons the longer we continue our slow progression into the abyss.

My imagination runs away from me for a bit, envisioning this trek ending in a melting lake of lava, or a weird government bunker where they experiment on captured Nephilim.

I snap back into reality and realize that not only have I not been on my guard, but I've also lost Steel.

Not a speck of light penetrates the passageway. My fingers skim over the rough cut walls of the shaft. Sediment has built up under my short nails, but I don't dare remove my hand from the only lifeline I have. I'll be walking completely blind if I do, likely to conk my head on something hard or trip on a divot in the uneven ground.

What scares me now is that I don't sense Steel anywhere. He can travel this path as quietly as a ghost, but a few minutes ago I'm sure I felt his presence. Now I don't.

Slowing my steps to a stop, I concentrate on the enclosure around me. Even though it doesn't make a difference, I close my eyes and strain my hearing, hoping to pick up on even the barest hint of sound from his feet or breaths, but I sense nothing.

That is until something warm covers my mouth.

35

"*D*on't make a sound."

Steel is so getting throat punched later for freaking me out. I thought my heart was beating hard before. I was wrong. It's like the organ has been replaced by a bass drum.

I press a palm to my chest, hoping the pressure will calm it.

With his hand still covering my mouth, Steel's warm breath washes over the shell of my ear and cheek. When he bends forward, his lips brush my earlobe.

Squeezing my eyes, I order my body not to react.

"There's a split in the tunnels a hundred feet ahead. We're going to take the path on the left. I hear voices that direction. Stay close and alert."

Steel's hand slips away from my face after I nod, and he cautiously brushes past.

I swallow a gasp when he snags my hand, engulfing it with his bear paw.

I can't say that I mind. His grip is warm and dry and comforting. I'm sure he only took my hand to make sure I don't fall behind again, but for a few minutes, I pretend he cares enough to want to offer me a small measure of comfort.

It's a silly thought, but if I'm going to die tonight, I wanted to go out with the memory of a boy holding my hand simply because he wants to. I've never had that before.

Touch is something I've always been denied. I didn't get butterfly kisses when I scraped my knee, or cuddles after a hard day at school. Unbeknownst to me, my Nephilim side was a natural deterrent to the foster families I lived with.

I haven't truly understood how much I crave skin-to-skin contact until this very moment. Something as innocent as a person holding my hand is threatening to unravel me.

I'm suddenly unnerved and unsteady in the most wonderful way possible.

When the tunnel forks, I bumble along behind Steel. The ground starts a steep decline and I'm forced to place my free hand on the craggy rock wall to keep my balance. The rocky ground below us degrades as well, slowing our decent. The air begins to feel thick, and I taste the hint of dirt on my tongue.

I decide then that I really don't like mines.

It's not long before sound tickles my eardrums. Steel was right: there is someone down here.

At first it's a barely perceptible murmur, but in time, voices float from somewhere ahead of us. But the words I detect are uttered in a guttural tongue I don't recognize.

Steel slows his steps, and I follow suit.

Within a few minutes, I catch the cool glow of bluish light.

After a dozen more steps, beams of blue rays light another fifty feet of tunnel before the path cuts to the right.

Steel halts before the turn, and I take the opportunity to catalog everything in the narrow space, Steel included.

He stands stone-still, a hundred percent of his attention dedicated to whatever lies around that corner.

The pressure of his hand around mine becomes painful. I bite the inside of my cheek and count to offset the discomfort. The lonely part of me doesn't want to sever our connection.

I get to the count of eighty-six before Steel releases my hand.

Curling and stretching my fingers several times, I try to work out the feeling of his hand on my own, as well as get the blood flowing again.

It was nice for a moment, but I don't want to remember what I'm missing.

"Stay here," Steel whispers over his shoulder.

Yeah, I don't think so.

I mirror his steps when he inches forward. When he realizes what I'm doing, he shakes his head, but doesn't try to stop me.

There is no way we're splitting up now.

As Steel is about to inch his face around the corner, one of the voices speaks up.

"Ishic favit nador!"

Whatever that means.

"Who are you calling ugly? Have you taken a look at yourself in the mirror lately?" That sweet voice belongs to Aurora.

The gasp that Steel sucks in is barely audible, but being so close, I feel as well as hear it. The intake of breath is followed by a low growl only one level above feral.

"Shut it, freak."

"Who are you calling a freak?" This time it's Blaze who

shoots back at his captor. "You and your buddy here are the most unnatural creatures in this mine."

A snarl raises the hairs on the back of my neck. It's quickly followed by the smack of flesh hitting flesh.

"Don't touch him!" Aurora screams.

Having the sense to know that Steel is about to do something very foolish, I step forward and place both hands on his back.

His body shakes in fury.

I slide my hands to grasp his biceps, not having any illusions that I'll be able to hold him back if he decides to go all Rambo on me, but I'm crossing my fingers that the slight restraint will give him a moment's pause.

Pressing up onto the balls of my feet, I rest my chin on Steel's shoulder and whisper into his ear. "Shhhhh. Bring it down a notch, Cow Boy."

Turning his head, our noses touch. He bares his teeth at me, but some of the tension eases from his body.

Mission accomplished.

Dropping down, I put space between us.

Steel presses his back to the rock wall. Resting his head against the hard surface, he squeezes his eyes shut. His jaw moves back and forth and I can see a vein pulsing in his neck.

When his eyes reopen, his irises glow teal. Fastening that blue blaze on me, he executes several quick hand movements.

Ummmmm . . . I have zero idea what they mean. Is he telling me to go long?

I'm sure there's a look of utter confusion splashed across my face and it must convey my complete lack of understanding because with gritted teeth, Steel takes hold of my head and brings his face level to mine.

"Just follow my lead."

Did he really need all those hand gestures for that simple command?

Taking a deep but silent breath, Steel turns toward the bend in the tunnel. He inches forward until he can peek around the corner. I tiptoe along with him, staying only a hair's breadth away from his back.

Without warning, he charges forward and disappears around the corner.

Crap!

This is happening—without being able to phase or a single real weapon between the two of us.

We're in so much trouble.

Steel's angry battle cry spurs me into motion. Whipping around the corner only a few paces behind him, I watch Steel race forward with the rage of a rabid animal.

Thirty feet away, the tunnel opens to a circular cavern. Stalactites hang like muddy icicles from the rock ceiling several stories in the air.

Two large, bulky figures are crouched low in the middle of the space. Their animalistic stance tells me they have to be Forsaken. Their fingers are bent and ready to attack, but in the mortal realm they don't have claws.

On the floor behind them, illuminating everything around it, is a ball of blue fire about the size of a volleyball. It's hard to see the object clearly with the two Forsaken prowling in front of it, but I'd bet my gilded armor that isn't a normal fire. It's a perfect sphere of shining light that hasn't even scorched the ground beneath it.

That's some magic fire burning over there.

Steel lets out another angry yell and the Forsaken hiss

back at him like the bottom-feeding creatures they are. As I was ogling the strange fire-orb, Steel engaged in battle.

The Forsaken saw us coming—it's not as if our ambush was stealthy—but Steel's wrath is palpable. He's going to rip the two of them apart with his bare hands, which I fully approve of. He's already bloodied one of the creatures up pretty badly.

Leaving the beasts to Steel—and forcing the strange fire-ball out of my mind—I search for the twins. They are huddled together on the opposite side of the cavern with their knees pressed to their chests. Aurora's arms are locked around Blaze. One side of his face is swollen and there's a trickle of blood flowing from his nose.

The sight of the two children causes fury to poison my blood. It runs hot through my veins, melting part of my rational being away. The familiar feeling of liquid fire races up and down my spine.

Am I phasing?

I don't want to phase. Aurora and Blaze are in this reality, not the other one.

A hot knife sinks deep into the soft spot between my spinal cord and shoulder blades. It slices downward, splitting the flesh and allowing my warm blood to run free.

The pain brings me to my knees.

I land hard, cracking bone against stone, but the sting from my fall is nothing compared to the sizzling magma racing up and down the ridges of my vertebrae.

The knife pierces me a second time and drags an agonizing trail of fire down the other side of my spine. The smell of char fills the air, and I realize the clothes are being burned from my back.

My neck cranes at a seemingly impossible angle. The back of my head skims the space between my shoulder blades and my mouth opens in a silent shriek.

The agony comes to a sudden stop when matching razors punch out of either side of my spine and my golden wings flare wide.

I'm still wearing my regular clothes—no gilded-corseted armor—just the remains of my sweater, undershirt, and coat. Only an inch of fabric wrapped around my waist keeps the top covering in place.

I spot the twins, now standing and staring at me with wide eyes.

Unfolding my body to my full height, what has happened finally hits me.

My wings appeared, but I'm still in the mortal realm.

That's not . . . It's not possible.

No time to ponder the impossibility of what's happened; I have a job to do.

To my left, Steel battles a Forsaken. He's dumped the ugly lumberjack coat and is fighting in his long-sleeved shirt and jeans.

A trio of angry scratches runs down his face from forehead to chin. They weep a steady stream of blood and he's favoring his right side, but he's doing awesome. He managed to actually rip an arm off one of the beefy Forsaken.

Nice.

The bloody stump left behind drips an oily black substance, but the creature is coming at Steel like it has two good arms instead of just one.

The other Forsaken is slumped up against the cavern wall. I'm not even sure if it's still alive.

I search the ground for a weapon, but can't find anything. There isn't even a large rock to use for clobbering.

Steel and the Forsaken are battling each other in hand-to-hand combat.

Running to join the fray, I leap on the back of the one-armed Forsaken. Wrapping my forearm around its neck, I yank back.

My wings aren't light, so my weight throws the monster off balance. It backpedals a few steps, waving its remaining arm and arm stump in the air to steady itself.

Steel delivers a front kick to its gut, sending it crashing to the ground . . . with me still attached to its back.

Ouch.

Using my wings like an extra pair of arms, I push off the rocky floor and flip us over. I shove the monster's face into the dirt.

It flops under me like a fish out of water, but I don't loosen my grip. If anything, I squeeze harder.

Something crunches under my forearm, and the Forsaken under me gurgles.

I've crushed its trachea—it's suffocating to death.

Good.

The sounds of the monster battling to suck in air aren't pleasant, but I don't feel bad.

I've become savage, unfeeling.

Eventually the Forsaken stops struggling and his body stills. Only then do I wrench my arm free and rise.

36

"*S*teel! Stop!" Aurora breaks free from Blaze and darts past me. Swiveling, I spot Steel punching the limp form of the second Forsaken. One hand is fisted in the front of the creature's bloody and torn shirt, and the other jackhammers blows to what is left of its face—which admittedly, isn't a lot.

The wet sound of flesh connecting with pulverized Forsaken face is a little gruesome, even for me.

Aurora reaches her older brother and wraps slender arms around his middle.

It takes him a moment to settle, but he finally drops the battered and broken body of the Forsaken. Taking in a shuttering breath, he engulfs Aurora's slight frame. Bloody chunks of Forsaken flesh and brain matter are splattered on the stone wall behind them, but neither sibling seems to notice the gore surrounding or covering them.

Feeling a tickle along my wings, I cast a glance over my shoulder. Blaze snatches his hand back and shoots me a wide-eyed look—or rather a one-eyed look, as his right eye is swollen shut.

"I just wanted to see what they felt like," he admits.

"It's okay."

"Those are wicked cool."

Biting a lip to keep from smiling at the awestruck look painted across Blaze's face, I fold the gilded feathers close to my body and turn, dropping to a knee in front of the boy.

"May I?" I ask before raising my hands to probe Blaze's injured face.

He lifts one bony shoulder and drops it. Standing in front of me in his thin and ripped t-shirt, stained with drops of his own blood, he strikes me as both frail and fierce. His young-boy body is all awkward angles and thin limbs, but even with a swollen face he stands with his chest puffed and legs braced apart, ready to take on the world.

He is going to be a force once his body catches up with the warrior spirit living inside.

I gently examine Blaze's face. I'm no expert, but I don't think anything is fractured except maybe his nose. There's nothing to be done about that now. A quick scan of his body assures me he's going to be just fine.

Warmth coats the backside of my body a moment before Steel speaks. "Come here, bud."

I shake my wings, hoping my body's involuntary reaction to Steel's closeness will slide off with the movement.

Blaze marches up to his brother and holds his fist out for a bump. After tapping his hand with his own, Steel wraps Blaze in a giant bear-hug—one that includes lifting the boy off his feet and a few hearty shakes.

"Steel!" Blaze squirms and bats at his brother. "I'm not a baby," he complains, sliding me a covert look.

Aurora tugs on Steel's sleeve after he sets his brother down.

"We can't stay here. There are more of them." Concern drips from her gaze as she wrings her hands.

He nods gravely. "Yeah, we know."

"And we have to take that with us." Aurora's delicate finger points to the blue fire in the middle of the room.

Steel's face is unreadable. I can't tell if he knows what the orb is or not. Without answering her, he gives Aurora a brotherly pat on the head.

When he turns to me, Steel's gaze ticks over my body, checking for injuries. I might only be seeing what I want to, but some of the tension leaves his ridged posture when he registers that I'm unscathed.

"Those are new." He addresses me for the first time since we ran into the cavern, guns blazing.

I tilt my head in acknowledgement. "Looks like I'm full of surprises."

His brow arches as if to say that's an understatement.

I don't disagree.

"We have to be ready to fight our way out."

"I just wish we had a weapon or two."

"Maybe we do." Steel ticks his chin up and cranes his neck, looking over my shoulder. "Those can't be for looks alone."

I open and close the wings, testing their weight.

"I'm not sure what I can do with them," I admit.

I can't use them to fly in an enclosed space this tiny. In this situation, their only purpose could very well just be aesthetic.

324 | JULIE HALL

"Those feathers are constructed of tougher stuff than a typical Nephilim's. Maybe you can use them in a fight."

"Maybe. But even if I could, it's not as if I have the time to train with them now."

Steel's gaze becomes thoughtful.

"Come here. I want to try something." It's as much a command as it is a request.

I clench my jaw.

His demands are getting old and we don't really have time for experiments, but arguing will only eat up more precious moments we don't have.

Tugging me over to one of the cavern walls, he motions for Blaze and Aurora to stand back before getting behind me.

"Stretch them."

Heat races to my face as I extend my wings. Steel most likely has no idea how uncomfortable it is to have him inspect a part of me so closely.

A tug is followed by a small burst of pain. I peer over my shoulder.

"Did you just pluck one of my feathers?"

It's a rhetorical question because Steel now holds a gold-dipped quill between his thumb and index finger.

Peeved, I swing around. My right wing clips his arm. He grunts and stumbles back. Moving into his space, I jam a finger into his chest.

"Hands off my wings. Got it?"

Instead of answering, Steel holds up the feather he's stolen. It's approximately a foot long and the tip gleams. Lifting his hand, he pricks his finger on the end. A bead of blood blooms.

"Looks like we have a weapon after all."

I feel extremely silly creeping through the underground labyrinth clutching a metal tipped feather as my only defense. But it could be worse. I could be Steel right now.

Not only is he holding a feather, but he has some sort of magic orb or light ball wrapped in his coat and secured under his arm. It looks like he's smuggling a watermelon.

Aurora was adamant that we take the strange object with us—to the point of growing hysterical when she thought we'd leave without it. When she mentioned the orb was preventing us from phasing, Steel finally relented.

Throwing his discarded coat over the top of the orb, he picked it up and shoved it underneath his armpit. The thick material of the ugly covering kept most of the sphere's brightness concealed, but not all of it. We use the glow to find our way through the tunnels, hoping the Forsaken on guard duty are still outside, searching the forest.

The mouth of the tunnel yawns in front of us. Silver beams of moonlight illuminate patches of the snow-covered ground outside, tempting us with freedom.

"You ready to do this?" Steel waits for acknowledgment from each of us. "Blaze. Aurora. I want you two to stay behind us. Preferably, behind Emberly's giant wings."

"I can fight," Blaze argues, "You know I can." His little boy face is hard with determination.

Steel's eyes soften. "I know you can, bro. But I want you to concentrate on taking care of your sister."

Aurora rolls her eyes, but doesn't contradict Steel's statement. After considering the request, Blaze puffs out his chest and nods once.

326 | JULIE HALL

"Let's get out of here. We could all use a shower."

He's not wrong about that.

Steel glides forward, his feet gobble up the distance to the tunnel opening. After a short pause, he steps into the night and gestures for us to follow—this time with a simple wave rather than a complicated hand signal.

With Blaze and Aurora quickly shuffling behind me, I join him.

Goose bumps break out along the exposed patches of my back. My top is still hanging on by the remnants of my sweater—thank goodness—but not much else. The unforgiving winds tug at the singed edges of my clothes and slips underneath the material. Icy coolness slithers across my skin. I'm about to wrap my wings around myself when I notice Aurora and Blaze shivering.

"Where should we go?"

I really hope Steel has a plan, because there's no way we're going to be able to get back to the academy the way we came. Especially with the young twins, who are most likely half-starved by now. We need shelter, pronto.

Encouraging Blaze and Aurora to stand beside me, I curl the edges of my wings around the three of us, hoping it will buffer some of the gusts of frosty mountain air.

Taking my free hand, Aurora smiles her thanks up at me.

"We have to find a road. We can follow it until we come to a house or gas station or something and call Sable from there."

I'm not positive we're going to make it, but I'm not about to voice my concern in front of the children. Instead I nod, knowing my assured gesture doesn't reach my eyes.

"We'll make it. We're built tough."

Steel's sharp gaze scans the trees in front of us. "I'm more concerned about avoiding the other Forsaken. Everyone on alert."

Moving as silently as we can, we strike out heading west. The only reason I know that's the direction we're traveling is because there's the slightest bit of pink beginning to brighten the sky behind us.

That's good. Forsaken can't be out in the daylight. Once the sun punches over the horizon, our concerns will be limited to the elements.

Aurora tugs on my hand and when I glance down she slowly shakes her head.

My brow furrows. I don't know what she's trying to communicate.

"The night doesn't hold them anymore," she whispers.

As soon as the words leave her mouth, the world explodes around us.

37

*J*ust because Nephilim can't phase, doesn't mean the same rules apply to the Forsaken.

That really sucks.

It also would have been a nice factoid to know before over a dozen enemies pop into existence all around us.

The Forsaken are not nearly as scary in this realm. Since most are possessed angel-borns, they retain the beauty of their host bodies—except they all have the pallid complexion of the severely anemic. The inability to withstand sunlight and a creepy dependence on other people's blood will do that to a creature, I suppose.

This group of Forsaken is a bit more imposing, though. It isn't just the number of creatures surrounding us—don't get me wrong, I don't love our four-to-one odds—it's that they've clearly come prepared for a rumble.

The Forsaken hold wicked-looking weapons in their hands. Swords with serrated edges, double-sided axes, daggers with curved blades, and even a few firearms. These are weapons Nephilim train with, not ones Forsaken fight with. From my limited experience, and from what I've learned at Seraph Academy, the Forsaken favor a more animalistic form of battle, using their speed, strength, claws and teeth to take down Nephilim. I don't know what to make of the group that closes in on us, but it can't be good.

"Steel?"

I'm looking to him for direction. I may have the magic wings, but I'm still very much a newbie.

Steel keeps his eyes glued to our enemies, even as he addresses me. "Do you think you could fly with Aurora?"

That thought hadn't crossed my mind. Maybe because having wings is new for me? Regardless, it's a good idea, but my body locks up in rebellion at the thought of leaving Steel and Blaze to be picked apart by the bloodthirsty creatures closing in on our small group.

"Steel," I hiss, "I can't just leave you and Blaze here to die."

Spinning in my direction, he grips my biceps. "We don't have time. Please save her."

The desperation splashed across his face makes my heart ache.

I'm not strong enough to do what he's asking of me—to sacrifice some so others can live. That shouldn't be a choice anyone has to make, but it's one I'm facing now.

Steel's hands squeeze my arms, his fingers tight enough to bruise. "Please."

Nodding once, I crouch to Aurora's level and stare into her eyes. She knows what's coming. Her chin trembles and trails of tears slide down her face.

"I don't want to abandon my brothers," she argues.

"I know, I don't want to leave them either."

"How would we live with ourselves?" she asks.

That's not a question I can allow myself to dwell on now. I've been asked to protect something precious to Steel, and I'm going to honor that request.

"Put your arms around my neck, Aurora. This is going to be a bumpy ride."

Despite her objections, she wraps her twig arms around my neck. Flexing my wings, I ready for a takeoff I'm not quite sure how to make.

"That's not wise, young one," comes a booming voice. It echoes off the trees and mountains surrounding the valley.

"Go!" Steel urges.

Thrusting my feather weapon at Steel, I rip my gaze away from his tortured eyes and spring into the air with one strong flap of my wings. With the second downward stroke, Aurora and I are several body lengths above everyone. With the third, I angle us away from the circle of Forsaken. I'm preparing for the fourth flap when something goes askew. There's a sharp tug on my left wing and Aurora and I plummet to the ground.

Twisting the best I can mid-fall, I absorb the bulk of the collision.

Thank the Creator for the several feet of snow built-up over the hardened soil and stone. Snow detonates into the air around us. I blink groggy eyes with Aurora clutched against my chest as fat flakes glide lazily back down to the earth. I would consider it beautiful if I weren't so stunned.

My wings took the brunt of the fall. There's a dull ache at the root where they attach to my spine, but other than that, I think I'm fine.

I'm about to sit up and test them when I'm hauled to my feet.

Rough hands grip the top of my wings, painfully forcing them to fold against my back, effectively thwarting another attempt at an aerial escape. Aurora is ripped from my grasp and thrust somewhere to my right. She lets out a panicked scream before the brute in front of me yells, "Someone shut the small ones up."

I'm forced back to my knees in the snow.

Steel is thrown to the ground beside me. His face is covered in white flakes and blood. He labors to his knees. Rubbing a hand from forehead to chin, he wipes the snow off and spits a glob of blood onto the ground. Red splatters over the white, grotesque gore contrasting with virgin snow.

He isn't holding my gilded feather or the weird orb of blue light anymore. The Forsaken must have relieved him of both.

Craning my neck, I search for the twins, finally spotting them behind us. They're gagged and their hands are secured in front of them with rope. Their gazes plead with me to do something.

"Stand them up. I want a better look at them."

I recognize that voice.

Stepping around the giant in front of us—this Forsaken is truly the largest human-like being I'd ever laid eyes on—is the female I fought in the alley several weeks ago.

Lilith.

A pair of angry hands wrench my left wing.

I hold in a shriek of pain as I stumble to my feet. I don't want our enemies to know how sensitive my wings are. No need to give the Forsaken extra ammunition. The odds are already stacked against us.

"I can stand on my own," Steel snarls at the Forsaken

manhandling him. It earns him a crack on the head with the butt of a handgun.

The blow sends Steel to his hands and knees, where two Forsaken haul him back up. He isn't immediately steady on his feet.

"Looks like all that waiting finally paid off," Lilith muses while circling us.

She's creepy.

Her perceptive eyes rake over us, taking in my wings and all our injuries. I feel covered in goo when she finishes.

"Took long enough," the goliath Forsaken snarls. "Those small ones were a pain to keep alive."

Lilith's apathetic gaze takes in the small Durand siblings behind us. "I suppose there's not a reason to do so much longer. They're so small, I'm not sure any self-respecting Fallen would even want to take them as a vessel."

"Don't be too hasty. I'm not done with them yet." A voice rises from deep within the pack of Forsaken.

I can't see her, but I watch the sea of bodies part as the speaker moves through the crowd.

When she skirts the last Forsaken and reveals herself, someone starts choking beside me.

Steel sinks to his knees. Anguish is painted over the angles and planes of his face.

Forcing my attention to the figure sauntering toward us, I catalogue her features. They are all typical to angel-borns: tall, slender, dark-haired, beautiful. I don't see anything remarkable about this female outside of what is remarkable about every Neph.

That is, until she stands only feet in front of me and my eyes lock with hers.

Twin aqua pools assess me. An eye color so unique, I've only ever seen it once before.

The breath I inhale is audible. Loud enough to be heard by the creature whose calculated gaze fans over my face. Loud enough to be heard by the surrounding group of monsters.

"Perhaps not a dumb blonde after all." A conspiratorial smile dances on her lips and she winks. "Time to get a better look at my prize. The snare we set to trap you was quite elaborate, after all."

Our captor starts a slow circle around me. When she passes out of view, I try to catch Steel's attention—silent questions scream inside me—but he's too focused on the Forsaken sizing me up.

"Interesting." She strokes one of my feathers. The sensation of slimy worms crawling over my wings follows the path of her finger.

"Hey, hands off!" I yell as I flare my wings and spin.

I want the sharp tips of my feathers to slice into her flesh.

No such luck.

She jumps out of the way too quickly for me to inflict an injury.

"Testy." She holds her hands up in front of her, imitating a posture of innocence. "I was just curious."

"Sil—Silver?"

The broken word is ripped from Steel's gut. He's on his feet now, but far from steady. He fists his hair—his grip so tight it stretches his hairline back a half-inch.

"In the flesh," she answers as she throws her arms out and does a quick pirouette. "I look pretty hot for being dead, don't I?"

Only then does Steel's shock melt away.

His hand drops from his head and balls at his side. His spine slowly straightens until he towers over both of us at his full height.

The sadness bleeds from his eyes, leaving them deadened even as a drop of moisture falls from one. The glossy trail that curves down his cheek is now the only evidence of the emotions that spike inside.

If this is truly Silver, that means she didn't perish on the mountainside so many years ago. And if she didn't die, and is standing here as a Forsaken, that means she met a much darker fate.

Feigning disappointment, Silver's mouth downturns and her head tilts. The moonlight bounces off her shiny sheet of raven hair, the color and texture so similar to Steel's own.

"Are you not happy to see your long-lost sister, Steel?"

"You are not my sister," Steel says through clenched teeth.

"Aren't I though?" Silver asks with a notched eyebrow. "It's an interesting question, don't you think? In all the history of the Nephilim, it's hard to believe that no one has ever stopped to ask how much of the angel-born remains after possession. Perhaps the nature of the Forsaken is more symbiotic than any of you realize?"

"That's not possible. Silver's soul was released when you got your putrid claws in her."

"This makes for a very interesting moral dilemma, doesn't it, sweet brother?" She taps a finger against her lower lip as if considering something.

"Would you really be able to slaughter your Nephilim brothers and sisters so easily if you knew they were still inhabiting these bodies?" Silver gestures to herself. A sly grin lifts both corners of her mouth.

If Steel is shaken by her words, he hides it well.

"There isn't a bit of my sister left in that shell. What you're speaking of is blasphemy."

A rich laugh rolls out of Silver. "Like I care."

"If there was even a sliver of my sister left inside, there's no way she would have offered our siblings up as bait."

"But they were so young when I was embraced by the dark. Just babies, in fact. Remember how much Aurora used to cry all night long? Such a nuisance. Why would you think I'd be attached to the mongrels after all these years?"

Something like uneasiness flickers across Steel's features.

Something akin to doubt.

Could her tidbit about Aurora crying all night have been true?

I don't know whether or not the Forsaken retain their host body's memories, but from Steel's momentary lapse, I don't have a good feeling about this conversation.

Silver takes a step closer to Steel, invading his space. She tilts into his body. Her voice drops to a whisper I can barely hear.

"I'll let you in on a little secret—something the Fallen and the Nephilim Council don't want getting around. There are pieces of angel-born living in every Forsaken. For some, only the whisper of the soul remains, but for others . . ." A wicked smile spreads across her face. "Well, you see for some of us, rather than spending an eternity as a spectator in our own bodies, we choose to live another way. We choose to bond with the Fallen inside, becoming one entity. One immortal being." Leaning back far enough for Steel to take in every bit of her expression, she finishes with, "I'll let you guess which one I turned out to be."

"Lies." The word hisses between Steel's lips.

"I wouldn't have told you, except—" she shrugs a delicate shoulder, "I don't expect there to be much, if any of you, left to spread the word."

A warning I didn't mean to release rumbles in my chest. Taking a menacing step toward them, I wedge a foot between the Forsaken and Steel.

Silver's head whips in my direction. The action is more bird-like than human.

"Looks like I was right. This one *does* have an involuntary attachment to you." Silver's unsettling gaze remains on me, even though her words are meant for Steel. "If it weren't for the circumstances, I'd say you were very lucky, brother. She'd make an excellent guard dog."

"Watch it." Steel shoots the words at her like bullets. "Emberly has nothing to do with this. It's me you want."

"Is that what you think?" With a raspy chuckle, she pats his cheek with just enough force to leave a red print behind. "I shouldn't be surprised. You were always full of yourself. But no, you're not our prey this time. You're simply part of the bait that lured her here. Like I said earlier, she's the prize. This mortal shell she wears will soon be shed, and she'll become the savior we've all been waiting for."

Fire sparks in Steel's eyes.

Before fear has a chance to spike at Silver's words, Steel lashes out.

His fist connects with her jaw, and her head snaps to the side.

Two Forsaken are on Steel in an instant. They lash ropes around his arms and force him back. It takes another two to hold him as he struggles for freedom.

"You keep your hands off of her!" Steel shouts, still fighting his captors.

I twist to help him escape, but something nicks my throat, sending warm blood trickling down my neck.

I freeze.

Silver stands to my left, her arm outstretched, a sword with a long, slightly curved blade clutched in her hand. The sharp end of the katana bites into my neck.

"I wouldn't make any sudden movements if I were you," she cautions. "I'm very fast."

I believe her.

Holding my hands up in surrender, I back up a slow half-step. More blood slides down my neck when the blade pulls free, but I can tell the cut isn't deep.

A beam of morning sunlight breaks through the sparse tree cover and lights the side of Silver's pale face.

My eyes saucer as the natural light continues to bathe her skin rather than burn it.

Catching my look, the side of her mouth upturns in a knowing half-grin.

"We're full of secrets."

38

"Where's the orb?" Silver calls.

A scrawny Forsaken steps forward with the fireball, still covered by Steel's coat. I suppose not all Forsaken are angel-born. A willing human can be possessed as well. And there is no way, with his five-foot-six height and boney frame, this creature could have been a Nephilim.

"Get that ugly thing off of it," she orders.

The gaunt creature peels Steel's coat away and the glow from the orb emanates across the space. Many of the Forsaken around us close their eyes and turn toward the radiance. Sucking in a lungful of air, their chests expand and muscles flex as if they are absorbing energy from the pulsating ball of light.

"You see," Silver starts conversationally as she lovingly strokes the object, her fingers passing through the flames unscathed, "what prevents you from phasing into the spirit realm is the same thing that protects us from the sun's rays.

It's a charming win-win—for us, of course. For you, I imagine it's quite inconvenient."

"What is it?" Steel asks.

"Just a little something taken from the spirit realm."

"That's not possible," he scoffs.

One of the first things I learned when coming to Seraph Academy was that nothing from the spectrum world could be transferred to the mortal realm, so I understand Steel's disbelief.

"Oh, it certainly used to be. But you see, our worlds are in transition. Your girlfriend here is going to help bring about even more changes."

"What are you talking about?"

"I think I'll let the Fallen tell you once you two merge."

"I'd die before I let that happen."

"We'll see about that."

Turning her back on Steel, she addresses her group. "Bind and gag him, it's the only way we'll get back to the stronghold without having to listen to his squawks."

Something whistles through the air and strikes the Forsaken about to gag Steel. Its prone figure falls to the ground—an arrow sticking out of its face.

Steel takes advantage of the moment of surprise to jab another Forsaken in the throat with his elbow and free himself.

I search the area for the twins as figures charge the group of Forsaken. The Forsaken who bound the twins have already been dispatched. One is now missing its head, and the other is lying face down in a black slushy of its own dark blood. The twins are being led away from the erupting battle by Ash.

A wave of relief breaks over me.

The sound of metal striking metal is music to my ears.

All around, Nephilim are fighting Forsaken, and this time we outnumber *them* four-to-one.

I prefer these odds, but the fight is still close. Forsaken pop in and out of the spectrum world to attack Nephilim or escape blows.

I spin in a circle, not knowing exactly where to jump in.

Sterling and Greyson tag team a Forsaken to my left. Whenever he phases into the spectrum world, the twins go back-to-back so they aren't taken unaware by his reappearance.

Sterling fights with a fierce double-bladed ax, and Greyson twirls a spear.

Not far behind them, Nova delivers a series of kicks to a stunned Lilith and then jumps on her back and does some really cool-looking wrestling move that brings her to the ground. Once Nova has her down, Hadley, with glasses still fixed on her face, decapitates the creature.

Whoa, who knew she had it in her?

A blur catches my eye and I twist to see Sable lop off the arm of a Forsaken. What she doesn't notice is the creature creeping up behind her with a curved saber, ready to run her through.

I sprint three steps in her direction before I'm tackled to the ground.

"Not so fast," Silver says as she grinds my face into the blood-splattered snow. She wrenches a wing back while pressing her knee into my spine. "You're coming with me."

I huff a half-laugh into the copper-scented ice. She's going to have a hard time hauling me out of here without anyone noticing. And there's no way I'll go without a fight.

"You can die trying."

"Not today."

Brightness blinds me. When my vision blinks back into focus, the snow beneath me has a lavender hue. Angry waves of light roll through the air. The sky is painted in pastel strokes.

From one breath to the next, I was sucked into the spectrum world with Silver.

"How?"

Jerking my wings, she forces me to my feet.

I watch in horror as Forsaken appear and disappear, using the spectrum world to fight and escape the Nephilim still in the mortal realm.

Silver's appearance has altered along with our surroundings. Her once-gleaming sheet of raven hair now hangs from her scalp in limp black dreads. Fangs indent her lower lip. Her cherry-red lips have mutated into a deathly shade of bluish-purple. And sharp black claws extend from the tips of her fingers.

"Just because you can't phase with this around," Silver hefts the orb she carries under her arm, "doesn't mean I can't pull you here with me."

She tugs my wings again, using them like a bridle to force me in a direction of her choosing. Her claws shred through a few of the feathers and sink into the flesh around the top joint.

I've had enough.

Gathering my strength and ignoring the lance of pain in my wings from Silver's manhandling, I flare them wide, knocking her off balance.

Spinning, the daggered tips of my feathers bite through

the soft flesh of her shoulder. A spurt of black blood sprays into the air.

Clamping a hand against her wound, the orb drops from her grasp and sinks into the purple-tinted flakes at her feet.

I snap my foot out, striking her in the chest and sending her soaring until her back connects with a tree. She flops to the ground like a rag doll.

Digging my hands into the snow, I snatch the ball. The second my fingers connect with the object, a bolt of gold lightning streaks across the sky, bathing the spectrum world's atmosphere with gilded sparks before they fade.

The orb's blue glow changes into undulating waves of golden light that spread from the source like ripples on the surface of a pond.

But these ripples pack an angry punch.

The blast hits me first. Heat sears my body, but I smile when I recognize what's happening.

When the blast dissipates, I stand tall in my fully morphed armor—handy weapons attached to the cuffs on my arms and legs.

I start toward Silver, who is standing wide-eyed with her hand pressed against her oozing shoulder wound. Grabbing the dagger off my leg, I aim for her eye, figuring embedding the metal in her skull is enough to put her down.

Unfortunately, she snaps out of her shock and dives out of the way before the blade finds purchase.

Suddenly, Nephilim phase into the spectrum world all around us. The orb's effects have been neutralized.

Silver takes a skittish look around, most likely coming to the same conclusion as me, and bolts. I give chase, but smash into an angel-born who appears in front of me. We both go down, and by the time I regain my footing, Silver is nowhere in sight.

"Yo, Emberly!" Greyson waves his hands in front of my face. "Are you okay?"

Looking down, the now gold orb is lying in the snow. Radiant light still pulsates off it in waves.

"Emberly." Greyson snaps his fingers in front of my face. "I said are you okay?"

I refocus on him. The fighting around us is dying down as the remaining Forsaken scatter and run for cover from the sun's rays.

"Yeah, I think so. It's good to see you, Grey."

39

Sable's office isn't large enough to fit all of us, so the cafeteria doors have been shut to give privacy to this impromptu meeting. It's funny how I don't mind being underground at the academy anymore. That itchy, claustrophobic feeling is completely gone and I'm just glad to be back. Happy to finally be somewhere safe . . . even if my body hasn't gotten the memo yet. It still buzzes from the last several hours of action.

"How did you find us?"

Steel asks the question from the table next to mine. We're spread out among several round tables. Steel isn't waiting patiently in a seat, like the rest of us. Instead he's settled on the tabletop with his feet planted on the chair below and his arms resting on his knees.

His posture may look casual, but I can tell he's ready to strike.

He's fierce with his grime-and-gore-streaked face. The scratches he got during the brawl with the Forsaken in the tunnels have faded to white lines. His partially shredded shirt is spatter-painted in red and black blood. His jeans are ripped at the knees, one of which is bleeding and trickles red droplets on to the plastic chair under his feet.

And we both still need a shower. Badly.

It's not fair he looks hot all grungy and blood-soaked and I just look . . . homeless.

I covertly touch my hair. Gah! It's rancid. I'm going to have to take at least three showers to get the newly formed dreads out.

The only clean thing on my body is a borrowed sweater. When I phased back into the mortal world my wings hadn't transitioned with me. I had to hold what was left of my shirt over my front. Ash fetched a new one from our dorm room for me the moment we returned. I pulled it on over the charred remains of my last sweater.

R.I.P. pink angora sweater. You were cute, and kept my boobs hidden from the Forsaken and most of Seraph Academy. Thank you for your service.

"I want to know why you didn't find them sooner. I have five children at this school, and I was just this close to losing three of them because of gross incompetence."

The Durand patriarch is seated next to his wife. They are the first set of parents I've met at Seraph Academy. It's jarring to see not only how closely they resemble their children in appearance, but also in age.

Laurent Durand's hair is several shades lighter than Steel's —it most closely resembles the middle twins'. He sits in the plastic cafeteria chair like he's seated at the head of the table in a board room. His back is erect, his shoulders pushed back, and the look he is sending Sable would make most grown men weep.

"I can understand why you're upset, Laurent, but this situation was highly unlikely. We are still trying to sift through all the details. We will get to the bottom of this, but the important thing to focus on at the moment is that everyone was recovered without any serious injury."

His lips thin and eyes narrow, a clear sign of his displeasure.

After clearing his throat, Deacon takes a half-step closer to Sable. He silently shows his support of her with his arms crossed over his broad chest, feet planted shoulder-width apart.

I wait for the pissing match to start between Deacon and Laurent. They both keep their mouths shut as they glare at each other.

"I want to find out what happened so we can prevent an incident like this from occurring in the future." Eloise Durand shoots her husband a look that dares him to contradict her. "I agree with Sable. I, for one, am glad that my children are back safely and would like a moment to be thankful for that."

Breaking his testosterone-filled stare-down with Deacon, Laurent rubs a hand up and down his wife's back. Gracing him with a grateful smile, she goes back to fussing over Blaze's swollen face for at least the eighth time since we entered the cafeteria.

Watching Eloise is eerie. Her long-lost daughter is almost a perfect carbon copy of her mother, except for about a ten-years age gap in appearance. Eloise has the same glossy sheet of raven hair as Silver, and delicate facial features that make both of them appear fae-like.

Slap a pair of pointy ears on her and she'd be ready for a *Lord of the Rings* fan convention.

My gaze skips across the room during the momentary lapse in conversation. Greyson and Sterling are seated at the table with Steel. The former is sitting in a backward chair with his arms draped over the seatback. His attention ping-pongs from Sable to the members of his family.

Sterling is sprawled across two seats, his butt in one, his legs propped up on another. With his arms folded in front of him and his head a little askew, I'm not sure if he's even awake anymore.

Ash told me both middle twins hadn't slept the entire time we were missing. They had searched in the wrong direction the whole time, so I can understand Sterling's exhaustion.

I'm at the middle table, splitting the Durand bunch in half. Steel, Greyson, and Sterling sit to my right. Aurora, Blaze, Eloise, and Laurent to my left. Ash sits next to me, and surprisingly, Nova chose to flank my other side.

Everyone looks a little worse for wear. We won the battle, but didn't escape completely unscathed. We're a bloody and bruised bunch, but overall, I'm relieved we didn't lose a single student or teacher during the fight. It's basically a miracle.

"Will someone tell me something," Steel barks, causing his mother to start and Sterling to fall out of his make-shift bed.

"I didn't do it!" he shouts from the floor.

"It was the anomaly that tipped us off," Sable begins to explain. "It wasn't long after we realized we couldn't phase that we discovered there was a geographical correlation. There were certain areas we could phase, and certain areas we couldn't. We started to test the borders of the anomaly and established it was a circle. Or rather, a bubble. We took a chance that you and Emberly were caught in the middle of the mess, and that you'd found your siblings."

"Don't forget the glitter bomb," Sterling says as he settles back into his chairs.

Sable clears her throat. "Well, yes. There was that, too."

Huh?

"Huh?" Steel looks as confused as I feel.

"Right, well, there was someone . . . or rather something . . . that helped us pinpoint your exact location."

"Dude, there was this sparkly glitter bomb that flew through the air, peeing out sparkles or something. It was trippy. Nova found it and convinced us to follow it."

Everyone's attention swings to Nova, and for once it doesn't seem like she's enjoying all eyes on her. Sinking lower in her chair, she fiddles with her bracelets.

"What? It seemed like the logical thing to do at the time. You see something otherworldly flying through the air, you follow it." She holds her palms up in a *duh* gesture.

"Oh, that." Some of the tension leaks from Steel's contracted muscles. "We're familiar with that particular . . . Tinker Bell, wasn't it, Emberly?" He gives me a side-eye. "It appeared to both of us at separate times."

I cough into my hand.

"You named it?" Greyson asks.

"That's rad," Sterling adds.

"So, what exactly *is* it?"

I can't be the only one who wants to know. Collectively these people are walking libraries of supernatural information. Which is why I'm surprised by the elongated silence that follows my question.

"You don't even have an idea?"

I turn wide eyes on Sable.

"The council is looking into it, but at the moment, no." Her hair swings as she shakes her head. "We've never seen anything like it. Especially in the mortal realm. We obviously believe it is something preternatural."

Wow.

I lean back in my chair, my mind whirling with questions. This whole hot mess is so confusing. And I hate that I'm part of it. I just want to blend into the shadows. Is that too much to ask?

Straightening her back, Sable addresses the lot of us. "Let's see if we can start making sense of all of this."

Three hours later, we're still trying to sort through all the details. My lids feel weighted with concrete and lined with sandpaper. My clothes are stiff with dried blood and several days' worth of mountain gunk. My nails—yuck. The crescents that are usually white are caked with black dirt and grime.

My sore muscles started to ache in protest hours ago. The worst are the spots on either side of my spine where my wings attach. I don't know if I have special muscles there, or what, but something back there is angry.

I fantasize about a shower—the warm water massaging my tender muscles and bruised skin, rinsing away the build-up of grossness suctioned to my body. Breathing in the lavender scented steam. Running my fingers through my hair, free of mats and—

"Emberly!"

"What? Who?" Jolting, I grab the tabletop to keep from sliding off my chair and onto the cafeteria floor.

"Classic," Sterling snickers.

I don't bother shooting him The Look. Sterling would just find that funnier.

"The orb glowed blue before turning gold, right?" Steel raises his eyebrows as he waits for my confirmation.

I turned the orb over to Sable after the last of the Forsaken had fled. Where Sable is keeping the object now, I don't know. And I can't muster the energy to care.

"Yeah, exactly. The moment my fingers brushed it, the color changed and you guys started to phase into the spectrum—I mean spirit realm. Even Silver seemed surprised about it."

The room stills. I shouldn't have brought her up again. I need to start referring to her as She-Who-Must-Not-Be-Named.

"Someone who is like Emberly took it from the spirit realm." Aurora's sweet voice fills the silence.

"Someone like me?" Nervous energy tickles my belly.

Eloise squeezes her young daughter, who is settled on her lap. "How do you know that, sweetie?"

"The Forsaken said so."

"I didn't hear them talking about it," Blaze adds.

"Oh," Aurora tucks a piece of hair behind her ear. "It was when you were sleeping." She drops her gaze and plays with the ends of her hair.

Something about her answer feels off.

A crease forms between Blaze's eyebrows, but he nods. "Oh, that makes sense."

"What do you mean 'someone like Emberly'?" Sable's mouth tweaks to the side and she furrows her brow.

Yeah, exactly. That. I want to know that.

Leaning forward, I suck my bottom lip into my mouth and start gnawing.

Aurora scrunches her nose and she shrugs. "He's a prince. He's like Emberly because she's a princess."

Come again?

"You think this girl is a princess?" I'm not sure I appreciate Laurent's tone or the look on his face as he takes my measure with a skeptical scan up and down my body. It's clear he finds me lacking.

"Emberly is special," Aurora insists.

Laurent's inspection gets even more uncomfortable. His gaze narrows and he tips his body forward, partially blocking his wife and daughter from view. "Yes, but what exactly do we know about her?"

"*This girl* is sitting right here and can hear everything you're saying," I remind him. Does he hope to intimidate me by refusing to refer to me by name? I've been called way worse than "her" and "this girl," but intentionally being belittled still gets my hackles up.

"Emberly is none of your concern." Sable's voice rings clearly in the cavernous room. If I were closer, I'd slap her a high five.

"The hell she isn't."

"Nor is she up for debate right now."

"Oh, snap," Ash whispers beside me.

"Yeah, apparently she's a princess. You don't mess with royalty, Dad."

Oh, Sterling. Gotta love him.

Laurent leans forward even farther to glare at his son. I half expect frozen projectiles to shoot from his ice blue eyes. Sterling ducks and mumbles, "Just sayin.'"

"Lay off her, Dad." My back straightens when Steel speaks up. "If it weren't for Emberly, you'd be searching for my frozen corpse right now. Not to mention the whole lot of us would have been slaughtered by the horde of Forsaken."

Okay, I didn't exactly do anything except touch a mysterious object, but I'm not about to point that out.

Laurent opens his mouth to argue when his wife places a hand on his back, stopping whatever flow of words he was about to expel. "Emberly helped save our children, even at the risk of her own life. We owe her a debt of gratitude, not our suspicion."

After a beat he leans over and cradles his wife's face in his hands, placing a chaste kiss on her lips. His actions are so sweet, so caring, that watching them makes my heart twist. True love and respect exist between the pair. A rarity in this messed-up world.

It would be beautiful to watch if Laurent hadn't just demonstrated what a grade-A jerk he can be.

Looking into Eloise's eyes, Laurent nods once before turning his crystal gaze back on me.

The air of superiority and hostility is absent from his mannerisms and speech when he says, "Apologies. My wife is right; we owe you much."

"You're . . . welcome?"

Wow. That was a speedy change of heart. What sort of witchcraft does his wife practice to be able to unruffle his feathers so quickly?

Eloise catches my eye and a conspiratorial smile lifts the corners of her mouth. She winks.

She may look like Silver, but I'm beginning to see where Sterling gets some of his charisma.

Greyson lets out a wet cough, catching everyone's attention.

"Bro, you bleeding again?" Sterling asks his twin.

Lifting a hand from his side, it comes away with a coat of fresh blood. "That blows. I really did like this shirt." Greyson seems way more upset about his ruined clothing than the fact he's leaking fluid from his gut.

"All right, everyone," Sable says. "We can talk more in the morning, after everyone has had a good night's rest and their injuries treated properly. Greyson, I'm looking at you."

"Yeah, yeah. I'm off." Pushing up from his seat, Greyson's the first to leave the room, but he starts the mass exodus. Most of us are past the point of exhaustion, so there's a lot of shuffling going on and a bit of grunting.

"Emberly, can I talk to you?"

My lids flutter. I'm half asleep already. "Sure."

With a hand gently wrapped around my arm, Sable leads me off to the side, out of hearing range from the group. Ash shoots me a questioning look, but I wave her off. When he spots us, Steel stops, a frown pulling down the corners of his mouth. My mind is too fuzzy to work out what he's displeased about.

"Do you know how you manifested your wings in the mortal world?"

Mentally dismissing Steel, I fix my attention on Sable, rubbing a hand back and forth across my forehead. "I know we have to figure this out, but I'm not sure I have the bandwidth to tackle that topic right now. I have a feeling it might have something to do with that magic orb. I wasn't able to phase back into the mortal world with them after I touched it. But you know I'm still trying to figure out how all my powers work." I rub my eye with the back of my hand. My eyeballs are scratchy and dry. "I just don't know. That could be coincidental." I can't quite keep all the frustration out of my voice.

She nods, but the look in her eyes causes a ball of anxiety to roll in my belly. "I get that." She takes a deep breath and purses her lips before continuing. Whatever she's going to say, she's having a hard time getting it out. "I hate to tell you this, I really do, but I'm going to have to reveal your skills to the Council. All of them. I can't keep you under wraps any longer."

And there it is.

"We need to get some real answers, and I've hit the end of my resources."

A cafeteria door slams shut, startling me. We're alone. Even Steel has gone.

I stare at the exit. The familiar desire to flee rides me hard. I have a choice to make. I can follow through with my plan to leave Seraph Academy, or I can stick it out.

I suck my top lip into my mouth, my teeth press into the soft flesh.

I want to know the truth, but the Council is scary. I can't forget my friends' reactions the first time Sable mentioned contacting them. I thought Greyson and Sterling were going to put me into their own version of witness protection. But Sable just dangled a juicy carrot in front of me.

Answers. An explanation for what I am, where I came from, who my parents were and why they abandoned me. The chance to fully discover my potential. The Council may be the key, and I could lose the chance to unravel my own mystery if I leave. This hidden world of the Nephilim I so recently discovered would also be out of reach. The logical side of my brain thinks about resources and centralized knowledge, but another part of me snags on the people here. If I leave, I'll be leaving them, too.

Sable waits patiently while I process my options. Her clasped hands and the tension on her face tell me she's anxious for my response, but she's always been good about knowing when I need a few moments to myself. Sucking in a gulp of air, I release it slowly.

"This is pretty far out of my comfort zone, but I think the Council will help us get some answers." Goodness knows I don't have any.

Sable nods her agreement. "Your wings, the orb—they're pieces of the puzzle. Once we collect enough pieces, the full picture will start to make sense."

I guess. But if I'm one of those crazy five-thousand-piece jigsaw puzzles, it's going to take a lot of clues to reveal the full story.

Sable tips her head toward the exit. "Go get cleaned up and then get some rest. I won't report anything to the Council until tomorrow. We'll sit down and talk it all through before I reach out to them. I want you to know what's going on. I don't want you to be in the dark about anything. I realize trust is hard to build and I'm not interested in taking yours lightly."

Sable's efforts to make this easier on me warm my heart and set me at ease, if only fractionally. Time and time again she's proved that she has my best interests in mind, and it's time I returned the favor. But my confidence in her doesn't extend to this enigmatic Council. I'm not going to let my guard down, but for today, my brain—and body—has had enough.

"A shower sounds like heaven." It truly does. And I can't wait. I smile just thinking about that warm water sluicing over my skin. I can almost feel it.

My smile turns wooden as I remember something. Sable actually doesn't know about all my shiny new powers. I suppress a groan and force the confession out of my mouth. "Wait, there's something else you should know. I can shoot fire balls out of my hands that are strong enough to turn boulders into dust. I mean, I did it once, so I'm assuming I'll be able to do it again . . . maybe." A grimace follows the confession.

Sable's eyes widen until I can see white around her irises. I swear she doesn't blink for twenty-three whole seconds. "Come again?"

We're going to be here a bit longer.

40

*A*fter another thirty minutes of back-and-forth with Sable, she finally lets me go. I rub my eyes as I trudge down the hallway. Both of them are full of grit.

Maybe I should put off cleaning myself until after I've had a nap?

My hand accidentally comes into contact with the crunchy hair at my forehead when I scratch an itch on my face.

So much yuck. I will not be skipping that shower.

Heaving a frustrated sigh, I catch the rays of the dying day filtering in through the west-facing windows. The orange light is tinted with gold and the dust in the air makes the beams shimmer, reminding me of my gilded wings.

I'm lost in thought about glowing orbs and metal-tipped wings and magic fireballs when movement outside catches my eye. Grinding to a halt, I stare down at a figure bent over a black and chrome motorcycle. He's securing a bag to the side.

I haven't spoken to Steel alone since before the battle with the Forsaken, but instinct tells me he's not preparing for a joyride.

"Did you at least say goodbye to your siblings?"

Steel doesn't turn, but he stops messing with the leather saddlebag at the side of his motorcycle. The breath he sucks in is big enough to move his shoulders up on the inhalation, and back down when he exhales.

After a stretched moment, he rotates to face me. Leaning against his bike, he shoves his hands in his pockets.

"Just going on a little trip. No need to sound an alarm for that."

Does he really think he's fooling anyone?

Sucking my bottom lip into my mouth, I bite down on it while I consider what my next words should be.

Reaching out, Steel gently tugs it free with his thumb.

"That lip is too pretty to abuse."

Whoa.

Heat sweeps down my body and twin tingles run up and down the lines on either side of my spine where my wings emerge.

Clearing my throat, I lick the lip Steel just freed.

Steel's eyes blaze as he watches me.

"What about Nova? I'm sure she'd be interested to know about your 'little trip.'"

His chest overextends as he breathes in a giant gulp of air. His eyes take on a faraway look before they clear and his gaze latches back onto me. "I didn't realize what was going on right in front of me. I've been . . . distracted the last few months." I don't miss the pointedness of his words.

Did he move closer? It feels like the heat from his body is buffeting against me. Not sure I like that. I probably stink.

"Even so, I should have caught on sooner. There's no excuse for taking her for granted. I had a talk with her. We're straight." His eyes cast to the side. "Or at least, we're okay for now."

His confession causes something to lighten inside my chest. I tell myself it's relief for Nova's sake—she's been living in a world of uncertainty and assumption for too long—but I'm not sure that's really it.

The reason I sought Steel out presses down on me, compressing the lightness from my chest.

"What do you plan to accomplish when you find her?" I ask.

A wall slams down over his features and his body. He sways away from me. The dead space between us suddenly stretches for what feels like miles. But it's better that way. Whatever weird connection I have with Steel really should be broken.

I don't understand the part he plays in my phasing—or spontaneous wing growth—but I need to learn to do it on my own. Now that I know there's a horde of Forsaken gunning for me, I have to learn to protect myself. Myself and the people I'm beginning to care about.

And all this inner cave-woman stuff—the "Mine," the growly noises—um, no. Don't like that at all.

Stepping back, I give Steel even more space.

"Are you staying?" he asks, notching his chin toward the academy behind me.

"Yeah, I think so," I answer honestly.

"I'm glad."

His reply surprises me. It was only yesterday—or was it earlier today?—that he was telling me to go to another academy.

"People here care about you. I was wrong to try to take that away from you."

And now I'm not just surprised, but floored . . . and utterly speechless.

This is the first genuine note of care Steel has shown me. Yes, he's shouted a few times that he didn't want me to die, and he's protected my physical body on a number of occasions, but up until now, he's never shown me real compassion.

"But . . . what about your siblings?" I finally get out.

"I think . . ." He looks toward where the sun is hanging above the western horizon. The warm light bathes his face, bronzing his skin and making him appear soft for once. "I think you can learn to protect each other, for now."

He turns his face to me, a half-smile quirking the side of his mouth.

"Besides, you have some pretty badass skills and abilities. There may not be another Nephilim alive capable of protecting them as well as you right now . . . besides me, of course."

Holy kraken balls! Did he really just compliment my fighting ability?

I glance down at the ground, expecting ice shards from a frozen-over Hell to shoot through the ground at any moment. When nothing happens, I return my attention to Steel.

"Who are you and what have you done with the moody angel-born I know?"

He chuckles before sadness tugs at his features.

"I have a lot of regrets right now. The way I've treated you is at the top of the list."

Again, I don't know what to say, so something really stupid comes out of my mouth.

"Going after Silver by yourself is a really bad idea."

A muscle jumps in his jaw. I imagine he's grinding his teeth pretty aggressively. Steel hates people telling him what to do. And when it comes to his family members . . . Well, the smart thing to do would be to save my breath.

"It's not your concern," he finally grits out.

His eyes flick to the left in annoyance and his arms fold over his chest in the universal sign for "back off."

Of course, I ignore it.

"If you go to Sable, I'm sure she'd figure out a way to get a team—"

"She already said no."

"You asked?" The words fumble from my mouth.

"Yeah, I did. And she denied the request. She said that in light of . . . recent events . . . we needed to concentrate on keeping the academy students safe."

A little bit of my heart cracks for Steel. Once again, I'm the cog keeping his world from running smoothly.

"I'm so sor—"

"Don't."

Steel pushes off his bike and turns to secure the latch on his saddlebag. He throws a long leg over the sleek chrome and black machine before giving me his attention again.

"It's better this way. She was right—they need all the resources the academy has now. The priority should be keeping all of you safe, not hunting down a single Forsaken."

"I could . . ." Am I really going to do this? "I could come with you. I can help."

Steel clearly wasn't expecting me to say that. His head jerks back and his lower jaw drops an inch.

I plow forward.

"Silver wants me." I point at my chest. My words grow more impassioned. "I'd be the perfect bait. And this way . . ." This is the most important part of my whole spur-of-the-moment plan. "Steel, this way I wouldn't be putting anyone else in danger. Things would go back to how they've always been at the academy."

Vulnerability drips from my words and I have a sinking feeling my heart shines from my eyes.

What the heck happened to my resolve to sever our connection?

It melted in an instant, like spun sugar in water.

Steel just stares. He blinks half a dozen times before taking any action, but with his mind made up, he moves swiftly, like the predator he is.

Snaking his leg off his bike, he reaches me in two purpose-filled strides.

His hand slips around the back of my head and his mouth covers mine in the delicious way I'm starting to worry only his can.

The kiss is soft and sweet. Something it's never been before.

But it also feels a lot like a goodbye.

When he pulls back he cradles my face in his warm palms.

"No. You can't come with me. This fight is mine."

He slides his hands off my cheeks and mounts his ride once again.

"Stay safe."

He starts the engine and a moment later I watch him drive through the academy gate.

He doesn't bother with a backward glance, and in a way that's a small mercy, because if he looked back, he would have seen the tears dripping down my face.

41

*T*he first time I phased into the spirit dimension that co-exists with our own, the air smelled like fresh honeysuckle. Light danced in the air on iridescent waves of sound. Pale pink clouds lounged in a lavender sky. I'd never seen beauty of that caliber. The world was filled with wonder and joy I hadn't known in my short life.

It was a glorious five minutes.

Until it wasn't.

The monsters appeared in short order, and what I'd mistaken for paradise was actually Hell in disguise.

I haven't thought of that day in some time. Maybe watching the blood and gore slide off my skin and snake toward the drain shakes the memory loose. Certainly the tang of exhaust left on my tongue from Steel's retreating motor-cycle has nothing to do with the melancholy settling over me like a heavy blanket. I'd have to care about him for his sudden departure to cause me even a drop of sorrow, and I resolved not to be weighed down by regard for the maddening angel-born. So it has to be something else.

The water running off my skin has gone from reddish-brown to a pink hue that might be considered pretty if it wasn't tinted with my own blood. As a Nephilim, I heal quickly, but even so, my body is marred with faded green bruises. I'm sure a few hours ago, I was covered in black and purple marks.

I scrub with a coarse loofah until I'm free of dirt and grime and my skin is pink from abuse. After a final rinse, my hair and body are free of the physical evidence of the last several days. Mud, sweat, and blood circle the drain before being washed away for good.

If only memories could be disposed of so easily.

I reach for the dry towel hanging neatly on the rack outside the shower and pain spikes from twin slashes on opposite sides of my spine. Snatching the cloth, I wipe away the layer of moisture fogging the mirror and twist, convinced I'll see scars, but my skin is unmarred, having knitted together perfectly after my gold wings folded back into myself.

How over twelve cumulative feet of wingspan is able to disappear into my back is a mystery I'm not likely to solve.

Steel's whole body expands when he shifts forms. How does that work?

Shaking my head, I remind myself I'm not allowed to think of him right now. Chalking the unknown up to magic, I nudge him and other curiosities out of my mind.

I pull the tie on the terry cloth robe tight before opening the bathroom door. Taking a fortifying breath, I do my best to shrug off the despondency. We just located the missing Durand twins and won a battle against the Forsaken, and every angel-born returned to Seraph Academy—perhaps a little worse for the wear, but alive. All things worthy of celebration, not mourning.

Ash is my favorite person in the world, but the girl doesn't know the meaning of personal space. I'm not in the right head space to answer questions, so I need to leave this bathroom looking as if I don't have a care in the world.

Using a hand towel, I squeeze the wetness from my hair and then emerge from my hiding place. A wave of steam heralds my entrance. "That was the best shower of my entire—"

"Ahh!" Ash's squawk interrupts the sonnet I'm prepared to spew about my love of running water.

She's hunched with a textbook raised above her head, staring at the bookcase. I almost miss the streak of sparks that zips from under my bed to the messy shelf.

I blink and the streak fizzles out.

"What the angel-fire is that?" Ash asks me, the textbook still raised in the air.

"I'm not sure?" That wasn't supposed to come out as a question. "But I'm worried I may have an idea."

Tiptoeing forward, I stretch my arm to reach for an overturned book on the shelf.

"Emberly," Ash hisses. "What are you doing?"

"Trying to figure out what—yikes!"

Something flies at my head and I hit the floor.

Ash drops down beside me a nanosecond later. Throwing her arms over her head, she curls into a ball.

"Kill it!" she screams.

"Did you see what it was?" I yell back. Whatever it is, it's flying or bouncing around the room, shoving books off our desks, lotion off our nightstands, and knocking into the walls and ceiling like an over-caffeinated pinball.

"It's some sort of demon squirrel."

"That's a thing?"

"I have no idea. We didn't know *you* were a thing until you showed up. Maybe demon squirrels are next."

"Seriously, Ash?" I lob a glare at her.

With her arms over her head and her legs tucked, she still manages a small shrug and a sheepish grin.

"I am not a demon," a high-pitched voice complains from my bed.

Ash's eyes grow to the size of saucers and I'm sure mine have done the same.

"Or a squirrel. I find the fact that you thought either of those things highly offensive."

Peeling ourselves off the floor, Ash and I shuffle to our knees and peek over the side of the bed.

Balanced on its back feet on top of my pillow is . . . a flying squirrel.

The creature taps its tiny foot.

Ash and I exchange twin looks of disbelief before drawing our eyes back to the furry, five-inch being.

"Well, what do you have to say for yourselves?" it squeaks. Its raised arms show off the fur-covered, parachute-like membranes connected from wrist to ankle. "Anyone can see I'm not a rodent or a demon. Insulting, is what that comment was."

"Am I still asleep?" Ash asks. "Because that would explain quite a bit."

"But . . . you *are* a squirrel," I insist.

It shakes its tiny fist in the air. If it had a complexion, I imagine it would be turning red right about now.

"Tell me, can a squirrel do this?"

The little guy throws his arms down and shoots into the air. Gold glitter-filled sparks follow in his wake as he zips around the air above our heads.

"Is that squirrel shooting glitter out of its butt?" Ash leans over to ask.

"I think so."

It lands back on my pillow and crosses its arms. "You see? Not a squirrel."

"Or maybe you're just a squirrel that farts glitter . . . and talks."

I snort a laugh at Ash's response. We're both still on our knees on the hard floor, staring at the creature who is definitely not a typical squirrel, but looks like one.

The little creature scrunches his tiny face in displeasure.

"I didn't want to have to do this because of your delicate Nephilim sensibilities, but just remember, you drove me to it."

"Should we be scared right now?" I stage-whisper.

"It seems to think so."

Beady black eyes narrow on us before they close. The glitter-farting rodent begins to vibrate and both of us shuffle back until we bump into the wall behind us.

The squirrel explodes in a ball of bright sparks.

I throw my hands up to protect my face.

When the light dims, a monkey the size of a medium dog sits crossed-legged where the squirrel had been.

Which means I now have monkey butt on my pillow as well as squirrel feet. I'm throwing that thing away later.

"Sooooo . . . not a squirrel. But a monkey?" Ash asks.

The monkey slaps a hand across its face and drags it down slowly.

"You're not too bright, are you?"

I glance at Ash. She shrugs. "What? It looks like a monkey."

The monkey leaps off the bed and lands with a soft thud, startling both of us. "You two are hopeless. Do they not teach you anything in this academy? Let's try one more time."

Once again the creature vibrates and explodes in a shower of golden sparks.

This time, when we open our eyes, a pitch-black panther sits in front of us, licking its front paws. Its jowls stretch in what might be a feline smile.

"Boo."

Ash and I launch ourselves for the door on the other side of the room at the same time.

Squirrels and monkeys are one thing, but that jungle cat can tear us to shreds. It's not as if the robe I'm wearing is going to protect me from its claws.

As my hand closes over the brass knob, a strange hiccupping laugh starts.

I spare a quick glance over my shoulder as I turn the doorknob. The large cat rolls around on the ground, holding its tummy with its blunt paws, doing some sort of weird, hissing cat-laugh.

The sight is strange enough to stop me in my tracks.

Ash—not having the same moment of indecision—plows into me.

Going down in a tangle of limbs, we push and pull at each other until we bounce to our feet.

The creature is back to its flying squirrel form, lounging on my pillow.

"That was amazing. I knew Nephilim could move fast, but that was some serious hustle, girls."

Okay, enough is enough. It's time to figure out what this creature is, and what it's doing in our dorm room.

Planting my hands on my hips, I march to my bed. Grabbing its feet, it rolls around my pillow like a small ball.

"All right, little beastie. Spit it out. What are you and what are you doing here?"

It stops and cocks its walnut-sized head at me.

"I didn't hear the magic word."

With an aggravated huff I plop down on the mattress, causing the fur-ball to catapult a foot in the air.

"Is that the thanks I get for saving your heinie?"

"What are you—" The squirrel transforms into a flickering ball of light and starts to float in a circle around my head. Familiar sparks shoot off the flying sparkler before it descends to the bed and converts back into a gliding rodent.

"Tinker Bell?"

"That is not my name."

"Then what is it?"

It tips its nose in the air. "You wouldn't be able to pronounce it. It's a combination of sounds too advanced for your vocal cords."

O-kay.

"You can call me Your Majesty."

Ash and I exchange a look. The corners of her mouth twitch. "Yeah, no. We're not calling you that."

Its hands land on its hips.

"Why not?"

"It kinda reminds me of Sterling, right?"

Ash agrees. "Just what we need."

"I'm gonna call you Tink," I announce.

Putting its fist under its chin, the creature seems to be considering the suggestion. "No. I think I like Tinkle better."

Ash slaps a hand over the lower part of her face to keep from laughing.

"You want me to call you . . . Tinkle?" I can't keep the corners of my mouth flat to save my life right now.

"Yes. It's a good, strong name. Dignified, like me." Tinkle tilts its chin up and tries to look down its nose at me.

I deserve a medal for not busting out in laughter.

"Shall we shake on it?" I ask, extending an index finger in its direction.

"We shall."

Reaching out its little paw, Tinkle grabs the tip of my finger and pumps its arm up and down. Ash rolls on the ground, no longer even trying to contain herself. Snorts intersperse throughout her snickers.

"Now," Tinkle starts, flopping down on my pillow. "I'd like to discuss your extreme stupidity—both of you. I get why *you* don't know what I am, but that one over there," Tinkle points a tiny finger in Ash's direction, "has had proper schooling."

Ash collects herself and sits upright, holding her hands in the air, palms up. "Yo, we do not get educated about glittery balls of shape-shifting—" She cuts herself off, crawls over to the bed, and plops down on it, pressing three fingers to her mouth.

"No, it can't be," she mumbles.

"I think I just saw a light bulb go off. Not used to exercising your brain very often, are you? Poor thing. Maybe she's not completely useless." Sniffing the air it turns to me and says, "Although I think I smell charred brain matter. I hope she hasn't permanently injured herself. That would suck."

"Are you a Celestial?" Ash asks in a whisper.

"In the flesh, sweetheart."

"What's a Celestial?"

"It's like the Neph version of a fairy godmother," Ash answers. "Our parents tell us stories of them at night before they tuck us in. Complete fairy tale stuff."

"Pfft." The little squirrel snuggles deeper into my pillow. "Obviously not."

"They're guardians. Make-believe, though. We don't know exactly when the stories of them started, but no one has ever seen one."

"Come on, angel-born. You should know all stories are based on a kernel of truth."

This is wacky.

"So it was you who led me to Steel when he was in trouble, and Steel to me when I passed out in the snow?"

"Don't forget how I brought the horde of Nephilim to save your bacon against the Forsaken. Oh, and the small task of masking your presence from evil for your entire life. That was me too." It buffs its claws against its chest in a gesture of self-satisfaction.

"You've been around my whole life? But . . . why haven't I seen you until now?"

"Those were the rules set out for me, sugar buns."

Sugar buns?

"I couldn't reveal myself to you until you'd embraced your angel side. Took you long enough, by the way."

Too many questions. Where to even start?

I stare at the bookshelf, not really seeing anything, but

trying to work this all out in my head. If this creature has been around my entire life, it knows more about me than even I know about myself. It could know answers about where I come from, even who my parents were and why I was abandoned as an infant.

I come back to myself with a shake of my head. "Does everyone have a Celestial . . . ah . . . guardian?"

"I'm not sure," Ash says. "Up until two minutes ago I didn't think they existed. I thought that thing was a demon squirrel."

Our heads swivel in Tinkle's direction.

"No, of course everyone doesn't have one of us. We're very rare."

A bubble of something that very well may be hope is growing in my chest. It's hard to identify because "hopeful" is an elusive emotion for me. But this tiny shape-shifting creature has just given me something to hold onto.

"I have a million questions. But, er, I gotta get changed first. I cannot have this conversation in a soggy robe."

I go to the dresser and grab some clothes. When I turn around, Tinkle blinks up at me.

"You have to turn around."

"Why?" The tiny squirrel seems confused.

"Because I don't want you watching me change."

"Why?"

"Because it's weird."

"Why?"

"Because you're a dude, er, maybe? And it's creepy."

"I'm male, but you don't have to worry. I have no bits or bobbins."

"Bits or bobbins?"

"Yeah, you know, bits," he leans over and points to the

space between his legs. "And bobbins," then he grabs his furry chest with equally furry hands. "Those parts you people are always so obsessed with. Nephilim and humans like to play with each other's parts. I wasn't born yesterday. I see things."

I cover my face, and Ash starts choking.

"Forget I asked. Wait, if you don't have any . . . bits . . . then how do you go to the bathroom?"

Tinkle wiggles its eyebrows. "Wouldn't you like to know?"

"Ew! Nope. Sorry, forget I asked that as well. I don't want to know at all. I'm changing in the bathroom. And I'm locking the door."

42

I'm in and out of the bathroom in record time. I'm pretty sure my shirt is on backwards, but that's not important. Ash sits cross-legged on her bed and shouts the names of different animals, which Tinkle transforms into the moment the words leave Ash's lips.

I've now lost track of how many different animal butts have been on my pillow. I'm burning the thing the first chance I get.

Spotting me, Ash stops the rapid firing of animal names, leaving Tinkle in sloth form. Raising his hand in slow motion, he wiggles his long-clawed fingers at me. I take a quick step back.

"Please pick a different form. Sloths are creepy."

In an explosion of dissolving sparks, he pops back into his flying squirrel form.

"Better. Thanks."

I settle on the end of the bed, mirroring Ash's cross-legged position. "Tinkle, who sent you to watch over me?"

I hold my breath as I wait for the tiny creature to answer. The little beast takes his time, tilting his head back and forth several times as he regards me. I can't read the expression on his face because he's a dang squirrel.

The tension builds until I'm sure my head is going to explode. I'm milliseconds away from grabbing the creature and shaking him.

"I think it should be obvious, but your kind is apparently more obtuse than your predecessors. Who else could have sent me besides your father?"

Ash gasps, but I don't move a muscle.

"*Sent* as in past tense. You mean before he died?"

"Died? Who said anything about Camiel being dead? I don't even think it's possible to kill a seraph."

Boom. The destruction from the emotional grenade leaves me mute.

"But there aren't any seraph Nephilim." Ash's voice is a notch above a whisper.

"Who said anything about a Nephilim? Do you know nothing?"

"Are you telling me my father is an actual Fallen?" I exchange a look with Ash and she shakes her head, just as surprised as I am. According to everything I've been taught, that shouldn't be possible. There hasn't been a first generation Nephilim born in over four thousand years, and as far as anyone knows, there's never been a seraph angel-born.

"No, of course not. That's blasphemous to even consider."

Oh. Well, now I'm confused.

"Camiel would never oppose the Creator. To think that he would do so is offensive. I won't mention you even brought it up the next time I see him. You're very lucky I'm good at keeping secrets."

"Ash."

I look to my best friend for answers because my mind isn't computing this information properly. It can't be, because what I hear him saying is that not only am I a first generation angel-born, but the daughter of a full-blown seraph angel.

Not a Fallen—an actual legit angel. That would make me a double—no, a *triple* impossibility. I would be the only one of my kind in existence.

The loneliness that accompanies that thought presses in on me, making our dorm room uncomfortably hot.

"We need to talk to Sable."

"No. Wait, not yet." My voice comes out as a croak. "I have more questions. What about my mother?"

"What about your mother?" Tinkle stares at the ceiling. I glance up, but don't see anything interesting.

"Who is she? Where is she?"

"How am I supposed to know that? I'm all-powerful, not all-knowing." He says the last part as he holds on to his feet and rolls back and forth, the tip of his tail dangling over his nose.

"Emberly, we need to talk to someone else about this. This is a lot of information. And if what he's saying is true—"

"Then it means I have a father out there who left me to be raised by strangers. Ha. Forget strangers, he left me to be raised by an entirely different *species*. Sounds like an awesome guy. Can't wait to meet him." I don't even try to keep the bitter note out of my voice. Shock mixes with fury and my emotion scales start to tip toward the latter.

A hand rests on my shoulder. When I look up, Ash stands

above me, sympathy pooling in her eyes. "I don't think we're going to get much more out of him at this point. Maybe he needs a nap or something?"

Tinkle is back to staring at nothing on the ceiling, but his eyelids do look a little droopy. I'm not ready to back off now. That little being contains a mountain of knowledge.

I open my mouth, ready to shoot off more questions, but before I can utter a syllable Tinkle tips over, face-planting into my pillowcase. Soft snores rise from his tiny nose.

Did that really just happen?

"Do you think he's narcoleptic?"

"Come on."

"I'm fully serious. Did you see how fast he nodded off? That can't be normal."

She has a point.

Squeezing my eyes shut, I rub the bridge of my nose. Another tension headache brews. My emotions are so intertwined, I don't know how to separate them. Fear and anger and hope and joy slosh around inside my brain, battling for dominance.

"Will you let me tell Sable about what Tinkle said about my . . . father? I want to feel out the situation a little first. And I need a minute to process some of this." All of this.

"Yeah, of course."

Thirty minutes later, Tinkle is perched on my shoulder. After a fifteen-minute power nap, his eyes popped open and he started bouncing around the room like a caffeinated gremlin. It took another fifteen minutes to calm him down enough to get out the door.

There's a sharp tug on my earlobe followed by something being shoved down my ear canal.

"Ahh. What the heck." My hand smacks the side of my head, protecting the sensitive area. "Tinkle, did you just stick something in my ear?"

Twisting my head, I do my best to take in the small creature as we navigate the academy halls on the way to Sable's apartment. I've never been there before, but Ash assured us she knew the way.

"I most certainly did not stick *something* down your ear."

"Well then what was—"

"I merely wanted to see if my arm would fit in this hole."

"So you *did* put something in there." Creepy little dude.

"I did not. It was my arm."

"Your arm isn't something?"

"No." I contort my neck to see a blurry image of his triangle head. His beady black eyes blink back at me. "My arm is part of me."

Ash snickers under her breath. "Weird Celestial logic?"

"I guess."

I follow Ash through a set of doors and up a flight of stairs.

"The teacher's quarters are on a separate floor," she says by way of explanation.

It's an effort to keep from hammering Tinkle with questions as well as keep my pace steady. The desire to get to Sable drives me hard. I need answers, one of which is whether or not this creature is reliable. I'm counting on Sable to fill in the blanks.

Ash leads us to a part of the academy I've never been to before, but the stairs we're ascending are dark stained wood, just like all the other staircases in the sprawling U-shaped building. Carved floral designs decorate the banisters, also typical. The walls are a familiar chalky white. Nothing new there.

At the landing there's another set of thick wooden double doors. When Ash pushes them open, the world is flipped on the other side.

"Are we in a spaceship?" I genuinely want to know.

The plaster walls of the academy have been replaced by white plastic panels. Rows of them cover the walls and curve onto the ceiling, creating a tunnel that bends at the end of the hallway.

"Wait, it needs to scan us."

"What?" I squeak.

The panels to our left and right, as well as the ones overhead, light up blue and then flip to angry red a moment before an alarm starts.

"Shoot, I forgot about the little guy. He must have tripped the alarm."

Several staff members in various stages of undress pour out of doors on each side of the hallway tunnel. One of them is Deacon. Seeing us, his face pulls down into a frown. After hitting some buttons beside his door the blaring noise stops and the red lights fade.

I shake my head to rid it of the ringing in my ears. The movement displaces my hair and covers the little beastie on my shoulder. I can feel his little rodent hands grasp and tug my hair as he parts the strands like a curtain so he can peek through.

Deacon waves off the people who have exited their rooms and they lumber back inside their apartments. Most have bed head and a few are wrapped in towels. Dark smudges mar the skin under their eyes and the men sport heavy five-o'clock shadows.

I cringe.

The academy faculty has been working tirelessly over the last several days to find Blaze and Aurora and then Steel and me when we went missing as well. Nephilim might not require the same amount of sleep as humans, but they deserved a rest.

"What are you two troublemakers up to now? And which one of you set off the alarm?"

How are we supposed to explain this one?

Deacon's unshaded gaze bounces back and forth between the two of us the longer we remain mute.

"Well..." I start.

Deacon's hand shoots out, grazing my right cheek. Grabbing a handful of my hair along with Tinkle, he tries to yank the little creature off my shoulder.

I yelp as my head is jerked forward, just as Tinkle shouts, "Unhand me, you beast."

Deacon's brows shoot up, which is just about the most animated I've ever seen him.

"Can you let go of my hair and my . . . Tinkle please."

"Excuse me? Your . . . Tinkle? Ow!" Deacon jerks his arm back. The little Celestial glides to the ground. Strands of my platinum blonde and red-tipped hair float to the floor with him. Pretty sure I have a bald spot now.

"It bit me." Deacon blinks down at the animal at our feet. "What is that?"

"That's what we're here for. We need to see Sable." Ash answers as I bend over and scoop up the pissed-off looking squirrel. He brushes his hand down his body as if trying to rid himself of Deacon's touch. I'm so deliriously exhausted I don't know whether to laugh or cry right now.

"Is it . . . safe?" Deacon's head tilts left and right as he inspects the Celestial. Reaching out a finger, he pokes Tinkle in the stomach like he's the Pillsbury Dough Boy. Tinkle bats his hand away and bares his tiny teeth at the large Nephilim.

"Touch me again, Gigantor, and you're going to lose more than a finger."

"Everything all right down there?" Sable calls from the bend at the end of the hallway. "I heard the alarm."

Twisting in her direction, Deacon answers her. "I think this is something you have to see for yourself. Come on, girls. Let's get out of the hallway."

I carry Tinkle in my hands as we traverse the spaceship-like hallway. Turning on a heel when we reach her, Sable leads us past four doors before stopping at the one at the end of the corridor. After punching a code into the lighted panel recessed into the shiny wall, she nudges the door open and gestures for us to follow.

We enter a small living area. A tendril of unease weaves its way through my belly. Eloise and Laurent are seated in sofa chairs around an oval coffee table. Eloise presses a teacup to her lips, sipping some of the steaming liquid. Pulling the cup back, she tilts her head as she regards our group.

Laurent stands as soon as the door shuts behind us. "What's happened?"

"That's what I'd like to know." Deacon settles his shoulder against the doorframe before folding his arms across his chest.

Ash and I exchange another weighted look. She shrugs a shoulder, which I take to mean that this is all me.

Shifting from side to side, I side-eye the Durands. I'm hesitant to share this news with them in the room. I don't really know them and this is important information.

Okay, it's only Laurent that gives me pause . . . Eloise seems cool.

"Emberly?" Sable prompts.

Oh, fine.

"Yeah, so . . ." This is so awkward. "We found this." I bring my cupped hands up and forward for the adults to see. Tinkle is on all fours. His nose twitches, but besides that he's frozen.

"You found a squirrel?" Sable squints as she regards the rodent in my hands. Her eyes flick to me, her face scrunched in confusion.

"Ah . . . no." How is it that the Celestial hasn't reacted to being called a squirrel yet? "Come on, Tinkle. Do your thing."

There's a gurgle and Eloise's porcelain teacup rattles against the saucer. "Did you just call that creature 'Tinkle'?"

"I did *not* name it." I'm quick to defend myself. "That's what he said he wanted to be called."

A feminine giggle escapes Eloise's lips. She brings a hand up to cover her mouth. I don't blame her—this whole thing sounds ridiculous.

"Yo, dude." I bring Tinkle up to my eye level. "Shoot some sparkles out your backside or something."

He cocks his nutshell head at me, his dark eyes unblinking black beads.

"What's going on here?" Laurent asks. "Is this some sort of joke?"

"No, I swear. I'm being a hundred percent serious. This is a Celestial. He's just in the form of a flying squirrel right now. And up until five minutes ago he was a Chatty Cathy. I don't know what his problem is now. I think he's messing with me."

"There's no such thing as Celestials." Laurent scoffs as he retakes his seat. "We tell stories of those mythical creatures to our children to sooth their fears of the spirit realm. Can we please get on with our discussion, Sable? Entertaining these two is an obvious waste of our time."

Nice to know where Steel learned his people skills.

"Excuse me, sir, but that's what I thought too." The Durand patriarch has Ash pulling the "sir" out. I have to press my lips together to keep from smiling. "That is until I watched this little imp fly around our room while shooting fire sparks. And then he changed into a monkey and panther. As you know, Emberly didn't grow up in our community. She doesn't know the stories, but I do. I know how unbelievable this sounds, but it's true. That is a Celestial."

"I think I heard it talk," Deacon adds from outside the circle. He hasn't left his sentry position by the door. "It bit me, too."

"Well," Sable plops down on a loveseat to the right of Eloise. Reaching a hand up, she rubs the corner of her eye. "I'm not sure what to say right now. Girls, I'm sorry, but it just looks like a rodent to me."

Tinkle launches himself from my hands and glides to the coffee table, startling almost everyone in the room, including Laurent, who shoves his chair backward a foot.

Scurrying to the middle of the table, Tinkle grabs a piece of round shortbread off the tray and makes a valiant attempt to shove the whole thing in his mouth. He's too small to accomplish the task though and ends up jamming the cookie against his face, his thin fingers clutching around the edges.

"Gotta be bigger," he says right before he explodes in a burst of sparks and dissolving glitter. In the next instant, Tinkle is lying on his back in the form of a large tabby cat. The whole plate of shortbread is gone. Only crumbs remain. Tinkle licks his paws, purring happily.

"See!" I shout, pointing at the feline.

"Oh. Wow. That just happened." Eloise brings her teacup to her lips, but forgets to take a sip. Her eyes are wide and the cup quivers as she sets it on the saucer.

Out of the corner of my eye I see Laurent lean forward, his hand reaching for Tinkle.

"I wouldn't—"

The sound that comes out of the Celestial is straight hellcat screech. He slashes a paw full of sharpened claws at Laurent, who manages to yank his hand away with the speed of a seasoned warrior.

I tried to warn him.

"It doesn't like to be poked," Deacon deadpans. He would know.

"*He* is not a pet," Tinkle says, before leaping to the seat next to Sable. Circling twice he settles on the cushion. Sable scoots closer to her armrest. "Now, I'm assuming you all have questions?"

43

*D*espite their best efforts, the adults haven't been able to get much useful information out of the Celestial in the last forty-five minutes. All we've learned is that Tinkle doesn't physically age and can render himself invisible in both the spectrum world and mortal realm. The former I don't care about and the latter is something I could have guessed.

"This has been a very strange week." Rising from her chair, Eloise shakes her head once, as if to rid herself of bad memories. "If you don't mind, I'm going to say goodbye to my children. Laurent and I have to leave soon." She turns sympathetic eyes toward Sable. "I do not envy you right now. Best of luck sorting all this out.

"Laurent, I'll give you a few minutes to wrap up here, but I expect to see you in Blaze's room in the next ten minutes."

Guilt prickles my skin. I need to say something about Steel, but as Eloise floats toward the door, my vocal cords freeze. I manage to punch through the ice covering them when her hand turns the knob.

"Steel's gone." The words burst from my chest, brittle but loud. Eloise's head snaps in my direction.

"What do you mean, 'gone'?"

I swallow in an attempt to wet my dry throat. Screw Steel for putting me in this position. I shouldn't be the one who has to tell his parents he's gone to destroy one of their other children.

"I saw him packing up his motorcycle a few hours ago and went outside to see what was going on. We only talked for a few minutes, but I didn't get the impression he planned on heading back anytime soon. He left the academy grounds just before sunset."

Eloise's eyes dart to the window. The night is so completely settled, only blackness greets us.

"He's gone after Silver," Laurent correctly assumes. A heavy sigh leaves his chest. "We should have known something like this would happen."

Crossing the room to her husband, Eloise wraps her arms around his waist and settles her head against his chest. Laurent lifts a hand to rub circles on her back as they comfort each other.

"When he found out she was alive, it was just a matter of time." Eloise's eyes are squeezed shut, but a single tear still manages to break free and run down her cheek. Taking a deep breath, she leans away from her husband and wipes away the wetness. After pressing his lips to her forehead, the pair break apart. "Thank you for letting us know, Emberly."

"Yes, thank you," Laurent echoes his wife.

Wait, that's it?

"I'm very sorry we can't make finding her a priority right now. I'm sure that contributed to Steel's rash decision," Sable says, her voice ringing with sincerity.

Steel's parents knew he'd gone to Sable to get help locating Silver?

"We understand." Although not embracing anymore, the couple's hands remain clasped together. They exchange a look and Laurent nods at Eloise before continuing. "There are bigger priorities right now. We made peace with the loss of our daughter, but I'm afraid Steel never has. He's not a child anymore. His decisions are his own, regardless of whether we agree with them. Out of all of our children, Steel has always been the most resolute. There's not much to be done about it except hope he reaches out to someone."

"We'll let you know if we hear anything from him," Sable offers.

"We'd appreciate that. I think I'll accompany my wife. You have much to discuss." Laurent and Eloise brush past me on their way out. Eloise offers a sad smile as she moves toward the door, but Laurent pauses.

"Thank you for telling us about our son. It's better to find out about this sooner rather than later."

I give a small nod, unsure if he's looking for another reaction, but knowing I have nothing else to offer him and his wife.

"It looks like I may have been hasty in forming my opinion of you." He casts a meaningful glance at his wife, who nods encouragingly. "My apologies. Sometimes my protective nature overrides good sense."

Ah, another personality trait his son has inherited.

"You've not had an easy life, but the strongest spirits are

often forged in adversity. I do hope you unearth the answers you're searching for."

His head turns, and I follow his gaze to Tinkle, who is scurrying along the top of the coffee table, searching for cookie crumbs. "I have a feeling you're going to face some unique challenges." His hand settles on my shoulder, startling me. I meet his eyes, which are so much like Steel's that something twists in my chest. "Our family is here for you. All you have to do is reach out."

I'm floored. This is the same man who threw eye-daggers at me several hours ago. What could have changed during that time?

"Thanks," I croak, my throat thick with unwanted emotion.

"Let's let them finish their conversation in private," Laurent tells his wife.

After a gentle squeeze, his hand drops from my shoulder. Eloise goes up on her toes to kiss his cheek and offer him an encouraging smile. She must have had something to do with her husband's change of heart.

I'm struck for the second time today by what a strong and palpable bond the pair share. Is that an angel-born thing or unique to their relationship?

After the Durands leave, Tinkle won't stop scrounging for food on the tabletop. Sable clears her throat to get his attention, but it doesn't faze the Celestial with a one-track mind. Sighing, she leaves her seat and returns a few minutes later with a fresh plate of cookies. Chocolate chip this time.

"Mine!" Tinkle shouts and attacks the plate the instant she sets it down.

Sable waits to resume her questioning until he's lying on

the table with a bloated belly and sucking the chocolate from his claws.

"So, if I have it correctly, you were charged with protecting Emberly from the Fallen and Forsaken until she found her way to us?"

"More or less. I can shield her presence, which has been necessary because of her father's bloodline. She would be a particularly tasty treat for the Fallen."

I hope he doesn't mean that literally.

A smile breaks over Sable's face and her eyes shift to me. "You know who Emberly's parents were? This is great news."

Nope. Don't want to go there just yet.

"If you could shield my presence," I cut in before Tinkle can open his furry mouth, "then why was I still attacked so many times? Does it not always work or something? Are there limitations to your abilities?"

Tinkle lumbers to his feet and plops his hands on his hips. "I'm going to pretend you didn't just insult my superior supernatural abilities." It takes supreme control not to roll my eyes. "But if you must know, I had to sleep sometimes. Naps are very important for growing Celestials."

Oh. My. Gosh.

"Are you telling me . . ." I suck in a deep breath and hold it for three long counts before releasing it, trying to control my blood pressure. "Are you saying the times I was attacked happened when my fairy god-Celestial was literally sleeping on the job?"

Un-flippin'-believable.

I flex my fingers, curling my hands in and out of fists.

"You should just be grateful your father had the foresight

to send you a protector at all. If not for me, you'd have been felled by a Fallen's blade. . . or worse."

My lips are sealed as I breathe loudly through my nose. Sable, Ash, and Deacon all stare at me, but this is the best I can do to compose myself.

"Tinkle, who is Emberly's father?" Sable asks, trying to lower the tension in the room, but this is the truth I'm not sure I want brought to light. At least not yet.

Ash's fingers brush my arm. "I think you should let them know."

"You already know?" Sable asks. She leans forward, waiting for one of us to speak. Deacon remains silent, but his gaze rests on me so heavily, it feels like a physical touch.

I take a moment to fortify myself before opening my mouth to spill the details, praying I'm not making one of the biggest mistakes of my life.

"Do you know of an angel named Camiel?"

44

"The Angel of War? What does Camiel have to do with any of this?" Sable blinks as her gaze trips between me and Tinkle.

"War?" My eyes grow a size or two. "Ash, you didn't mention that."

She throws her hands up, palms facing the ceiling. "Yo, I didn't know. I don't have every angel in the codex memorized."

War. That's heavy. Shuffling to the couch, I plop down in the space next to Sable and angle toward her.

"Tell me everything you know about him."

"Hey, why is no one asking me? I'm the one who knows the mighty warrior." My eyes flick to Tinkle for a brief second before refocusing on Sable.

"Hold up. Your father can't be a descendent of Camiel. At least not the one I'm thinking of. Camiel is a seraph."

I glance at Ash. "She's going to flip." She nods her agreement. "According to Tinkle, my father isn't descended from Camiel; my father *is* Camiel."

It's Sable and Deacon's turn to exchange a look. After a beat, Deacon strides over and sits in the chair Laurent vacated. Ash has found her way to the other armchair, so we're all seated, huddled around the odd little Celestial who has resumed rolling around the table like a soccer ball, haphazardly knocking into teacups and saucers.

Deacon rests his elbows on his knees and leans forward. "Tell us everything. Start from the beginning."

"There's not much to tell." I take a moment to catch them up on what little information Tinkle provided.

Sable steeples her hands under her chin when I finish the quick recap. "It just can't be. Not a single seraph angel fell from grace during The Great Battle. And Nephilim are descended from the Fallen. An angel has never sired a child with a human before."

"Just because it's never happened before doesn't mean that it can't. That's a weak and rather ignorant argument, don't you think?"

Tinkle has a bit of a point.

"But you are right about one part. There's never been a union between an angel of grace and a human." Matching looks of confusion blanket our faces. Tinkle's words seem contrary. "Angels can only procreate with the angel-born themselves."

"Are you just making this stuff up on the spot?" Every detail Tinkle reveals just gets more bizarre.

Tinkle stops his rolling and glares at me. "You make it sound like I'm lying. Celestials are incapable of lying. It's not in our nature. We only tell truths . . . and occasional half-truths."

"Well, there you have it," Deacon declares with a slap of his hand on his thigh. He leans back in the wingback chair and crosses his arms over his chest. "The seraph, Camiel, isn't your father. The little rodent got some of the details mixed. Maybe Camiel was just tasked with your protection?"

"Who are you calling a rodent? You brute!" Tinkle pops to his feet and puffs out his chest. "Camiel *is* Emberly's father. He came to me himself the day her mother was murdered and asked me to protect her. And I've done my job all these years."

Every molecule in my body comes to a screeching halt.

Murdered.

My blood turns to sludge in my veins. I can feel it, thick and viscous, as it forces its way through the narrow passageways. Its slow progression pounds in my head like the beating of a bass drum.

Murdered.

I'd given up the dream of finding loving parents years before. Finding out one of them was no longer alive confirmed what I'd always believed to be true, yet still . . .

Murdered.

The word hangs heavy in my heart. "But you said you didn't know where she was."

Tinkle blinks up at me. "Because I don't."

Sable's lips are moving, but I can't make out the words over the drumbeat in my ears. Tinkle has resumed rolling on the table, as if he didn't just drop a bomb that rocked my whole world. Deacon's mouth is moving, the space between his eyebrows pinched, but I can't hear any words.

Daughter of a murdered mother and an angelic father. Who would have thought?

Something takes hold of me and shakes my upper body, snapping me back into the moment. With her hand on my shoulder, Sable's face is expectant as she waits for my response to her unheard question.

"I asked if you were all right?"

I shake my head slowly. "No. So not okay right now."

Pressing her lips together, she nods. She gives my shoulder one last squeeze before pulling her hand back.

"Understandable." Her gaze travels to an oblivious Tinkle before landing on Deacon. "We have some digging to do."

"How much are you going to tell the Council?"

"I don't know." She pinches the bridge of her nose. "I suppose the right thing would be to just download all the information we know, but . . ." That *but* hangs in the air for several bloated seconds. "Maybe we should wait until we're able to verify some of the information we learned here tonight."

"How are we supposed to do that?" Deacon's gaze shifts to Tinkle. "If the rodent is correct, Emberly is one-of-a-kind, at least as far as our knowledge of the world extends. Short of putting in a call to Camiel and asking him to do a paternity test, I'm not sure how we're supposed to authenticate her parentage."

"Is it possible to reach out to the angels?" I'm suddenly very interested in knowing how such a thing might be done.

I've learned some things about angels in my Nephilim history class, but in general I know very little about the other-worldly beings. From what I've gleaned, angels spent their time in the spectrum world fighting Fallen and defending territories. Like a human military, they cluster in hot spots. And if angels are the military, Nephilim are the supernatural police working in smaller groups spread out over a larger geographic area. We each have our parts to play, but rarely overlap with each other.

Angels have partnered with Nephilim against the Fallen and Forsaken at various times through history, but the accounts of those times are rare and littered with holes in the Book of Seraph. The same goes for stories of angels crossing into the mortal realm. It's believed—but never verified—that angels can only pass into our world with the permission of their Creator.

"I'm sorry to say angels don't carry cell phones." Sable's words are heavy with regret.

The chair beneath Deacon groans as he leans back. A stern look creases his brow. "And even if they did, I doubt they'd give us their numbers."

"They aren't our biggest fans," Sable says. "The general consensus is that they tolerate us."

Deacon snorts. "And by 'tolerate,' Sable means plenty of them wouldn't shed a tear over the demise of our entire race."

"We're on the same side. Yet they . . . resent us?"

"We're the offspring of their fallen brethren," Sable explains. "In their eyes we never should have existed. We were created as vessels to allow evil into the mortal realm. Some angels even hunted us until the uprising."

"But angels are tasked with safeguarding humanity."

"Since the first of our kind was born, our inclusion in 'humanity' has always been subjective."

My view of our angelic ancestors is tipped on its side once again. I used to think they were lyre-playing, downy-winged messengers of God, caretakers of humankind. My perception shifted after coming to Seraph Academy. I now picture them as strong and benevolent—if emotionally and physically distant—protectors with an impeccable moral code. Proud warriors who fight for truth, justice, and all that jazz. But a darker image begins to take shape. Their characters are splattered with malignant influences and prejudices. Thirsty for the blood of not only their enemies, but their innocent offspring as well.

Is there nothing pure in this world? If the almighty angels could be tainted by hatred, what hope is there for the rest of us?

"Tinkle, what else do you know about Emberly's mother?"

The little creature is plopped in the middle of the cookie plate, licking its surface. He releases a happy squeak every time he manages to slurp up a crumb.

"What of her?" he asks. "She's no longer in this realm or the next."

Something tightens in my chest at the reminder.

"Yes, but what did you know about her when she was alive? Did you ever meet her? Do you know what angel line she's descended from?"

"Does it matter?"

I'm unable to hold my tongue. "Yes! It matters a great deal."

"No need to get feisty. Do you know I had to watch over you when you were getting your butt cleaned as a babe? That was frightful work. And the smell!"

"Tinkle," I warn.

"Fine. Let's see if you can figure it out. What line do you think the Angel of War would take as a bride?"

"Is this supposed to be a trick question?"

"They really do need to raise the bar at this institution." Sable shoots Tinkle a slanted look that he ignores. "He would only take a mate from the more fearsome line fighters, of course."

"Cherubs?" I guess

"Maybe powers?" Ash adds.

Deacon crosses his arms over his chest, leaning back in his chair. "Could be archangels."

Tinkle rests his tiny head in his tiny paws. "Imbeciles, all of you."

"Is he always so complimentary?" Deacon asks.

"We've heard worse."

"I'm talking about the Nephilim who are the most highly-trained and impressive of all when it comes to battle." We all just stare, waiting for him to get to the point. "The angel line."

It's quiet for a beat, and then everyone starts talking over each other. Deacon accuses Tinkle of fabricating details. Sable nerds out and regurgitates what little she knows about the fabled Nephilim line. Ash lobs questions at no one in particular.

It's a lot of noise for only a few people. As their voices climb, I don't react. At least not outwardly. Inside, my synapses are going off like fireworks.

Daughter of a seraph and angel Nephilim. A phrase that wouldn't have made sense to me a few months ago, but is now my new reality.

"I know what we have to do." I'm not loud, but the others go instantly quiet. Three sets of light, angel-born eyes and the black orbs of the Celestial fix on me. A tar pit of apprehension bubbles in my gut. Chances are I'm setting myself up for more heartache and pain, but there's only one way to get to the bottom of these mysteries.

"We need to find my father."

STEEL

I jolt up in bed, throat raw from shouting in my sleep. The thin, scratchy sheet I pulled over me before falling asleep is twisted around my legs.

Sweat doesn't just bead on my chest, it streams down in rivulets. My hair is so saturated, I could shake drops off like a dog.

As the last vestiges of the nightmare dissipate, my brain tricks me into thinking I can smell sweet honeysuckle and taste the warm cinnamon of her skin on my tongue.

It's torture, but I close my eyes and hold on to the senses until they fade.

When they do, my muscles are a shaking mess of Jell-O.

I stumble out of the ratty twin bed and lurch to the bathroom. I'm on my knees in front of the toilet before the nausea churning in my gut bubbles up my throat.

I know the drill.

Her spicy taste is wiped from my mouth after I expel a

liquid mess of bile and half-digested food. Now all I can smell is my own sickness.

I flush the toilet and watch the vomit circle the bowl before being swallowed.

On shaky legs, I pull myself into the shower stall and turn the water on. The pipes sputter and groan before giving up chilly water.

This place is a dump. Maybe next time I'll spring for the full-star motel instead of a half-star.

From experience I know it'll be a few minutes for the spray to heat, but the cold is good for me. It wakes me up and chases the dreams away.

The visions. They started months ago, well before Emberly entered my life, but her presence sure did amplify them.

They'd been beautiful at first. I'd wake with hazy memories of a golden-winged goddess. My heart ached for her at the same time it soared. I was drawn to that beautiful creature like I'd never been to anything else.

And then, as if by a miracle, she appeared to me in the flesh.

My fiery-tipped blonde warrior princess. A fierce package wrapped in gold. My dream, brought to life.

A legion of Fallen wouldn't have scared me more.

And like the emotionally stunted coward I was, I used every weapon I had to push her away.

The dreams began to darken and morph, turning what was once beautiful and pure into a morbid nighttime terror I relived almost every night. When I succumb to sleep, I'm forced to watch the wounds I inflict on her weep blood onto my hands. Her eyes always ask one question—*Why*—even as I drive a knife into her again and again.

For weeks, the horror has ended the same way, with shadow arms wrapping around her middle and dragging her away from me, into darkness. The sound of her tortured screams echoes in my head even after I'm roused.

As lukewarm water pounds my back, I close my eyes and replace the Emberly of my nightmares with my last memory of her.

She stood in front of me in skinny jeans and a heather gray sweater. The evening sun kissed her features, making her light hair look like it was truly aflame.

The uncertainty in her posture had been all my doing, and when she lifted those beautiful sapphire eyes after offering to help me, the vulnerability in her gaze left me speechless.

I wasn't supposed to kiss her. She'd already warned me against it, but I couldn't help myself from taking one last taste, not sure I'd ever have the opportunity again.

Her lips had been so soft and pliable under mine. So sweet.

I didn't have the guts to look back when I sped off, knowing she would tempt me to stay.

And I couldn't stay. There's something I have to do. Or rather, something I have to undo.

Twisting the shower handle, I stop the flow of water and step out of the stall, hastily wiping the moisture from my upper body before securing a towel around my waist.

The sun hasn't risen yet, but that doesn't matter. There's no way I'm getting any more rest tonight.

I dress swiftly after taking only two minutes to cram my meager belongings in my bag.

Once dressed, I start strapping a small arsenal to my body. It takes longer to weapon-up than it does to dress.

When I left the academy, I stole as many weapons as I could secure to my person.

The particular Forsaken I'm after can't be underestimated.

My greatest defense and offense against any foe is the animal forms I shift into, but there is no guarantee the fight I'm anticipating will be hosted in the spirit realm.

I've been tracking Silver for weeks and am beginning to think she's merely taking me for a ride. But I know sooner or later she'll slip up and I'll find her.

She's already made a grave mistake by letting me know she's alive at all.

I slide the last dagger into the holster at my ankle, hidden under my jeans. The neon vacancy sign in front of the motel flickers rather than blinks when I exit my room and head for my ride.

I double-check my route on my phone's navigation app before revving the engine.

It's time to hunt. The prey? My sister. I'll carve a knife through her chest if it takes me a lifetime.

After leaving her on that mountain to die, I owe her that much.

ANGELIC CLASSIFICATION
IN ORDER OF SPHERE

Angelic Spheres – The nine classes of angels are divided equally into one of three spheres. Each sphere has related roles and responsibilities and it's believed—but not proven— that the most powerful angels are from the first sphere with decreasing power down to the third.

Seraphim – Literally translated as, "burning ones," seraphim are the highest angelic class and considered the most powerful. Part of the first sphere of angels, these supernatural beings are said to have six wings and protect the throne of their Creator. There are no known Nephilim from the seraphim line, because not a single seraph angel rebelled and therefore there are no seraph Fallen.

Cherubim – Part of the first sphere of angels, cherubim are the highest angelic class that rebelled. The Nephilim of this line can typically shift into one of three different forms in the spirit realm: a lion, an eagle, or a bovine. It's very rare for a

Nephilim to be able to shift into two or all three of these forms.

Thrones – The thrones are part of the first sphere and are said to be natural protectors. Nephilim of this line can manipulate and build wards to protect the academies and compounds from supernatural enemies by pulling on energy contained in underground springs.

Dominions – Part of the second sphere of angels, Dominions regulate the duties of the lower angels as well as govern the laws of the universe. Dominions are considered to be divinely beautiful with feathered wings of various colors. The Nephilim of this line value friendship, family, and loyalty and tend to be the peacemakers of the angel-born world.

Virtues – These angels are known for their signs and miracles. Part of the second sphere, they ensure everything is acting the way it should, from gravity keeping the planets in orbit, to the grass growing. Nephilim of this line can control natural elements in the mortal world, but their abilities are more powerful in the spirit realm.

Powers – Part of the second sphere, these angels are considered the warriors of the angel hierarchy. As such, they are always on the frontlines of battle. They are known to be single-minded and focused on their cause. Nephilim of this line are skilled in combat and have a knack for military strategy. They are able to manifest wings in the spirit realm.

Rulers – As part of the third sphere, these angels guide and protect territories and groups of people. They preside over the classes of angels and carry out orders given to them by the upper spheres. They are said to be inspirational to angels and humankind. Nephilim of this line tend to manage and govern different bodies of angel-born. Their natural talents veer toward shepherding and their powers manifest as defensive rather than offensive.

Archangels – These angels are common in mortal lore. Part of the third sphere, they appear more frequently in the mortal world than other classes of angels—with the exception of the angel class. Tasked with the protection of humanity, they sometimes appear as mortals in order to influence politics, military matters, and commerce in their assigned region. Nephilim of this line are skilled chameleons. They have the easiest time blending in with humans and many of them work as Keepers.

Angels – Perceived as the lowest order of celestial beings, angels—sometimes called "plain angels" or "guardian angels"—belong to the third sphere. Their primary duties are as messengers and personal guards. Nephilim of this line are believed to have been murdered over two millennia ago. As a result of their weak powers, Forsaken and Fallen targeted this line for elimination. Not much is known of what their powers and abilities were.

GLOSSARY

Angel – A winged supernatural being who protects both mortal and spirit realms from Fallen and Forsaken.

Angel-born – The common name for Nephilim. An elite race of supernatural warriors born of human females and male Fallen, and their descendants. They have varying powers and abilities based on their Fallen ancestor's angel class. They are stronger, faster, and their senses more enhanced than humans.

Celestial – A fabled supernatural being that acts as a protector for angel-born. Nephilim tell their children fairy tales about these creatures, but their existence has never been confirmed.

Council of Elders – Comprised of the oldest Nephilim in each of the seven existing angelic lines: cherub, throne, dominion, virtue, power, ruler, and archangel. They are the closest thing to a ruling body the Nephilim have, yet—unless there is a global threat—their normal duties are to act as judges to help settle disputes between angel-born.

Fallen – Angels who rebelled and were banished to Earth as punishment. They retained their strength, immortality, and wings, but lost their class specific angelic powers. They are unable to access the mortal world.

Forsaken – Fallen who have merged with a Nephilim—or willing human—and taken on the form of their host's body. They are able to travel between each realm unencumbered. Their appearance is hideous in the spirit realm, reflecting their true nature. Forsaken thirst for blood—although it's not their primary source of sustenance—and are unable to withstand the sunlight in either realm.

Keeper – Nephilim tasked with monitoring and collecting information about the human race.

Mortal World/Realm – The dimension on Earth where humans reside.

Nephilim – The proper name for angel-born.

Seraph Academy – One of nine secret academies around the world devoted to the education and training of Nephilim children. Nephilim youth attend the academies from age eight until twenty, at which time they are considered fully trained. Seraph Academy is located in the Colorado Mountains near the town of Glenwood Springs.

Spectrum World – What Emberly calls the spirit realm.

Spirit Realm – The plane of existence that can only be accessed by supernatural beings. The spectrum of colors differ in this realm and sound can be seen as ripples through the air. Angels spend the majority of their time in the spirit realm warring with Fallen for control of territories. Nephilim's angelic powers activate in this realm.

The Great Revolt – When the Nephilim rose up against the Forsaken and Fallen who had enslaved and used them as vessels for Fallen.

PLEASE WRITE A REVIEW

Reviews are the lifeblood of authors and your opinion will help others decide to read my books. If you want to see more from me, please leave a review.

Will you please write a review?
http://review.StealingEmbers.com

Thank you for your help!

~ Julie

FORGING DARKNESS

*M*oist air caresses my neck and the bed shakes rhythmically with each heavy heave from the large animal behind me. My tank top is plastered to my skin and my cheek rests on something damp.

Turning my head, I'm face-to-face with a black and white Great Dane snuggled up against me. Its hind legs stretch over my hip and waist, and its tongue lolls on my pillow. A drool stain the size of the massive dog's head spreads across the pillowcase.

Nasty.

I'm gonna kill Tinkle. The idiot likes to shift into large animals and cuddle with me at night.

My pillow buzzes. I reach underneath it and grab my cell —the first phone I've ever had. Aside from the occasional group text, and the random gifs Sterling likes to send me,

I hardly ever use it. It's basically a glorified alarm clock.

The screen is lit up with one word: Unknown.

My heart starts to beat double-time. This is the fifth unknown call this month. Most of them have come through in the early morning or middle of the night. When I answer,

I'm only ever met with silence—total serial killer stuff—but my gut tells me who is on the other line.

Maneuvering out from under the dog sprawled across my comforter, I pad to the bathroom, making sure Ash is still asleep. She's a lump under the covers, slowly inflating and deflating with her even breaths. Only a few clusters of ringlets peek out from under her blankets.

Shutting the door as gently as possible, I scurry to the far end of the small room, anxious to answer the call before my voicemail picks up.

I hit the green button on the screen and hold it to my ear for several ticks before saying anything.

"Hello?" The word passes my lips as barely more than a whisper.

As usual, I'm greeted by silence.

My stomach bottoms out in disappointment.

Is he ever going to talk to me? If not, why does he even bother calling?

I slide down the wall until my butt settles on the chilled tiled floor, and pull my knees to my chest.

"Steel?"

I know it's him. I haven't told anyone about these calls, mostly because there's nothing to tell since he never talks. Also, I don't want to explain how I know it's him. With every call there's a tug on my heart that only ever happened when he was around.

Audible breathing on the other end of the line should probably be creepy, but it's not. It's a connection to Steel I'm desperate to hang on to. The last two months he's been gone have been . . . hard.

I'll only admit it to myself, and under duress I'll deny it to my dying breath, but I miss him.

The frustrating part is that I can't put my finger on what exactly I miss. Steel was a grade-A jerk to me ninety-five percent of the time. He pushed me and aggravated me and didn't let me get away with anything. He never took it easy when we trained, and the tender moments we shared were few and far between. But since he left, I feel the hollowness inside more acutely. I'm over trying to figure out why.

My grip on the phone goes white-knuckle as the silence continues.

"If you're not going to talk to me, please check in with your family. They're worried sick about you."

His parents and siblings haven't heard from him since the day he rode off. The youngest twins seem to be taking Steel's absence the hardest. They've practically adopted me as a surrogate. I've even found them hiding in my dorm room a few times. They claimed they were making sure I hadn't been devoured by monsters, but I knew better. They missed their older brother and were looking for some sort of connection to him. Unfortunately, they weren't going to get what they needed fighting the dust bunnies under my bed.

Even though Steel and I had buried the hatchet—kinda . . . sorta—he probably wouldn't be okay with them seeking me out. When it comes to his siblings, his protective instincts run deep, and who's to say I don't still have a target on my back?

"Steel, at least tell me if you're okay," I say. I don't hold out much hope that he'll respond, so when he does, my heart stutters.

"Em . . . I found her."

I stop breathing.

There's no mistaking who he's talking about: Silver, his twin sister, thought to be deceased up until we learned she orchestrated the youngest Durands' kidnapping to lure me into a trap. It didn't work, but it was a close call. I still don't know what the Forsaken want with me, but if the Nephilim from Seraph Academy hadn't tracked us down that day, I have no doubt I'd be dead now.

Steel has been hunting her since the day he found out she was alive.

My lungs start to burn, reminding me I need oxygen. I drag in a ragged breath. "Tell me where you are, Steel. I'll talk to Sable and she'll send help. Please don't do this alone."

Steady, Emberly. He spooks easily.

I press a hand to the floor beneath me. The thought of Steel going up against his sister sends earthquakes of trepidation thundering through my body.

Silver isn't your average Forsaken. She's cunning and strong and somehow seems to have retained part of herself even after being possessed by a Fallen. She's dangerous in a way I don't fully understand.

Steel doesn't want to admit it, but he needs help.

My fingers curl as the silence stretches and pulls. My nails scrape across the porcelain tiles as if dragged against chalkboard.

"I have to." And then the line goes dead.

I lower the phone from my ear, but my grip tightens until it snaps. I've broken the glass screen. A long fissure splinters its way from the bottom corner to the top.

I tap the screen and only feel a mild sense of relief that it's still working. What I really want to do is yell in frustration, but I don't want to wake Ash, so instead I simply

420 | JULIE HALL

squeeze my eyes shut and let my head fall back and bump into the wall.

Relief that Steel is still alive and safe wars with fury at his refusal to accept help. And although I'm glad he's at least checking in with someone, he's put me in an impossible position.

Now that I know he's actually found Silver, I don't know if I can keep this secret anymore.

The room brightens behind my shut lids and I blink them open. Ash stands in the doorway, rubbing her eyes. The pink eye-mask she wears is pushed up on her head, keeping her hair off her forehead.

The girl gets epic bedhead when she's too lazy to wrap her hair before sleeping, like tonight. The curls on one side of her head are squished flat against her scalp, and on the other they are fanned out in an afro. She's rocking a half-mohawk that's going to be a nightmare for her in the morning.

After shuffling a few steps forward into the bathroom, Ash catches sight of me folded in the corner. Her head tilts and eyebrows draw together.

"You okay?" she croaks, her voice heavy with sleep.

Pressing my lips together, I shake my head before pushing to my feet. This weight is too heavy for me to bear alone.

"We need to talk."

Continue Emberly and Steel's epic story at
www.ForgingDarkness.com

ACKNOWLEDGMENTS

Before I jump into the herculean task of trying to squish all the people I owe thanks to into a few condensed paragraphs, I'd like to take a moment to acknowledge the inspiration behind these first books in the *Fallen Legacies* series. After I wrapped up the *Life After* series, it was heavy on my heart to write a book that my daughter might be able to relate to one day. My husband and I adopted our daughter from Ethiopia when she was very young. We did our best to prepare ourselves for life as an interracial family, but I willingly admit there have been unexpected hurdles along the way.

My daughter was six when I started writing *Stealing Embers*, and even at that young age we watched her struggle to feel accepted in a sea of people who look very different to her. I will never fully understand what hardships people of minorities face in our nation, but I do have a front seat to the wounds my daughter sustains and the insecurities she battles daily.

As such, it was a deliberate decision to create a main character whose physical appearance is different from the supernatural race she is supposed to belong to. I set about to write Emberly and Ash (named after my daughter, Ashtyn) into this series with the hope that someday my daughter will read this series and find a little bit about herself woven into it. She's quite young, so I suppose I'll have to wait several years to find out if I've accomplished this task.

With that said, there are a number of people that deserve my appreciation and a basket of fluffy puppies (because puppies make the world a better place). First and foremost, my handsome husband, Lucas. He is not only the most supportive husband on the planet, but the engine behind my book publications. Without his IT genius, not a single one of my books would ever have seen the light of day. He is my rock and tether in this ever-changing world. I love you baby. #bettertogetherforever

I would also like to thank Amanda Steele. She has been a part of my writing journey for years and is an invaluable part of my team. She's not only a marketing wiz, but a beta reader extraordinaire, a superhero encourager, and a dear friend. Amanda, Sterling will forever and always be yours. #yourewelcome

Thank you, Carrie Robertson, for reading all the worst versions of my stories #imsosorry, for offering unwavering support throughout my author career, and for being such a true friend.

A special thanks to LeAnn Mason and Alyssa Muller for all their hard work in my Facebook group as well as the members of my Fallen Legacies Launch Team who take time out of their schedules to read and review my books (and hunt down those typos) and selflessly help me spread the word about new releases. I treasure your support and friendships! #pleaseneverleaveme

There is an army of authors who have offered me support, encouragement, and advice throughout my career. Literally too many to name, but I want to particularly thank Casey Bond, Cameo Renae, Audrey Grey, and Michele Israel Harper for taking the time to read *Stealing Embers* and provide me with their lovely endorsements. I know it wasn't a small ask.

My final note of thanks goes to you, the reader. I'm humbled to have you read my work and truly hope you've enjoyed spending time in Emberly and Steel's world. I hope you choose to continue this journey with me!

JOIN THE NEWSLETTER
GET FREE UPDATES & PRIZES

Please consider joining my exclusive email newsletter. You'll be notified as new books are available, get exclusive bonus scenes, previews, ridiculous videos, and you'll be eligible for special giveaways. Occasionally, you will see puppies.

Get all the snarky funsies:
JulieHallAuthor.com/newsletter

I respect your privacy. No spam.

Unsubscribe anytime.

JOIN THE FAN CLUB
ON FACEBOOK

If you love my books, get involved and get exclusive sneak peeks before anyone else. Sometimes I even give out free puppies (#jokingnotjoking).

You'll get to know other passionate readers like you, and you'll get to know me better too! It'll be fun!

Join the Fan Club on Facebook:
facebook.com/groups/juliehall

See you in there!

~ Julie

ABOUT THE AUTHOR
JULIE HALL

My name is Julie Hall and I'm a *USA Today* bestselling, multiple award-winning author. I read and write YA paranormal / fantasy novels, love doodle dogs and drink Red Bull, but not necessarily in that order.

My daughter says my super power is sleeping all day and writing all night . . . and well, she wouldn't be wrong.

I believe novels are best enjoyed in community. As such, I want to hear from you! Please connect with me as I regularly give out sneak peeks, deleted scenes, prizes, and other freebies to my friends and newsletter subscribers.

Visit my website:
JulieHallAuthor.com

Get my other books:
amazon.com/author/julieghall

Join the Fan Club:
facebook.com/groups/juliehall

Get exclusive updates by email:
JulieHallAuthor.com/newsletter

Find me on:

a amazon.com/author/julieghall

f facebook.com/JulieHallAuthor

BB bookbub.com/authors/julie-hall-7c80af95-5dda-449a-8130-3e219d5b00ee

g goodreads.com/JulieHallAuthor

O instagram.com/Julie.Hall.Author

▶ youtube.com/JulieHallAuthor

BOOKS BY JULIE HALL

Stealing Embers (Fallen Legacies Book 1)

www.StealingEmbers.com

Forging Darkness (Fallen Legacies Book 2)

www.ForgingDarkness.com

Huntress (Life After Book 1)

www.HuntressBook.com

Warfare (Life After Book 2)

www.WarfareBook.com

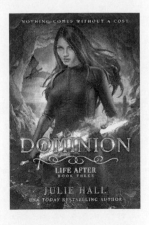

Dominion (Life After Book 3)

www.DominionBook.com

Logan (A Life After Companion Story)

www.LoganBook.com

Life After - The Complete Series (Books 1-4)

www.LifeAfterSet.com

AUDIOBOOKS BY JULIE HALL

My books are also available on Audible!

http://Audio.JulieHallAuthor.com

Made in the USA
Middletown, DE
05 March 2021